Lieberman's Choice

"Lieberman is endearing, wise in his crotchets, weary with his wisdom.... The pacing is sure and sharp throughout, with a snappy flow that keeps you moving rapidly and easily among the several strands to the final confrontations."
—*The Washington Post Book World*

"Kaminsky gets his details exactly right.... Tightly plotted... The best mysteries work on multiple levels, and this one is no exception."
—*The Chicago Tribune*

"Enough explosives to blow the North Side of Chicago to kingdom come... Kaminsky mines plenty of suspense."
—*The New York Times Book Review*

ALSO BY STUART M. KAMINSKY

Toby Peters Mysteries

Bullet for a Star
Murder on the Yellow Brick Road
You Bet Your Life
The Howard Hughes Affair
Never Cross a Vampire
High Midnight
Catch a Falling Clown
He Done Her Wrong
The Fala Factor
Down for the Count
The Man Who Shot Lewis Vance
Smart Moves
Think Fast, Mr. Peters
Buried Caesars
Poor Butterfly
The Melting Clock
The Devil Met a Lady
Tomorrow Is Another Day
Dancing in the Dark
A Fatal Glass of Beer

Abe Lieberman Mysteries

Lieberman's Folly
Lieberman's Choice
Lieberman's Day
Lieberman's Thief
Lieberman's Law
The Big Silence*

Lou Fonesca Mysteries

Vengeance
Retribution*

Nonseries Novels

When the Dark Man Calls
Exercise in Terror

Biographies

Don Siegel: Director
Clint Eastwood
John Huston, Maker of Magic
Coop: the Life and Legend of
  Gary Cooper

Other Nonfiction

American Film Genres
American Television Genres
  (with Jeffrey Mahan)
Basic Filmmaking
  (with Dana Hodgdon)
Writing for Television
  (with Mark Walker)

Porfiry Rostnikov Novels

Death of a Dissident
Black Knight in Red Square
Red Chameleon
A Cold, Red Sunrise
A Fine Red Rain
Rostnikov's Vacation
The Man Who Walked Like a Bear
Death of a Russian Priest
Hard Currency
Blood and Rubles
Tarnished Icons
The Dog Who Bit a Policeman

*forthcoming

Stuart M. Kaminsky

LIEBERMAN'S LAW

A TOM DOHERTY ASSOCIATES BOOK
NEW YORK

*For Leora Benishay and
all the Benishay Family*

LIEBERMAN'S LAW

A Forge Book
Published by Tom Doherty Associates, LLC
175 Fifth Avenue
New York, NY 10010

www.tor.com

Forge® is a registered trademark of Tom Doherty Associates, LLC.

ISBN: 0-812-57533-4

First mass market edition: December 2000

Printed in the United States of America

0 9 8 7 6 5 4 3 2 1

You cannot call him back from the river of Hades, that all must cross, with weeping and lamentation, with helpless sorrow and grieving beyond all reason. You'll sicken to death; no tears can lighten the labour of trouble past; must you still cling to misery?

—Chorus in *Electra* by Sophocles

Somewhere in Israel Near the Jordan border in 1973

ALI WAS WORRIED.

The exhaust pipe of the battered Dodge van clattered against the stones in the dirt road every time Ali hit a bump. In spite of the pieces of wire that held it up, the badly rusted pipe was definitely exhausted, but it would have to do for a while. He would slip under the van in the morning with more wire.

But it wasn't the clanging exhaust that bothered Ali most as he drove along the road late that night. Nor was it the chatter of his own children and those of his brother-in-law and sister-in-law in back complaining about having to get up early. The visit to his wife's mother had gone on too late, too long.

The moon was almost full. That helped a bit because even on high beam the headlights of the van were in need of replacement. One light had been flickering and waning for more than a week.

Farrah, Ali's wife, stepped over their daughter who was

shouting loudly at her cousin about a boy they both knew who was supposed to be a thief.

"Anything?" Farrah said softly.

Ali shook his head no, scanning both sides of the road as he passed a few small houses, looking for, praying against hostile movement in hostile Israeli territory.

They were close to home now, their own gray town of Arabs and the smell of familiar night food.

Hassan called out to Ali, "What do you think?"

He didn't know what Hassan was talking about. He saw a movement here, an outline there, as he always did on such nights. Ali shrugged in answer to his brother-in-law's question.

"See," said Hassan, a thin man of forty-one years who had been bald since he was a little over nineteen. Ali had come to the conclusion that his brother-in-law argued so much because he thought Allah had played a cruel trick on him. His mustache was ample and dark, but the top of his head shone brightly and burned easily in the summer sun. Hassan wore a small cap on his head whenever he was out of his home. Ali was sure that it was less a sign of piety than vanity.

And so Hassan argued about everything: King Hussein's failures, the duplicity of the Israelis, the indifference of the Russians, the lies of the Americans, the lust for power of the Syrians, the price of grain in the market, the British royal family. If he could not have hair, he could have opinions.

Ali rubbed his eyes. He was nearing fifty. He was tired. He was worried about how he could keep the van running on his salary. The Israelis paid what the market would bear and Ali was an expert at his job, but his pay was meager. He could assemble the parts for the photograph frames faster than anyone else in the small factory. Assemble, glue, and clamp. Haim Vesh, a Jew who did not believe in God and who had only come to Israel two years ago from Brazil, knew enough to praise Ali for his work. They spoke in Hebrew. Ali's Hebrew was far better than that of Haim Vesh. Ali had lived his life among the Jews traveling nearly

40 miles to the factory each morning and 40 miles back home each night. He took their language across the border to where he worked and left it at the border when he returned home.

They were close to the checkpoint and safety, but they were still in hostile territory and difficult times. Ali tried to remain alert, but he was tired and the noise of the two families behind him had given him a headache. He got headaches easily and tried any and all remedies to relieve them. Nothing ever really worked. He had such a headache now, but it was forgotten when the windshield in front of him suddenly shattered.

There were screams behind him, people rolling on top of each other. Ali marveled at how perfectly the windshield had shattered and blown away completely, almost as if it had suddenly been cleaned and he could clearly see the road before him. He tried to drive on, his hands shaking, unaware of the bleeding cuts on his face. A voice, that of his fourteen-year-old nephew, Amin, cried out behind Ali. A shot passed Ali's face and Amin's cry stopped.

The fear of his entire life was coming to pass on this stretch of empty desert road. The images of robbers and crazed Jews were never far from his imagination. Shots from outside. Definitely shots. He turned his head briefly to see who had been hit. He thought he saw the bloody face of Amin. He panicked and looked for his own family in the darkness as he pressed the gas to the floor. His brother-in-law, the babbling Hassan, leaned over Ali's shoulder and began to fire his rifle wildly into the darkness.

A rattle of shots sprayed through the van as it zagged from one side of the road to the other and Ali lost control. Perhaps a tire had been hit. Hassan had taken a bullet and slumped back with a groan. The van careened. Ali tried to call his wife, his daughter, his son, hoping that their cry would be evidence that they lived.

More shots. In the working headlight, Ali saw a man in the middle of the road. He was bearded. He held an automatic weapon and stood firing at the swerving truck, mindless of the fact that it might run right over him, which was

what Ali tried to do as his head went mad with pain from
the screams of his family. The van rolled drunkenly in the
general direction of the bearded man who continued to fire.

The van rocked once to the right and then fell on its left
side screeching forward along the stone road. Children,
women screamed behind him as the van skidded noisily,
sending up sparks and screeches that sounded like pain.

Ali was on his side, his face inches from the road through
the now shattered glass of the side window. A body, his
nephew, lay on top of his as he uselessly and automatically
tried to steer the dead vehicle. And then the van stopped,
partly on the road, partly in the scrub of sand and weeds
along the roadway.

Ali, his hands shaking, pushed the body of his nephew
out of his way, through the missing windshield. He had
skidded past the man in the road. At least he thought he
had. Ali had no time to think. His wife, his daughter were
behind him. He heard a moaning in the darkness. His
nephew faced him, dead and bloody, just beyond the windshield now.

As Ali eased himself out from behind the wheel he called
back, "Anyone who can move, come quickly, through the
front window, quickly."

He reached back, took a hand, his ten-year-old niece,
Kala, weeping, trembling. If only there were no moon they
might escape into the open field, be lost in darkness. A
single headlight of the Dodge was still on, a screeching
noise of automotive death shivered the van as a wheel continued to turn.

"Out, out," he shouted, trying to ignore the blood that
blocked the vision of his left eye.

They came slowly, sobbing, looking around as if they
were emerging after a decade in a dark cellar. Jara crawled
forward. She was six. Her arm was twisted and her white
dress was red. She was pulling at her mother, Farrah, who
lay silent, eyes closed, face red with blood, almost certainly
dead. Hassan, who had apparently only been wounded, was
in the road now, confused, being urged back by his scream-

ing wife. Ali reached back for Jara's hand and pulled the girl forward. She wept in fear and pain. The child had been shot or cut by flying glass. Her right shoulder was covered in blood. Through the window, onto the road. For the first time, Ali felt for the old pistol that he carried under his jacket for a moment like this, a moment he frequently prayed would never come.

"Massad," Ali called into the darkness. He thought he heard a low groan that might have been his four-year-old son. No time to look now.

"Off the road," he whispered, patting his little daughter, "into the darkness. Quietly," he added fruitlessly, knowing that she, like he, would not be silent in their fear and grief and the pain of their wounds. Jara slumped to the ground.

On the road, out of sight because of the fallen van, Hassan heard a terrible shout of rage from his brother-in-law and a cry of fear from his sister-in-law followed by a fresh blast of the automatic weapon. And then there was silence.

Ali hurried to pick up his moaning daughter and carried her toward the brush, weeping for his family, praying to Mohammad for help. Ali was not a leader. He was a gluer of photograph frames. He looked back in the darkness behind the van expecting the Jew with the automatic weapon to suddenly appear.

"Quickly," he shouted, putting down his daughter and waving for her to run to the field ahead of him.

Ali turned to look down the road through his one unblinded eye for the Israeli checkpoint, which should have been visible in the distance. What he saw was impossible. The bearded Jew with the weapon was advancing, firing, but coming from the wrong direction. He must have run in the scrub along the opposite side of the road and gotten ahead of them. Ali could see the man's face now, a man younger than Ali had thought. There was no hatred. Nothing. Only a dead, drugged look.

And then Ali understood what had happened. The van had skidded around. It was not facing toward the checkpoint but away from it toward the road behind them. The checkpoint was behind them, behind the van. The Jew began chanting. With shaking hand Ali managed to pull out his pistol and, peering through his non-bloodied eye, he fired. The shot hit a stone in the road a few feet in front of the Jew who kept moving forward and began firing again.

Ali fired again also, a volley of three shots from his old pistol. The Jew isn't a good shot or they would all have been dead by now, he thought, but Ali knew he was better. The bearded young man moved closer. Ali fired again. No sign of dust in the road. Perhaps he had hit the man, but it had not stopped him nor slowed him down.

The decision came to Ali without thought amid the carnage surrounding him: His dead wife, his slaughtered in-laws, his daughter sobbing on the road beside him, his son's life uncertain. Ali advanced toward the Jew as quickly as he could. The pistol was no match for the automatic and though he hadn't counted, he knew he had no more than a bullet or two left, if any. He would fire in hope, die in anger.

"Jara, run," he shouted as he rushed toward the man in the road.

The Jew fired, bullets chopped up the ground in front of Ali who realized that his run was less than a run. His left leg had been hit. But he moved forward firing his pistol again.

And then there was a second figure behind the Jew, or Ali imagined a second figure, another attacker, as if another was needed.

The figure spoke in the dark in clear, precise Hebrew. His voice was young. His voice was loud and demanding.

"Stop," the figure shouted.

The Jew heard, turned.

The figure, a young border guard, was faintly visible in the now flickering light of the wrecked van. He held a weapon at the ready.

The Jew gave him hardly a glance and turned again to fire at Ali, a new burst from within two dozen yards. But this time it was the Jew who fell to his knees, dropping his weapon and saying something unintelligible, something that sounded like the beginning of a prayer. And then the Jew fell forward on his face.

The border guard moved forward into the light. He was very young, maybe nineteen or twenty, and wearing glasses. The world had changed now for Ali, the gluer of photograph frames. He had been warned all of his life that this moment would come. Now he saw not a border guard but another Jew. He limped forward and aimed the gun at the young man in uniform who shouted, "Stop," first in Hebrew and then in Arabic.

Ali's madness drove him forward, amazed that he had any bullets left. He fired one into the body of the fallen Jew who had murdered his wife and maimed his child and then he turned on the young border guard.

As he pulled the trigger on an empty chamber, the guard fired. The bullet struck Ali in the chest, turning him around in surprise. He faced his fallen daughter in the distance. She crawled toward her father as the border guard stepped forward.

The guard watched, himself shaken and trying not to show it. As Jara reached the body of her father, the guard tried to mouth an apology but none came as the girl looked up at him with hatred, the hatred of more than two thousand years.

Jara could not know that Tsvi Ben Levitt, an off-duty bor'der guard on his way home, the Jew who had killed her father, had also saved her life and that of her brother. She did not know that the dead Jew was the half-mad fanatic cousin of Tsvi Ben Levitt from the nearby kibbutz. And now the boy soldier would have to explain that he had killed the beloved physician of the commune to save the lives of Arabs.

The eyes of the girl and the young soldier met: his in sadness and confusion, hers in hatred. In the instant of silence, there came a distinct frightened moan from the van.

The border guard motioned to Jara to remain where she was and he hurried to the vehicle, reaching it just as the single flickering headlight died.

ONE

Chicago, Today

THE MORNING RUSH hour at the Edgewater Restaurant, which was little more than a small diner, was over. Traffic hurried by in the late spring rain. People scurried with and without umbrellas down Lawrence Avenue. There were only three customers in the diner; two of them were Korean businessmen who owned shops in the area, one a cleaning store, the other a shoe store. They were sitting in a booth finishing a late breakfast and arguing in Korean about something. The only other customer, a burly, weary-looking white man, sat in the booth behind them drinking coffee from a white mug and reading the *Sun-Times*.

The old counterman in a white apron filled white ceramic containers with packets of Sweet'n Low, Equal, and sugar. When the diner door opened, letting in the sound and smell of falling rain, the counterman barely looked up. The burly man sipped his coffee and turned to the sports pages in back. But the two Korean businessmen turned, rose from their unfinished breakfast and hurried to the counter to pay. One of them placed a ten-dollar bill near the cash register.

The other businessman, the one with the shoe store, tried not to look at the trio who had come into the restaurant, one of whom was now closing the door behind him.

"I'll add it up," said the counterman, putting aside his packet container and wiping his hands on his apron.

"No need," said the cleaning store operator. "You keep change."

"Suit yourself," said the counterman with a shrug and reached for the ten spot while the businessmen made their way around the three men who had just entered.

The three were in their twenties, Korean. Two were dressed in black jeans, nicely laundered white button-down shirts, and identical leather bomber jackets. The third Korean was slightly older than the other two and wore a black London Fog raincoat and sunglasses. The three moved to the counter and sat as the old counterman smoothed his white mustache and asked, "What'll it be, gentlemen?"

"Mr. Park," said the one in the middle, the one wearing sunglasses.

"Park's sick," said the counterman. "You wanna start with coffee?"

The three young men sat silently, barely wet from the pouring rain, their car probably parked within a few feet of the diner. The three men watched the old man pour them coffee. Their cups sat untouched. The old counterman put out the sugar and sugar substitutes and a small metal pitcher of milk.

"When will Mr. Park return?" the young man with glasses said, without a trace of accent.

The old counterman shrugged his thin shoulders and said, "Couldn't say. Pretty sick. Something with his stomach. Hypotonectosis. I'm talking over the place for a while, maybe a long while." The counterman heaved a heavy sigh and looked around the place. "Thought I was safely retired, but . . . what'll it be? Hotcakes, eggs, fruit and yogurt cup? Strawberries are fresh."

"Fruit and yogurt," said the young man, removing his glasses to clean the rain off with a napkin.

The old man looked at the flankers who shook their head without speaking. The old man shrugged and called the order back to someone in the kitchen. Then he moved from behind the counter with the coffee pot in his hand to give a refill to the burly man who grumbled something about the Cubs having no pitchers again, about someone named Dickerson giving up two runs in the eighth.

The old man shook his head sympathetically as he retreated behind the counter and returned the pitcher to the hot plate. He picked up the fruit cup and delivered it to the young Korean whose glasses were now cleaned to his satisfaction and back on his nose.

"We have come to collect," said the young man. "I am sure Mr. Park informed you that we come in every other Friday to collect."

The old man looked puzzled. "Park got sick suddenly. Rushed to the hospital. I talked to his daughter, said I'd take over. Park's an old friend. How's the yogurt cup?"

"These strawberries are not fresh," said the young man. "They were frozen."

"I swear on my mother's life," the old man said shaking his head. "I thought we had fresh strawberries. You want me to take it back? No charge."

He reached for the cup. The young man grabbed his wrist and held it tightly. One of the other two men looked at the man reading his newspaper. The burly man didn't seem to be paying any attention.

"We collect one hundred dollars every two weeks," the man in the glasses said softly. "Today is collection day."

"Collect?" said the counterman, trying to pull his arm away. "For what?"

"Protection," said the young man.

"From who, what?" the old man said, still trying to free his arm.

"From us," the young man said softly. "Park pays. We don't break his windows. We don't mess the place up. We don't mess up Park or his family. What we could do to Park, we could do to you. Hypo . . ."

". . . tonectosis," the old man finished.

"You'll wish you were in the hospital with it next to Park. You understand?"

"This is a shakedown," the old man said, frightened but also angry. "This is blackmail."

"Now you understand," the young man said, letting go of the counterman's arm. "Every other week we collect one hundred dollars from every Korean business in the neighborhood."

"I'm not Korean," said the old man.

"As of right now, till Park returns, you are acting Korean," said the young man, adjusting his dark glasses as the counterman rubbed his wrist and looked at all three of the young men. The one on the right smiled slightly.

"Blackmail," repeated the old man.

"Extortion," the young man with glasses corrected.

"I'm not paying," said the old man, backing away from the counter.

The young man in the middle, the leader who had grabbed the old man's wrist, put his palms together and touched his hand to his lips as if in prayer.

"Then," he said, "we will begin by breaking two of your fingers and destroying the kitchen."

The two young men flanking the leader got up from their stools. One of them moved around the counter heading for the counterman. The other headed slowly toward the kitchen.

"You hear all that?" the counterman said.

"Clear as spring rain," answered the burly man, still looking at his newspaper.

"Leave now," the young man with glasses said to the burly man. The man who was heading for the kitchen paused at the customer's table and a knife suddenly appeared in the young man's hand, a long, thin-bladed knife. He pointed it at the burly man.

"OK," said the old counterman, wearily stepping back in front of the bespectacled Korean.

The young man smiled and then, to his total surprise, the

old counterman reached over, grabbed the front of his jacket, and with an unexpected strength yanked the young man onto the counter, overturning the yogurt plate and one of the cups of coffee. The young Korean was appalled to find the barrel of a pistol pressed up against the right lens of his glasses.

When the other two young men moved to help their leader, the burly man lowered his newspaper, revealing a pistol in his hand. "Stop there," he said.

The two ignored him and took a step forward. The young man looking into the gun barrel shuddered.

"I said 'stop' in clear, plain, loud English," the burly man shouted, firing his weapon into the ceiling.

This time, the two men stopped.

"You OK, Rabbi?" the burly cop said, sliding out of the booth, weapon aimed at the frozen young Koreans.

"Lovely, Father Murphy," said the old man, releasing the young man with the glasses but keeping the gun leveled at his head.

"Tape?" asked the burly cop, knocking the knife from the hand of the young man nearest him.

Gun still leveled, the old man reached beneath the counter and pulled out a small tape recorder. "I'll leave it running in case these gentlemen have anything more to say."

None of the three Koreans spoke as the two policemen handcuffed them behind their backs.

"Let's set a record booking 'em," said the burly man, pushing the two young men toward the door. "Iris and I have an appointment with Father Parker about the wedding."

"You could've told me earlier," said Lieberman, removing his apron and pocketing the tape recorder.

"Slipped my mind," said Hanrahan.

"Slipped his mind." Lieberman said to the bespectacled young man as if they were friends. "You believe that?"

The young man said nothing as Lieberman guided him around the counter and had him join his partners at the front door. The young man was known only as Kim to his small gang and to the Korean businessmen he robbed. Kim's goals in life were to look as dry as Clint Eastwood and as cool as a young Robert Mitchum and to become very wealthy and respected. He and his gang had been at this extortion game for almost a year. They had done well. Until now. Kim was humiliated, beaten by a skinny old man.

"I'll get the car," Hanrahan said, putting his gun back in the holster under his jacket.

"I'll entertain our visitors," said Lieberman.

Hanrahan opened the door, looked at the downpour and turned to say, "I'll have the door open. Get 'em in fast."

"Like the Flash," said Lieberman, and his partner dashed out into the rain. "You know the Flash?"

The question was directed at the three handcuffed young men. The one nearest Lieberman was having trouble keeping his glasses on his nose with his hands cuffed behind him.

"The Flash was in the comics," said Lieberman with a sigh at the lack of education of the young. "When I was a kid he wore a tin helmet with wings, like Mercury. Then they stuck him in a tight red suit."

The Koreans seemed even more bewildered.

"OK now?" came a timid voice behind Lieberman.

"OK now," Lieberman answered.

From the kitchen two people emerged, Park and his wife. They were in their fifties and held back in fear, not completely sure that what they had done was the right thing.

"We will talk again," the young man in glasses said to the couple.

"That would be a bad idea," Lieberman said, moving to Kim's side. He moved close enough to whisper in the man's ear. "Much to my regret and in the hope that God has forgiven me through my prayers, I have killed four people and cooperated in doing very unpleasant things to about six others. If anything happens to the Parks, if anything happens to this diner, if he even tells me that you or one of your gang has returned here, I'll find you and I'll shoot you."

The young man twitched his nose trying to keep his glasses on. Lieberman helped him by pushing the glasses back with the barrel of his gun.

"You believe me?" asked Lieberman.

Kim didn't answer.

"You know the Tentaculos?"

The three men looked at the skinny cop with the almost white hair and the white mustache. He looked a little like an undernourished old dog, one of those dogs with the sad, tired faces. They didn't answer, but Lieberman knew the answer.

"You get in touch with El Perro," Lieberman said in his ear. "Tell him that El Viejo said he would shoot you. Ask him if you should believe me."

"You're threatening me," said Kim.

"You are a very perceptive young man," said Lieberman softly. "I turned the tape recorder off long before I did it."

"You are the Jew cop. Liebowitz," the man in sunglasses said calmly. "You are the one who has been talking to our clients, costing us business. I've heard of you."

"It's nice to be famous," said Lieberman. "The name is Lieberman."

Three quick honks of a car horn. Lieberman nodded the trio out into the rain. He turned and smiled sadly at the Parks, who were pressed close to each other. Mrs. Park raised her hand slightly in what was probably a wave.

Lieberman ushered the three onto the street and into the back seat of the unmarked blue Geo. It took about ten seconds. Lieberman closed the door and slid into the passenger seat. He was almost as soaked as Hanrahan who gunned the car into the dark wet traffic almost colliding with a bright, white, double-parked Lincoln Town Car.

"That your car?" asked Hanrahan, nodding at the Lincoln as they passed it. "Bockford Towing gets them in minutes around here, even in the rain."

"I'll book 'em," Lieberman said, running his hand

through his hair and glancing back at their silent prisoners. "We'll get you to the church on time."

"Meet you back at the station at noon?" asked Hanrahan, now driving merely recklessly instead of insanely through traffic.

"Make it one," said Lieberman. "I've got an appointment too. You three comfortable back there?"

The three men in the back seat started to talk in Korean.

"Silence," said Lieberman, half turning in his seat and pointing his gun at them. "I might think you're planning some kind of escape. You don't want me to think that. You have long lives and short prison terms ahead of you unless we find you're wanted for something else."

The young man directly behind Hanrahan said something in Korean. He was clearly frightened. The one in the middle, with sunglasses, answered him with two or three clipped words and the frightened one grew quiet.

"I think, Father Murphy, that we have a winner in the back row."

Hanrahan nodded. If one of them was wanted they would work him over, make a deal with his lawyer, get better counts on his partners. On the other hand, all three of them could be back on the street the next day. The ways of judges and lawyers were a mystery to Hanrahan. He checked the car clock and his wristwatch. He had a little over half an hour to pick up Iris and ten minutes after that to get to St. Bart's. There was just enough room between the Bekin's truck and an old Dodge. Hanrahan sloshed through, heading up Broadway.

"What the hell is hypotonectosis?" asked Hanrahan.

"Made it up," said Lieberman.

"Why didn't you just give him a real disease?"

"Spring is the mischief in me," said Lieberman.

"What?" asked Hanrahan.

"Robert Frost," said the bespectacled prisoner. "It's from Robert Frost."

Lieberman looked at Kim.

"English major," Kim said.

Lieberman sat forward and shook his head. He listened to the torrent of rain on the car roof and thought about his lunch meeting with Eli Towser. Capturing the three in the back seat was like eating a strawberry danish at Maish's compared to what he expected from Eli Towser.

In spite of the faded jeans, the red-and-black flannel shirt, and the little black *kepuh* on his head, the beard gave Eli Towser away. He was not just a Jew, he was very much an Orthodox Jew. In fact, he was not just an Orthodox Jew, he was also a rabbinical student and had come highly recommended by Rabbi Wass of Temple Mir Shavot. Since Rabbi Wass was neither Orthodox nor particularly brilliant, Lieberman had been suspicious of the lean young man who had appeared at his door a little over a month ago. The young man had introduced himself seriously, touched the mezuzah on the doorway and entered.

Eli Towser, no more than twenty-five years old, had explained that he and his wife made a modest supplement to his scholarship, she with the money earned by a part-time job while she too went to school, and he by tutoring Jewish boys for their bar mitzvah and Jewish girls for their bat mitzvah. Towser had been dressed more seriously the day he first met Lieberman, Bess, and their grandson Barry. Winter had just made up its mind to depart but left a late chill behind and the young man before them had worn a black suit, hat, and coat.

He answered all of their questions and assured them that Barry's being bar mitzvahed in a Conservative temple would be no problem, and they came to a price. Bess took care of the payments and Barry had reluctantly prepared. If there had been no reluctance from a twelve-year-old boy, Abe would have worried. For the first four sessions—two per week, after school on Tuesdays and Thursdays—the rabbinical student and the resigned boy, who bore a distinct resemblance to his father, were left alone in the Lieberman kitchen.

They practiced. Much of what Barry had to learn was simply memorization. His reading of Hebrew was going slowly. The whole process was about to go even more slowly.

Now sitting among the early lunch crowd a Kopelman's Kosher Restaurant, Lieberman said "Eli," as he pushed aside his bowl of rice pudding, leaving just enough left to delude himself that he was indeed eating with moderation.

The rabbinical student was methodically dipping mandel bread cookies into his coffee. With each dip, Towser smoothed down his beard to make room for the dripping delight. Four pieces of the almost oval cookies remained on the plate.

Lieberman had to speak loudly to be heard over the early lunch crowd at Kopelman's Kosher Restaurant. Lieberman felt the first twinge of a coming stomach ache. He was getting them more and more often. Two blocks east of them on Devon was the T & L Deli, owned and run by Abe's brother Maish, but the T & L wasn't kosher. Kopelman's was.

Towser had consumed a lunch that would have made Marlon Brando proud: salad, pot roast, a side order of kishke, and a large glass of orange juice before coffee and desert.

"Yes?" asked Eli, reaching for a second piece of mandel bread.

"You have any idea of why I asked to have lunch with you?"

"To *take* me to lunch," Towser corrected, pointing a piece of cookie across the table at Lieberman.

At the table inches away from them, one of the two women working on their kreplach soup said, "Be sensible, Rose. If he were cheating, would he give you her name?" Lieberman thought it a distinct possibility that Rose's husband would give the name of the woman he was having an affair with. It would depend on how smart the husband was and how much Rose was willing to pretend not to know.

A few more details and Lieberman could have given a definitive answer.

"None at all," Towser answered Lieberman with a small smile of anticipation.

"Politics," said Lieberman, nodding at the waiter who had come to refill Towser's cup and offer coffee to Lieberman. Lieberman had been a master of restraint for over a month, rigidly watching his diet, eating the inedible, drinking massive amounts of water, moderate amounts of coffee and envying all who could consume enormous quantities of fat and salt without being warned by their doctors about blood pressure, cholesterol, and inflamed intestinal walls. Today Lieberman had eaten a toasted onion bagel with nothing on it and a bowl of cold beet borscht with no sour cream. He had consumed a small bowl of rice pudding and was now working on coffee.

Towser paused mid-dunk to look at the man across the table who had taken pains to tuck his holster and pistol well beneath his armpit under his jacket. There would be no hint of anger or intimidation. Abe had promised Bess.

"Israeli politics?" Towser asked.

"In a sense," Lieberman answered, dreading the rest of the conversation and smelling a brisket being served to the betrayed Rose and her sympathetic friend.

"You are the president of temple Mir Shavot, aren't you?" Eli Towser said.

"My wife is," said Lieberman. "I adroitly managed to escape that trap, only to find myself maneuvered onto the building committee."

"I've seen the new temple on Dempster," said Towser. "Very contemporary." There was a faint touch of criticism in Towser's observation.

"It used to be a bank," Lieberman said.

Towser dunked and nodded his head.

"You're a good teacher," Lieberman went on, his hands in his lap. "Barry's learned a lot and he's learned fast."

"Thank you," said Towser. "Am I here to get a raise?"

"No," said Lieberman, "you are here to be told politely

to stop teaching your own political views to my grandson.
Your job is to prepare him for his bar mitzvah."

Towser put his piece of mandel bread aside and leaned
toward Lieberman. "There is no line between the politics
of Israel and the process of being a Jew," said the young
man.

"What we want is a bar mitzvah for my grandson," said
Lieberman, trying to ignore the smile of recognition from
a man in a booth across the room.

"And he'll have it," said Towser.

"He's talking about driving Arabs out of Israel, a return
to war against the PLO," said Lieberman. "He doesn't even
know what he's talking about and you've got it in his
speech."

"Where it belongs," said Towser.

"He's twelve," said Lieberman.

"My father bombed a British hotel in Jerusalem when he
was twelve," said Towser intently. "Jewish boys become
men when they bar mitzvah. A thirteen-year-old stands with
us in a minyan."

Lieberman was far more familiar with what twelve-year-
old boys are capable of than Eli Towser was. That was
Lieberman's point. He knew how ready they were to follow
a leader into violence and their own sense of group respect,
survival, and often a creative or idiotic sense of honor or
territory. A minyan, a gathering of ten adult, bar mitzvahed
Jews needed in order to pray, required no political posture.
"I don't want my grandson to be taught hate," said Lieberman.

The man who had smiled at Lieberman rose from his
booth, put down his napkin, and headed through the crowd.

"Over and over throughout recorded time, the Lord Our
God has delivered us from those who would take away
Israel," said Towser, his eyes scanning Lieberman's face.
"But he does not just deliver us with miracles. He tells us
to take up sword and return to the days of Samuel. Do you
understand Hebrew?"

"No," said Lieberman.

Towser sighed and said, "First Samuel, chapter seven, verses eleven through fourteen: ' . . . and the hand of the Lord was against the Philistines all the days of Samuel. And the cities which the Philistines had taken from Israel were restored to Israel, from (Ekron even unto Gath); and the borders thereof did Israel deliver out of the hands of the Philistines.' "

The rabbinical student's voice was rising now. Rose and her friend stopped talking and tackled their food with religious intensity. The man from the booth made his way between tables and past waiters juggling steaming trays.

Everything smelled good to Lieberman. Everything looked like trouble.

"You told Barry that it was the responsibility of every Jew to be prepared to take arms against Arabs and anyone who supported them anywhere in the world," said Lieberman.

"Yes?" said Towser.

"Sounds too much like terrorist rhetoric for my wife and me," Lieberman said.

"And Barry's parents? What do they say?" asked Eli Towser, his white-knuckled hands now gripping the table.

"His father is a gentile," said Lieberman. "He teaches Greek literature at Northwestern. He thinks politics stopped over a thousand years ago, but I bet he can quote you a line of Aeschylus to counter anything you come up with from the Bible regardless of which side it takes. My daughter Lisa, Barry's mother, is in Los Angeles seeking her Self. She thinks that a bar mitzvah for her son is a waste of time, a waste that probably won't hurt him. She walked out on her husband and left her kids with us."

"So?" asked Towser expectantly.

The man from the booth across the room was now hovering over their table grinning widely. Abe pretended not to see him. He wanted his moist eyes focused on the rabbinical student.

"So, the decision is mine and my wife's. So we ask you to stop the politics."

"I can't," said Towser.

"I didn't think so. I've seen too many people, young and old, with the look you have in your eyes," said Lieberman. "True believers." Lieberman reached into his inner jacket pocket, pulled out his wallet and found a check, which he handed to Towser. It was all made out. "Payment in full," said Lieberman.

"I'm fired?" asked Towser looking at the check, off guard.

"Dismissed," said Lieberman.

There was more to say but Lieberman was certain it would have no effect. He could talk about the anger Eli Towser needed to control, but Towser would have responded with indignation and examples from Jeremiah, the Likud Party, and the *New York Times*.

Eli Towser rose. People in the restaurant were looking at them. Most assumed it was an argument between father and son and lowered their voices to listen or raised them to drown out the battle. This was lunch time at Kopelman's.

Towser pocketed the check. "I deserve this payment," he said.

"I agree," said Lieberman with a nod to Eli, who walked away shaking his head. Lieberman looked up at the hovering man who was casting a shadow on his now tepid cup of coffee.

"Lieberman," the man said jovially. He was plump, around Lieberman's age, early sixties, and had a pink, healthy face and a businessman's smile. His suit wasn't new, but it was definitely made from good material. Lieberman knew good material. His mother's father had been a tailor on the West Side on 12th Street even before it became Roosevelt Road.

Lieberman looked up, wanting very much to be alone, and not recognizing the man though Lieberman had a reputation in both the Clark Street Station and Congregation Mir Shavot for never forgetting a face or a name. It might take him a while and he might have to imagine a historical context, but he seldom missed.

"Hoover," said the man, surprised that Abe did not recognize him. "Ira Hoover."

No bells rang for Lieberman. He did not really want to listen for them. The two women at the next table watched the exchange while they nibbled at a small plate of rugalah. Rose ate slowly.

"Itzak Hoverman," the man prodded.

"Izzy?" said Lieberman, looking at the man again.

"The one. The only. The same. In the flesh. Only more of it," said Hoover. "Izzy Hoover."

"Haven't see you around," said Lieberman.

"For good reason," said Hoover taking the seat Eli Towser had recently left. "I've been away from Chicago for more than thirty years. I'm in the front office for the Supersonics. Moved up from a USBL team in Texas about four years ago."

"How's Seattle?" asked Lieberman.

"Nice. Wet," said Hoover. "I hear you're a police officer?"

Lieberman nodded, dearly wanting to be alone with his thoughts rather than reminiscing with someone who looked like the greeter at a posh Michigan Avenue men's store. He did not want to see this nearly bald man with a fringe of gray hair and a pink face who had once been Izzy Hoverman, one of the best shooting guards in Chicago. At Marshall High School back in the 1950s, the Commandos Juniors, 5'8" and under, four blacks, six Jews, were the best in the city, probably the best in the country. Abe's brother Maish was three years ahead of Abe, but they got to play together for one season, the best season. Abe, the ball handler, remembered every pass, every assist, every jumper he made that season. At least he thought he remembered. Izzy and Billy "Springfeet" Springfield were the only ones who had gone on to college ball. And Billy, who had suddenly shot up to 6'6", had even been drafted out of college by the Celtics, but he hadn't made the team.

Abe didn't want to remember. He didn't want to talk basketball or old times at Marshall High.

"You see *Hoop Dreams*?" Izzy said. "The gym looked the same. The cheerleaders were leading the same. Déjà vu, you know? That Agee kid reminds me of Billy, even looks like him."

Lieberman nodded and drank some cool coffee.

"You got stuff on your mind," Izzy observed, standing. "I know how that is. Listen, I got to get back to my booth. My cousins. I don't get back here much. You know how it is. How's Maish?"

"Fine," said Lieberman, not wanting to go into the recent death of Maish's son.

"Nothing bothers Maish," Hoover said. "City championship game. No time left. We're down by two and Maish has a pair of free throws. I'll never forget. Chicago Stadium. Maybe ten thousand in the audience. School winning streak in his hands. And calm as you please, Maish sinks 'em both. We all run out, jump all over him. Pick him up. Never cracks a smile."

"I remember," said Abe.

"Won't keep you any longer," said Izzy, reaching into his pocket. "Maybe you can use these." Izzy handed Lieberman an envelope pulled magically from his inside jacket pocket. He reached out to shake hands and Lieberman shook. "You look like you need a vacation, Abe. You ever get to Seattle, look me up. I mean it."

And Izzy was gone. Lieberman was alone with his cold coffee. The two women at the next table were gone. A busboy was quickly clearing their table. Lieberman opened the envelope and pulled out four passes behind the Sonics bench for a Bulls-Sonics game next season. Abe looked up for Izzy, but like the ladies at the next table, he and his cousins were gone.

TWO

IF THERE IS such a thing as a typical American Catholic church, St. Bartholomew's is not it. St. Bart's priest is Sam "Whiz" Parker, a thirty-eight-year-old African-American, former All-American running back at the University of Illinois and former Green Bay Packer. Father Parker's congregation consisted almost totally of Vietnamese and Koreans who moved slowly into the previously Polish neighborhood in Edgewater when the Poles moved out. St. Bart's had a homeless shelter. Most of the homeless who made their way west from Broadway, north from Devon and east from Western, were white with a few blacks, never an Asian.

Result: A congregation of Catholic Asians with a black priest was running a shelter primarily for white men and women.

The few white parishioners, like Detective William Hanrahan, were there, more or less, by mistake. A murder investigation two years earlier had brought Hanrahan in search of a homeless man and back to the church. The policeman, who had himself been a *Parade* magazine All-American football player from Vocational High School, had bad knees that drove him from big-time college ball to a mediocre career at Eureka College and no draft pick.

The two men spoke the same language.

"You know," said Father Parker, looking across his cluttered desk in his cluttered office, "I can't marry you."

Hanrahan nodded and patted the hand of Iris Huang who looked nervous. Hanrahan was a little past his fiftieth birthday. So was Iris, but she could easily be mistaken for thirty.

Hanrahan sat back and looked at the familiar walls filled with photographs, mostly football players. Most were signed. There was even one of a young Bill Hanrahan, obtained by Parker when he was a boy. A light, chilly spring rain was still falling outside. Parker, wearing sneakers, a pair of jeans and a white button-down shirt, looked out at the rain and listened as it hit the pebble-covered parking lot next to the church. "Advice, suggestions, Sam," said Hanrahan. "We've got a problem here."

Father Parker turned back to the man and woman who were holding hands. "Maybe," said the priest, rubbing his neck.

"I've been sober for almost two years," said Hanrahan.

"Bill," Parker said softly. "It's not your sobriety or lack of it. You've been divorced in a civil court. Even if I wanted to, I'd have to check with the Archdiocese who would have to check with. . . . You can see how it goes. I might even go all the way to the Vatican where some ninety-year-old Italian cardinal will automatically say 'no.' Right or wrong, the Church has circled the holy wagons and is drawing lines in Our Savior's blood around the circle. One line clearly reads that you can't cross it on this issue."

"I'm a Catholic, Sam," Hanrahan said. "Iris is more than willing to convert if necessary. We don't want a Justice of the Peace. We don't want a Protestant."

"Best I can give you is an Episcopalian," said Father Parker. He paused and added, "That's a joke, Bill."

"Hard to laugh, Father," Hanrahan said with a sigh.

"Miss Huang?"

"My family, my father, has learned to accept William. My uncles, aunts, cousins, and others are more cautious."

"How about an ex-priest with a Korean wife who heads a Universalist congregation in Des Plaines?" asked Father Parker.

"Another joke?" asked Hanrahan.

"Nope," said the priest standing up. "Vincent DiPino. Went to the seminary with him. Ordained with him. He dropped out of the church four years ago, got married, runs a computer system update business out of his house, and has a congregation triple mine."

"A football player?" asked Hanrahan.

"A little high school soccer," said Father Parker, sitting on the edge of his desk after moving a pile of books and papers. "Can't have everything."

Hanrahan looked at Iris, who smiled back at him and squeezed his hand.

"The ex-priest would be fine with me," said Iris softly.

Hanrahan shrugged. He had waited for years for his ex-wife Maureen to return. She had obtained a civil divorce, unrecognized by the Church. He had waited for his sons to forgive him for his drinking, his fights with their mother, his not being around when they grew up. He had kept the small house in the old neighborhood on the other side of Wilson spotless, like an ad on television, in the hope that Maureen would return, not so much that she would see what he had done and return to him but that she would see that he had not fallen completely apart. He had done that even when he was carrying his badge and suffering as an alcoholic.

What had put him firmly on the wagon happened the night he met Iris. He was supposedly watching the front entrance and a window in a high rise on Sheridan. He had sat inside the Black Moon Chinese Restaurant. Iris had waited on him. Hanrahan had spent several hours drinking and watching through a rain not much different from the one now falling, but it had been darker that night and he had missed the closing of the drapes signal from Estralda Valdez that she needed help. By the time Hanrahan noticed the signal, made it across the street, and up to the apartment, Estralda Valdez was a bloody corpse. Lieberman covered for his partner. Hanrahan had stopped drinking and carried his guilt to Sam Parker. He had also joined AA, though at first he had felt little confidence in their beliefs.

How many times? How many guilts had Bill Hanrahan confessed to Sam Parker? And how in the name of the Blessed Mother could Father Parker continue to absolve him and remain his friend?

"Call the ex-priest," said Hanrahan with resignation, looking at Iris who nodded. "Am I risking excommunication?"

"That one I think I can deal with," said Parker, burrowing through the clutter for a black address book.

Hanrahan's pager suddenly went off. Usually, he turned it off when he entered the church. This time he had been more than a bit nervous. He asked to use the phone, called in to Nestor Briggs on the desk at the Clark Street Station. Nestor reported that the Korean extortionists had been booked, printed, and scowled at. Nestor gave Hanrahan a number to call. Hanrahan made the call. Identified himself, listened, nodded his head, and said nothing.

"Got to get back on the job," said Hanrahan, checking his watch.

"I'll stay and make the arrangements," Iris said.

"You sure?" Hanrahan asked standing.

"I am sure," she said.

"I'll give Miss Huang a ride home," said Sam Parker, as he found DiPino's phone number in his book. "I've got hospital calls to make."

Hanrahan gave Iris a chaste kiss, said he would call her later, and said to the priest, "Thanks, Father."

Father Parker was already dialing the number.

Hanrahan hurried down the aisle of the empty church, stopped, looked up at the stained glass image of Jesus on

the cross, rain on the other side of the window running
down his face like tears. Hanrahan knelt, crossed himself,
and prayed. He used no words and thought none. He simply
gave himself over to prayer.

The blue, flat cushions on most of the benches in the main
worship hall of Temple Mir Shavot had been ripped by a
sharp object. Padding puffed out like gray-white intestines.
No windows were broken, but the ark had been opened and
three of the four Torahs had been unfurled and torn and
thrown toward the congregation seats like sheets of wall-
paper. The fourth Torah was gone. The walls were spray-
painted in red, hurriedly with no style or graffiti grace and
pride.

"Kikes eat our babies," was dripping down one wall next
to, "Jews get out or die." The other messages were equal
in kind and hatred. "Yids will die in the street," "Soon we
will cut off your. . . ." Hanrahan stopped reading and
looked at Lieberman, who showed no emotion. Lieberman
stood in the center aisle of the temple looking at the damage, noting that no windows had been broken, that the vandals had taken care not to be heard. Lieberman absorbed
each act of sacrilege and blasphemy.

Hanrahan was sure he himself would be feeling enormous rage if St. Bart's had been desecrated like this. But
Hanrahan had learned that his partner's facial expressions
and feelings might be quite different.

The other man looking at Lieberman was in his late forties, thin, dressed in a gray suit with no tie on his white
shirt. A white yarmulke rested atop his head. Lieberman
and Hanrahan wore similar little round black caps, which
they had taken from a box that had fallen near the entrance
of the chapel. The man in the gray suit was wearing no
socks and his shoes were untied. His eyes through his
glasses were fixed on Lieberman, watching the detective's
eyes, trying to read in them something, anything that would
help him make sense of the abomination around him.

"You got the call?" Lieberman said.

"Around ten," said Rabbi Wass. "No, a few minutes before ten. Mr. Timms called. I think he was crying. Then I got dressed, came over and . . . this. I tried to reach you, left messages. Sat, prayed. . . . The Torah, the blue velvet Torah, it's missing."

Lieberman nodded.

"Mr. Timms, Albert," said Rabbi Wass, "was here last night till after ten, cleaning up, and then came back this morning, saw all this, and called me."

"Where's Mr. Timms?" asked Lieberman.

"In my study," said the young rabbi who had replaced his father, the Old Rabbi Wass, as leader of Temple Mir Shavot six years ago. "He's not a young man. He has a bad heart."

"Your study is . . . ?" Lieberman began.

"Thank God," said Wass looking at Hanrahan. "It's untouched. No other room but this was touched."

"Thank God," Hanrahan said not sure of what he should say. It was Hanrahan whose fists were clenched in anger as he looked around. Lieberman continued to look, as he always looked, like a sad, old man with gray hair and the face of a beagle.

"You haven't called the police?" asked Lieberman.

"You're the police," said Wass, holding out his hands. "I called you."

"I'm a Chicago police officer," said Lieberman. "The temple is in Skokie now. You call the Skokie police. Let's go back to your study, talk to Mr. Timms, and call a friend of mine who can help. Detective Hanrahan will keep looking around."

Hanrahan was only a few feet away from an obscenity on the wall in dried blood. As they walked out of the large chapel that had once been the lobby of a bank, Rabbi Wass looked back at the devastation in bewilderment and fear.

"How can we get this cleaned up for services? Who did such a thing? What . . . ?" Wass said as they stepped into the hallway near the entrance of the temple. The white

prayer talliths were draped evenly over wooden rods next
to the box of black yarmulkes on the floor. The rack of
rods had been pushed or kicked over against the wall. On
Dempster Street outside, cars sloshed through rain and pe-
destrians with umbrellas made their way quickly down the
sidewalk.

"First, Rabbi," said Lieberman. "I am here in my capacity as building committee chair. Calling me was a logical
thing to do."

"But the repair of desecration doesn't come under the
building committee," said Rabbi Wass. "At least I don't
think so. You are a policeman. I called you. There is no
precedent. I mean no precedent in our congregation, not in
my father's time, not in my. . . ."

They entered the rabbi's study, bookshelves along both
walls, desk near the window, small conference table near
the door. Seated at the end of the conference table, looking
up at the two men who had entered, was Albert Timms.
Albert was very black and very old and remembered being
hired by the Old Rabbi Wass when the old temple in the
converted grade school had opened. The present Rabbi
Wass had been a toddler when the Old Rabbi hired Albert
Timms.

Albert always wore clean, sturdy blue slacks, a crisp,
clean denim shirt—except on Jewish holidays when he
dressed up and on Sundays when he went to the same Bap-
tist church he had gone to on Harrison Street since long
before his wife died more than twenty years ago. Albert
had suffered at least two heart attacks, but Dr. Ira Shulman,
cardiologist at Rush-St. Luke's and member of the Temple
Mir Shavot congregation, had said that retiring Albert
Timms would probably kill him faster than letting him continue to work.

"I didn't do that," Albert said as soon as he saw Lieberman come through the door. "Had nothing to do with it,
Mr. Lieberman. You know that."

"That, Mr. Timms, I am very sure of," said Lieberman.
Albert looked relieved. Lieberman moved behind Albert

Timms to the rabbi's desk, picked up the phone, and dialed a number he got out of the small address book in his pocket. The custodian and the rabbi exchanged looks of confusion and fear as Lieberman dialed.

"Detective Benishay," Lieberman said. "Thanks." Lieberman put his hand over the mouthpiece and said, "We're in luck. He's there. If . . . ," and then he removed his hand from the mouthpiece and said, "Leo, Abe Lieberman. I'm over at Mir Shavot. We've had some overnight vandalism. You think you can take the call yourself? . . . Good. . . . I'm here with Bill. A favor: no sirens, no lights, no marked car. Good."

He hung up and looked at the two men. "He'll be right over. You and Mr. Timms just sit down, don't come out and touch anything. Detective Benishay will be here soon to have a look."

"Abraham, there have been threats," said the rabbi softly, hands folded before him.

"Threats?" asked Lieberman.

"Since the madman in Israel murdered those praying Arabs. I've had calls, against me, against the congregation, against the temple."

"And you didn't tell me? Didn't call the police?" Lieberman asked with a weary sigh.

"Many rabbis, many congregations have received such threats over the years. Even Jewish schools and community centers. There have just been more since the shameless massacre. And until this. . . . Should I call Mrs. Lieberman?" asked the rabbi.

"Yes," said Lieberman.

Bess Lieberman, Abe's wife, was the president of Mir Shavot, a job Abe had deftly maneuvered to her when it looked as if he were going to be backed into the position. Bess had proved, as Abe knew would be the case, that she was a much better president than he would have been. Thin, well groomed, and looking fifteen years younger than her fifty-eight, she had been a rallying dynamo, attending meetings, pushing the building committee that Abe had been tricked onto, mediating disputes, raising funds, and taking care of their own two grandchildren.

Lieberman returned to the chapel and looked across the aisles at his partner who shook his head. Hanrahan had not found the missing Torah.

"I'm going to find whoever did this," said Lieberman, turning his eyes to an unfurled Torah, the sacred first five books of the Jewish Testament, the holy word.

"We're going to find him," Hanrahan corrected.

Lieberman nodded. There was nothing to say. Mir Shavot was a Conservative congregation and Lieberman had really only become an active member a decade ago when he was fifty. His grandfather had been a stern Orthodox Jew, complete with long black coat, hat, and beard. His grandfather, his mother's father, had refused to speak the language of America just as he had refused to speak Russian in the old country. He spoke and read Hebrew in his prayers and spoke Yiddish in his home and that of Abraham's mother and father. He had insisted that the boy and his older brother, Morris, accompany him to services, hours of standing and sitting, praying in a language the boys didn't understand, dreading the knock of their grandfather at the door to take them back to the mysterious boredom of the synagogue on the West Side. Neither Abe nor Maish had ever had faith. And when their grandfather had died, and old men and an ancient rabbi had told them that their grandfather had been a great and pious man, both boys decided that they had seen their last days as practicing Jews.

When he had married Bess, who came from a Conservative Jewish family, they had agreed that she would continue her practice and he would be left alone. At first he had joined her in only a few annual social events. Then he had decided to accompany her once to Friday night services, just to see if it brought back the same feelings, the ghost of his grandfather.

There were no ghosts at the service. There was almost as much English as there was Hebrew and though he thought he would feel uncomfortable at praying and thanking a God in whom he did not believe, Abraham Lieberman found himself briefly at peace. He could still read the Hebrew he had learned more than thirty-five years earlier. He still could not understand what he was reading, but it gave him a meditative calm, and gradually, it put him at peace with the ghost of his grandfather. There were even times when Lieberman had gone to services alone, especially when the horror and pain he was forced to witness in his work made him wonder at the meaning of his own life. There were never answers, but there was solace and comfort.

And now, he looked around the chapel, his refuge, and knew the fear, memories, and images of the Holocaust would slap each member of the congregation, would sting.

Leo Benishay arrived speedily with a team of photographers and techs and they set to work, Leo giving Abe a sorrowful and sympathetic look as he surveyed the damage. Leo Benishay was a devout Jewish atheist, as Abe had once been, but he would work at this because, atheist or not, he was a Jew and he was a good cop. That, however, was not going to stop Lieberman from finding who had done this in the very room where his grandson was to be bar mitzvahed, the room where he had found some peace. What Lieberman felt was more powerful than Hanrahan's rage; it was a resolve that no one could be allowed to come into his home and that of his people, and get away with doing this. No one. Somewhere in the Torah it was written that the wrath of the Lord could, when He deemed it, be swift, powerful, and without mercy.

Even if the Lord didn't tell him what to do, and Lieberman was certain that the Lord would not since He had never done so before, he would emulate the Lord.

And then, in the middle of the desecration, he thought of Eli Towser, the unforgiving rabbinical student he had fired no more than an hour ago. And Lieberman knew that even with what he saw about him now, he would still have fired the wild-eyed young man.

*   *   *

Within half an hour, they began to come to Mir Shavot. The first to arrive were Abe's brother, Maish, an older, heavier, even sadder version of Abe, and Maish's wife, Yetta. With them were the Alter Cockers, the klatch of old Jews and one Chinese, Howie Chen who, it had been established long ago, was a distant cousin of Iris Huang, Hanrahan's fiancée. Terrill, the new short-order day cook, was with the Alter Cockers. Terrill had spent three years in Stateville on a drug count. Lieberman had set up the job for Terrill after his release, and he turned out to be the best short-order cook the T & L Deli had ever had.

"Clean-up squad," said Syd Levan.

"Let's get to work," said Herschel Rosen, a gnome in a Cubs baseball cap.

"We're ready," said Al Bloombach, who suffered from asthma, was almost eighty, and shouldn't have been there.

"Howie's kids and a few of the grandchildren are coming over," said Syd. Howie Chen nodded solemnly.

"We've got to wait till the Skokie police are done with the photographs and fingerprints," said Lieberman, holding back the rising number of congregation members and friends who were now choking the corridor.

"Leo," called Herschel Rosen.

Leo Benishay stepped through the door into the corridor and looked at the growing throng. Bess was trying to get through with a group of women, some of whom were the wives, daughters, and granddaughters of the men who had first arrived.

"Mr. Rosen," Leo called back. "If everyone will just wait a minute or two more. . . ."

"I was at his bris," Herschel told those around him. "He was a little pisher. Now he's a policeman giving orders."

"We've got the photographs," said Benishay softly to Lieberman. "No point in trying for prints except on the things that were torn and thrown around. Lab says the walls are so full of prints it would take us forever to get them and check them against the FBI lists and we'd have to fingerprint every member of this congregation. My men are gathering the things that have been tossed and torn. We'll call the FBI and have them go over them. Might take some time."

"Take some time?" Lieberman said, as Bess made her way through the crowd and moved to her husband's side taking his hand.

"Five synagogues were attacked last night," said Benishay, suddenly looking very haggard. "This one and four in the city. One in your district, B'nai Zion. The FBI is going to be very busy."

"So . . . ?" asked Lieberman.

Benishay shrugged. "We seal off the chapel. Wait for the FBI. They give the OK and your people can clean up."

Rabbi Wass suddenly appeared from his sanctuary. The noise level was high. An old woman in the back was shouting something about Arabs. Wass looked at Bess, who took him in her arms and said, "Be strong, Rev. Be strong."

Rabbi Wass shook his head, wishing his father were here, that his father were still the rabbi of Mir Shavot, but he was over a thousand miles away in Florida with a weak heart. Wass shook his head and stood up straight.

"The police still have work to do," Bess shouted. She was wearing a yellow dress, her cleaning dress. Her short silver hair was perfectly in place and she had taken a moment to put on makeup while she made her phone calls.

Some in the front heard her. Those in the back shouted, talked.

"Please," shouted Rabbi Wass. "Quiet." They grew silent.

"The police still have work to do," Bess repeated. "They'll tell us when we can start cleaning up."

"What did they do?" shouted someone.

"Graffiti on the walls," said Lieberman. "Some pews and prayer books damaged. The podium on the bema smashed." Lieberman looked over at the rabbi who adjusted his glasses and stood erect.

"They destroyed three of our Torahs," Rabbi Wass said. People gasped. A woman began to weep. "And they stole the velvet Torah."

Now there were wails, people clutching each other in confusion and fear, a few, both young and old, with a look of anger on their faces Lieberman had never seen before. Herschel's daughter Melody stood at her father's side. She was a quiet woman, who had lost her husband in a car accident almost ten years earlier. Now she worked at Bass's Department Store on Devon not far from Maish's T & L. There was anger, death, and determination clear and frightening on her face.

"We'll go into the small chapel," said Rabbi Wass. "I think we can all fit. Mr. Timms can bring extra chairs."

"And what do we do there?" said Bloombach in asthmatic exasperation.

"We pray," said Rabbi Wass. "We pray, talk, and wait and let the police do their jobs." There was some grumbling but they had all heard. When giving his sermons the usually soft-spoken rabbi could project with clear enunciation.

"When will it end for us, Abe?" Syd Levan said, as he filed past with the rest.

"Probably never," said Lieberman.

Syd, the youngest of the Alter Cockers, had lost a son who had moved to Israel and become a soldier and the victim of a terrorist bomb. He shook his head and looked very old.

Maish, a bulky bulldog with sad eyes, had not prayed or come to a service since the murder of his own son by a robber a year earlier. Not only that, but his pregnant daughter-in-law had been shot and lost her baby, Maish's grandchild. He paused when the others were finally in the chapel. He and God were engaged in a bitter feud, a feud which helped to give some sense of meaning to his damaged life. He had lost his faith in God as a young man, regained it before his brother and had it still, but he no longer believed that he could understand the pain of the innocent, which God could stop. He would not quite pray at home, alone, but he would talk to God, imagining answers to his questions, debating them, pointing out God's errors in thinking. It sustained him.

Benishay had returned to the large chapel. Bess and Abe stood facing Maish and the Chen clan.

"Why don't you all go back to the T & L?" Bess said, taking her brother-in-law's hand and looking at the Chens and Yetta who, she was certain, did not wish to pray in the small chapel. "I'll personally call as soon as the police let us clean up."

"They took your most valuable Torah," said Sylvie Wang, Howie's granddaughter, a nice-looking girl in thick glasses. "I heard the rabbi tell someone."

"We'll get it back," said Lieberman, thinking, "I'll get it back if it still exists."

There was a chance the vandals, the anti-Semites, had not destroyed the blue velvet Torah. There may have been some among them, perhaps only one, who knew its value. Simply put, the missing Torah was priceless. More than four hundred years old, about a yard long, made by Spanish Jews during the reign of the Moors, when Jews were allowed not only to hold office in Spain but to worship as they chose. Each of the first five books of the Old or Jewish Testament, the Torah, had been meticulously and beautifully written out in a fine hand with the first words of each chapter in real gold.

The small chapel was only a few feet from where they stood and the doors were not particularly thick. There was only silence and a few sobs from behind that door.

"I'd better go in with them, Abe," Bess said, touching her husband's arm, kissing his cheek, and turning to the Chens. "You're all welcome to join us, but I thought you might feel more comfortable at the T & L."

Howie nodded and said something to his family in Cantonese. They answered and began to leave the temple with Maish and Yetta.

"I'll stay," said Howie, heading for the small chapel.

Bess moved with him and glanced at her husband. He nodded.

Maish, his wife, and the Chens filed out past Bill Hanrahan, who nodded at them as they left. Lieberman had seen his partner coming in moments earlier and caught the look that made it clear he knew or had discovered something.

When the corridor was clear, Lieberman could see a pair of unmarked cars pulling up in front of the door. The FBI.

"Rabbi," Hanrahan said, glancing at the cars out of which men in dark suits were emerging quickly. "I think I've found a witness."

Abe moved toward him. This was not their town, not their jurisdiction, and legally not their investigation, but it was Abe Lieberman's congregation. He followed his partner out the door as the FBI men moved briskly past them as if they knew just where they were going.

It had been a busy night and there had been too few of them. Most of the Arab students at the universities—Chicago, Northwestern, DePaul, Loyola—had simply refused to join in the desecration and the older Muslims in the city had categorically said that they were Americans and had no intention of breaking the law.

"If you do this, they will blame us, punish us," Mohammed Ach Bena, a highly successful rug dealer in the Loop, had told the young man who had tried to enlist him or at least make a donation. "I am not a terrorist."

The group, which called itself the Arab Student Response Committee, had wound up recruiting a total of fifteen to join them in their night of desecration, the anniversary of the date the madman had murdered innocent Arabs at prayer. Even so, when the moment came to attack the Jewish temples, some of the active members of the committee chose not to show up.

Those who took part were mostly young men and a few young women. After the coordinated attack at the Jewish houses of worship, they sat in the meeting room the University of Chicago provided for campus groups. About half of them were students. They were tired. A few were unsure. A few closed their eyes. A few smiled at their success.

"And no one was seen?" asked the young woman, a graduate student, who stood before them. "Except those we wanted seen."

Heads nodded. A few voices said, "Only the ones you wanted seen."

At her side stood a tall Arab in a gray suit and tie. He was well groomed, clean shaven, and very big. His face showed nothing but a broken nose and scar tissue that bolted over both eyes. He was clearly a man who had seen and suffered violence.

"The scrolls?" she asked the man. "The Torah? Where is Howard?"

"Safe," Massad said. "The Torah is safe."

"The call?" she asked.

"Made," he answered.

She nodded and told the group that they should leave, a few at a time, quietly carrying the books that were provided at the door if they did not have books of their own.

One hour earlier, the big man with the broken nose had made two phone calls, one to the FBI and one to the Chicago police in South Rogers Park were they had struck two of their five targets. He had called from different phone booths, speaking quickly, calmly, and precisely to the person who answered the phone and saying the same thing: "We have struck our next blow to free the so-called United States and bring down the corrupt government run by Jews and their money. In the name of the memory of our too-long-dead Führer, we will bring the Jews and those who support them to their knees and shoot each one of them in the back of the head as they shot Adolf Hitler. We are his ghosts, his new army. Heil Hitler." And with that he had hung up, wiped the telephone clean with a handkerchief and gone to his nearby car.

They would wait a week, maybe more to be sure they hadn't been seen and then take the next step. She had already planned it, had already imagined the frightened faces of the Jews. She was concerned that Howard had not come to the meeting as he was supposed to have done, but she would deal with him later. The attack appeared to have been a complete success. If so, this was but the start.

It would be almost twenty-four hours before she realized what Massad had done, what he had not told her or the committee, and why Howard Ramu had not been there.

THREE

"I DRINK TEA but I don't like it," the old woman said, pouring a cup for each of the policemen who sat in her small studio apartment on small unmatching furniture. The furniture was of acceptable size but not texture for Lieberman. Hanrahan chose to squeeze himself into one of the chairs near the window that the woman had offered and to take the tea.

"Thank you," said Lieberman, taking a sip of the tea as he stood looking at rows of mounted photographs on the walls. "Very good."

"My departed husband was a photographer as a sideline. They are good, aren't they?"

Lieberman had meant that the tea was good.

"You'll notice there are no people in Carl's photographs. No animals either for that matter. Trees, flowers, empty parks and playgrounds, buildings."

"Interesting," said Lieberman.

"You sure you wouldn't like more sugar? I like lots of sugar."

Lieberman drank tea socially when it was offered to him by strangers but he didn't like it. Coffee was his drink.

The old woman, whose name was Mrs. Ready, Anne Crawfield Ready, was covered in a flowered shift. Her hair was dyed an odd reddish orange and she looked far too overweight for any of the frail chairs. "Noisy out there this morning," she said, nodding at the two windows of her apartment.

The apartment was across the street from the front entrance of Mir Shavot, in a small square above a real estate branch office that wouldn't be open for another hour, a photography supply store, and a baseball card shop.

"Yes," said Lieberman. "My partner tells me you have trouble sleeping?"

"Insomnia," Mrs. Ready said, touching Lieberman's arm and speaking quietly as if the condition were something to be kept secret. "I watch television, read."

"I know what you mean," Lieberman said. "I have insomnia, for years. I take hot baths. I read. I watch AMC, nothing works."

"Tea is no good," she said.

"Never helped me," Lieberman said, turning his baggy eyes down to the dark brew. "Detective Hanrahan says you saw something last night."

"About three in the a.m.," she said, moving to the third and last chair in the room and easing into it. "Heard something. Usually quiet out there except for the cars on Dempster. I like the rushing of the cars. Soothing. You know the wind sound, changes when they pass the street. It's like a what-do-you-call it, a meditation. Relaxing. I read a book on it. Buddhist. I'm an Episcopalian myself."

"The sound you heard that was different?" prompted Hanrahan.

"Oh," Mrs. Ready said as she downed her tea in a single long gulp. "Like something breaking. I looked out the window and saw him coming out of that Jewish church where the bank used to be. Jews are quieter than the bank. Surprised me when they moved in, but they're quieter and I don't mind listening to them on Friday night and Saturday morning."

"What did you see?" Lieberman asked.

"Young man, leather jacket, bald head," she said. "One of those German swastikas on the back. I turned my light out so he couldn't see me, but he looked right up."

"And you said he was carrying something?" Hanrahan asked.

"Yes, something that looked a little heavy and maybe blue. Street lights are not the best, but I'm not complaining."

"Where did he go?" asked Lieberman.

"Down the street, right below me. Watched till I couldn't see him. Then I thought I heard a car start."

"And that was it?" Lieberman asked.

"Bank was here for more than ten years and never got robbed," she said ruefully. "I watched, hoped I'd be able to identify a bank robber, but this is good too, isn't it?"

"Very good," Hanrahan said, sipping his tea.

"You'd know him again if you saw him, the bald man in the jacket?" Lieberman asked.

"Can't be one hundred percent," she said. "But I watch television, CNN, WGN. He was one of those skinheads."

"We'd like to tell the local police about this, have them come and talk to you," Lieberman said, rising.

"The FBI too?" Mrs. Ready asked excitedly. "I saw those cars pull up. Look just like the FBI guys on television."

"Probably," Hanrahan said, also rising. The chair beneath him creaked in relief.

"I don't get out much anymore," the woman said. "Embolism in my left leg. Friend of my daughter from college days does the shopping for me and takes me to the doctor. Almost all my family is in Salt Lake City. A few are Mormons. Well, tell the other police and the FBI to come on over. I've got lots of tea, herbal and otherwise."

"You've been very helpful," Lieberman said, taking her hand in both of his.

"I've seen you go in there more than once," she said.

"I've got 20-20 without glasses. You're a Jew."

"One of the chosen people," Lieberman said, with a touch of irony that only his partner caught.

"My husband, Carl, rest his soul, wore thick glasses and had swollen toes. Stuck it out at the postal office never letting on his constant pain to a soul. Died two months after he retired, leaving me the pension and Social Security and the photographs."

"Anything else you think of, tell the local police or the FBI," said Hanrahan. The two men moved to the door. Lieberman opened it.

"Aren't you going to ask me about the girl?" the old woman said.

The two policemen turned toward her, door partly open.

"Girl?" asked Hanrahan.

"Pretty, standing at the door right under the night light. Bald guy moved right past her. She was back in the shadows. Then when he was gone she looked back into the glass door and moved the same way the bald guy had gone. She was dressed all in black. Looked pretty from what I could see. Long, black hair, turned once to look up at my window, but I still had the lights out."

"And you'd recognize her again if you saw her?"

"Yes," said the old woman. "I figured she was out late, heard the noise, and tucked herself back in the dark so she couldn't be seen by the bald guy when he came out. Pretty girl. I hear there've been rapes within blocks of right where I stand." She pointed at the floor and badly faded gray carpet.

When the policemen were down the stairs and in the curious bustle of gawkers who knew something was happening even if they weren't sure what, they spoke as they walked back toward Mir Shavot. "How do you figure it, Rabbi?" Hanrahan said. "Skinheads like the lady says?"

"Could be, Father Murphy," said Lieberman. "The girl worries me."

"If there was a girl," said Hanrahan as they crossed the street. "And if Mrs. Ready really can identify her."

"And if there was a bald young man," said Lieberman. "A bald young man carrying something heavy and blue."

"The Torah," said Hanrahan.

Lieberman glanced back across the street toward the window of the old woman. She was looking down at them with a proud smile. She was perfectly clear and so, he was sure, were they, even in the rain, but in the middle of the night it might be different. Lieberman had the feeling that the woman was reliable. Maybe because he wanted to believe that she was.

Howard Ramu had stuffed his skinhead jacket and the Torah in the oversized Reebok gym bag and put on his wig as soon as he had gotten back into the car. He had driven home carefully, not too slow, not too fast, sticking to streets that were reasonably busy even at three in the morning— McCormick to Devon, Devon to Western, Western south, avoiding the expressways.

He went back to the apartment he shared with two other Arab students, one of whom was his cousin and both of whom disapproved of the Arab Student Response Committee and Howard's participation in it. They had, in fact, asked him to leave the apartment at his earliest convenience. He had readily agreed.

It was a little before four in the morning when Howard Ramu parked on Woodlawn, picked up the bag, and locked the car doors. He was lucky to find a space so easily. Bag in one hand weighing heavily and his other hand in his pocket holding a small gun, Howard hoped that he would not be confronted by one of the wandering bands of black teens who came into the university neighborhood during the night and sometimes during the day looking for some student or faculty member to trap and rob. Woodlawn was an all-black neighborhood surrounding Hyde Park and the University of Chicago, an unofficial boundary that was not always respected.

Howard made it back to his room in the six-flat brick

building, opening the locks as quietly as possible. The living room was dark as he entered. Even through the closed door he could hear the loud snoring of his cousin. He placed his gym bag on the top shelf of the closet near the door, confident that his roommates would not touch it, and then he felt very, very tired. The bag contained not only the heavy Torah but six lightweight Israeli Uzis, but lightweight or not, the bulging bag had been extremely heavy and straining at the seams. He had taken no more than four steps from the now-closed closet when he heard the tap at the apartment door. He froze. It came again. A voice whispered.

"Everything all right?" came the man's voice still in a whisper. "Can you hear me in there?"

Howard stood still, gun now out and in his hand. The man knocked harder. Howard looked toward the closed bedroom doors. His cousin snorted but continued to snore.

"Everything is fine," said Howard softly, moving to the door.

"Saw someone going in there," said the man. "I'm with campus security."

"It was me," said Howard. "I live here."

His cousin was no longer snoring.

"How do I know you're not a burglar just telling me everything is fine?" said the man in the hallway.

"My name is Howard Ramu," Howard said with exasperation. "I live here."

"Could have gotten the name from the bell downstairs," said the man. "I'll have to ask you to open up."

Howard's cousin was clearly awake now. The snoring had stopped and the bed springs vibrated as if he were rising.

"How do I know you are campus police?"

The man shoved a card under the door. Howard picked it up and examined it. It was a photo ID of a heavyset man with a dull American face. Howard adjusted his wig, put his gun back in his pocket keeping his hand on it, and opened the door except for the chain link. Behind him,

Howard heard his cousin's door open and his voice sleepily saying in a heavy accent, "What on earth is happening?"

Before Howard could answer, the chain link snapped and the door flew open, sending Howard backward into a small table. A man came in, neither in uniform nor resembling in the least the photo of the heavyset, dull American. The man, whom Howard Ramu well knew, held a weapon in his hands, a weapon Howard recognized. The man closed the door.

"Where?" asked the man, stepping into the room with a decided limp. "I saw you come in with it."

Howard said nothing. His cousin stood frozen.

"Where?" the man with the automatic weapon repeated.

Howard's hand came out of his pockets. He did not think nor pray nor hope. He knew the man meant to kill him and that his little gun was no match for what the man carried. Before his hand cleared his pocket, the intruder fired, the sound breaking a still-night silence, tearing into Howard Ramu, who dropped his pistol and fell backward, dead.

Howard's cousin turned back to his bedroom and the intruder fired, tearing red-black dots into the white pajamas. The gunman moved toward the closed door of the second bedroom. He kicked open the unlocked door and fired as a voice cried, "No."

In spite of the noise and the certain arousal of neighbors, the murderer put down his weapon and began looking under the small secondhand sofa. He searched quickly, determined. Gunshots were not new to this neighborhood; neither were they likely to be ignored. Someone would call the police.

The gunman threw open the closet and immediately saw the oversized Reebok bag on the shelf. "Found it," he said to himself. He unzipped the bag, folded the metal stocks of his weapon and put the compact gun on top of the Torah, then zipped up the bag. The bag was even heavier now, the zipper beginning to tear, the seams already tearing. He hurried to the front door, his limp made more pronounced by the weight of the bag. At the door, the killer stopped to pick up the fake ID from the floor and pocketed it. He pulled a small, black yarmulke from his pocket, knelt at Ramu's body, and touched the little cap to the blood. Printed inside the cap, black against white lining, was "Temple Mir Shavot" with the temple's address. He stood up and dropped the yarmulke in front of the body of Howard Ramu.

He left the apartment, closing the door behind him, not worrying about noise. He had already made ample noise but no doors opened. Everyone was afraid to look. The man ran down the stairs and out of the building as quickly as his heavy bag and limping leg would allow. The streets were still clear. A drunk tottered toward him. He was black and ragged, humming to himself. The man brushed past him and the drunk sullenly shouted, "What the fuck you think you are, goddamn Newt Gingrich?"

He had parked illegally next to a fire hydrant. He placed the gym bag on the back seat, slid behind the wheel, closed the door and moved into the night. He had only a few blocks to go. He made it without lights on and, he was sure, without being seen. He pulled into the campus overnight parking lot using a key code card, parked in the rear where most people preferred not to leave their cars, and hurried out, carrying the heavy bag.

He moved quietly up the rear stairs in his sneakers and stopped at the second floor to rest his leg and shift the bag to his other hand. He unlocked the door to his apartment on the third floor, stepped inside, put down the bag and reached back to lock the door behind him.

Outside a police siren cut the night.

"You got all six?" said the man with the shaven head.

Berk had left his tiny, neat, cell-like apartment minutes earlier to buy a cup of coffee at Denny's and stand at the phone booth in front of the restaurant. No one would bother him and no one would try to use the phone if he indicated to them that he was waiting for a call. He was not tall but he was broad like a wrestler and in good condition. In fact, when he hung up, he planned to go back to his apartment and continue his workout. He had finished 110 push-ups and four hundred sit-ups before he put on his jeans and a T-shirt and ran the two miles to Denny's, which he would have done no matter what the weather. He planned to run back home after the call came.

William Stanley Berk wasn't worried about his phone being tapped. One of his men had worked for the phone company and checked it out regularly. Besides, if they had been tapping, they—the cops, FBI, whoever—would have pulled him in by now and played him the tape to break him. The line was safe. Tuckett would tell him if and when it wasn't. Even so, Berk never called or received a call at home that might incriminate him. At the end of each call, they would designate who would initiate the next call and at what time. The person to receive the call would give the number of a public phone where he would be waiting. It was awkward, but it was safe. Some people, in fact, were too safe, like the man he called Mr. Grits. Mr. Grits would never use the telephone like this as safe as it seemed. Mr. Grits made it even more elaborate. When Mr. Grits and Berk spoke on a phone designated by Mr. Grits, Mr. Grits was always pleasant, reassuring, and matter-of-fact. There was only one clear rule. Berk was not allowed to see Mr. Grits.

But the man on the other end of the line now was not Mr. Grits. He was an Arab fanatic named Massad, whom Berk treated with what seemed like true respect.

"All six," Massad said proudly, breathing hard.

"And the prayer thing?" Berk said. He knew it was a Torah. He knew what to call it, but he had an image to present to his caller and he didn't want the caller to think Berk was as smart as Berk knew he was. Berk was a reader. Berk had educated himself, like Gary Gilmore.

"The Torah, got it," said the man.

"What's the problem?" asked Berk, sensing something in the man's voice.

"I had to kill Ramu," he said.

"Couldn't have been any other way," said Berk. "I told you."

"And two others who were with him," Massad went on.

"Civilians?"

"Arabs," said the man softly. "More Arabs have died. Three Arabs and not a single Jew."

"Breaks," said Berk. "We'll talk later. We stay with the plan. Give me a number and a time." The man gave Berk a number and a time. Berk said the number was fine, but he would call him at seven, not midnight. If Massad could not get to the phone, he would call at seven the next morning.

Berk almost added, "Put the guns somewhere safe," but that was a given and he didn't want the man looking down on him for suggesting the obvious. Berk hung up and looked to see if anyone was watching him, was fairly certain there was not, and threw his empty plastic coffee cup into the nearby garbage before running home.

When he got to the small apartment, he was greeted on one wall by a large poster of George Lincoln Rockwell. Once he had put up a photograph of Adolf Hitler taken from an old *Life* magazine he bought legitimately from an old bookstore on Damen, but now Berk had read a lot of Hitler, his life, his speeches. No substance. All ego. He had seen movies. Hitler was a great speaker, probably the greatest, though Berk couldn't understand German, but putting his picture on the wall had been something a kid went through. Berk was no kid. Rockwell had been calm, held a pipe in his hand, wore a Nazi uniform, always sounded reasonable even if he proposed cutting the balls off a Jew politician.

Berk didn't like dealing with the man he had spoken to on the phone in front of Denny's, but he had no choice. It was part of Mr. Grits's plan. Bruce Willis in one of those *Die Hard* movies would call it a double-cross, but Rockwell would have understood. Expediency. He would make it work and he would convince others to help him make it work.

Berk had risen fast. He had gotten in trouble as a kid, petty stuff, snatch-and-grab, a few purses. His father had always given him mixed messages. Once, when they caught Berk, he couldn't have been more than ten, his father had come to pick him up and had hit him on the side of the head, but not as hard as Berk had expected. His father was a sober, hardworking Irish fireman.

"You know why I'm not beating you, William?" his father had asked.

Berk had said "no" softly as he sat next to his father in their shit-brown Mustang.

"Because you stole from a Jew lady," he said. "I don't want you stealing. I don't want you breaking the law, but if you got to do it, do it from a nigger or a kike or any colored bastard who should never been in this country in the first place."

Berk nodded and listened. He had heard it before. The United States had been ruined by people who didn't belong here, colored people. Berk's father could be colorful and inconsistent on the subject for hours. Recent immigrants from Europe, any country in Europe as long as they weren't communists or Jews, were fine. White. Always dealt with him straight enough. Berk's mother knew enough to mind her business when this subject came up. She went to watch television or call her sister when Berk's father got on the subject.

Meanwhile, Berk did some juvenile time, not much, for breaking into a coffee shop at two in the morning. He and his buddy had found thirty-six dollars and some change and loaded up a bag of getting-stale donuts. They were barely out of the broken window when the police picked them up.

When Berk got out, he played his father's boy, did reasonably well at school, announced that he, like two of his brothers, wanted to be a firefighter. While he prepared himself for the job, with the help of his father and his skeptical brothers, he was very selective about the crimes he committed at night, well-spaced robberies of women alone on dark streets. He worked alone then and always wore a ski mask.

He had actually apprenticed as a firefighter in Chicago when he made it through high school. His father had some clout and it was clear that Berk had already been well prepared by his family. He had been assigned to the same station as his brother James W. Berk, Jr.

One night he had gotten back to the station after a massive blaze at a building on the South Side where his unit had been sent as backup. A whole block was on fire. Stores. Flames threatening to jump the street. Looters running right past the firemen and the few cops and grabbing what they could.

Berk, covered in dirt and smoke, smelling like death, had called his father, woke him from a sound sleep and said, "They shot at us. They fuckin' shot at us. The niggers shot at us. Jimmy has a bullet in his foot. We're puttin' out their fire and they're shootin'. And this guy on the sidewalk with a bullhorn and one of those velvet hats on his head, black son-of-a-bitch is telling the people to stop us, to let the Jew stores burn. A bullet came this fuckin' close to my head. For what? To protect a bunch of Jew and Korean stores?"

"To pick up a good paycheck, make a living, and retire young," his father had answered. "Which hospital did they take Jimmy to?"

Berk had told him, hung up, quit the department, teamed up with four friends and convinced them to shave their heads and put on leather jackets after he read about skinheads in England. Skinheads were pure white and took no shit. Their group had grown. They started as vandals, joined up once in a while with some neo-Nazi groups and a handful of Klan guys for joint marches and rallies, but Berk soon realized that he was bigger, smarter, stronger, and a better speaker than any of those guys, and by the time he realized it, he had more than two dozen young men who had joined him. And there were girls. He stayed away from the ones who wanted to be hurt. He didn't want that kind of trouble. There were plenty of girls who were happy with what he gave them. He stayed nice to the Klan and the neo-Nazis who gave him a little money. They didn't seem to have all that much, though they claimed rich backers out of state. One of the television station commentators, an old fart, had given Berk's group a name, the Chicago Skinhead Hate Mongers. Berk liked it. It sounded like a hockey team. Eventually, they became known simply as the Mongers.

When something else wasn't going on, Berk's Mongers wore baseball caps and delivered pizzas or dished out pieces of fried chicken.

One night on television, Berk had seen the nigger in the velvet hat, the one with the bullhorn who had egged on the crowd at the fire, the one who had gotten his brother Jimmy shot. The nigger's name was Martin Abdul. Berk knew the name. Abdul had risen fast, started a Muslim church, pulled in big bucks, built a big mosque, appeared on talk shows with Jesse Jackson. Martin Abdul was one dangerous nigger, but a smart one. He had big bucks.

Ever since Mr. Grits had shown up, Berk's financial prospects had risen considerably. He had first been contacted by Mr. Grits the night after he had spoken to the Mongers, their girls and some people, many of them older, some of whom he knew were friends of his family, in the park not two blocks from where he had grown up. The police were there. They were always there. They always found out, showed up, ready to break up the crowd if they got the call from a sergeant watching from a car that it was getting too big or surly. They could always stop him for lack of a public permit, but it was easier to let him speak, even come close to inciting riot, though there was no one within miles of the neighborhood whose family wasn't Irish, Polish, German, or British. There was a family of Indians who ran a 7-11 on Oakton, but they weren't worth the trouble of bothering. Not yet anyway.

Berk had spoken loudly to cheers: two of his brothers in the audience including Jimmy, Jr., people saying, "He's right," laughter at his jokes. When he finished, he went with two of his people to an all-night place on Touhy where the waitress and manager weren't happy to see them, but treated them with polite blandness.

Three young men had approached Berk's group at a table, said they wanted to join. Berk welcomed them. So did the others. One said he'd probably lose his job clerking at a shoe store when he shaved his head but he wanted to be a Monger. Berk said he could get him other work.

That was when it happened. The waitress, a skinny rag in a wrinkled uniform with heavy bags under her eyes had come to the table and said, "One of you Berk?"

"Yeah," Berk had said.

"Phone," the waitress had said and then headed for the kitchen and their meager orders. She didn't expect much of a tip and was fairly sure they'd hang around until the place closed. She shuffled away and Berk went to the front of the coffee shop where one of the two pay phones was off the hook resting on the metal platform.

"Berk?" asked the man with a smile in his voice and the joy of a car salesman.

"Yeah."

"Heard you talk tonight," said the man who would never give his name but because of a slight Southern accent, Berk would always think of as Mr. Grits. "Son, you were good. Right up there with the best."

"Thanks," Berk said, going over the faces of the people who had been in the crowd, not being able to put one of those faces to this voice. Berk didn't ask how the man had found him, gotten the phone number. He knew the man must have followed him and must be calling from not very far away.

"You should be much bigger," said Mr. Grits. "Doin' much bigger things. More doing, less talking. We've been talking about the niggers, the Jews, the Chinks, the Indians for more than a hundred and twenty years. It's time for doing."

"Yeah?" said Berk not sure if he might be talking to a cop or even the FBI.

"I can get you cheap briefcases filled with unmarked money," said Mr. Grits. "Not Washingtons wrapped in bank paper and lined up in neat lines so it looks like a lot but turns out to be a few thousand. I'm talking about big money for you, personally. Handle it the way you want. Just get a job done for us, a job that will fit quite nice with what I heard in the park tonight."

"What jobs? How do I get the money?"

Mr. Grits had hung up. Berk had asked the night manager behind the counter, an older male duplicate of the waitress, if he had seen anyone come in and look at or use the phones. The man shrugged, said he'd gone to the can, thought maybe he had seen a man in a suit, wasn't sure.

Mr. Grits returned three days later. Berk had run three miles and went back to his apartment, his sweatshirt soaked. Pinned to the door was a note. The note said, "Bring this note with you. Go down to your mailbox. Take out the unstamped letter. Bring this note and the letter outside. When you finish reading the letter, burn it and this note right out on the street next to the fire hydrant."

Berk had done as the note asked, feeling that the man he now called Mr. Grits was probably some kind of nut, but there had been cash in the envelope, a lot of cash. There was also a note asking him if he had thought about the call he had received and telling him he could keep the money no matter what.

Berk had walked outside, held up the the letter and the note so that someone watching could see and burned them both. Mr. Grits was really watching out for his own ass. Berk decided to keep a couple of sheets of paper and some envelopes like the one he had just burned. If he got more messages from Mr. Grits, he would burn the fakes and pocket the real notes which might come in handy.

Berk visited his mother who was pushing seventy and working part-time at the Christian Resale Shop on Devon where the few dollars that were made went to the inner-city needy. Mrs. Berk didn't care if the needy were black, white, Jew, or Hindu. She had read the words of Jesus herself and heard Father Brian every week since before the boys were born. She had held her peace, kept to herself, and gone to work for the Resale Shop three weeks after her husband died in a parking garage fire.

Berk rarely visited his mother. She made him uncomfortable and he had the clear feeling that she was not always happy to see her youngest son. He always dressed neatly when he visited her and even took the earring out, but his shaven head and occasional pictures of him on television kept him from carrying off the role of peace-loving, dutiful Christian son.

Berk visited his mother that day, though. She was cordial, made him coffee, cut him a slice of cake, told him about his brothers and their families, and listened to him tell a few lies about what he was doing. Then, before he left and without his mother knowing, he hid the money from Mr. Grits inside the broken slat of wood at the back of his old closet. He had already put a few dollars there. He would put a lot more in that closet. Berk had plans beyond making speeches and getting into fights.

Then Berk waited, talking, marching, even doing a local television talk show and acting calm, intelligent, and highly and sincerely bigoted, insisting that his group never started violence, that they simply responded to it when someone tried to abridge their freedom to speak publicly, that it was television that had named him and his friends the Chicago Skinhead Hate Mongers. As far as the group was concerned, they were just friends who shared his ideas and wanted to protect the United States. He talked about the failure of immigration laws, the government's appeasement of lawbreakers if they were minorities—Mexicans, Haitians, Cubans, Chinese.

"They couldn't do anything about it if they even wanted to," he had said on one show. "The law is too screwed up. There is no two-party system, just people out to get votes from foreigners so they can keep their jobs and their blood money. My grandparents came here legally. It should have stayed that way. Now, it's too late. It's people like us who have to take care of the problem."

About a third of the audience, not counting his own people, had applauded. About half had booed and jeered, and the white-haired host had shaken her head at his statements.

And then he heard from Mr. Grits again. Little kid had stopped him on the street while he was running one morning handed him an envelope, and ran away. Berk had opened the envelope, found more money and a note saying, "Public phone on the right about half a block. Tear this up now into two pieces and dump it in the trash can on your left."

Berk had done what he was told. He was beginning to understand Mr. Grits. The phone rang when he was no more than three feet from it. While he was on the phone, out of sight of the trash can, he was sure someone who worked for Mr. Grits was already picking up the torn note.

"Are you ready to talk seriously?" Mr. Grits said, as if this were the most beautiful day the world had yet experienced. "Or do I hang up and hope you make good use of the money you have been blessed with?"

"We talk."

"Good," said Mr. Grits. "There is a booth at the Burger King half a block away. Go there. Go to the toilet. Take your pants down. Lock the door. When no one else is in the room, we'll talk. If you try to see me, perhaps even succeed in seeing me, you'll never hear from me again. There will, however, come a time soon, when you will have accepted so much money from us that the option of ceasing our negotiations will be void."

Mr. Grits hung up. Berk went to the toilet in the Burger King and talked to Mr. Grits in person though all he could see of the man were his neatly pressed tan slacks, brown socks, and expensive brown walking shoes.

The plan was a bit complex, but Berk understood. He would follow the plan and, in return, would receive a great deal of money and a substantial bonus when the job was done.

"After all," Mr. Grits said with a slight laugh, "we don't expect you to plan the details of and execute the murder of perhaps several dozen people without reasonable compensation."

And the money had come. Berk had planned and rethought his life. When he finished exercising that morning, Berk would practice the speech he planned to deliver that night to his followers. They would think he was making it up standing right up there at the front of the room, but he wrote it out longhand and memorized it, practiced in front of his mirror like Hitler, checked the time so he would not lose the real dummies who would be sitting there.

Berk thought he heard rain. That was fine with him. He would do his sit-ups and run another mile in the rain, feeling his T-shirt cling to and slap against his body. He'd laugh as he ran and people would get out of his way or cross the street if they saw him. He would run till he was exhausted and then go to Fran's apartment, wake her up, and screw her dripping wet, a little cold, tired. Fran's roommates would mind their business.

It would be a perfect morning.

Less than a year earlier, Alan Kearney looked like a young man. Dark groomed hair, strong chin, straight nose, Irish green eyes. Youth had left him fast after his ex-partner had been killed. Shepard had died cursing Kearney for seducing his wife.

Kearney, who had been headed for the top, including a well-placed society wife and a long-term move up to Commissioner, had gone empty. He was still Captain of Detectives and head of the brown brick police station on North Broadway. He did his job, put in the hours, praised, complained, pushed, and assigned, but Lieberman knew the ambition, the real fire, was out. Kearney might even marry yet. Every Irish cop, including Bill Hanrahan, had a woman for him, a cousin, a friend, a sister. Once in a while Kearney tried, but all the women reported that his idea of a good time was going to a bar, looking at his glass, and listening without saying much. It was even rumored that Kearney had made it to bed with Michael Horrigan's sister, Eva. The rumor was never confirmed and their single date never repeated.

At Bess's urging, Lieberman had once invited Kearney to the house for a Shabbat dinner. To his surprise, Kearney had accepted. That was when Lisa was home, separated from her husband. There had been no thought of match-making, at least on Lieberman's part, but Bess had been disappointed that Lisa and Kearney had little to say to each other and had left shortly after dinner. They paused only to say goodnight to Melisa and Barry, who had decided that Alan Kearney, their grandpa's boss, looked like a real po-liceman.

Now Kearney stood in the day room of the stone-walled Clark Street Station with very little day coming in through the narrow windows. The room was often used for inter-rogations. It looked like rain was coming. The sound of thunder grumbled far in the distance.

He stood in front of a white board, a red marker in his hand, and looked around the room. The whole squad of eight men and two women was present, plus a thin, dark man who sat at a scratched table. Kearney did not introduce him. No one looked at him or said anything.

"Lorber, you charge Gonzalez today by noon or he walks," said Kearney. "You got enough to charge?" Kear-ney ticked off something with his marker on the yellow, lined pad before him on the table.

Lorber, who had once been a department weight-lifting champ, had kept in shape, but not the shape he had been in. Time had made the weights heavier. He was still strong enough to lift most perps off the ground and batter them against a wall till they'd hear Chinese gongs, but station-house banter had Bill Hanrahan six to three if the two of them ever had to stand it out. Hanrahan had stopped drink-ing and held most of his strength as a gift of heredity rather than practice as Lorber had. Lorber was a station house grouse.

"I'm talking to a lawyer downtown today," said Lorber, taking a drink from his Styrofoam coffee cup. "I think we've got enough for illegal possession, resisting and . . ."

". . . but not for murder," Kearney finished.

Lorber shrugged.

"We've got three Jewish synagogues desecrated in this district," Kearney went on. "And a fourth in Albany Park."

"And a fifth in Skokie," added Lieberman, whose hands were folded in his lap.

"And a fifth in Skokie," Kearney amended. "What do we have?"

"What we don't have is more to the point," said Lieberman. "The FBI is taking prints. Most of them are matching congregants who don't like being printed. It's taking time. Perps may have worn gloves. We're working with the Skokie police. I stopped at B'nai Zion. Torn apart. The rabbi is old, the congregants are few and old. Rabbi Zechel was crying."

Kearney nodded and passed around a stack of color photographs, each one marked on the back with the name of the desecrated synagogue where it was taken.

The squad looked over the photographs slowly and passed them along. The man none of them recognized looked especially closely at each photo before passing it on. Lieberman and Hanrahan did not look. They had seen them all, been in all of the desecrated synagogues.

"What's this?" asked Harley Buel, putting on his glasses.

"Which temple?" asked Lieberman.

Harley, a balding man in his forties who looked like a grade school principal, always seemed baffled by new information. Harley wanted his crimes clear, his suspects found quickly, and a quick plea bargain. Testifying in court was Harley's great fear. He had lost more than one case by his fear, which turned to surliness on the witness stand. He showed Lieberman the photo.

"That," said Lieberman, "is a pile of shit."

"They shit in the . . . ?" Harley said, handing the photograph to Rene Catolino, a woman with the body of a model but a face that was hard and surrounded by a helmet of forbidding, straight, short black hair. She was, Lieberman thought, the best cop in the room other than Hanrahan and himself. Her father had been a cop. Lieberman had known him. Vince had gone through life in a blue police car showing no ambition and was happy when retirement came. Rene was different. She was ambitious.

She said, looking at the photo, "They brought it with them and dumped it on those white scarves.

"Talliths," Lieberman corrected. "Prayer shawls."

Rene Catolino looked at the other pictures slowly, carefully, and passed each picture on as she finished. "Not very creative," she said, looking at the racial comments on the walls in the photographs.

"But effective," said Lieberman.

"This is a mess," said Kearney, moving to the board. "Late last night a call came in to both the FBI and to this station. The call came before the public was informed about the attacks. The caller talked like a neo-Nazi. Suggested we hadn't heard the last of his group. He added the usual anti-Semitic remarks. We've got tape. You can all listen."

"Same call to the feds and to us?" asked Catolino.

"Same caller. Same message. Seemed to be reading it," said Kearney. "You can judge for yourself. At two of the sites, the one on California and the one in Skokie, bald men were seen leaving the attacked sites. One was definitely identified as wearing a jacket with Nazi markings. The other was also wearing a leather jacket with markings but the person who saw the possible suspect could not say for sure if there were any Nazi markings."

"Skinheads," Tony Munoz sighed. Tony was the youngest person in the room, a cynic at twenty-eight, and a little more reckless than Kearney liked. Tony, whose parents were born in Puerto Rico, was particularly interested in all hate crimes and participated willingly in his own brand of hate directed toward skinheads, neo-Nazis, overboard militias, the Klan, anti-Semitic groups, terrorists and, above all, anti-Hispanics. It was suspected that Tony, who had a nice wife and a two-year-old boy, had shot and killed a Nazi during a confrontation following a demonstration. Nothing was ever proved. Nothing was ever charged. Tony's weapon had been checked and proved to be clean, but many cops, especially ones like Tony, also carried an untraceable weapon they could throw away or put into the hand of a dead or half-dead suspect.

Kearney wrote the name of each defiled temple on the white board. He wrote in red. The marker squeaked. Lieberman was surprised that Kearney spelled each one correctly. At the right of the board, he wrote: "Call from supposed perp. Claims responsibility. Racist reasoning."

Below this, in the center of the board, he wrote: "Possible sightings of skinhead at two locations. Sighting at one location of a young woman; white; long, dark hair. Witness says she may be able to identify the woman."

"There was also an early a.m. shooting of a suspected Arab terrorist which may be connected," said Kearney. Kearney turned to see what effect the last item would have on his squad.

"Who?" asked Lieberman.

"Howard Ramu," said Kearney without referring to his notes. "Cheesed in his apartment in Hyde Park. A part-time student at the University of Chicago and a member of a radical Arab group on campus, the Arab Student Response Committee. The killer or killers used automatic weapons. They killed Ramu and his two Arab roommates, neither of whom appear to have any ties to anti-American or anti-Semitic organizations. They were just in the wrong place."

"Anything else?" asked Hanrahan.

"Howard Ramu's head was shaved," said Kearney. "There was a jacket in the front closet with a swastika on it."

"Skinheads don't let Arabs in," Munoz said knowingly.

"But Arabs can make themselves look like skinheads,"

said Catolino, still looking at the photographs and passing them on.

"Maybe they shaved his head before they killed him," said Munoz.

"Take too long," said Buel.

"Forensics says his head had been shaven at least twelve hours earlier," said Kearney. "It was already growing back."

"The Torah?" asked Lieberman.

"No sign. Nothing more than the jacket and shaved head and the fact that he was murdered to attach him to the attacks. Killers escaped. No sign but one item that appears to have been left by the killers or fallen from the head or hand of Ramu, a yarmulke, inside of which were the words 'Temple Mir Shavot.'"

"You think a Jewish radical may have killed Ramu?" asked Lieberman. "The vandals could have taken a dozen yarmulkes from the box at Mir Shavot. It just sits there for people who forget their own or don't own them. But a militant Jew would have his own yarmulke." Lieberman's dresser drawer was almost full of yarmulkes, ones he had forgotten to return to the box, a blue one from the Temple Brotherhood, several of many colors from weddings, bar mitzvahs, and one a gift from his granddaughter with his name painted on it in Hebrew.

"What we're supposed to think," said Kearney, "is that a bunch of skinheads vandalized five Jewish temples and then a radical Jew went after a known Arab activist and gunned him down in his apartment in revenge. It stinks."

"What now?"

"We set up a task force," said Kearney. "We work this, even the bad smelling leads, and we keep up with our other cases and whatever new comes through the door. But we do have some help." He looked at the thin, dark man at the end of the table. "Detective Said, Ibraham Said from downtown," said Kearney, putting the cap on his marker with a 'pop.' "Detective Said is . . . he can speak for himself."

"Thank you," said Said, looking around the room at the

less than welcoming faces. "Yes, I am an Arab and Muslim. I'm also an American and a specialist in Arab terrorist and hate groups in Chicago. I've been trained by the FBI and have spent time in Iran, Iraq, Syria, the Sudan, and Ethiopia. I speak Arabic and passable Hebrew, have since I was a child. There are Arabs who consider me a traitor and there has been at least one attempt on my life. Most of my friends are Muslims and Americans, far more of them than there are terrorists and fanatics. If you have questions, shoot."

"He heading the task force?" Hanrahan asked.

"I'm heading the task force," said Kearney. "It could all blow up. The Commissioner can take it all away from us. Depends on how he can handle the press and public when the six o'clock news figures out the connections and starts making screwy conclusions. The FBI liaison is an agent named Triplett, but my guess is he'll make a token appearance or two for television and leave us alone for a few days. If we don't come up with something, the FBI will take over."

"Where is he?" asked Munoz. "He know about this meeting?"

Kearney shook his head and said, "Agent Triplett told me that he would check with us to see if we can turn anything up. Triplett worked the Oklahoma City bombing. Meanwhile, he's working on his own with his own leads. We'll put it all together later."

"When?" asked Munoz.

"When Triplett and the FBI are fucking good and ready to feel like humoring us," Kearney said, slapping the red marker on the tray at the bottom of the board. "Everybody start checking your sources. If you come up with anything, bring it in, clean or dirty, and pass it on to me. More questions? Good. Go to work."

Kearney left the room with the door open behind him. The photographs were collected by Lieberman as the squad members filed out one at a time. Munoz and Catolino stayed back when the others left.

"Sorry about what they did to your temple, Lieberman,"

said Munoz. "If they did something like that to St. Anne's, I'd . . . I don't know what I'd do."

Lieberman nodded and said thanks.

Catolino simply touched his arm and gave a very rare supportive smile before she left. And then all that remained were the white board with red markings, a pile of photographs, an Arab, a Jew, and a Catholic.

"The man who was murdered in Hyde Park was known to me," said Said, looking at the other two men across the table. "He was not normally bald. I did a preliminary examination of the body. I agree his head had been shaved within the last day."

"So," said Lieberman, "you think all this might have been done by an Arab terrorist group, not skinheads, in spite of the call."

"A good terrorist, an adequate hate monger, takes credit only when it suits his cause," said Said. "When it does not suit his cause, he blames others, spreading more hate, fear. The goal of Arab terrorists is an ideal state of Arab unity and the death of those who have been their enemies. When they bother to envision a distant future, it is an Arcadia of Islamic perfection, a Utopian state which I have long been convinced is unreachable for any group. I would prefer to be tracking down renegade militias, Nazis rather than Arabs, but I have special qualifications and so. . . ."

"Any ideas?" Lieberman asked.

"Ramu," said Said, putting his hands together as if he were about to pray. "There is to be a rally in his honor this afternoon at three. The Arab Student Response Committee will meet at the University of Chicago on the quadrangle steps of the Administration Building to swear revenge and probably blame the Jews or the police for Ramu's death. They have already circulated leaflets, put up signs, and called those who would not normally be part of their folly. There will be more of them than usual, the active members are few. I will be there. I believe that as a group the Arab Student Response Committee might well vandalize a house of worship and carry on marches and rallies, but they are not killers."

"We'll all be at the rally," said Lieberman.

Said held up his hands in acceptance and went on, "A photographer would be helpful. There will probably be several news photographers and television crews. We may get a photograph of the dark-haired girl or another pseudo-skinhead wearing a wig. They have already called the media to alert them to the meeting and the murder of one of their members. There will be a crowd."

"You're sure?" asked Hanrahan.

"I'm sure," said Said. "A little more than a decade ago I was a graduate student and a member of the Arab Student Response Committee. Actually, I was one of its founders. Militancy diminished our number. I was one of the first to leave. Many others followed. One who stayed with uncertainty keeps me informed."

"You'll be recognized," Lieberman said.

Said was smiling. "Those who walked away are still my friends. Those who stayed have all graduated, gone home, changed their minds. This is a new group, a far more dangerous group, but not killers."

"Lunch?" asked Hanrahan, getting up.

"Yes," said Said.

"I know just the place," said Lieberman.

FOUR

THE MAN WATCHING the softball game looked Chinese, at least to Barry Cresswell. The man sat alone on the bench. He wore a raincoat, which made sense considering that morning's rain and the dark sky and distant thunder. What didn't make sense was the man's sunglasses.

Barry almost always stopped to play after school at the softball fields behind the Jewish Community Center on Touhy. His grandparents' house was only a few blocks away and like his grandfather, but unlike his father, softball and baseball were almost the meaning of Life.

There were only six on a side this afternoon. The weather was keeping some of the less committed away, but the die-hards had been known to play with as few as three or four on a side with an infield of mud. With six or less, right field was usually "out." Hit the ball to right field and you were out even if it was a grounder. With five or less on a side, the batting team had to supply a catcher. The batting team also supplied the umpire. There were no called pitches. You kept getting pitches till you hit one or till you struck out swinging. The umpire called plays on the field.

Barry adjusted his Cubs cap as he stood waiting for the next pitch. All was forgotten. Homework. Bar mitzvah lessons. He watched the pitcher. He watched the ball. Since he batted left-handed, Barry had to be particularly aware of hitting to the opposite field.

He couldn't help himself. He glanced again at the Chinese man who sat, arms folded. Now, Barry was sure that behind those glasses, the man was looking at him.

The ball went by and the pitcher shouted, "What the hell was the matter with that one?"

Barry shrugged apologetically. The pitcher had the ball again and lobbed it toward the plate. It was outside and high, but Barry swung and the ball sailed up and out into left field. Barry dropped his bat and ran for first. His team was shouting at him to go for second. The other team was shouting at the left-fielder to catch the ball. The left-fielder, Jerry, Barry didn't know his last name, tried to keep from falling on the wet grass as he moved under the ball. He had time to think about catching it, too much time. When it came down in his hands, Jerry bobbled the ball. It went into the air in front of him. Jerry lunged, caught it, and fell in a patch of grassy mud.

Barry walked in from the base path and stood at the sideline not looking at the Chinese man. Barry tried to concentrate on the game, cheer on the batter, a fat, slow kid called Mike, though his name was really Meyer. Mike could hit the ball. The muddy outfielder backed up and Barry glanced toward the Chinese man. He was gone. Barry was relieved. He looked to his right to see if the man was still in sight. He was, no more than a foot from Barry. It was like magic.

"Hit straight across," the man said. "Level. Line drives. Forget the long ball. It will come on its own."

The man was watching the game. He adjusted his glasses. He had no accent. Barry didn't answer. "You're a Cubs fan?"

Not hard to figure that considering the cap on his head. Barry nodded.

"I like the Sox," the man said. "Less colorful, but steady. I figure the Sox for the pennant this year. What do you think?"

Mike fouled a ball down the left field line or where a line would have been. The team was urging him to tear the next one.

"Don't know," Barry said. "I don't want to be rude, but my grandfather told me not to talk to strangers."

The man nodded.

"Good advice, but your grandfather and I are not strangers. I'm really here to give you a message for him."

Barry wondered why the man had not simply gone to the house and seen his grandfather. And then Barry wondered how the man had known he would be behind the JCC playing ball. Unless the man had followed him from school.

"What message?" Barry asked as Mike grounded hard to third. The third baseman had trouble with the ball, but Mike ran like a turtle.

"If he and his partner do not stay out of my business, something very bad will happen to you or your sister or your grandmother," the man said.

Barry looked up at the man and backed away.

"Just describe me to him," the man said. "He will understand. Remember, an even swing, not up and don't take bad pitches."

The man turned and walked slowly away from the field toward Touhy Avenue. Barry watched him, wanting to run, but not wanting to run home alone. He watched until the man disappeared on the sidewalk and then Barry picked up his books, told his team he was feeling sick enough to barf, and ran for the low iron fence. He scrambled over the fence into the large open field of weeds and ran toward the block of high-rises on Kedzie. His grandparents had friends who lived there. A lot of retired people—Jews, Catholics, even

Hindus and one or two Chinese and blacks—lived in the towers.

Barry ran, sneakers turning mud-black, jeans a soaking mess. He took off his Cubs cap as he ran and jammed it into his pocket, starting to lose his breath as he ran in the humidity and the weeds. When he cleared the field and found himself in the concrete courtyard of one of the buildings, he stopped, panted, and went for one of the buildings. The Chinese man in the dark glasses stepped out from behind a pillar, adjusted his glasses, and took a slow level swing with an imaginary bat. And then he was gone.

"So?" the woman asked, looking around at those gathered in the living room of the small apartment. There were eleven of them, all but two were young men. They sat on the sofas and the floor. They sat silently listening to the dark-haired woman. It was clear to her that at least two of the men, possibly three would vote with her simply because they loved her. It was also clear to her that at least three or four would vote against her because they drew the line at actual violence against people.

"So," said Ahmed, who was within a year of finishing medical school. "We murder two of them. Then they murder three of us and soon . . ."

"They murdered Ramu," the young woman said. "They murdered two others who had nothing to do with our cause. To them, all Arabs are the same. We have no choice."

"It's too soon." said a small young woman on the sofa. She spoke very quietly.

"We raided their temples only last night," said a thin young man with thick glasses.

"And Ramu was murdered almost as soon as we finished," the young woman countered. "We may have a spy among us."

"We have no spy," the young man in glasses said. "We know each other. They must have followed him."

The young woman looked at him as if he didn't exist

and then one of the young men, Mustafa Quadri, whom she counted on, said, "We have to organize. We have to blame the skinheads again."

"Two members of the Jewish Defense League," she said. "Perhaps three. We know who they are. We know they probably killed Howard. We kill three of them."

"To warn them," a dark man named Omar said supportively.

"To kill them," the young woman said. "We vote."

The vote was against her call for murder. Only three voted with her. Hands went down.

"All right," she said. "Those of you who voted against honorable vengeance should leave now. Those who voted for it should remain."

"You are destroying our organization," a young man said, standing.

"The organization remains," she said. "What we do outside of it is not your responsibility."

One of the three who remained was the tall Arab with the scarred face. He walked to the door with a decided limp, closed it behind those who had departed, folded his arms, and leaned against the wall to listen to the young woman. He had no intention of participating in what she might be planning. In fact, though he was easily the most militant member of the Arab Student Response Committee, he would see to it that whatever she might devise would not take place for at least a week. He had his own plan and had already murdered three of his fellow Arabs to ensure that it would work.

There was a new, neatly painted sign at Maish's T & L. It was in red letters. It was pinned to the wall behind the counter and said, "Thank You For Not Smiling."

There was little at the T & L that Said could eat so he simply said that he was not hungry. He sat alone with Lieberman at one of the booths. The place was nearly empty. Maish and most of the Alter Cockers had returned to Mir

Shavot and had begun the cleanup, probably arguing about what they could do about this outrage and reluctantly concluding that they should leave it to the police.

The short-order cook, Terrill, wearing a white apron, took Lieberman's order for a lean corned beef with hot mustard and a cup of coffee. Neither was good for his stomach, but there were things on the menu much worse.

"Those two old men are staring at me," said Said calmly, hands folded on the table top.

"Alter Cockers," said Lieberman. "Part of the furniture. Probably haven't heard yet about what happened or just don't have transportation to get to the temple. You want a salad?"

"That would be fine," said Said. "No dressing."

Lieberman called out the order. Terrill grunted back.

"This food will kill you," Said said, watching Lieberman eat when he was served.

"So I've been told," Lieberman said. "By my doctor, my wife, my daughter, a few friends, and some people I don't even know. To live without pleasure is to not live at all."

"Is that from your Torah?" asked Said as the salad was placed before him.

"Columbo," said Lieberman. "You think this Student Arab Response Committee tore the temple apart."

"I think it is a possibility, at least a possibility for some of them," said Said. "We are dealing with angry, intelligent young people without a homeland. They are attacked, called names by your press and people, suspected of all acts of supposed terrorism, awakened by phone calls in the middle of the night with threats."

"And for all this, they blame the Jews?"

"They are not anti-Semitic. We Arabs are Semites too. They are not against Jews. They are against Israel and against the American Jews who support it with their dollars. Against the government of the United States, which protects Israel. Do I look like an Arab?"

"Not particularly," said Lieberman, feeling a definite discomfort in his stomach.

"Could you mistake me for a Jew?"

"Could," said Lieberman.

"Semites. We are all Semites. Were we to band together in the Middle East we could build an economic empire to rival Western Europe, Japan, and the United States."

"Umm," said Lieberman, eyeing the last bite of sandwich and then wolfing it down.

"You've heard this before?"

"Frequently," said Lieberman. "Right now I don't care about it. I care about finding who desecrated the place where my family and I worship, where I get the only damned sense of sanctuary from what I see every damn day. I care about getting our Torah back if it still exists. I think you'd feel better if you had a half pastrami instead of pieces of lettuce."

"Were your parents born in this country?" Said asked.

"Yes."

"Grandparents?"

"No," said Lieberman. "My mother's parents were from the Ukraine. Had a farm north of Kiev, a few miles from Chernobyl. My father's parents were from Vilnius in Lithuania. Does it make a difference?"

"Yes," said Said. "My parents were born in Cairo. I was not taught by them to hate Jews. I was encouraged by them to become a successful American."

One of the two Alter Cockers at the table set for eight called over to Lieberman, "Where's everybody? Where's Maish? This a holiday?"

Lieberman explained and the two men had a conversation and stood up and walked over to the booth.

"Nazis?" asked old Braverman, squinting through amazingly thick glasses. He was thin and stooped and almost completely bald.

Lieberman shrugged.

"Nazis," Braverman confirmed, looking at Moscowitz who looked ten years younger then Braverman, though both were seventy-six.

"Maybe Arabs," said Moscowitz, looking at the two policemen.

"Nazis," insisted Braverman, "maybe working with Arabs. Arabs are crazy. They blow themselves up. Nazis don't die for their hate."

Said sat silently. Old Braverman's sleeve was pulled up. On his arm was a still-vivid concentration camp number.

"Shoot them dead on sight, Lieberman," Braverman said with calm certainty.

"Let's go to the temple instead of sitting here repeating ourselves, see if we can help," Moscowitz said, taking Braverman's arm. "I'll call my daughter-in-law. She'll take us."

As Moscowitz turned, Braverman said, "Well, was I right or was I right? Arabs or Nazis. Or maybe the Klan."

"I don't know," said Lieberman.

"There's right and right," said Moscowitz, as he and Braverman went to the pay phone near the washrooms to call Moscowitz's daughter-in-law.

"They think I'm a Jew," Said said. Lieberman nodded and worked on his coffee. "I'm as American as they are. Maybe more so," Said continued, watching the men make their call.

"Children?"

"Two," said Said. "Don't tell me you want to see their pictures."

"If I don't tell you, how do I communicate the information?"

Said reached into his jacket pocket, came out with a wallet and opened it to a photo of a pretty, dark woman and two remarkably beautiful children, one a boy, the other a girl.

"Beautiful," said Lieberman, handing Said his wallet open to a picture of his daughter and two grandchildren.

"Also beautiful," said Said.

Lieberman took back the wallet and looked at the photograph as if he had never seen it.

"Not beautiful," he said. "That's Lisa, my daughter, and

her two kids. Lisa is too serious to be more than pretty and too stubborn to work on it. The kids are fine. Barry looks like his father, which is good, and Melisa looks like her mother which makes her, I'd say, on the verge of good-looking."

"And now?" asked Said.

"You and I go see some of the people Howard Ramu knew," said Lieberman.

Said nodded and opened his wallet to take out a five-dollar bill. Lieberman stopped him. "At Maish's, my guests don't pay." On the way out, Lieberman called out his thanks to Terrill, who was nowhere in sight.

The phone was ringing.

Bill Hanrahan sat in his immaculate living room in his perfectly clean little house in Ravenswood not far from the Ravenswood Hospital. He and Maureen had raised their boys here, fought here, made love here, and very seldom had any visitors because of Bill's odd working hours and his drinking.

The phone was ringing.

Bill Hanrahan had been an alcoholic. He probably still was but he didn't drink, though he occasionally wanted to. A woman had died because of his drunkenness and he had stopped drinking with the help of AA and Smedley, his sponsor. Hanrahan had always been a big man. Without the booze, he had grown even bigger. He wondered why Iris, calm, determined, beautiful, even-tempered Iris wanted to marry him.

The phone was still ringing.

Iris said she didn't mind living in the house when they were married. They had made love here once, on the open-out couch in the living room, the couch on which he now sat looking at the phone. No, he couldn't keep living here. There were ghosts and memories on every shelf, in every corner, on every piece of furniture. He had kept himself busy the night Maureen left by cleaning house. The boys were already grown and on their own clearly wanting nothing to do with their drunk of a father.

He had never struck Maureen and never wanted to, though, ironically, she had frequently, toward the end, tears on her cheeks, slapped Bill, slapped him hard and he had taken it, knowing she was right.

He had cleaned the house better than she had ever done and he waited for years for her return, waited for her to come to the door and see what he had done, the shrine he had kept to their marriage and family.

The phone did not stop ringing.

Hanrahan had finally realized that she was not coming back. He had been attacked by a murderer during an investigation and was hospitalized with critical head wounds. Maureen had come. One of his boys, Bill Junior, had come. There had been no love in his eyes. A touch of sadness. A tic of regret. A quiver of sympathy. Maureen and their son had come once, heard that he would live and had departed after a few words of bitterness from Bill Junior. His younger son, Michael, had refused to fly in to see his father. Maureen had said little, but had made it clear that she had a new life, was seeing other men, had a decent job in an insurance office, and as a good Catholic, had no hope in seeking a divorce or annulment within the church. Instead, she had pursued a legal divorce and obtained it, though she told herself that she would have to live out her life in the eyes of the church still married to William Hanrahan.

Hanrahan picked up the phone.

"Father Murph," said Lieberman from his car phone.

"Rabbi," answered Hanrahan.

"I'm heading for Hyde Park with Said."

"Be more specific and I'll meet you there," said Hanrahan.

"How about you get the short list of neo-Nazis and skinheads and start paying them a visit instead?"

"Right," said Hanrahan. "Watch yourself."

"I'll check my well-groomed mustache in the mirror right now. Catch up with you later," said Lieberman.

"Abe."

"Yeah, Bill?"

"Forget it. See you later."

They hung up. In this room were ghosts, even the ghost of the man he had murdered, the madman with the gun, Frankie Kraylaw, who Hanrahan had set up before the man could kill his own wife and little boy.

Hanrahan stood up. It was time to leave the ghosts. He'd sell and send half the money to Maureen, though the house was in his name and she had not asked for it in their quick civil divorce. She had asked for no money and no support, wanting none, knowing that Hanrahan probably wouldn't have it even if the court ordered him to pay. She wanted all chains cut. They had paid off the house years ago. She deserved half. He thought she'd keep it, but she might send it back to him.

What had brought all this back? The sight of destruction, anger borne of a hatred Hanrahan could not understand. He had simply stood there while the Skokie police and the FBI had gone over the chapel. He had read the signs, seen the destruction.

He really needed a drink. He called Smedley Ash, who answered after three rings. "Smed? It's Bill Hanrahan. The bottle's calling."

Smedley Ash was an alcoholic. He had been sober for a decade. Ironically, Bill Hanrahan had arrested Smedley on two occasions for disorderly conduct. Now Smedley was sober and working as the manager of the Now Boutique on Oak Street. Smedley was quietly but proudly gay.

"What happened?" Smedley asked.

Hanrahan rambled for about ten minutes about Maureen, his kids, what he had seen earlier that day, Iris.

"I'll be right over," said Smedley.

Hanrahan sighed. "No," he said. "It's passing and I've got to get to work. I just needed to let it out. I don't even know what it is."

"OK," said Smedley. "I'll give you a call later, maybe we can talk after work."

Hanrahan thanked him and hung up. He put on his shoes, checked his gun, holstered it, put on his jacket, and headed for the door. The phone rang. Hanrahan considered ignoring it, but he had no answering machine, and he picked it up.

"Bill?" came a woman's voice.

"It's me," he said. "Bess?"

"Yes," she said, trying to speak calmly and evenly. "I've got to find Abe. Someone threatened to kill us, came right up to Barry when he was playing baseball in the park, said he'd kill us if Abe didn't leave him alone."

"How's Barry?"

"Considering, he's all right. Scared but all right. I didn't tell Melisa. Find Abe."

"I'll find him," said Hanrahan. "Did Barry describe the man? Would he recognize him again if he saw him?"

"I don't think so," said Bess. "Maybe. He wore a raincoat and dark glasses. He was Chinese."

Hanrahan paused. Or Korean, he thought.

"I don't know," Bess said. "I woke up this morning and the world went crazy. Fanatics deface my synagogue, lunatics threaten my family."

Hanrahan knew the feeling.

The phone rang.

Barry was in the kitchen drinking chocolate milk and eating Oreo cookies. Melisa was in the living room watching something about manatees on the Discovery Channel. Melisa had asked if she could go down the street and play with Sarah Horowitz. Bess, who desperately wanted a shower because she was covered in paint and reeked of filth from the start of the cleanup at the temple, said no. She wanted them together, in the house. Melisa had asked why she couldn't play. Bess said that she needed her granddaughter's help in making cookies. It was a weak excuse, but Melisa didn't question it and was soon absorbed in the manatees.

The phone rang again. She picked it up automatically, expecting an Asian voice, the repeat of the threat and warning that had been given to Barry. It turned out to be almost as bad.

"Bess?" asked Lisa.

"Yes."

"Are you all right, the kids, Abe?"

"Yes. Why?"

"I don't know. I just had a feeling."

California was doing something to Lisa. Bess wasn't sure whether it was good or bad. Lisa, her biochemist daughter, who showed little affection and no capacity for or interest in intuition, was on the phone showing concern for something she didn't even know had happened.

"Well, everything is fine. How are you?"

"Making it," Lisa said seriously.

After she first left her husband, Todd, he had pressed for months for her and the children to return. He'd finally given up. At the very moment that Lisa had finally considered a return to her husband, Todd had taken up with another professor in his department, a woman ten years older than he and, what was worse, a woman Lisa liked. And so they divorced and Lisa had left her children with Bess and Abe, and had taken off for California with the idea of settling and sending for the children.

"Good," said Bess, aware of her reeking dirty clothes. "Would you like to talk to Melisa?"

"Yes, and Barry."

"Barry isn't here," said Bess, eyes closed as she lied. "He has a ball game at the J."

"Then Melisa."

"Lisa?"

"Yes?"

"We love you. Your father and I."

"I know," she said. "And since I know I'm not lovable, I'm beginning to appreciate it. Bess, I'm seeing someone."

"Is it serious?" asked Bess.

"Very," said Lisa.

Melisa, having heard part of the conversation during a commercial, ran to the phone and took it from her grandmother.

"Mom?"

"Yes, Missy. How are you?"

"OK. Did you know manatees are almost extinct?"

"Yes."

"Did you know that grandma's temple was torn up by Nazis?"

"Torn up by . . ." Lisa said with a gasp.

"They wrote things on the walls and everything. Grandma helped clean up. She's still wearing smelly clothes. We're going to order Domino's pizzas delivered. I've got a tape of *Lion King*. When are Barry and I going to California?"

"You want to come to California?"

"I guess. Maybe not. It doesn't get cold there, does it?"

"Not very. I'll talk to you again soon. Tell Barry I called."

"You can talk to him. He's in the kitchen all muddy eating cookies."

"Put Grandma back on."

Melisa handed the phone to Bess and returned to the television set.

"What is happening?" Lisa said even more calmly than usual.

Bess sighed and told her from beginning to the present. Then she said, "Lisa? Are you there?"

"I'm here, Mother," Lisa said. Lisa rarely called her mother and father anything but Bess and Abe. It was a sign, but of what Bess was not certain. "I think I may take the children now," Lisa said.

"It's the middle of the semester," Bess said. "Barry's about to have his bar mitzvah."

"It's the beginning of their lives," Lisa answered. "They'll be safe with me."

"Los Angeles is safer than Chicago?" asked Bess.

"It is where I live," she said. "And I don't live in a house with a policeman whose family gets threatened because he deals with lunatics, drug dealers, gangs, and killers."

"Lisa," Bess pleaded. "You've got a full-time job. You couldn't even be home for them after school. And the cost of day care . . ."

"Mother, I . . ."

"Lisa," said Bess. "I'm too dirty, too depressed, and too tired to do anything but tell you the truth, a truth you and I both know."

She looked back to see if the children could hear. Melisa was already back in the living room. Barry had left the kitchen.

"The truth is, Lisa, you don't want the children. You'll come here, take them, uproot them, put them in after-school programs, and regret the nights you have to deal with their growing up."

"Which means," said Lisa evenly, "you don't think I've grown up."

"That's part of it," said Bess wearily.

Lisa hung up the phone.

FIVE

BRAHAM SAID LOOKED at Lieberman who looked back at him. The message was clear. Said knew the beautiful young woman with the long, dark hair who was speaking to the crowd, and was suggesting that she might well be the one for whom they were looking.

"Listen," the woman said holding up her hand for quiet. "Listen, for the sake of the dead, for the sake of those who have died for a homeland for their children, for the sake of justice."

The crowd grew quiet and paid attention. A muscular young man with blond curly hair stood with his arms folded, shaking his head. He had heard this before.

"Her name is Jara," Ibraham whispered. "Jara Mohammed. One of the most militant of the Arab Student Response Committee. Her younger brother, Massad, is probably around someplace."

Lieberman didn't bother to turn around. He knew a police photographer was getting the woman's picture, a picture Lieberman could show to Anne Ready, the old woman who lived across from Mir Shavot.

"Three of our people died yesterday," the woman said, holding up three long fingers and snapping them down one at a time. "No more than a half-mile from where we now stand arguing. If we are not strong, the Jews like this one . . ." She pointed at the muscular young man with folded arms, "will slaughter us as they have slaughtered us for five thousand years."

"A body count?" the muscular young blond man said suddenly, shouting, angry, his hands held out. "I am an Israeli. I have seen body counts. I've been in the army on military patrols and seen the bodies of slaughtered Jewish children in a school bus. The numbers of our dead civilians, our children, our mothers is part of the attempt throughout history to eliminate the Jews and a Jewish State. The Nazis, the Arabs, the British have all tried and failed. They looked behind themselves and there was their dark shadow and they called it Jew and tried to destroy it, but you can't destroy your shadow. Never." There were some shouts of approval from the crowd and other shouts and insults aimed at the young Israeli.

Lieberman knew the quadrangle of the University of Chicago well. Standing at the rear entrance to the Administration Building with Said at his side, Lieberman watched and listened and remembered. Twenty-five years ago, he had stood in about the same spot just off the grass. He had looked around at the matched, heavy gray stone buildings that made the university look English, ancient, and serious.

Two and a half decades ago, the Weathermen, primarily a group of university students, had protested the war in Vietnam at a massive rally right where Abe now stood. With bullhorns, intelligence, hate, and paranoia, they had rallied a few hundred students into a boycott of classes and a take-over of the Administration Building, a sit-in until demands were met including the university's pulling out all its investments in unacceptable companies and unacceptable countries. The targets were the U.S. government, South Africa, chemical companies. The students wanted change.

Lieberman had been assigned to that protest. Even at

thirty-five he looked at least fifty and was taken for a professor by most of the students. One of the Weathermen, a young man with long hair and skin as clear as a model's, had approached Lieberman and asked, "Are you with us or against us?"

Lieberman had answered that he hadn't chosen sides.

"Then you're against us," said the young man. "Don't you know what's going on here?"

"A hundred or so students," said Lieberman, "are going to go into that building and sit around making demands, getting their pictures in the paper, going to jail, accomplishing very little."

"Then we'll think of something bigger," said the young man with great sincerity. "Ask him. He knows." The "him" who supposedly knew was a black photographer named Jim Cooper who had been hired by the university to take pictures of the crowd so that leaders could be identified and later expelled. The young man who had pointed to him certainly did not know that Cooper was employed by the university the young man was attacking.

Jim was philosophical about the matter. He was older than Lieberman and had been through two wars carrying a camera. Now he made a living freelancing and shaking his head at all people who carried banners, made threats, and assumed he was one of them because of the color of his skin. Jim had told Lieberman over a beer at a bar on 57th Street that these were middle-class and rich white kids, smart, and feeling guilty because they weren't black and poor and hadn't had to live with hate and poverty and despair. "Headlines and a few busted heads," said Jim.

Lieberman had nodded, looking around the tavern at students and faculty slowly downing beers and eating cheeseburgers.

Lieberman and Jim Cooper had stayed in touch over the years. Cooper had opened a studio just north of the Loop on Wells Street and had succeeded in making a living by doing everything from portraits to car collisions. But his big break came only a few years ago when he developed a secret process for printing color photos, mostly of musicians, so they came out looking like eerie suggestions of life, abstract disturbing forms. Jim won prizes, had articles written about him and his work, and actually sold most of his work at a price that kept him and his wife comfortable.

So, given the fact that Jim Cooper was a success and was at least seventy it was no little surprise today for Lieberman to see Cooper, hair completely white, a slight stoop to his shoulders, standing at the fringe of the growing crowd, taking pictures with a telephoto lens, a black bag slung over his shoulder.

A thin young man was the next to speak. He had conviction. He had zeal. He also had a pair of glasses that he had to keep on his nose with an occasional squint. He had no charisma.

Lieberman told Said he would be right back and moved toward Jim Cooper who greeted him with a smile and a handshake. "What the hell are you doing here?" Lieberman asked.

"Last time I was here for something like this," said Cooper, "I felt something. I couldn't get it in the photographs, the hate, confusion, the colors of anger and fear, the shapes. No, Abraham, this time I'm here for me."

"How've you been?" Lieberman asked, as Jim Cooper raised his camera to take the picture of an arguing group of young men and women who paid no attention to the young man with the bullhorn. Cooper clicked off about five photographs, held the camera at his side, and said, "Pretty good."

Bess Lieberman had spoken to Jim's wife, Amanda, no more than a month ago. Jim Cooper had triple bypass surgery. He also had a stomach cancer that the Veteran's Administration Hospital was managing to hold their own against.

"How are you, Abraham?"

"Nothing. A little cholesterol problem. Stomach. Kid doctors who know what they're doing but don't know people."

"Tell me about it," said Cooper, looking down at his camera.

"You gonna take a lunch break?" asked Lieberman.

Someone was arguing vehemently with the thin man carrying the bullhorn. Someone in the crowd. The young bespectacled Arab with the bullhorn made the mistake of trying to reason with the crowd. "We must find a way to live in peace," he said. "We, Arabs and Jews, are cousins fighting over the legacy of a common father, Abraham. The five pillars of Islam and the ways of Judaism are the same. We both bear witness to God's oneness. We pray five times a day. You pray three. We have Ramadan, a time of soul-searching, fasting, self-examination. You have Yom Kippur. We must give alms and so must you. Islam has much more in common with Judaism than either faith has in common with Christianity. We . . ." Something orange, rotten, and wet hit the neck of the young Arab. He stood bewildered, bullhorn in hand.

"Raincheck on lunch," said Cooper, picking up his camera and moving around so he could see the faces of those in the crowd.

Lieberman moved back to Said. The crowd had grown to about forty. Uniformed police were in cars on the other side of the building, but they wouldn't move without an OK from the campus police who took their orders from a vice president.

"You should at least get your facts straight," shouted the blond Israeli at the man with the bullhorn.

"Your 'straight facts' are Jewish lies," said the young man. He was standing on the steps of the administration building now, about three feet above the crowd.

"I'll give you dates, times, body counts of innocent Jews, children, murdered by Arab terrorists in my country," shouted the Israeli.

"And I'll give you more accounts of Israeli attacks on the innocent in Lebanon, Jordan, and Palestine," said the man with the bullhorn.

"All right," said the Israeli. "Give them. You describe

and I'll describe, each mutilation, each threat to kill us all or drive us into the sea."

The Israeli, with a mixture of encouragement and boos pushed forward with the help of a pair of friends and strode up the steps reaching for the bullhorn. He was much bigger than the Arab student, with the arms of a weight lifter. Lieberman noted that one of the two men who had helped part the crowd so he could step up was Eli Towser, the man he had fired as his grandson's bar mitzvah tutor. Towser looked around. His eyes met Lieberman's for an instant. Towser shook his head and turned back to watch the coming battle for the bullhorn.

But before the muscular Israeli could take the bullhorn, the young woman Said had earlier identified as Jara Mohammed reached for the horn. The bespectacled young man gladly relinquished it to her.

Mohammed wore a sacklike green dress that covered her arms and went down to her ankles. There was no belt at her waist to show the shape of her obviously lean body.

The young Israeli hesitated, reluctant to wrestle the bullhorn from a woman.

"Listen," she said into the bullhorn. "For the sake of the innocent dead. For the memory of those who struggled and died."

The muscular Israeli had heard this before. He folded his arms and looked at her with a sigh that said he knew what was coming.

Lieberman did not turn around. He hoped and assumed that the police photographer would get a good enough photograph for Abe to show to Anne Ready.

"For five thousand years, the Jews have slaughtered our people and taken their land," she said. "Sometimes by the thousands. Sometimes one or two at a time. Yesterday, not more than half a mile from here, three Arab students were slaughtered."

"Ridiculous," the muscular Israeli shouted, unfolding his arm, screaming so that the sinews of his neck stood out like thin red pillars. "For five thousand years the Germans, the British, the Arabs have denied us our small piece of land, have waged war against mothers and children, have vowed to drive us into the sea. We will not be driven into the sea. We will fight and we will win if we must. The countries that surround us are coming to understand this and come to a table of peace. It is Hamas and the mad men and women like this one who will be the cause of more slaughter, more dead, more hatred on both sides."

"They're repeating themselves," Lieberman said.

"Yes," said Said. "A bad sign. Violence will be next."

As if to fulfill Said's prophecy, there were arguments in the crowd now. Small surging groups pushing, shoving, shouting.

"Listen," shouted the girl with the bullhorn. "This is not the time or place to fight. We will have justice, a justice we cannot expect from a country and a political system that sees Israel as the fifty-first state in the union."

Someone, it may have been Eli Towser, threw something at the woman. It was a ripe tomato that splattered against her breasts. She wiped it away ignoring the attack. "Those of you who now believe in our cause," she shouted. "Those who knew Howard Ramu and our other dead brothers. Those of you who know the truth of what I have said should sign the membership list that is being passed among you. We must organize. Even if you are not an Arab. If you believe. If you know, it is your duty to join us, to sign, to be prepared to protect freedom of speech, to stand up for a maligned minority that seeks only justice."

The muscular Israeli threw up his hands in disgust and went back into the crowd where the shoving and arguing were growing more vehement.

Lieberman tapped Said's shoulder, turned his back on the scene and the growing noise. Fights would break out in the next seconds. The campus police would try to handle the situation. They might succeed. They might not.

"She got what she wanted," Said said as they walked. "Six or seven students have created a riot that will give them publicity on television and in the newspapers."

Now clear of the fringes of the crowd Lieberman looked back. Standing on the lowest step of the Administration Building, Jim Cooper was slowly, calmly taking pictures.

"Lieberman," a woman's voice called. Rene Catolino was moving toward him, her voice raised over the battle behind him. She wore a light black jacket that billowed as she moved. "Hanrahan's been trying to reach you. Says to meet him at your house fast. No one's hurt, but something's going down."

"Go, we will meet later," Said said.

Lieberman nodded at Catolino, who, hands on hips, watched the battle of people wielding books, fists, a bullhorn and one or two metal bars brought for the occasion. The tall young man with a limp took several steps toward Eli Towser and swung a bar at him. Towser blocked the blow with his arm and punched the man in the face.

"These are the smart kids," she said to Said as Lieberman moved as quickly as he could toward his car. "I went to Northern Illinois and we never had anything as fucking crazy as this."

"Intellect and violence are often in harmony," said Said, his back to the battle. "It was the one problem with Plato's theory of choosing the wisest man in the nation to be king."

"Because the wisest man wouldn't necessarily be peaceful," said Catolino, her eyes following the clumps of battle.

"He might even be mad," said Said. "In fact, I believe Plato would be puzzled by the number of wise men who lead their people into slaughter."

"You were a philosophy major," said Catolino.

"Theoretical Biology," Said said. "Right here. In that building to our right. Excuse me."

Said turned around suddenly, scanned the crowd, saw what he was seeking, and sailed in. Without knowing where the man was going or why, Rene Catolino followed. They pushed through flying fists and screams of hate. Something hit Rene in the back of the head. She touched the spot. There was no blood. Said got to the front of the crowd with Rene close behind. He found Jara Mohammed sitting on the steps, dazed, blood coming down her forehead. Catolino helped Said lift the confused young woman. They moved to the entrance of the building. The door was locked. Rene led them to the edge of the steps where Jim Cooper took their picture as they moved down and through the edge of the crowd.

The campus police were wading in weaponless, trying to calm small battles, talking, keeping their voices even, doing everything they had been taught to do in such a situation and wanting simply to bash a few heads, cuff a few of the worst, and get this over quickly. Instead they reasoned, got between combatants, and found themselves under attack. By the time the city police waded into the crowd, two campus police were down and ambulances were arriving.

Rene Catolino and Ibraham Said moved away, the young woman between them, heading for an ambulance.

"What else could you expect from them?" Jara Mohammed said, blood still trickling down her forehead in a rivulet past the right side of her nose and down along her cheek.

"What else can you expect from yourself?" Said asked.

Jara tried to grasp the question but before she could answer two medics took her in hand. "She been shot?" one of the medics, a very young man with a very thin mustache, asked softly.

"Hit by a tomato," Said said. "And probably on the head with a bullhorn."

The medic nodded and hurried to help Mohammed, leading her toward the nearby ambulance.

"Well," said Catolino. "We've got some work to do."

They both turned to look at the students running from the front of the building, running away from the Chicago police. A few sat on the ground either hurt or in protest. The two campus security guards who had fallen were being helped up. Television cameras turned silently.

By this evening, the battle would be the subject of more than one talk radio show.

*   *   *

They were waiting for Hanrahan outside of his house when he went home to change his shirt, right on his doorstep, hands folded in front of them. They could have been about to ring the bell or they could have been standing there for half an hour. Hanrahan recognized them immediately, Woo's two "associates," both immaculately dressed in matching blue slacks, navy blue jackets, white button-down shirts, and striped ties. Both men were Chinese, but the resemblance stopped there. One man was small and from his neck and the fit of his slacks, Bill Hanrahan could tell he was capable of significant damage without the need of a weapon. The other man was taller, broader, and wore a considerable bulge under the right side of his jacket. "Mr. Woo would like to see you now," said the smaller man.

"Mr. Woo will have to wait," said Hanrahan to the men barring his way.

Mr. Woo was a man of considerable influence in the Chinese community. Officially, he was an importer-exporter with a thriving business in Chinatown just off of Cermak Road. Unofficially, Mr. Woo was more than suspected of trafficking in a variety of goods including opium, prostitution, illegal immigrants, and stolen Asian art objects. Mr. Woo was a man to be feared in the Chinese community. He was a man to be respected, and it was respect he wanted most. At least this was the opinion of Iris Huang's father who had known Woo in China. Woo had been a shoeless, orphaned street thief in Shanghai. He had moved up significantly with age and, with the help of several major bribes to Chinese communist officials, made his way across the border to Hong Kong where further bribes to British officials secured him official immigration to the United States. All that had occurred when Mr. Woo was young. He was no longer young. When he died, he planned to leave his considerable fortune to the Chinese community and have that fact announced immediately after his death. He planned for and was assured of the biggest funeral service in the history of Chinatown. Mr. Woo would prefer to have the streets lined with sincere mourners.

Meanwhile, Mr. Woo was far from dead and saw himself as something between a protector and a rejected suitor of Iris Huang. He could have forced himself on Iris, but the humiliation of such an act was definitely beneath him. What Mr. Woo had made clear on three occasions, accompanied by the two men in front of Bill Hanrahan, was that he did not like Hanrahan and did not want him, marrying any Chinese woman, particularly Iris Huang.

"Mr. Woo told us to ask you politely," said the smaller man in perfect English. "I give you his assurance that this will not take you long nor far out of your way."

"How do you know where I'm headed?"

The smaller man shrugged. There were no smiles from either of Mr. Woo's men. "Mr. Woo is waiting for you now at the Black Moon Restaurant," said the smaller man. "He is having tea with Mr. Huang."

Hanrahan stood for a moment considering. He could take out the smaller, tougher man in front of him with a sucker punch that would drop him down the steps. He could probably get his own .38 out before the clumsy bigger man. But the bigger man might not be as clumsy as he looked and . . .

"I'll give him ten minutes," Hanrahan said.

"Mr. Woo will be grateful for whatever time you can give him out of your busy schedule," the smaller man said with what Hanrahan took as well-veiled sarcasm that would probably elude anyone but a cop, a priest, or a hooker.

"I drive my own car," said Hanrahan.

"And I will accompany you while my associate drives behind us," said the smaller man.

Hanrahan nodded, went upstairs with the men to change his shirt, and fifteen minutes later was sitting in a booth at the Black Moon Restaurant directly across from Mr. Woo whose cane was propped up on the seat as if it were a third party to the conversation.

It was mid-afternoon. There were no other customers and no one at any other booth or table except for the two men who had come with Bill Hanrahan.

Hanrahan was sure that Woo had arranged the seating so

that the policeman could look out the window and across Sheridan Road at the apartment building where a woman had died because Hanrahan had been too drunk to save her.

Mr. Woo was unwrinkled. His thinning black hair was brushed straight back. He wore a serious gray suit that complimented the clothing of his associates, but stood out by being a bit more expensive. The army of Woo was certainly well dressed.

"Tea?" asked Woo.

"Tea," Hanrahan agreed though he didn't particularly like tea.

"Mr. Huang and his daughter are in the kitchen," said Woo pouring tea into the small white cup in front of Hanrahan and then into his own cup.

Woo nodded at the cup and Hanrahan took a sip. It was hot, strong, and Hanrahan found it surprisingly good.

"I brought my own tea," said Woo. "I can see that you appreciate it. The tea served in almost all Chinese restaurants is tasteless and without tradition or civility."

"It's good," Hanrahan conceded.

"But other beverages are better?" asked Woo, taking a small drink.

"I don't have to answer to you, Woo," Hanrahan said. "And neither does Iris or her family."

Woo shrugged almost imperceptibly.

God, he plays the part well, thought Hanrahan with more than grudging admiration.

"I haven't had a drink in almost two years," said Hanrahan. "I don't intend to ever have one again. I have an official divorce, papers and all, State of Illinois. I pay no alimony or maintenance to my ex-wife. Her idea. She's got a job that pays better than mine. My sons are grown and on their own. I make enough to support a wife and I've got a little in the bank. But you know all this."

"Yes," said Woo. "I would prefer that you not marry Iris Huang. I have, however, given up the hope that she might willingly marry me. By doing so, she would be a wealthy woman while I live and even wealthier when I die. She would help her family and make what remains of my days on earth more enjoyable."

"You said you've given up hope of her marrying you willingly?" Woo nodded and poured Hanrahan more tea. Hanrahan couldn't keep his eyes from the building across the street.

"I would prefer that she marry someone worthy. Someone Chinese," said Woo. "Did you know that you and your people have a particular odor, which my people often find offensive? Negro people also have an odor."

"We call them African-Americans now," said Hanrahan.

"I have no need to keep up with such fickle conventions," said Woo.

"Woo, is there a point to all this?"

A tic, however slight, touched Woo's right eye. There was a proper way to carry on a conversation. Though Woo had been of low birth, he had studied, had even learned Mandarin and turned his street Cantonese into grammatical Cantonese. He wished, above all, to be civilized, but the United States was filled with those who had no sense of civility or interest in it. He sat across from an example now.

"You are finding it difficult to get someone to perform a wedding," said Woo. "And what I offer is something Mr. Huang, his family, and I would like very much. You also want a Catholic wedding. About that I can do nothing, but we both know that such a wedding would not be sanctioned. So, you will be married by a fallen priest in an eccentric church."

"You're saying that you can get someone to marry Iris and me in a Chinese wedding?"

"I can arrange it," said Woo.

"Why?"

"Mr. Huang and his daughter wish it," he said. "I am informed that though she tells you it is not of great consequence to her, in fact it is causing her great . . . distress. I do not like policemen. My entire life has been a series of bribes and confrontations with the police and rarely have I encountered one who showed civility or respect. I will add that I am prejudiced against your race, but, I believe, for good reason. Added to this, I have a particular aversion to you. There is a saying in Mandarin that once a man weds the bottle, there can be separation but no divorce. You are also a very violent man who has committed murder."

"I shot Frankie Kraylaw in self-defense," said Hanrahan, his eyes directly meeting Woo's.

"Please repeat that," said Woo.

Hanrahan sat back.

"Your motives were honorable and violence is sometimes a necessary part of business," said Woo. "More tea?"

"No, thanks."

"Then we have an agreement?" asked Woo.

"No strings?" asked Hanrahan.

"The strings are many," said Woo, "but they will not involve you. My community will view this as a sign of weakness, possibly the failure in thinking of an old man. There may be those who try to replace me because of this. It will take much work to heal wounds and restore honor."

"I'll try to appreciate your position," said Hanrahan.

Two couples came into the restaurant, one straight, one gay. They came in together, anticipating with smiles the punch line of a joke from one of the gay men who said, ". . . and the doctor said, 'Two Wongs don't make a white.' "

The quartet, including the man who had told the joke, laughed and found a table across the room from the booth where Woo and the policeman sat, Woo's men between them.

"If," Woo went on, palms on the table, "you resume drinking, betray Miss Huang, dishonor her family, or cause her pain in any way starting from this moment, I will have you killed. It will be an accident."

Hanrahan choked back anger and an obscenity. It was what Woo was trying to provoke. A test. Hanrahan tasted bile and sweet tea and said, "I will treat Miss Huang and her family with respect and give neither them nor you any reason to regret your decision."

"I will discuss the arrangements with Mr. Huang. I understand you are on duty and late for an appointment," said Woo in obvious dismissal.

Anger just short of rage came close to overcoming reason, but Hanrahan stood, looked back toward the kitchen where Iris had come out to serve the couple still telling jokes across the room. She glanced at Hanrahan. He smiled and she smiled back with relief.

Hanrahan headed toward the door without looking at Woo's two associates. He had work to do and someone to see who deserved no civility.

SIX

LIEBERMAN WASN'T PREPARED for the gathering that greeted him when he walked into his house. Bess hurried to meet him at the door and whispered, "I couldn't stop them. They just showed up."

They included Rabbi Wass, looking like a pudgy and decidedly anguished Claude Rains; Irving Hamel, attorney, member of almost every temple committee, not yet 40, and expected by the congregation to attain great things in politics; Ida Katzman, ancient Ida, the major benefactor of Temple Mir Shavot. Ida and her husband had started the original temple and helped to hire the now retired older Rabbi Wass. Ida's husband had left her a chain of jewelry stores, five in Chicago, six in the suburbs. Ida's hearing was going. Her eyesight was going and while her pockets were deep, Lieberman thought that her patience must be going. They sat at Lieberman's dining room table drinking coffee. A place remained open at the head of the table for Lieberman.

"Barry and Melisa?" he asked Bess softly, hanging up

his jacket in the front closet taking off his holster and gun
and reaching up to put them on the high closet shelf. Normally, when he came home. Lieberman locked the gun in
the night table next to his and Bess's bed. He wore the key
to the drawer on a thin gold chain around his neck. Clinking
against the key was a gold star of David given him by Bess
on their thirtieth wedding anniversary.

"The children are upstairs," Bess whispered.

Lieberman moved to the table, shook hands with Hamel
and the pale Rabbi Wass and nodded respectfully to Ida
Katzman who had declined in the past few months from a
cane to a metal walker that stood next to her chair.

"We are in crisis," said Rabbi Wass. "I've called my
father in St. Petersburg and he agrees."

Bess filled the empty cup of coffee in front of her husband and sat at his side. The coffee was decaffeinated and
the slice of cake he took was fat free, cholesterol free, su-
garless, and without distinctive taste, though it tried to
make up for its deficiencies with texture and color.

"What does he agree to?" asked Lieberman.

"That we are in crisis," said Rabbi Wass. "And something must be done. These desecrators must be found and
punished. Our Torah must be returned. Do you know where
that Torah came from?"

Lieberman knew but he listened as Ida Katzman said, in
a hoarse but not particularly weak voice with a slight accent
of Eastern Europe, "When my husband and I went to
France soon after we were married, a year after the war
ended, and before Morris was born, we found the Torah in
a small town where there were no longer any Jews. The
Catholic priest had it. It had been given to him to protect
during the war. The Rabbi who had given it to him had left
no name, no place to return it. My husband made a donation to the church and we took the Torah. In New York,
Menachem Mushevitz himself, a great scholar, examined
the Torah and declared it priceless, from the Moorish oc-
cupation of Spain."

Ida looked at Rabbi Wass who acknowledged in his pious nod that Mushevitz was the essence of scholarly greatness.

"Mushevitz was already an old man." Ida went on with a story everyone at the table had heard many times before. "Mushevitz said the Torah had certainly been commissioned by a great artist at great cost and done with loving care that would be the envy of any congregation in the world. My husband pressed him for a value. All Mushevitz would say was, 'priceless.' "

"So," Ida Katzman continued. "We brought it home to Chicago where we had opened our first store on Madison Street and we brought it to the old Rabbi Wass who made it the heart of our congregation. Scholars have come from all over the world to see it, touch it, study it. And now . . . ?" Ida Katzman suddenly became silent, having nowhere to go.

"Rabbi Wass has been contacted by phone," Hamel said, briefcase with laptop computer at his side.

"They want money for the Torah," said the Rabbi, looking down at his untouched coffee. "First they desecrate . . . not just our temple but also others. There are rituals I will have to get from the Board of Rabbis to cleanse the temple. There are . . ."

"The call," lawyer Irving Hamel reminded him, stealing a glance at his watch.

"Two hundred thousand dollars," said Rabbi Wass. "Two hundred thousand. And who knows how many thousands it will cost to finish the cleaning, repair the damages. Our people are working. Sam Shapiro will donate materials and time, but he is not a wealthy man. He'll need compensation."

"Are you sure it was the same ones who . . . ?" Lieberman began.

"They gave details, told me the filth they had written on the walls, told me what they had done, described the Torah in detail down to the small piece missing from the lower right handle of the scroll."

"How do they want the money and when?" asked Lieberman.

Rabbi Wass adjusted his glasses and shrugged. "Who knows? They said they would call someone in the congregation with that information. They said they will destroy the Torah if we do not do as they say."

Clever, thought Lieberman, phone taps and tapes couldn't be set up for every member of the congregation.

"They won't destroy the Torah," Lieberman said. "If they don't get the money from us, they'll sell it in Europe."

"There probably isn't a congregation in the world that wouldn't recognize our Torah," said Ida Katzman.

"You know best," said Lieberman who, in fact, thought that the people who had mutilated the temple and taken the Torah were very likely, indeed, to destroy it, whether they got their money or not. "We'll just have to get the Torah back. We've got good leads, which I can't talk about now."

"I'll pay the money," Ida Katzman said.

Ida had, in her lifetime since the death of her husband and later that of her only son in Vietnam, made the congregation her life, her child. Rabbi Wass estimated that she had donated more than a million and a half dollars for everything from the building fund to new benches and books to guaranteeing the salary of the rabbi.

"Let's hope that's not necessary, Ida," Lieberman said.

"That's very generous of you, Mrs. Katzman," Rabbi Wass said with tears in his eyes.

"The Torah is insured for one hundred and fifty thousand dollars," said Irving Hamel. "That is the worst case situation."

"We all want the Torah back," said Ida Katzman insistently.

All present nodded. Bess looked at Lieberman. It wasn't telepathy. It was nearly a lifetime of silent communication developed between a husband and wife. Bess's face said she was afraid the Torah was already destroyed and Lieberman's eyes closed for an instant to let her know he shared her fear.

"The cleanup is progressing extremely well," said Bess. "It should be completed in two or three days with volunteer help. With Rabbi Wass's agreement, I'd like to hold an open discussion with the congregation following the sermon."

"The president always has that right," said Rabbi Wass. "I welcome it."

Ida Katzman nodded her agreement and Irving Hamel said yes and added, "One occasionally wonders why God has singled us out for five thousand years of suffering and insists that we are the chosen people."

Irving had frequently stood ready to argue and disagree, battle and even hold an occasional grudge, but never had Lieberman heard him speak out as he just had with such emotion. Irving Hamel was a contract lawyer. Irving Hamel was an ambitious young man, but above all, Irving Hamel was a Jew. When Hamel was at his worst, Lieberman sometimes referred to him as Irwin Rommel.

Bess offered more coffee and cake. All declined. Hamel had to get back to work. Rabbi Wass had to get back to help with the cleanup and be available for counseling the troubled and weeping members of the congregation, and Ida Katzman, who had a driver in her 1984 Cadillac parked in front of the house, simply rose with dignity and used her walker to make it slowly to the door, Lieberman at her side.

The rabbi and the lawyer left first. Ida hung back till they were gone, looked at Bess and Abe, and said, "Is it gone?"

"I don't know," said Lieberman. "I don't think so. Not yet. If the Torah still exists, we'll get it back."

The front door was open. Ida Katzman nodded. Her driver, a Mexican named Raul, hurried to help her down the steps. The Liebermans watched till the Cadillac had left the space in front of the fire hydrant. A car racing down the street behind them pulled straight into the empty space. The car was a Geo Metro, red, new. The driver stopped, not quite parallel to the curb but close and definitely illegally parked in front of the hydrant.

Todd Cresswell, wearing jeans and an unzipped wind-breaker over a shirt and tie, jumped out of the car, slammed the door, and looked up at Bess and Abe Lieberman.

"I talked to Melisa and Barry," Todd said. "My teaching assistant's taking my class. What's happening?"

Lieberman motioned his former son-in-law into the house. As he did, he scanned the street. Two cars behind Todd's, an Asian man in sunglasses sat behind the wheel and looked directly at Lieberman.

The man who had killed Howard Ramu and his two room-mates and had taken the Torah sat looking at the two things he had placed on the wooden table before him. On the right was the Torah. To its left an automatic weapon, an Uzi, one of six he had taken from the dead man.

He had gone to the rally, participated in the fight. Managed to bloody the enemy and get bloodied himself. He had also managed, along with other Arabs, Jews, and people who chose not to mind their own business, to be arrested. At the station, Jews and those who supported them, who were few, and Arabs and those who supported them, who were slightly more numerous, were placed in separate rooms, given a stern and insincere warning that there would be prosecutions the next time, and released or taken to the hospital for treatment.

After being treated at the University of Chicago Hospital, Ramu's killer went to his apartment, got the weapon and the Torah from the closet, and placed them on the table before him.

It was not over. While they still existed, still demanded, one major battle would be fought, and, if necessary, he would fight it alone.

He picked up the weapon and slowly, carefully, with the tools and equipment from the small box at his side on the floor, he began to clean it. He now had a total of seven weapons and though the number of those he had been assured were committed was small, their number at least matched that of the weapons he had collected.

Pig Sticker sat in the corner of the back booth at the Waffle House looking out the window and at everyone who came in. All of the customers looked at Pig Sticker. He was a skinhead far from his friends and his home and what passed for a neighborhood where he lived in a rented one-story house with three other skinheads. The house was the unofficial headquarters for the Hate Mongers. He and Fallon had an apartment in the house as did Luther and Smith the Axman.

Pig Sticker's real name, which only the man across from him ever used, was Charles Kenneth Leary. Leary wore a fading leather jacket covered in Nazi insignias, laughing skulls, and a link chain attached to the neck of a kneeling black man. Pig Sticker weighed close to three hundred pounds. His head was shaved and he looked like he would welcome a question he didn't like.

"Fast," said Pig Sticker, scooping in a triple order of potatoes and grilled onions.

Hanrahan wasn't eating. He was drinking a diet cola. "Simple," said Hanrahan. "What do you know?"

"About the Jew churches?" asked Pig Sticker.

"No," said Hanrahan. "I'm interested in your views on term limits, balancing the budget, and whether a girl should go all the way on the first date."

"You're not funny," said Pig Sticker, finishing his snack and pushing the plate away. A piece of onion stuck to his chin. Hanrahan nodded and rubbed his own chin. Pig Sticker wiped his chin and looked at a skinny old guy on the counter stool nearest their booth. The old guy needed a shave and probably a square meal. He knew enough to mind his own business.

"We had nothing to do with it," said Pig Sticker.

"What about the other skinhead gangs, Nazis, Klan, militia?" asked Hanrahan.

Pig Sticker shook his head and said, "I woulda heard by now."

"Charles Kenneth Leary," said Hanrahan. "You wouldn't be lying to an old friend."

"You're not my friend," said Pig Sticker, his face going red, starting to rise.

"Sit down, Charles," Hanrahan said. "I could probably take you. I sure as hell could shoot you. You got six people in here would probably cheer and swear you came at me with a side order of cole slaw."

Pig Sticker sat down.

"You listen. You ask. You tell me. I find out that you know something and you didn't tell me, I talk to your friends, Luther, The Axman, Stevie Spikes."

"I'll listen," Pig Sticker said, holding in his rage with clenched fists.

Normally, the old waitress would have cleaned up their plates. Instead she dropped the check and hurried off to check waffle batter and make some coffee, or pretend to.

"That's all I ask, Charles," said Hanrahan.

"What about the Nation of Islam, the Arabs?" asked Pig Sticker with a challenge. "Or this guy Martin Abdul and his ignorant black-assed Muslim jokes?"

"You can ask about them."

"We don't move in their circles," Pig Sticker said.

His jacket was open. Beneath it he wore what looked like a new white T-shirt.

"Day or night," said Hanrahan. "You know the number."

"I know the number," said Pig Sticker, standing up. He was massive. He made the papers whenever there was a skinhead rally or incident that made the news. There he would be. The biggest, the scariest, saying nothing, arms folded, scowling protectively above the heads of his buddies doing the talking.

What his buddies did not know that William Hanrahan knew was that Pig Sticker's father had been a cop. No problem there. He had probably told the Hate Mongers and said his father taught him about the alien shit on the street and how it had to be cleaned up some day. Ted Leary didn't talk like that. Didn't think like that. He lived and died a street cop who kept it all to himself and looked as if he carried a sad secret.

No, what Pig Sticker's friends did not know was that Charles Kenneth Leary's mother was a Jew. Hanrahan knew but it wasn't common knowledge. Hanrahan knew from table and living room conversation when he was invited to the Leary house. Shirley Levitt Leary had no family in Chicago. Her people were up in Minneapolis and though she sometimes visited them, they never visited her. Not the least of the reasons the Learys had few visitors was Charles Kenneth, who was almost taller than his father by the age of eleven. Charles Kenneth was an angry child. Hanrahan had witnessed one of the boy's rampages over not being allowed to take the family car one night. Charles Kenneth had been a long-haired fat boy with no friends.

And then, probably to spite his father, shame his mother, and feel that he belonged somewhere, the massive child had moved out of the house at the age of sixteen. Two months after that he had shaved his head and begun saying things his usually quiet father could not tolerate, especially when they were made against his wife's people.

There had been a fight, a real fight, which Charles had obviously expected to win. Instead it had ended within seconds when Ted had hit his block of a son with an elbow to the boy's neck and a knee in the stomach, and the boy leaned over spitting blood on the living room carpet.

Hanrahan had not been there. Shirley had told him about it at her husband's funeral, a funeral Charles Kenneth "Pig Sticker" Leary did not attend. "Lord, forgive me," she had said, held up on one side by Bill Hanrahan and on the other by Maureen Hanrahan. "I was afraid Charles would show up."

It was shortly after that that Bill Hanrahan had talked to Pig Sticker about an incident in which a group of Chicago Hate Mongers had been in a small battle with a beret-wearing group calling themselves the Jewish Protection

Army. The Jewish Protection Army wore armbands, blue armbands with white letters saying, "NEVER AGAIN."

Hanrahan had found himself talking to the huge creature in the small interrogation room on the second floor of the Clark Street Station. Hanrahan had asked the captain if he could handle Charles and one or two others individually. The captain Hughes, who was black, didn't care. He had only warned that there be no marks on any of the Mongers beyond the ones already inflicted by the Jewish Protection Army. From the information that had been brought to Hughes, he had figured the battle between the two groups had been close to a draw.

It was in that small room sitting across from Charles Kenneth Leary that Hanrahan had struck pure double-eagle gold. After two or three minutes of "I-don't-give-a-shit-if-you-do-know-my-family," Hanrahan had asked the great hulk if his friends knew he was half-Jewish.

The Pig Sticker's face had gone as white and flat as his gang wanted the world to be.

"I tell them and you're a dead half-Jew," Hanrahan had said. "Your mother won't tell. She's ashamed of you. Her family won't tell. Hell, they don't even know what happened and wouldn't recognize you if they saw you on the news. And your father has no living kin in this country. It's just you and me, *boychick*."

"What the fuck do you want?" asked Pig Sticker, sitting down, more than a little like a slightly deflated balloon.

"You always let me have a number where I can reach you," Hanrahan had said. "I'll say I'm your cousin Carl from Germany. You can tell your buddies I'm from your mother's side of the family and your grandfather was a lieutenant in the SS. From time to time, I come through town and we get together."

"And I answer your questions or you . . . ?" Pig Sticker had begun and then let his voice drop.

"Right on the button, Charles Kenneth Leary," said Hanrahan, "son of Shirley Levitt."

And since then, Hanrahan had called on his American

cousin four times for a nice meal at a distant Denny's and some information. Hanrahan had had to protect Pig Sticker a few times on some minor counts, but it was worth it. The only ones who knew about his connection were Captain Kearney, who replaced Hughes, and Abe Lieberman.

Abe was back at the dining room table with a fresh cup of coffee. He had excused himself to make a phone call from the bedroom, leaving Bess to deal with a distraught Todd, who tried to keep his voice down. When Lieberman sat down at the table again, he reached for another slice of cake. Bess gave him a look of warning. Abe ignored it. He needed the cake.

Bess sat on his left. Todd on his right.

Todd Creswell, former son-in-law, father of Lieberman's two grandchildren upstairs now probably playing Nintendo instead of doing homework, and associate professor of classics at Northwestern University, was badly in need of a comb. Todd was a good-looking man rapidly approaching forty. He was also a worried man. He kept running his hand through his thick hair, taking his glasses off and putting them on, and generally looking as nervous as an innocent man who believes he is about to be arrested for a major felony.

"They can't stay here," Todd said.

"You live in a small one-bedroom apartment," Abe said.

"It's not that small."

"It's small," said Lieberman.

Todd pushed his coffee cup away. It was still full and growing cold. Todd didn't need any more stimulation.

"It's not that small," said Todd.

"You and . . . you and your wife are hardly ever home," Bess put in, a slight variation on what she had told Lisa.

"We have to deal with it, Todd," Lieberman said.

"The man who thinks he ever stood a chance against the Gods was born a fool," said Todd. He looked up and added, "Euripides' *Iphigenia in Tauris*. I can't help it."

Abe shrugged. Todd thought in terms of Greek tragedies and couldn't keep from quoting them, which normally irritated Lieberman. Today Lieberman was inclined to let it pass.

The phone rang. There was a rushing of feet overhead and Melisa's voice muffled.

"We talked to Maish and Yetta. The kids can stay there a while," said Bess.

"A while?" asked Todd. "Their family has been torn apart. Their mother moved to Los Angeles like a'...a... Meryl Streep in *Kramer vs. Kramer*. I see them once a week. Where's their stability? I'm sorry. You've both been fine, but now we're talking about threats. How crazy are these people, Abe?"

"Crazy" was not quite the word Lieberman would use. "Serious" seemed far more appropriate, especially after he had noticed the car parked behind Todd's Geo.

"It's for you, grandpa," Barry shouted from upstairs. "It's mom."

Lieberman sat still for several heartbeats as Bess got the phone from the table in the corner and handed it to her husband. Lieberman didn't like these remotes, never had. No substance. No heft. Everything was getting lighter, easier, and wearing out faster.

"I've got it, Barry," Lieberman shouted. "You can hang up."

More scurry of feet and Lieberman heard the phone, a sturdier old model, being hung up.

"Lisa," Lieberman said, looking at Todd who shook his head, fearing inevitably in the next few minutes he would have to talk to his ex-wife.

"If anything happens to my children," she said, "I hold you responsible. You and your job and the violence. I grew up with Bess trying not to show how scared she was when you showed up late or forgot to call. Tell me, Abe, were there times when those madmen threatened to kill me and mom? Times you never told us about?"

"First," said Lieberman, looking at Bess who strained to

understand what was going on from Lieberman's side of the conversation. "I accept the responsibility. I have no choice. Second, there were a few times when I heard threats about you and your mother. They were all just street punks who threatened everyone when they were caught, including me, the judge, the mayor, and their own families. When they went back on the street, they forgot threats, remembered that they hadn't lost face in front of the police. I was threatened on a regular basis. Still am."

"An honest answer," Lisa said, as if she were holding a checklist to see if her father would score the requisite one hundred points that meant she could leave her children with him and her mother.

Lieberman moved carefully into the conversation knowing his daughter wanted him to score high, didn't want to come flying back to Chicago to be responsible for her children. But if Abe didn't make the score, she might have to start making reservations.

"They're trying to scare me, Bill, the department, into letting them have their kingdom," said Lieberman, looking at Todd.

"They?" asked Lisa.

"A Korean gang," explained Lieberman. "I've already made plans to take care of the problem, maybe in the next day or two."

"What are you going to do? Have Bill kick down their door and the two of you go in with a gun in each hand, shooting surprised Koreans?"

"No. Hard diplomacy with something to back it up," said Lieberman. "That's all I can say. The kids will be safe."

"If anything happens to them . . ." Lisa continued.

"I'll have Bill kick down a door and shoot surprised Koreans," said Lieberman. "Then I'll shoot myself. But maybe first I'll shoot the furnace repairman who has been making his retirement money off of me and your mother. Then I shoot Sergeant Hurley, Curly Hurley, remember him? Works out of the Hyde Park. Anti-Semitic. Remember me telling you about him?"

"I remember, Abe," Lisa said impatiently. "I don't find you funny."

"You never did," said Abe with a sigh. "It was my curse. The kids will be fine."

"It would be hard to come right now," Lisa said formally. "I just accepted some additional lab responsibility, DNA testing for felony cases. But I might be making a trip soon for a few days. I'll be bringing a friend."

Abe had no idea where Lisa was working or on what. She had never volunteered the information and she had made it quite clear she didn't want to be asked.

"DNA, felony cases. You're a criminalist?" asked Abe.

"Los Angeles," she said. "I did a little work on the O. J. Simpson case."

There was a challenge in his daughter's voice that Lieberman did not want to face. His biochemist daughter who hated and was ashamed of her father being a policeman was now building a career in law enforcement.

"Your mother and Todd are here. Your mother wants to talk. You want to talk to Todd?"

"To Bess, not Todd."

Lieberman handed the phone to his wife and whispered to Todd, "She doesn't want to talk to you."

Todd's relief was punctured by a gentle exhalation, as if he had been holding his breath.

"So," said Bess. "Are you going to be staying here when you come in for Barry's bar mitzvah?"

Lisa spoke. She spoke for a long time.

"Socialism is a meaningless dying ritual," said Bess calmly. "Bar mitzvahs have been going on for over four thousand years. Are you coming? Are you not coming? You want to think it over some more? Think it over?"

This time Lisa did not speak long.

"The cleanup is going fine," Bess said. "It hit Rabbi Wass and Ida Katzman hard. They were just here. The children told you?"

Lisa answered.

"The children will stay with Maish and Yetta for a few

days. I'll call you. What's the best time? Can I reach you at work?"

Lisa spoke and Bess motioned to Abe for something to write with. He handed her his pen. She put on her glasses and wrote some phone numbers on the back of a telephone bill.

"I'm not going to tell you not to worry," said Bess to her daughter. "I'm not going to tell you to pray, which you wouldn't do in any case. I'm going to tell you that you should have faith in your father. He knows what he is doing. I love you."

Bess hung up looking slightly stunned.

"She said, 'I love you too,' " said Bess.

"Our daughter warms with age," said Abe, taking back his pen and clicking it closed. "The kids told her about the desecrations?"

Bess nodded her head.

"It was also in the *Los Angeles Times*, on television," she said. "Abe, I didn't tell you, but I agreed to let ABC interview me for the late news. They said they might even want me for 'Nightline' to talk about what happened."

"Ted Koppel used to be a Jew," said Todd.

"There's no such thing as 'used to be a Jew,' " said Lieberman, feeling decidedly hungry. "You are born a Jew. You call yourself what you want but everyone calls you Jew and when you die, even if you're a Franciscan monk, your fellow monks say prayers and call you the Jewish Brother."

"How do you know that?" asked Todd.

"I don't know it," said Lieberman sitting back. "I made it up like Sophocles."

Todd nodded. "Can I see the kids?"

"Whenever you want," said Bess. "You know that."

Todd got up and headed for the stairs. Looking back, he said, "What do you want me to tell them?"

"Whatever you want to tell them," said Lieberman. "Whatever you have to tell them. Whatever they ask. I'll take care of the problem."

"Dare death with us," said Todd, "which awaits you anyway. By your great soul, I challenge you, old friend. The man who sticks it out against his fate shows spirit, but the spirit of a fool. No man alive can budge necessity."

"More Euripides, I suppose," said Lieberman.

"Yes, *Heracles*." Todd ran up the stairs.

"He's feeling very Euripides today," said Lieberman, hearing the door upstairs open and Melisa shout, "Daddy!" in happy surprise.

"Avrum," Bess said, leaning toward her husband and taking his hand. "Are the children in real danger?"

"I'll see to it that they're not," said Lieberman.

Bess shook her head.

"So," he said. "What are you going to wear for Ted Koppel?"

"If they call me back, and if I do it," she said. "Very businesslike. Gray suit."

"With the pearls," said Lieberman.

"With the pearls," Bess said with her first smile of the day, albeit a small one. And once again, the phone rang.

"I'll get it," said Lieberman. "I'm expecting." He picked up the phone.

"Por supuesto," he said. *"Quisas. Pero . . . Deme cinco secundos."*

Lieberman put down the phone and moved across the living room to the front door. The Asian in the car was still there. He walked past Bess in the dining room holding up a hand asking her to be patient. He pushed open the kitchen door, and she heard him cross the room and open the back door. It closed almost immediately and when Lieberman returned he held a white envelope. He picked up the phone and said. *"Si, yo lo tengo. Hasta luego.* Yes, I'll say a Jew prayer for Sammy Sosa."

Lieberman hung up the phone, looked at his wife and bit his lower lip.

"Lieberman," she started, and then above them Barry let out an enormous cackling laugh. Bess changed her mind about asking her husband what he was planning to do. All she cared about was that it resulted in her grandchildren and her husband being safe.

"Don't do anything foolish, Avrum," she said.

"No man alive can budge necessity," Lieberman said. "You suppose a cheese and onion omelette from a woman who's going to be on 'Nightline' might be beneath her?"

"Sharp cheddar? Egg Beaters?"

"Perfect," he said, putting the envelope in his pocket.

SEVEN

"**BIG PILE,**" **SAID** Lieberman, looking down at the photographs on his partner's desk.

Hanrahan nodded. They had already exchanged information and had cups of strong coffee, Nestor Briggs's special brew, which required that the pots never be cleaned. Lieberman's stomach hurt after the second sip.

In the photographs, there were faces, puzzled faces, angry faces, faces Lieberman recognized, including his own. Lieberman didn't like looking at pictures of himself. The man in the pictures and the man he saw in the mirror was not Abe Lieberman. It was Abe Lieberman's grandfather. It was the silent, sad-looking man serving up his famous hot dogs with everything in the always packed hole-in-the-wall on Central Park in the heart of Jew Town.

Lieberman shook his head, kept flipping through photos, and found Ibraham Said and Rene Catolino, who the camera was kind to. It took most of the hard edge from her face. And here was Eli Towser holding his arm in pain. And the muscular Israeli blond. And there were three young men he hadn't noticed in the crowd. They were wearing berets and arm bands. And there were multiple pictures of the two people who had stood on the steps, the young woman and the young man. In some pictures she was tight jawed. In others she looked passionate. Lieberman gathered the photographs and put them in a large envelope along with a half-dozen movie stills and then made a phone call before they left in Lieberman's car.

On the way, Lieberman talked with Hanrahan about the threat from the Asian man.

"The Koreans," Hanrahan said. "Kim?"

"It would seem so," said Lieberman.

"And you left one of them sitting in the car at your house?"

Lieberman went straight up Clark till it turned into Chicago Avenue in Evanston and then kept going along the elevated train embankment on his left and then the business district leading toward downtown Evanston. He turned on Dempster and headed west.

"We could scare the shit out of him," Hanrahan suggested.

"It wouldn't work," said Lieberman.

"No," Hanrahan agreed. "It wouldn't work. Round the clock shift on the house, Bess and the kids."

"Think we can justify it on the basis of an Asian man talking to my grandson and another Asian sitting in a car near my house? Kearney would lose his job."

"Volunteers," said Hanrahan. "Off duties. I could set it up."

"No," said Lieberman. "It's got to end. I'm taking care of it."

"Meanwhile . . . ?"

"I've got someone watching the guy in the car," said Lieberman crossing McCormick into Skokie. "If he moves toward the house or the kids or Bess, he'll have a very big surprise. But I think he's parked out there to scare us off the Kim case."

"They don't understand, do they?" said Hanrahan with a shake of his head.

"No," said Lieberman, checking his car clock as he pulled into the small strip mall parking lot across from Temple Mir Shavot. "Bess is going to be on 'Nightline' tonight, maybe. About . . ."

Lieberman looked at the bank that had been converted less than a year ago into a temple and desecrated the day before. Hanrahan also looked at the temple building. A Skokie police car was parked in front of the door with two uniformed cops inside.

"We, Iris and me, are going to have both a Unitarian and a Chinese wedding," said Hanrahan, leading his partner through a door between a hardware store and a baseball trading card shop.

"*Mazel Tov,*" said Lieberman, as they moved up the stairs.

"If they have best men in Chinese weddings," said Hanrahan. "Would you . . . ?"

"I would take great umbrage if you asked anyone else," said Lieberman.

Hanrahan knocked at the door at the top of the steps. Anne Crawfield Ready opened the door, smiled politely, and backed away so the two men could enter. Leo Benishay was standing in the middle of the room. The policemen shook hands.

"You know Mrs. Ready has a collection of ceramic frogs in that cabinet," said Benishay. "Fascinating. And her husband, look at those photographs, professional. But those frogs." Leo Benishay was a con man from way back.

Mrs. Ready, smiling proudly, went to the cabinet in the corner and opened it, revealing shelves of ceramic, porcelain, and other frogs in neat lines. She stood back so the two policemen who had just come in could admire her collection.

On the bottom shelf were a camera and a bag.

"Frogs are mine," she said. "Camera was Carl's. You

can touch that but please don't touch any of the frogs. I'll
tell you about any ones that interest you."

"The tiny one, here on top, size of a pea," said Lieberman with genuine interest.

"Probably my most valuable," Mrs. Ready said beaming.
"Perfect scale, perfect detail, Chinese, about two hundred
years old, probably made for a member of the ruling class,
possibly even an emperor or someone in his family. I've
seen ones like it, but not as good, priced at seven hundred
dollars in catalogs. But I'd never sell any of them." She
reached out and touched one of the larger frogs. Most of
them were standard green or gray-green, a few were bright
yellow or even white, and some had spots.

"What got you into this?" Hanrahan said.

"I haven't the faintest idea," Mrs. Ready said with a
smile and a shake of the head to indicate this great mystery.
"I think my husband gave me one once and I've picked
them up ever since at garage sales, flea markets. Once in a
while, my nephew from Salt Lake City will bring me one
when he comes to Chicago on business."

"Magnificent collection." Lieberman said, as she closed
the cabinet door gently and turned the key in the lock.

"Magnificent," Leo Benishay concurred with an appre-
ciative smile.

"Could we show you some photographs, ma'am?" asked
Hanrahan, looking for permission at Benishay, who nodded.

Lieberman opened the brown nine-by-twelve envelope
he was carrying and handed the photographs to Mrs. Ready
who sat in her chair at the window.

The sun was bright. There were no lights on in the small
apartment.

"Just tell us if you recognize anyone?" Benishay said.
"Please take your time."

"All right," said Mrs. Ready, clearly enjoying the attention being given her by three men. She went through them
slowly.

"This one is you," she said, pointing to a photograph of Lieberman and looking up at him.

"Just skip the pictures of Detective Lieberman," said Benishay.

Anne Ready nodded and kept looking.

"This one is Winona Ryder, the actress," said Mrs. Ready looking at one of the photographs Lieberman had put in with the ones taken at the rally. The photo showed the actress in front of a crowd. She was wearing jeans and a flannel shirt. "She was wonderful in *Little Women*, but in *Dracula*. . . . Once a month my daughter-in-law comes in from Batavia and takes me shopping and the movies."

The three policemen nodded as she returned to the pack of photographs correctly identifying, in turn, Debra Winger, Benazir Bhutto, and Sally Ride.

"This one," she said, holding up the photo so the policemen could all see. "She was the girl in the doorway across the street the other night."

"You're sure?" asked Benishay.

"Positive, and here's another picture of her. Pretty girl, but so serious. What's that in her hand?"

"A bullhorn," said Lieberman.

Anne Ready nodded knowingly.

"Could we count on you to identify her in person?" said Benishay. "And, possibly, if it comes to it, to testify before a grand jury and possibly at a trial?"

"Like on television?" she asked with obvious excitement. "Like the O. J. Simpson trial?"

"Like that," said Benishay, "but probably not on television."

"I'd be happy to sit in a chair and take the oath," she said.

"And identify this young woman as the one you saw in the doorway?" asked Benishay.

"I've already said that I would do so," said Anne Ready. "Do you want me to bring my own pictures of her?"

The three policeman looked at the woman.

"I take pictures of people from my window," she ex-

plained. "With Carl's camera. Carl didn't like to take people. I collect people. I've got some of you," she said
looking at Lieberman. "You and a pretty younger woman
coming out of services on Friday nights. The Saturday
morning ones are best but you never go on Saturdays."

"My wife, Bess," said Lieberman. "The younger
woman."

"Ah," said Anne Ready, moving to the kitchen and coming back with a thick box she could barely carry. She
placed it on the table and sat with a sigh of relief. The box
was heavy.

She opened the box and looked through the photos, front
to back, saying as she searched, "In respect for Carl's art,
I don't put them up. Besides, I've got my frogs. Here, here
they are, three of them." Mrs. Ready handed the photographs to Lieberman who looked through them and handed
them to the other detectives. The girl was quite clear if a
bit grainy. The one shot of the bald man did not show his
face. He was more of a blur and he seemed to be carrying
something large under his arm.

"Grain, I know," said Mrs. Ready, watching the detective's face. "I used the telephoto with Tri-X and had them
develop it for one thousand ASA, which is pushing it, but
you can see, she's right under the light, and you see the
one where she looks like she's looking right up at me?"

"I see," said Leo Benishay.

"The one with the man in it is blurry because he was
moving fast out of the temple. I had to shoot pretty wide
open at two-point-eight and a little slow at one-fiftieth.
They're dated on the back," said Mrs. Ready. "Date and
time just like all my photographs. I've got a log for my
frogs too. Where I got them, when, how much I paid, or if
they were gifts."

"Can we keep these photographs of the woman?" asked
Benishay.

"You can have them," said Mrs. Ready, "as long as you
give me money for the cost of printing them again."

Lieberman was out first with the cash.

"Too much," said Anne Ready, taking the ten-dollar bill.

"Make an extra print of each and, if there's change, you'll give it to me when we come back," said Lieberman. "And we may still need you to testify."

"And show my photographs at a trial?" she asked.

"Yes," said Hanrahan.

"My Carl would be so proud, or jealous, or both," she said. "He was a complicated man."

Lieberman gathered the photographs and put them in the envelope with the ones he had brought.

"We'll get back to you soon, Mrs. Ready," said Leo Benishay taking her hand.

"Whenever you like," she said.

"You have a beautiful collection," said Hanrahan.

"Beautiful," added Lieberman.

"Frogs are my passion," Anne Crawfield Ready said, placing her hands on her heart to calm its beating.

And then the policemen were gone. She locked the door and moved to the window. The policeman who had come first was heading around the building. She couldn't see the other two. She moved to the other window and watched the policeman from Skokie go over to the packed police car and say something to the two men inside who looked over at her window. She waved to them. One of them waved back.

She got Carl's camera and hurried to her other window. She had daytime low ASA color film in it now.

At the other window, the two policemen from Chicago did not appear. There were very few conclusions to draw from this. One was that they were still standing in the hall or on the stairs, but she had heard them all go down. The other was that they had either stopped at Ace Camera Shop or the store where all the children went to buy comic books and cards with pictures of baseball players. The usual number of bicycles were parked in front of the baseball card shop even though it would soon be dark. She had so many photographs of these children that she had not yet filed all of them though she had dated them.

Anne Crawfield Ready stood for a long time looking out her front window. Finally, after about fifteen minutes the two policemen appeared in the parking lot.

Curiosity got the best of Anne Crawfield Ready. She slipped on her shoes, opened her door and slowly made her way down the stairs, holding the railing. When she stepped out onto the narrow sidewalk of the small mall, she opened the door of the photo shop. Mr. Shenkman said that two men had not just left his shop. The story was different in the trading card store.

There was a lull in the frenzy of small boys in baseball hats. Mrs. Ready always knew when it was baseball season. The shop was almost always crowded.

Mrs. Gantz stood behind the counter, an overweight woman of about sixty, wearing a satin-like Cubs jacket with a Cubs cap on her head. Mrs. Gantz was supposedly the daughter of a famous baseball player from a long time ago. Mr. Shenkman had told her this.

When Mrs. Gantz saw Anne Crawfield Ready, she interrupted her conversation with an adamant twelve-year-old to come out from behind the counter and greet her.

"Mrs. Ready," she said. "I think this is your first time in the shop since I moved in and you brought me the plate of cookies."

Anne Crawfield Ready nodded and watched the boys arguing, trading, looking. "Did two men just leave here?"

"Yes," said Mrs. Gantz. "Big one and a little Jewish one."

"They bought something?" asked Mrs. Ready.

Mrs. Gantz told her neighbor what they had bought. Mrs. Ready shook her head and said, "I thought collecting delicate frogs was almost unique, but . . ."

"We get all kinds," said Mrs. Gantz. "And you wouldn't believe what grown men will pay for a top grade card. I sold a Ron Santo yesterday for fifteen dollars."

Mrs. Ready didn't know what a Ron Santo was.

*   *   *

The weapons were cleaned, loaded, ready. What he needed was a shave and some help. There weren't many he could count on, though there were a few he could push, prod, intimidate, shame. He would use them all. He would use the one called Berk who strutted and shaved his head. He would use Berk as Berk planned to use him. In their few meetings, they had looked at each other with hatred and distrust, but they had struck a bargain from which there would be no retreat.

He had a book on the table in front of him. The book was not on his mind. The book was about the smallest known particles of matter. He had thought greatly about this. Each time the tools of science discovered an even smaller particle of matter or the movement of what appeared to be matter, a new scientist appeared with a new theory of the universe, how it operates, what it means. Meaning was back alongside Big Bangs and infinity as a time-space continuum. There were always alternative theories, but the one that emerged was the one whose wagon held the most room for the most scientists.

Then the philosophers, to whom no one listened, gave their explanations. At the same time, the priests, the gurus, the evangelists, came up with their own explanations and many listened and some believed, afraid that some massive technological machine working with some computer would confound what was thought of as the ordered universe.

Once he had cared about all this. Once he had feverishly sought information to present on a radioactive plate to be sifted through for answers the way an ancient or an oracle might sift through beads or the leaves of tea. Now, he had but one goal. It was simple. It was personal. It had no meaning in the total history of the universe, but he did not care.

Life, whatever it was, was precious. Life, whatever it was, did not endure for individuals in a species. Life was filled with fear and hate and at any moment it could be taken away meaninglessly. Small, ridiculous creatures fighting over which one was best because of the color of their skin, the power of their superstitions, the history of their people.

He had concluded long ago that there was no sin. There were fools on earth, mostly fools, who wasted time and life attacking, hating, fearing.

He had been labeled by birth and history. Why? It was the wrong question. A woman named June Singer had said that to ask the question, "What is the meaning of life?" is a waste of time. She was right. She suggested that a meaningful question was, "What is the meaning of *my* life?"

He had concluded from the violence and hatred that had reduced his family and people that the meaning of his life was revenge—pure, simple revenge. He had no illusions that acts of violence would change the world or that changing the world was even important. There were always smaller particles of energy, always deeper regions of space, and always older pieces of matter than had been found before.

Stephen Hawking, lolling in a wheelchair and unable to speak, had come up with the theory that black holes did not simply take in and consume all that came over their rim. Hawking had concluded from his calculations that any mass of energy—a small star, an astronaut—entering a black hole would sink and stretch, hit bottom and bounce out of the hole as a particle of compact energy, rejoining the univere. Too abstract. Too distant.

No, revenge was its own payment. Not reward.

He prayed with the others, but his prayers were different. He envisioned his God as a chance coming together of the particles that formed the universe. The ideal state would be for the universe to be stable and, for whatever particle he was, he would be part of it. Chance, will, madness kept clashing with the ideal tranquil universe. Nothing seemed able to change that. It was eternal. The ideal state would never be reached, just as the delicate butterfly gently flapping its wings against a steel ball the size of the earth would never finish its task of returning the ball to the dust of the universe because millions of steel balls existed for the butterfly when it completed its initial task. The trick, he had concluded, was to accept one's lot as that butterfly resigned to endlessly flapping his wings.

There were seven weapons. There would be six people, though not his people. He had made his pact with the devil. They would walk in and fire at whomever was at worship or meeting. The world would be appalled. Much of the world would hate him even more than they hated him already. Others would consider him and the Mongers heroes. And they would all fear him as they feared the lone mad butterfly that fluttered briefly from the iron ball and flew at the eyes of some leader of state.

The Torah lay in front of him on the table. He rolled it open randomly over the weapons. Oil from the weapons would surely stain the Torah. He didn't care. His Hebrew was very good. As good as his Arabic, his English, and his German.

He pointed a finger at the text. Genesis 49:27, "Benjamin is a wolf that raveneth; In the morning he devoureth the prey. And at even he divideth the spoil."

So be it. Benjamin was a realist. Monday, three days, there would be a devouring such as Benjamin never dreamed.

He rolled up the Torah. Then he closed the book, limped to the nearby bookcase, and put it away.

"A strike, a fucking strike. Everything is a strike, *Viejo*."

Emiliano "El Perro" Del Sol sat at Lieberman's side in the box seats fairly close to the Pirates bullpen so he and the Tentaculos could swear at the waiting pitchers, especially any of them unlucky enough to be told to warm up. Only the Hispanic pitchers escaped their grossest language, but they were not immune from attack.

The Tentaculos had all been sitting there, well into the first inning when Lieberman, using the ticket that had been left at his back door, found the box and sat down next to El Perro. Lieberman recognized most of the people in the box. Three of them sat in front of El Perro in the front row. One of them was Piedras, a hulk who had never learned English but knew how to kill with his hands and head. He had left his trademark more than once on a renegade Tentaculo, a rival gang member, or someone, El Perro just didn't like because of a look or remark interpreted as offensive.

Behind El Perro sat three more Tentaculos. El Chuculo, whose real name was Fernandez, sat directly behind El Perro. It was rumored that El Chuculo carried three knives sharper than the finest razors and that he could move, cut, slice between breaths. It was rumored that a man, woman, or child could die standing in front of El Chuculo without even knowing that blood was gushing from his or her neck.

El Perro looked at Lieberman and did something that must have been a grin. It was hard to tell. El Perro was not yet thirty. His face was a map of wild scars leading to dead ends. A scar from who knows what battle ran from his right eye down across his nose to just below the left side of his mouth. His nose was rough; red, and broken so many times that there was little bone, no cartilage. El Perro, when lost in thought, played with his nose, flattening it with his thumb, pushing it to one side absentmindedly. His teeth were white but uneven except for the sharp eye teeth, which looked as if they belonged on a vampire. Emiliano's black hair was brushed straight back. He thought it made him look like Pat Riley, the old New York Knicks coach or like Kurt Russell in *Tequila Sunrise*, one of his favorite movies.

Tonight, he wore a pair of gray designer slacks, an off-white shirt and a black silk zippered jacket. The rest of the gang wore their colors, blue satin jackets with a picture of an octopus on the back. The octopus had been designed and drawn by Emiliano himself. He had talent. He was also very crazy.

"They're calling more strikes because they want to make the games faster," Lieberman said, accepting some popcorn from El Perro who nodded his head in understanding.

"You're right," he said. "Since the strike, everyone is moving like they just woke up. You know?"

"I know," said Lieberman, who loved Wrigley Field. He sometimes took off a few hours in the afternoon to pick up a single seat and watch anything from three or four innings to a whole game. Wrigley Field and reading in the bathtub were his meditations. As time passed, the hot baths had less and less effect. He had grown impatient with them unless he was also reading and they had done nothing for his chronic insomnia.

"Sammy Sosa," said one of the Tentaculos in front of them. El Perro reached over and hit the young man who had spoken hard in the head with an open hand.

"I know it's Sammy Sosa, for Chris' fuckin' sake," said El Perro. "Sammy's on a streak. We shut up when Sammy bats."

Fans screamed and talked. Vendors hawked beer, popcorn, snow cones. The Tentaculos all went silent. The first pitch came. The ball went past Sosa. The umpire held out his hand as if pointing directly at the Tentaculos.

"See, a strike," said Emiliano softly. "That ball was outside."

Sosa hit the next pitch into center field just over the head of the shortstop. Sosa stopped at first.

"Hey." Emiliano said with a grin.

"I've got something for you," said Lieberman, pulling a thick package out of his jacket pocket. He handed the package to El Perro who opened it and began shuffling through the cards inside.

"Every Hispanic who ever played for the Cubs," Lieberman said.

El Perro tapped Piedras on the shoulder and handed him the package.

"Be careful with those," he said. "You check. See if everyone is in there. I trust you, *Viejo*, but it doesn't hurt to check twice."

"It doesn't hurt," said Lieberman.

The next batter struck out, stranding Sosa on first.

"Big guy like Grace," said El Perro, "you'd think he'd hit home runs. I hear he has some movie star girlfriend."

Lieberman shrugged. El Perro handed him a cup of beer. Lieberman took it and drank. Lieberman didn't like beer very much.

"Manny is watching your house," El Perro said. "He's a good man. He fucks up, I'll cut off his ear. I told him you were special. Manny doesn't look Mexican. He looks like that guy on television with the wrenches. Cops see a Mexican watching a Korean in your neighborhood, they'll haul both their asses in."

"Thanks," said Lieberman, taking a drink and watching the first Pirate batter defy the new odds by drawing a walk.

"I lost track, *Viejo*. Who owes who?"

"I'd say we're about even," said Lieberman, watching the Pirate runner take a big lead-off.

"Maybe." said El Perro.

The gang leader clearly liked the old cop at his side, liked the old cop's reputation in the community for being willing to get the law a little dirty to get what he wanted. Lieberman even had the reputation in El Perro's community of being a little violent and crazy when he was crossed. El Perro had never witnessed this, but he had talked to others who had.

Lieberman had, more than once, gotten a Tentaculo out of trouble for everything from drug dealing to the murder of a drug dealer. In return, El Perro had passed on information and on at least one occasion, assisted someone who had crossed Lieberman into jumping from the roof of a hospital. El Perro never knew why or how the man had crossed Lieberman. He didn't care.

"You know any of these Koreans?" asked Lieberman.

El Perro shrugged and shouted, "Pick off the son-of-a-bitch."

"They call themselves something I can't pronounce in Korean," said Lieberman.

El Perro held up his cup of beer without turning his eyes from the game and said, "The Protectors," drinking. "They stay on the North Side, out of our way, pick on their own people. Boss is a guy who thinks he's Clint Eastwood or something. Slant wears sunglasses, long coat. Name is Kim."

"Kim threatened to kill my family if I keep trying to stop him from robbing his people," said Lieberman.

El Perro shrugged and shouted, "He's taking off for second. He's stealing second. Did I tell him or did I tell him?"

"You told him."

"So, it's easy, *Viejo*. You blow Kim away."

"I'd have to blow them all away, Emiliano," Lieberman said. "You know that."

"I'd like to watch that," said El Perro with a mangled grin.

"By the time I blew them away, they'd probably get to my family," said Lieberman, who had no intention of killing a gang of up to twenty Koreans.

"And your buddies, your pals, your guys in the blue suits?"

"Can't protect us forever," said Lieberman.

"What do you want me to do about it?" asked El Perro. "Start a war?"

"Go to this guy and tell him to back away from my family for good," said Lieberman, downing what was left of his beer. "I'm going to keep coming after him, but my family is out no matter what happens. Can you do this?"

El Perro laughed. "These guys don't want a war with the Tentaculos," El Perro said, watching an infield pop-up to Dunston. "I'll talk to Kim."

"Thanks," said Lieberman, wanting to leave but knowing that he had to wait out the game till El Perro decided he had enough.

"You owe me big, *Viejo*," El Perro said.

"I owe you big," Lieberman agreed.

"You know how straight I'm trying to go?"

Lieberman knew that the Tentaculos had taken over small businesses in their near North Side neighborhood and even opened their own bingo parlor, but they still dealt in drugs, stolen cars, and death.

"I know," said Lieberman.

"Enjoy the game," El Perro said, patting Lieberman on the shoulder.

Lieberman nodded.

"You didn't ask me something," El Perro said as the inning ended with a weak ground ball.

"What?"

"Who busted up your churches," said Emiliano.

"You know?"

"I could ask questions," said El Perro. "Maybe. Maybe somebody who don't like Arabs or maybe even Jews like I do shot some guys in Hyde Park. They got big guns in this. You can't hide big firepower on the streets. Somebody knows. I'll see."

They sat through the entire game. The Cubs won 3-1. El Perro was happy. He stood up and so did Lieberman.

"We're still in first," El Perro said, slapping the head of a young man in front of him and showing a big smile.

Actually, the Cubs were tied for first with Cincinnati, but Lieberman had no intention of correcting Del Sol.

"You go first," El Perro said.

Lieberman nodded and stepped into the concrete aisle.

EIGHT

HANRAHAN KNOCKED AT the door. There had been a locked door downstairs in the lobby, but the detectives had not rung the bell of the apartment. Lieberman opened the lower lobby door with his credit card while Hanrahan looked out the window, admiring a dirty six-flat across the street.

"In," said Lieberman.

Hanrahan had turned and the two had walked up the carpeted stairs of the apartment building. The hallway was well lighted and, though the dark green carpeting was well worn, it was clean.

Something or someone stirred inside the apartment. Hanrahan knocked again.

The door came open and there stood the young woman, a white bandage taped just behind her left ear, a clotted cut below her nose to the top of her lip. She wore jeans and a loose-fitting blue-and-green sweater. In her hand, she held a pistol aimed at Lieberman's face.

"We're the police," Hanrahan said reaching toward his pocket to get his wallet and badge.

"Stop," she said.

Hanrahan stopped and put his hand back at his side.

"You were at the rally," Jara Mohammed said to Lieberman.

"Yes."

"You're a Jew," she said.

"Yes," said Lieberman.

"I don't want to talk to either one of you," she said.

"We're here to talk to you," said Lieberman. "If you don't want to talk, we'll arrest you and take you back to our station, all the way north."

"Arrest me? For being beaten up by Jewish fanatics?" she asked.

"For criminal trespass, destruction of property, desecration of a house of worship, and probably four or five other things the city lawyers can come up with," said Hanrahan. "And we can now add resisting arrest and threatening an officer with a weapon."

"Unless you want to put the gun away now," said Lieberman, "invite us in, and answer some questions."

"No," she said. "You cannot come in. You will have to arrest me," She lowered the gun to her side. "I have a permit. This is a dangerous neighborhood, especially for a woman. Would you like to see the permit?"

"No," said Lieberman. "But we'd like you to see a photograph."

He reached slowly for his inner jacket pocket.

"Open the jacket all the way," she said, holding up the pistol again.

Lieberman opened his jacket showing his gun and holster. He reached slowly into the inner jacket pocket opposite the weapon and pulled out a photograph. He handed the photograph to the young woman.

She held the gun steady and glanced at the photograph.

"So," she said. "You have a photograph of me."

"And the cooperation of the person who took the photograph of you coming out of Temple Mir Shavot just after it was torn apart last night," said Lieberman. "That person is ready to testify to the time and date the photograph was taken and it's a little hard for you to deny that you're standing in front of the temple door. The dark letters on the glass door are pretty grainy, but there's no doubt about where it is. And we'd like to know who that blurred bald man running past you might be."

"This is a police trick, a Jewish police trick, a fake, a fraud," she said. "I deny your accusation."

"Then," said Hanrahan, "we'll take you into custody for questioning in connection with the charges I've already stated plus possible knowledge of and complicity in the murder of three Arab students no more than four blocks from here."

"One of those students was a very active member of your group," said Lieberman. "Even looked a little like that blurred bald man in this picture."

"I will put the gun away but you will have to carry me," she said, placing the weapon back at her side.

"Resisting arrest," said Lieberman. "There isn't anyone out there to see you being carried, but . . . I'm afraid that'll have to be my partner's job."

"Anyone here with you?" asked Hanrahan.

She didn't answer.

"So," said Lieberman. "What'll it be? You invite us in to talk or we carry you out?"

She thought for several seconds and stepped back, opening the door wide enough for the detectives to step in. She certainly did not bother to hide the look of hatred she directed at both of them.

"Put the weapon back wherever you keep it," said Hanrahan, pushing the door closed behind him and looking around, particularly at the two closed doors across the surprisingly large and oddly furnished room. A couch and several chairs sat in a circle in one corner near the windows facing the street. The rest of the room was taken by a large table, larger than a dining room table and somewhat scarred. Folding chairs were arranged neatly at the table with more such chairs stacked against a wall next to a small rolltop desk.

Hanrahan headed for the doors across the room, took out his gun and pushed open each one in spite of Jara Mohammed's protests.

"Just put the weapon away," Lieberman said softly.

"No one here," said Hanrahan, putting his gun away. "Bedrooms. One has a computer and a copy machine."

The young woman moved to the desk, opened it, put her gun inside and locked it, putting the key in her pocket.

"Ask your questions, then leave," she said. "Or arrest me."

Her back was to the desk with her hands resting on it behind her. Hanrahan thought she was very pretty, small breasts, scratch on her face, patch of white and all. He liked long, dark hair.

"We're not here for a fight," said Lieberman.

"Can we sit?" asked Hanrahan.

Jara nodded indifferently. Both policemen sat. The big one pulled out a chair and sat at the table where he could see both her and the front door. The Jew sat on the couch on the other side of the room.

"How is your head?" Lieberman asked.

"Shaved patch, seven stitches. Would you like to see?" she asked defiantly, reaching toward her bandage. "Would you like to see what your Zionist animals did?"

"I just want to know how you're feeling," said Lieberman. "I have a daughter a little older than you. I wouldn't want to see her hurt in a brawl. You remind me of her."

"Of a Jewish daughter?" asked Jara with a disbelieving smile.

"Yes," said the old Jew and she knew he was telling the truth. He was concerned about her. It made no sense, even less when he added, "I'm a member at Mir Shavot. My wife is the president."

"Mir Shavot?" she asked, now folding her arms in front of her.

"Where your picture was taken after you and your friends

tore the place apart," said Lieberman. "After your friend
stole our Torah. We have a picture of that, too. Of him
carrying it away right past you."

Jara moved the hair that had fallen over her bandage and
returned to the arms-folded position before answering.
"You have no photograph of any man," she said. "Your
photographs are faked."

"No," said Lieberman. "Photos and a reliable witness.
We believe the man in the photograph is Howard Ramu
who was one of the three men murdered yesterday."

Hanrahan just kept staring at the young woman, knowing
that there was no way of identifying the fleeing man in the
photograph from the blur of movement.

"I was on Dempster Street several nights ago," she said.
"Not late but after dark. I was waiting for a ride. Whoever
took that picture and says it was last night or even the night
before is mistaken or lying."

"What were you doing in Skokie at night?" asked Lieberman.

"Visiting friends," she said.

"What friends? Where do they live?" asked Hanrahan.

"I do not choose to tell you," she said. "If it becomes
necessary to do so, if my attorney advises me to do so, I
will be prepared to give their names and address."

"Who was picking you up?"

"Howard Ramu," she said without blinking.

"Ah," said Lieberman with a smile. "And I suppose he
got out of his car and escorted you to it."

"Yes," she said. "I believe it was raining and he had an
umbrella."

Hanrahan and Lieberman didn't permit themselves to
look at each other and confirm what they were thinking.
This was one very clever and fast-thinking young woman.

"Why did Howard Ramu shave his head and why was
he wearing a jacket with a swastika on it?" Lieberman
asked.

She shrugged and answered, "I didn't question him about
it."

"An Arab dressed like a skinhead? If he tried to join any of their groups, they'd cut off more than his hair," said Hanrahan.

The light was small, but it was there, in her dark eyes. These policemen had tricked her. They had no photograph or no usable photograph of her with Howard Ramu, certainly no clear photograph of Howard in his skinhead clothes. She knew it. She wanted to bite her tongue till it bled. And then she remembered the old woman in the window outside the temple. Jara had looked up. The woman's face was almost pressed to the glass and then the woman had disappeared.

"We have fingerprints," Hanrahan said.

"No more," answered Jara, moving from the desk past the table to a telephone on the wall. "Unless you wish to detain me forcibly I will now call my attorney and I will say nothing further to either of you or anyone else concerning this without advice and presence of counsel."

Lieberman got up. So did Hanrahan. Neither moved to stop her from picking up the phone. "Tell him you'll be at the Clark Street Station," said Lieberman.

"I will tell *her*," said the young woman, making clear that the Jewish policeman was not only a racist but a sexist. She was dialing now.

"When you finish your call, we'll read you your rights and give you a few minutes to put some things together," said Hanrahan.

She glared at Lieberman. The phone rang five times before Charlotte Warren's secretary picked it up. "Ms. Warren's office."

"Tell her it is Jara Mohammed and I must speak to her immediately."

"She's in court all morning," the woman said. "Would you like to leave a message?"

Jara definitely did.

*   *   *

Kim was sitting in a booth at one of the several restaurants that he and the Protectors protected and from which they collected a significant but not crippling fee. Kim followed no pattern in where he ate. The presence of the two policemen in the diner a day ago was a complete surprise. The two must have been staking out the diner, possibly for days, possibly for weeks. Mr. Park who owned the diner and had more than cooperated with the police would have to be punished for his lack of gratitude for the protection provided for him. Mr. Park had a fourteen-year-old granddaughter. Kim would wait and think of the most effective way of dealing with this so that the community would know.

Kim and the two men who had been with him at Park's were out on bond. With his lawyer, a third-generation Korean who was kept on a respectable monthly bonus plus a fee per job, Kim had claimed that the policemen had trapped him, provoked him, that everything Kim had said had been misinterpreted, that Kim had simply made polite inquiries about the Park family, and sat down to wait out the rain, but the two policemen had pulled out weapons.

The judge didn't believe him, but she had little choice. Bond was set.

Meanwhile, Kim would keep low, have his people be particularly careful when they collected, and back away from trouble. He had already taken a significant step in getting the two policemen to drop their charges. Kim had seen to it himself. He had personally frightened the old Jew detective's grandson and had placed a man conspicuously parked across the street from the detective's house.

The police might suggest that Kim's man parked in front of the detective's house get out and stay out of the neighborhood. They might even arrest him or rough him up a bit. The young man would gladly take a beating. It was his entry into the Protectors. The young man named Fu Sun spoke very good English and was in this country quite legally. He might even welcome a beating from the police, though he had been told to be polite and start nothing.

Kim's booth was in the back of the small restaurant. He sat alone in his trench coat, wearing his sunglasses even though the lights were down and the day was slightly overcast, keeping out most of the sun. At the next booth, closest to the front door, two of the Protectors sat, not eating. Their job was to watch the door. When Kim was finished, they would be served while he sat and read the newspaper over a cup of strong coffee.

Kim did not carry a gun with him and would not do so again until the business of the arrest was resolved. He did keep a Colt King Cobra .357 Magnum in the glove compartment of his car and he knew that a compact Smith & Wesson .40-caliber pistol with no fingerprints was tucked under the cushion on which he sat.

He ate slowly, ignoring other customers who were beginning to come in for an early dinner.

The kitchen door behind the counter near the tiny restrooms opened. Kim did not look around. He continued to eat a very good slice of rare, thin-sliced beef. He did not even look up when he was aware that someone had moved into his booth opposite him. Instead, putting a forkful of beef into his mouth, he reached with his free hand under the cushion in search of the gun.

"Go for it, motherfucker," said El Perro. *"Por favor."* He had always wanted to say those lines and now that Emiliano Del Sol had been given his opportunity, he was in a good mood.

Kim looked up to see the grinning Mexican across from him. El Perro was wearing sunglasses and wore a trench coat mocking Kim who could see over the top of the booth in front of him that his guards were also facing a pair of Hispanics, though the young men were not wearing trench coats and glasses.

"You know who I am?" asked El Perro, reaching with the fork from the place setting in front of him to take a slice of beef from Kim's plate.

Kim nodded.

"You don't mind if I . . . ?" El Perro said, looking at the slice of beef he had already taken.

Kim nodded to indicate that he didn't mind.

"And my friend? He can have one too?"

The Mexican who had a reputation for unpredictable violence and insanity nodded to his left at the boy now sitting next to him. The boy was dark, almost black, very young, at least very young looking. He wore a red shirt and a jacket that Kim knew had a painting of an octopus on the back. These were the Tentaculos.

Still Kim did not speak. He nodded and accepted the insult as the young man reached for the last slice of beef not with a fork but with a knife that appeared suddenly. The blade of the knife was clean and sharp. It stabbed the beef and the young man swooped it toward his mouth.

Kim displayed no anger and the sunglasses hid what little one might see in his eyes. He put down his fork, placed both hands on the table alongside his plate, and waited for these madmen to explain. He guessed extortion, which Kim would have to meet with war. Kim did not want war, but he did not fear it. In any case, he could not allow any gang or even a crooked cop to move in on his business. He kept inside the Korean community and could not tolerate the thought of anyone entering from the outside.

"Good meat," said El Perro. "Got a name?"

"*Bulgogi*," said Kim. "Would you like to have another order brought to the table?"

El Perro's grin was broad now, showing remarkably white teeth. The scar on his face stretched white. The Korean was playing it cool. It was what El Perro expected, though he had been prepared for and would have welcomed a show of anger or action.

"No, *gracias*," said El Perro. "Chuculo?"

The young man at his side chewing shook his head no. Chuculo was cleaning his knife on a napkin as he chewed.

Kim didn't speak.

"I came to bring you some news," said El Perro softly. "I'm afraid it is not good news. I have a friend who is a crazy old Jew policeman. I think maybe you met him. Well, a Korean or a Chinaman sitting across from his house had a little accident." He nodded toward Chuculo, who was still chewing as he took a thick washcloth from his pocket and spread it open on the table. A bloody thumb rolled out.

"This Korean, Chinaman, whatever, he lost that about an hour ago. I give it to you. A gift. Maybe it's too late to sew it back on. Maybe not. When my friend here found him all cut up, he asked the guy what he wanted to do, but he din't answer. He just drive away somewhere. Maybe to a hospital." El Perro shrugged and continued, "Who knows. Anyway, you want the thumb, you got it. Gift. Me to you."

Kim reached for the thumb, placed it back in the washcloth and wrapped it up. He had no intention of doing anything with it other than throwing it away later. Right now he had an impression to make.

"I give you this gift in exchange for a favor," El Perro said, leaning forward and adjusting his sunglasses. "I would like you and your people to stay away from the Jew policeman and his family. I would like them not to be touched or threatened. I would like them to be safe. And maybe I don't like the big Irish *vaca* he partners with, but I don't want him bothered either. They do their job. And you do yours. I don' want your territory or even a small piece of it. We understand?"

"And if I do not stay away from these policemen?" said Kim.

Chuculo's knife came from nowhere. His hand swooped down swiftly, gracefully, and the blade dug into the wooden table between the thumb and forefinger of Kim's right hand. Kim neither blinked nor budged. There was no time. El Perro gave him the benefit of the doubt and pursed his lips in mock admiration.

"You bother *Viejo*," said El Perro, "and we cut off your cock and the cock of every one of your men and make you choke on them. This I promise." El Perro, though he had long since quit practicing anything that might resemble religion, crossed himself for emphasis. "You want war," El

Perro went on with a shrug, "jus' don't do what I say or, better, you come after me or let me know and I'll come for you. Well, what you say?"

"You stay out of my territory and off my back," said Kim, moving his hand carefully and pointing a finger at Emiliano Del Sol.

"It's done," said El Perro.

Chuculo carefully pulled his knife from the table and slid into the narrow aisle. El Perro slipped out and went through the kitchen door through which he had come.

"*Ahora,*" Chuculo said to the two Mexicans at the next booth who faced the two Koreans.

The Mexicans got up and all three backed out of the room into the kitchen. The two Koreans in the booth ahead of Kim leaped out and looked at their leader for direction. He motioned for them to sit down where they had been. He did his best to convey a sense of disgust at their inability to protect him.

When they sat, Kim looked at the hole in the table and the washcloth that held a thumb. He looked for a long time and then decided. There were too many Tentaculos and they were too crazy. El Perro had not asked into his territory, had in fact asked for nothing but that the two policemen and their families be left alone.

The decision was simple. He would do as the crazy Mexican asked but there would come a moment when this insult would be addressed. Even if it cost him his life, Kim would have his revenge or he would not be able to face an honorable death. For now, however, he had enough to deal with to keep his business going and stay out of jail.

NINE

LIEBERMAN, BESS, AND the children took a guided tour of the cleanup of the synagogue from Rabbi Wass himself.

An ABC crew had come to tape the damage and Jeff Greenfield had interviewed Rabbi Wass, Bess, a few members of the congregation, and, she later discovered, members of the Muslim community. Bess's brief interview never made it to "Nightline" and she was not asked to appear. The whole show had been preempted by a series of Supreme Court decisions. Lawyers appeared. Lawyers always appeared. But Bess was not brooding over the loss of "Nightline."

To those who had not seen the damage that had been done, the hatred that had ripped through the temple with the madness of a trapped animal, it looked much the same as it had before the attack. The speed with which the work had been done had been close to miraculous with donations of time, services, and furnishings coming in not only to Temple Mir Shavot but to the other temples in Chicago than had been vandalized. One rabbi, Tribenfeld, had a minor stroke when he saw the damage to his own house of worship. There was talk that Tribenfeld would retire now. He was old. He had been through too much in his life and had the number tattooed on his right arm to testify to it.

Lieberman and Bess could not see the temple through clear eyes. The double coat of white paint on the wall covered the graffiti, but Lieberman had photographs on his desk of the graffiti and all the damage and Bess carried in her memory her own version of what had taken place here. They could imagine where the words had been spray-painted. They could step down the carpeted aisle to the bema, the raised platform where the rabbi and cantor gave services, and Bess, as president, would make announcements.

Lieberman remembered the torn cushions, the wooden high-backed benches that had been broken and defaced and were now replaced with new, almost identical benches, contrasting with the few which had not been touched only by their newness. On the bema, the ark, the enclosure covered by a curtain behind which rested the temple's collection of Torahs, was closed but, Lieberman and his family knew, the ark was almost empty. One small Torah, the personal property of Herschel Rosen's sister brought from Kiev seventy years ago, sat alone in the ark.

"A good job," said Bess admiringly.

"Yes," said Rabbi Wass, looking around sadly. "Only those who had not seen the . . . what had happened can walk through and not remember, not imagine. It will never be the same. I can see it on your faces. I can see it in my own in the mirror."

"It looks fine, Rabbi," said Bess, touching his arm.

"Yes, it looks fine, but . . . perhaps it will serve as a reminder of what can happen to us, what has always happened, what God has given us to bear in return for choosing us as his people."

Barry and Melisa had hurried ahead and climbed the two steps up the bema to the platform. Barry stood behind the podium where he would stand and recite from the Torah for his bar mitzvah in less than a month. The sight of his grandson, hands on both sides resting on the podium, white *kepuh* on his head, looking out at the empty benches, imagining, showing just a touch of fear, touched Lieberman as it must have touched Bess, who suddenly kissed his cheek.

"We go on," Rabbi Wass said, looking at Barry.

Melisa stood before the ark. She knew that the big Torah, the heavy ancient blue velvet Torah, had been stolen. The ark had a new fascination for her.

"I fired Eli Towser," Lieberman said.

Rabbi Wass shook his head. He didn't have to ask why. Towser had shown nothing but scorn for Rabbi Wass's pacifist attitude, Wass's willingness to take the side of the moderates in Israel and not see the extent of the threat right in his own community. Towser was an angry, earnest, and very intelligent young man. Rabbi Wass had invited him to visit the congregation and earn some money giving bar mitzvah and bat mitzvah training. There was only one congregant who hired him who did not complain about Towser's focusing not on ritual but on politics with twelve-year-old children.

Rabbi Wass had tried to talk to Towser, who had answered that his own father had been an anti-British terrorist when he was twelve. It was clear from his tone that Towser respected neither Wass's political position nor his religious conviction.

Towser had come to services regularly over the past five months, both on Friday nights and Saturday mornings and on high holidays. He had been part of the minyan. As an honorary member of the men's club, he had launched into discussions of militancy and anger even when the club speaker was a Jewish sportscaster.

Rabbi Wass wished Eli Towser would go away. It was difficult to deliver a sermon or give a service without glancing at or being aware of the disapproving eyes of the bearded rabbinical student.

"I understand," said Rabbi Wass with a nod. He took off

his glasses and cleaned them with a handkerchief his wife had neatly folded, as she did each morning, into his jacket pocket.

Lieberman looked at his grandson who seemed to be trying to decide on the proper pose at the podium.

"So?" asked Bess.

Rabbi Wass put his glasses back on.

"So," said the rabbi, "I break a precedent. If you wish, I'll tutor Baruch."

"That would be wonderful," said Bess with a smile.

Baruch was Barry's Hebrew name. Melisa's Hebrew name was Malka. Abe's Hebrew name was Avrum, and Bess's was Sarah, as her mother's had been and as her mother before her and many generations back had been. When the conversation took even a slight religious turn, Rabbi Wass used their Hebrew names as he was doing now.

"But," Bess continued, "with everything that's . . ."

"It will be a relief, a pleasure," said Rabbi Wass. "I used to do it when I was a rabbinical student and I continued for a while when I got my first congregation. It will be good for me. Baruch," he called to Barry. "How would you like to finish your bar mitzvah lessons with me?"

"Sure," said Barry with ready acceptance if no enthusiasm.

"Tuesdays and Thursdays, after school. My study," Rabbi Wass said.

"He'll be here," said Bess.

Towser had come to the house. Getting Barry to the temple would make her busy life a little more difficult, but . . .

"So," said the rabbi. "Have you found anyone yet? The Torah . . ."

"In confidence, Rabbi," said Lieberman. "We think we know who did it, at least one person involved and others very likely. No lead on the Torah. It's a hard object to sell. And we'll have to face the possibility that it may already have been destroyed."

Rabbi Wass nodded in acceptance. "Nazis," said Wass.

"More likely a small group of Arab students," said Lieberman. "I'm telling you more than I should."

"And you think I would break this confidence?"

"No," said Lieberman.

"Tell me," asked Wass. "How many are in this small group?"

"Maybe ten, twelve," said Lieberman.

"Ten, twelve, fifteen people couldn't do the damage to all the synagogues that was done in a single night, a few hours," said Rabbi Wass.

Lieberman shrugged. It was a question that had also bothered him.

Bess rounded up the kids as Rabbi Wass said softly to Lieberman, "Oh, that I were as in the months of old, as in the days when God watched over me; when His lamp shined above my head. And by His light I walked through darkness."

Lieberman nodded as the children and Bess walked toward him down the aisle.

"Job," Rabbi Wass explained. "If Job could suffer and still believed, what has happened here is little enough to bear."

Lieberman agreed, but he also felt that it was not over, that there was more coming, that the attacks had been well planned and were but the first step in a campaign of terror. This was not the work of a few stupid children. Taking Jara Mohammed was only the first step in finding out what had happened and what might be about to happen.

He wished Jara did not remind him so much of his daughter. He wasn't sure if he should do the questioning or stand back and turn her over to Leo Benishay. Jurisdiction was a slight problem. Most of the synagogue attacks had been in the city, Lieberman's city, but the only attack on which they had evidence, Anne Ready's photographs, was in Skokie. And Jara Mohammed lived in Chicago.

Rabbi Wass shook Barry's hand and said he would see him on Tuesday, that Barry should bring whatever books or papers *Chaver* Towser had given him. After the good-byes were finished and Lieberman promised to keep the rabbi informed, the Liebermans left the house of worship.

"Are we going home, grandpa?" Melisa asked. "Or are we going to sleep at Uncle Maish's again?" She took his hand.

"We are," he said, "going home, but not before I exercise my rights as patriarch of this clan to take you to a restaurant of your choosing and to a movie we can agree on." He looked at Bess. She shrugged. He had spoken. He should have asked her first, but there was a need in her husband's eyes and she nodded.

"Nothing violent," Bess said.

"McDonald's," said Barry.

"Too violent," said Lieberman.

"Grandpa," Melisa said in a way that let him know his joke was ill timed.

"McDonald's," Bess conceded.

"*The Toy*," said Melisa.

"Yechh," said Barry. "The Jean-Claude Van Damme movie at the Old Orchard."

"Double yecch," said Melisa.

"We'll find something after we eat," said Bess, starting toward the car. The was a hint of coming rain in the air and a dampness in her soul. She was a dozen feet away when she turned and saw her husband looking up at a window across the street. Through the slightly parted curtains in the room, Bess thought she saw an old woman taking pictures of her husband with a rather large camera.

"Abe," she called.

He nodded and followed her to the car. There had not been enough Arab students in the entire crowd at the university to cause the damage he had seen. And he was sure that most of the Arabs had not participated in the attack, though many might be sympathetic to it. Then who had done the damage? His only link was the young woman and Lieberman had the feeling that something should be done quickly.

In his office, just before he picked up Bess and the children, he had received a call from Emiliano Del Sol saying that he guaranteed the Koreans would not bother him or his family. Lieberman had not asked how he had accomplished this. He didn't want to know.

"Thanks, Emiliano," Lieberman had said.

"De nada, Viejo," El Perro had answered. "We put it in the box, right?"

"En la caja," Lieberman agreed, the box of favors each man owed the other. "The Cubs won today. Cincinnati's a game behind."

"Bueno, Viejo. Piedras is putting all the cards you gave me in a big book."

Piedras, the Tentaculos prime enforcer, was big and silent, a silence that did little to hide his stupidity. Piedras's loyalty to El Perro was without question and Lieberman knew that Piedras had killed for his leader. But the image of Piedras carefully putting baseball cards in a book was too much for Lieberman to conjure.

The house was safe, but somewhere, he was almost certain, destruction was coming. He would definitely, if Bess did not give him too stern a warning, down two Big Macs and insist on a comedy.

Berk looked like Curly in the "Three Stooges," but Berk's body was solid, powerful, and without Curly's belly. He looked a lot like Curly but no one would ever tell him, certainly not Pig Sticker Charles Kenneth Leary, not if he wanted to live. It wasn't so much that a comparison to the looks of Curly would be an insult. Curly was a Jew. All the Stooges were Jews. Berk had a book he kept with him in which he wrote the name of every prominent person who he knew was a Jew. They were all part of the conspiracy. The Jews had no choice. Most of them were in it because they wanted to be. A few had to be pressured, threatened, but all Jews were part of it.

Berk did not despair. He knew what a handful could accomplish. From behind the table he looked out at the two dozen people who had gathered for a meeting. He looked at their faces. All wore leather jackets. All, with the exception of Pure Nell from Hell, were men. All, including Nell, were shaved bald. A few were drinking beer from amber bottles. None were smoking. Smoking was not permitted. Every member had to work out and stay healthy. If they slipped and were caught, they answered to Berk.

Berk was the oldest of the group. Berk was the toughest. Berk was the most confident. And they knew he believed in what they were doing. He had been involved in many beatings, two of which resulted in deaths. He had led marches, held rallies, screamed back at the Jews and niggers who had challenged him. Berk held his own and more in any group and he was afraid of nothing and no one.

They were in the basement of the Tip-Top-Tap on Montrose. Berk's brother-in-law owned the bar and agreed with most of what Berk believed. The Jews, the niggers, the Koreans were taking over everything. They had to be stopped. One of the daughters of Berk's brother-in-law was actually living with a Jew kid right now, somewhere in California.

Berk was sure that no one in the room would talk to the cops. They'd rather go to jail on a put-up charge than talk about what went on in this room. Jail was far safer than Berk's revenge.

"Meeting," Berk shouted, slapping his hand on the table. Everyone got quiet.

"Problem," Berk said. "You know what it is. Someone offed the Arab, Ramu, got the guns."

"It's what we get for working with fuckin' Arabs," said Nell from Hell.

Berk didn't get angry. In fact, he agreed with Nell. The alliance was supposed to be temporary. Berk thought the Arabs weren't any better than the niggers, but they had money, they had guns, and one or two of them were smart and didn't scare easily.

Berk leaned on the table with both hands. "Maybe. But we're in and we're gonna finish. I want whoever took those guns. If some Jew took them, I want to know. If some nut asshole on his own took them, I want to know. The Arabs think we did it. I don't give a shit what they think and as far as I'm concerned, three dead Arabs aren't gonna be missed by me."

Laughter. More than the joke was worth, but release.

They all knew what was going down. Someone had a lot of automatic weapons out there. Someone, particularly one of those crazy Jews, might come right through the door behind them, and open fire. Berk had placed a man outside the door and one upstairs at the bar to watch for just such a thing and to be ready, but he didn't expect it, not now. In fact Berk was sure an attack wasn't coming from whoever had taken the weapons because Berk knew who had the weapons. He had a plan, a plan he would share with only five people in this room, and only at the last minute. Berk wanted to be ready, always ready. While the niggers and Jews argued in their groups about what to do, Berk, as small as his group of skinheads might be, was the absolute final word.

His plan was simple. The group had grown, allied itself with whoever could help attain his ends, the Klan, militias, even Arabs who would eventually have to go. The Jews would go. The niggers would go. The Spics would go. The slants would go. This would be a white country like it was supposed to be. Berk was no fool. It probably wouldn't happen in his lifetime, but the movement would grow and the skinheads would be the most visible part of it. He imagined his photograph on the wall of meetings in the future. Meanwhile, he would make deals with the devil if it moved them toward a new America. He would also make deals with the devil if it meant making William Stanley Berk rich.

He thought briefly of Mr. Grits. Looked around the room and meeting eyes as if seeking dissent or a traitor. Berk, in fact, didn't know where the stolen weapons were, where the stolen religious scroll was, but he knew who had them.

"One more big rampage with the Arabs," he said. "And then we go quiet. We let the cops know. We let the Jews and niggers know we did it and then we go under and let them shit in their pants for maybe a year wondering what we'll do next."

"Right," the crowd shouted. Pig Sticker shouted loudest of all.

Berk smiled and folded his arms. He had seen pictures of Mussolini with his arms crossed. He wanted to look like that. Mussolini was a martyr to the cause even if he was a wop. Berk smiled. When it was all over, he planned to rape the Arab bitch with the big mouth. Maybe they'd all rape her. What could she do about it? Complain to the cops? She had a big mouth and she was too smart.

"Now," said Berk, "I'll tell you what we're gonna do next."

Pig Sticker sat forward to listen. He was sweating right on top of his shaved head. He looked around. No one else was sweating. He was afraid of what he was going to hear, afraid he'd have to tell it to the Irish cop. Maybe Pig Sticker would pack his bag, take a bus, and let his hair grow out. Maybe. But goddamn it, he believed in Berk, admired Berk, had never met anyone like Berk. Berk was the big brother who would stand up for him. Berk was the leader who would pat him on the back for a job well done. And what Berk said was right. But Berk could never find out that Pig Sticker was part Jew. To Berk there was no such thing as part anything. You were all or nothing.

Charles Kenneth Leary listened and wondered if he had enough money in his apartment to buy a bus ticket and rent a room in some town far away if he had to. It almost brought tears to his eyes. He did not want to leave Berk or the Mongers. It might be better to kill the cop, but if the Irish cop knew then maybe other cops knew too and would come after him.

It was too much for Pig Sticker to think about. He wanted to remain Pig Sticker. He liked it when Berk called him Pig Sticker. Shit. He leaned forward and listened, and since he was sitting in the back of the room, he waited for a moment when no one was looking back to lean forward and wipe the sweat from his head with the sleeve of his jacket. When he straightened up, Berk was looking directly at him.

Hanrahan was not very good at the game, but he promised Iris's father, Chi Huang, that he would work on it. It was simply that Hanrahan did not have that kind of memory, not even for his own painful football career; much less, movies. It wasn't that Hanrahan didn't like movies. He loved them. He had a battered VCR that played but didn't record, but mostly he would watch old movies on AMC. He just couldn't remember the details the way Lieberman could.

"They wept when I read my paper," Mr. Huang had said solemnly, sitting at his favorite booth in the empty Black Moon Restaurant. Iris sat across from her father at Hanrahan's side, touching his hand.

"I don't know," said Hanrahan. *"The Prize?"*

"Good movie. Good lines," said Mr. Huang. "Wrong movie. *Invasion of the Body Snatchers*. Original version. Kevin McCarthy came in here one time. I could not get myself to talk to him. I should have." Mr. Huang looked at the door of the restaurant as if hoping the actor would pay him a return visit. "Your Jew friend is much better at the game," he added thoughtfully.

"He has insomnia, watches old movies at night, and has a good memory," said Hanrahan.

"You bring him next time," said Chi Huang.

"I'll bring him for lunch soon," said Hanrahan.

"Wedding in three months," said Mr. Huang, returning his look to his future son-in-law and his daughter. "Mr. Woo has said that he would arrange."

Iris's father sat with his hands folded on the table. He was still wearing his apron. Perhaps a couple or two or a late-night party would still come. It was half an hour till closing. Iris would wait with him.

They sat in silence for a few minutes drinking coffee.

Chi Huang was not a tea drinker. Neither was Hanrahan. It made no difference to Iris, for whom it was just something social to do and she was pleased that her father and William were doing it. They finished their coffee and Huang said, "Confound it, man. I shall never be able to tell that story again."

It was another movie question. Hanrahan had no idea. Better to admit it than make a mistake. "No idea," he said.

"Four Feathers," said Chi Huang. "C. Aubrey Smith at very end. Next time you bring Lieberman."

Huang stood up and offered his hand to Hanrahan. Hanrahan also rose and took the hand. Iris's father had a firm grip in his small hand, a grip developed from more than half a century in the kitchens of Chinese restaurants.

Iris and Bill waited while her father moved toward the kitchen. Iris said her father was over eighty. It made sense. Though Iris could easily be taken for thirty-five, she was actually a few years older than Hanrahan. She was also, Hanrahan thought, quite beautiful.

When the swinging door closed behind Mr. Huang, Hanrahan leaned down to give Iris a kiss, a quick one. He knew she did not feel comfortable kissing in public.

"That was the longest conversation I've ever had with your father," Hanrahan said as he stood away from the booth.

"I think he is beginning to like you," she said.

"Now that I have Mr. Woo's approval," said Hanrahan, "my not being Chinese and being an alcoholic are not quite as important."

Iris stood, took his hand. "My father likes to hold on to some tradition," she said. "If you wish to make him truly happy, you might learn to speak a little Cantonese."

"I'm fifty-one years old, Iris," Hanrahan said with a grin, kissing her hand.

"My father is learning Spanish," she said. "Takes lessons every Thursday night at the Senior Learning Center. I think he is quite good."

"So," said Hanrahan with a shrug. "I learn Chinese."

"Cantonese," Iris corrected gently. "Not Mandarin. We cannot understand Mandarin."

"It's going to look a little silly for a big oaf of an Irish cop to be speaking Chinese," he said. "But for you . . ." He touched her cheek.

"Tomorrow," she said.

"Without a doubt," he said and left the Black Moon Restaurant, feeling the slight night breeze and the possibility of a drizzle.

He had parked his car quite illegally on Sheridan Road, a few doors down from the restaurant, and had pulled down his visor to show a passing cop who might be below his ticket quota that he should pass this one by. Normally, he would have driven straight down Sheridan to Foster, turned right and gone down to Western and then turned left for the drive to his house in Ravenswood, but this time he took the turn at Hollywood and went South on the Outer Drive. Then he turned at Lawrence and went a few blocks past the Weiss University of Chicago Hospital and made a left into some street. When he had gone two blocks, he was dead certain. He was being followed, had been followed from the moment he pulled away from the curb near the restaurant. He had seen the lights come on in the car parked about six car lengths back, behind a line of illegally parked vehicles, and watched it keep pace behind him.

He checked the weapon in his holster, a 9mm Luger automatic. It was fully loaded and he had more than forty rounds in a box inside the television set in his living room. He also reached down to slightly loosen the tape around the S&W Short Forty just above his right ankle.

Ever since an attack that had sent Hanrahan to the hospital for more than a month and had nearly cost his life, he had never left his house unarmed, though no weapon could have protected him from the attacker who had come on him from behind and struck him before he could react. He also had to admit to himself that when he was in the house he had needed the solace of a nearby weapon ever since he had killed Frankie Kraylaw right inside the front door.

It was the only subject over which he and Iris had nearly quarreled. She had been in bed in the living room in his house and found it difficult to make love with a large hand-gun within reach. She understood that he was a policeman, but she preferred not seeing the weapon. He had relented and placed it in the drawer next to the sofa bed in the living room where they were lying. Hanrahan couldn't bring him-self to take Iris to the bed and bedroom he had shared with Maureen. He, himself, frequently slept on the sofa bed, leaving the bedroom exactly as it had been when Maureen left him. However, he had begun to sleep more and more nights in the bedroom upstairs since he had murdered Frankie Kraylaw in the living room. The boys' rooms had been used several times, the last by Frankie Kraylaw's wife and little boy before Hanrahan had lured crazy Frankie into the house and killed him. Hanrahan had confessed his sin to Father Parker, but the Whiz had given him too light a pen-ance and had been too understanding. If there were a God in a heaven somewhere, he and William Hanrahan were destined for a long talk about good and evil. Hanrahan had also hinted to Lieberman about what had happened. Lie-berman had refused to use the word "murder," instead he had said "accident" and once he had said "execution."

Father Parker had given his view on the matter after Han-rahan had confronted the priest with what he viewed each day of his life, each torture and murder of a small child, often by the child's own parents, each rape of an old woman. Why didn't God save them? What did it prove or accomplish? Why was there a Frankie Kraylaw?

"The way I figure it," Parker had said in his office, ac-tually holding a football in his hands, a football full of the names of teammates Parker had played with on a winning Rose Bowl team, "God gives us free will, otherwise we're just puppets. He gives us free will and choices. We can do good. We can do evil. The ones who do evil may not know that what they are doing is wrong, is evil. They may say, and some have to me, that they killed the innocent wife or child to send them to a better life in heaven at God's side.

They may say that they have no choice, that something inside them, childhood abuse, a horrible, uncontrollable impulse, bad genes, whatever, made them do it. Some greater good, the saving of America, made them plant the bomb."

Hanrahan had looked up at that one.

"No, no one has confessed a bombing to me," Parker had said, throwing the ball to Hanrahan seated across the desk. "But I've seen as you have and I've heard. God created us and stands back, watching us make choices, exercising our will, often to do wrong or evil. We can make up excuses, blame others, say we are acting for an ultimate greater good, but one day we'll stand in front of our savior and have to explain."

"And he'll send the sinner to hell?" asked Hanrahan throwing the ball back.

"I don't know if there is a hell or what it might be," said Father Parker. "I believe there is judgment, on earth and after death. If I didn't believe that, I wouldn't be wearing a tight collar on Sunday, conducting masses, visiting the dying, blessing the newborn, listening to confessions, and talking to friends and parishioners over this table."

"And giving absolution," Hanrahan reminded him.

"Ultimately, I think that's God's business," said the priest. "I do it and then He has the power to overrule me. Like the Supreme Court."

Hanrahan wasn't sure that he felt better after that conversation. When God gave man free will, why did he also give it to monsters and madmen like Frankie Kraylaw? But, then again, what was free will if it was not a choice between right and wrong, good and evil. It was too much for Hanrahan. He had decided that he was going to go on being a cop, going after the bad guys—for he firmly believed in bad—and giving God a helping hand whether he asked for it or not. William Hanrahan had free will, didn't he?

There were a lot of ways to handle the situation he was now facing. He could park, go into a random alley or passageway, find a place to hide, and step behind whoever was following him if the person or people in the car decided to come after him. He could drive to the station, see if they parked, get some help, and confront his pursuer or pursuers. What he did was drive home, inside the speed limit, down main streets, checking his rearview mirror. But the guy stayed back. He could tell that the driver was a man. By the time he parked in front of his house he could tell that the driver was alone. There were plenty of spaces. The overflow from Ravenswood Hospital didn't spill as far as Hanrahan's house, though the hospital was expanding. A parking lot had gone up. Hanrahan had a garage in back, but he rarely used it except for winter nights when there wasn't much or any snow and the temperature dipped below 15.

The follower parked ahead and turned off his lights. Hanrahan picked up his mail from the box, opened his gate, and went up to his door. The nightlight was on. It was always on. The rest of the house was dark. Still, no one got out of the car, which he could now see was probably a Mazda. Hanrahan went inside, dropped the mail on the table next to the door, and took off his jacket. He turned the rocker toward the front door and sat in it with his gun in his lap.

He sat, gently rocking in the dark, listening, amazed that he didn't want a drink, frightened because he wanted whoever it was—some ex-con he had sent away, some gang member he had slighted, someone a cop offends and forgets—to come through the door as Frankie Kraylaw had. God help him, Hanrahan felt a little mad, as if he could shoot another bad guy coming through his door. He would understand, understand that God had chosen his fate, God had decided that William Hanrahan, planning a wedding, drinking no more, would have to kill, the very thing he no longer wanted to do, the very thing that had almost caused him to leave the force. But where would he go? What would he do? Be a security guard with a brown uniform? Or, if he was lucky, no uniform at all, sitting up all night at the desk in the lobby of some big company, watching surveillance monitors, and picking up a check every week?

The doorbell didn't ring. No one knocked, but Hanrahan heard the almost inaudible footsteps, heard the person pause in front of the door, heard someone insert a key in the lock and try to turn it, then remove the key. The lock had been changed with Frankie Kraylaw's death. All the locks had been changed.

Whoever it was hesitated and then rang the bell. Hanrahan got up, weapon in hand, and moved to the door. He opened the deadbolt and went back to the rocker.

"Come in," he said. "It's open."

The handle turned. A big man filled the doorway with the streetlight behind him. "Can I turn on the light?" the man asked.

"Turn it on, slowly, carefully," Hanrahan said.

The man closed the door and moved to the switch in darkness, giving it a click. The hall light was not bright, but it was enough. Standing before William Hanrahan was Michael Hanrahan, his son. The two men looked alike. Michael was thirty, as big as his father, wearing slacks, a white shirt, and a lightweight black jacket. He looked at his father who placed his gun on the table next to the rocker and rose, not knowing what to do. He walked forward and held out his hand. His son took it and they shook. Hanrahan wanted to hug his son but he held back. The last time he had seen him, almost two years ago, the meeting had been brief, cold. Hanrahan had been drinking, holding it well, but drinking. Michael knew, and he knew that his father knew that he knew. And Michael had not come to the hospital even when it had looked as if his father were dying.

"You followed me from the Black Moon," said Hanrahan, awkwardly facing his son.

"Black Moon?"

"The Chinese restaurant on Sheridan," Hanrahan explained.

"Before that, from the station," said Michael, his blue eyes looking around the house in which he had once lived. "Nothing's changed."

"Nothing," said Hanrahan and thinking, "Everything has changed."

"In the whole house, my room, Bill Jr.'s?"

"The same," said Hanrahan, looking at the room.

"Looks clean," said Michael.

"I keep it ready," said Hanrahan.

"What for?"

"For a moment like this," said Hanrahan.

TEN

THEY SAT AT the kitchen table, father and son, surprised at how quickly they had disposed of the history of half a decade.

"Seen your mother?"

"Yes, she's fine. Just got promoted. Still an office manager but a different office."

"How does she look?"

"Great," Michael had said, standing next to his father who had ground coffee beans in a little white Braun machine. It already smelled of deep darkness as it brewed.

Michael remembered the last machine, the one his father had let him press to grind the beans into a fine powder. His father had nodded his head when the powder was fine enough and Michael had stopped solemnly and poured the dark, wonderful smelling powder into the basket of the coffee machine. When he was old enough, Michael had filled the back of the machine himself with distilled water kept especially for making coffee.

"Your brother?"

"The same," said Michael, meaning he still wants to have nothing to do with you and blames you for the breakup of the family.

"His job? He still with that law firm?"

"No," said Michael. "He left there over two years ago, moved to California."

"Kids?"

"You mean Billy? No. Not me either."

"Work OK for you?" asked Hanrahan as they stood listening to the coffee perk.

"It's OK. Minneapolis is a good place to live. I keep trying to talk Mom into moving there, but . . ."

"Chicago's her home," said Hanrahan. "And Hallie?"

"Holly," said Michael. "My wife's name is Holly."

Hanrahan had met his daughter-in-law only once. She was small, dark, and pretty, but, given that it was the funeral of Hanrahan's mother, the meeting was brief and formal.

"And you?" asked Michael.

"If you mean the job, fine. If you mean the drinking, I haven't had a drop in almost two years." The coffee was ready. Hanrahan poured two cups, black and then remembered, "You like lots of sugar."

"Lots of sugar," Michael agreed as they sat and Hanrahan placed a spoon and the sugar bowl in front of his son. Michael recognized the bowl. It had belonged to his grandmother.

"One day you just stopped?" asked Michael.

"Drinking? Yeah. One day my drinking got a woman killed. I stopped. With a lot of help from AA and Iris and a man named Smedley Ash," said Hanrahan, taking a sip. It was hot and good, his best flavored beans.

"Ever get the urge?"

"When things get bad," said Hanrahan. "I fight it. If I can't fight it alone, I get help. I've been needing less help, but once in a while . . ."

"Like?"

"I killed a man, a crazy man who wanted to hurt a young woman and a child," said Hanrahan.

Michael looked at his father the way he had when he was a boy and overheard Hanrahan refer on the phone or to his mother to some act of violence that she blamed for his drinking.

"A man can't see what I see, do what I do, and not have a drink or two," he had once said.

"Abe doesn't need a drink or two." Michael's mother had replied.

"I'm not Abe," Hanrahan had answered, raising his voice. "And I'm not Harvey who got his ass kicked off the force for being drunk. Most cops drink. I'm an Irish cop. I drink a little. For Lord's sake, Maureen, I'm not a drunk." She had not answered him and Hanrahan had muttered something and gone back out slamming the door, unaware that his son was listening in the kitchen, seated just about where he was sitting now.

They drank their coffee in silence. Hanrahan waited and then said, "Do I guess or do you tell me?"

"Why I'm here?" asked Michael, putting down his coffee and looking around the room. He grinned. There was no mirth in it. "I used to hate you."

No news in that, thought Hanrahan who remained silent, drinking.

"I hated seeing you drunk, hated when you brought me some piece of junk candy and breathed on me and smiled. I hated the gun you wore, and was afraid every night you'd come home really drunk and shoot Mom, or shoot me and Bill. I hated you for not being a father."

"Did I ever hit you, Michael?"

"Never," Michael agreed, but this was old territory.

"About five years ago, maybe a little more or less," Michael said, not looking at his father, "I started to drink. Not much. A little. Drinks with the people from the office. Drinks at my boss's house. Then a drink or two when I got home. Holly commented on it long before I realized it. We had a fight. She threatened to leave me. I insisted that I wasn't a drunk, that I did perfectly well at work and no one complained. I looked at her and saw Mom. I listened to myself and heard you. And then I started to blame you. I drank because I couldn't get over what you'd done to the family. I drank because it was in my genes. I inherited it from you, your size, your eyes, your alcoholism. And I hated you more than ever."

Hanrahan took another sip of coffee, not looking away from his son.

"I followed you from the station to get up enough nerve to talk to you. I saw the Chinese woman." Michael had already said this, but Hanrahan didn't interrupt him. "Is she a good woman, like Mom?"

"She's a very good woman," said Hanrahan. "And I'm lucky she'll have me. We're gonna get married and I'd be pleased if you and Holly would come. I'll ask Bill, Jr., but . . ."

"I'll ask him," said Michael. "But I don't think he'll come."

"You stopped hating me?" asked Hanrahan.

"Yes, and I started maybe understanding you. Or maybe I kept hating you and started hating myself, too. Put us on the same field or in the same bar."

"And what is it you came down from Minneapolis to ask me?"

"I told you. I think I told you. I'm here on business. Company business," said Michael, forcing himself to look at his father.

It was in his father's blue eyes. That man had heard hundreds of lies from the best of liars, liars who often believed their own lies. Michael was not a good liar. "OK," he said finally with a sigh. "I'm on a long vacation, four weeks. Company shrink recommended it. Holly didn't want to come with me. She's got a job and she's just about had enough of me. Did you ever hit Mom?"

"Never," said Hanrahan. "I broke furniture. I hurt myself."

"I hit Holly," said Michael. "Last week. She just looked

at me surprised. It was a slap in the face. She didn't even reach up and touch the pain. She just looked at me as if I were someone else. I'm gonna lose her, Dad."

"You want to stay here, with me, for four weeks?" asked Hanrahan. "In your old room?"

Michael nodded.

"And you want me to help you start getting sober?"

This time Michael said, "Yes."

"You'll come to a couple of meetings with me, AA, and decide if it's what you need," said Hanrahan. "I can talk to you, give you the number where I can be reached, give you projects around the house to keep you busy, but this is a fight that'll go on your whole life, Michael. There aren't any quick and sure cures."

Michael nodded that he understood and Hanrahan thought he just might, a little.

"I've got to tell you this, Michael. Tomorrow morning there'll be a sign in front of the house. I'm selling. Too many memories, good and bad. They'd haunt me. They'd start haunting Iris." There was a long pause and then he continued, "I kept this house looking like this all these years in the hope your mother would come back. At first I hoped she'd come back to stay. Then I hoped she'd come back to visit, pick something up, who knows, and see that I'd kept the house almost like a . . . but like the bottle, I've got to put it away."

"I understand."

"You have a bag or two in the car?" asked Hanrahan.

"I'll go get 'em," said Michael, getting up from the table and starting toward the door. He paused, turned, and said, "Thanks, Dad." And then he was gone.

Twice in the course of a few minutes one of his sons had called him "Dad." More memories. He wasn't sure what he could do for Michael. Just be there. Bill Jr. would have been a bigger problem. As stubborn as his grandfather, as frail and good-looking as his mother. Bill Jr. seemed the more likely one to go for the family bottle.

The phone rang while Michael went for his luggage. Hanrahan picked it up.

"Hanrahan?"

"Yes."

"Pig Sticker. Twenty minutes. You know the little park on Rogers not far from Clark?"

Hanrahan knew it. The neighborhood was almost all black and Hispanic. Not likely another Monger would pass by and see him. Very likely a hostile local gang might be cruising and spot him. That would be big trouble, but obviously not as much trouble as Charles Kenneth Leary feared if they met in a place where another skinhead might see him talking to a cop.

"I know the place."

"Don't take your time," said Leary.

He hung up and Hanrahan called Lieberman. Barry answered and put his grandfather on.

"Father Murphy, what's up?"

"Pig Sticker wants to talk, little park on Rogers near Clark, twenty minutes."

"I'll be there," said Lieberman.

"Oh, Rabbi, my son Michael is visiting me for about a month. I thought . . ."

"We'll have both of you over for dinner."

"Maybe we can all get together at the Black Moon," said Hanrahan. "Iris's father wants to talk old movies with you."

There was a lot more that Lieberman wanted to ask. But they both hung up as Michael came back into the house with two suitcases.

"Packed heavy," he said. "Don't know if I'll be able to get back in the apartment when I get back to Minneapolis."

Hanrahan stood up. "I've got to go out," he said. "The job."

Michael nodded and said, "I'll be fine, watch a little television, get comfortable."

"There's nothing in the house to drink but coffee and orange juice," said Hanrahan.

Michael nodded again.

"First step," said Hanrahan, moving past his son and picking up his pistol and holster from the rocker. "Don't leave the house tonight. Search the place. Eat what you can find, but don't leave the house. Promise on your grandfather's grave."

"And in the name of Jesus Christ, our Lord," Michael said with a smile as his father put on his jacket.

"Amen," said Hanrahan and he went into the night.

When Hanrahan had called him, Lieberman had been in the middle of an important meeting in his dining room. He would have preferred taking his shoes off, getting in his favorite chair in the living room, reading his back issues of *Atlantic Monthly* or watching two Panamanian bantamweights go at each other on ESPN.

Barry and Melisa were asleep. Bess, Rabbi Wass, Leo Benishay, Syd Levan, and Lawyer Hamel were putting the finishing touches on their plan. Syd was the president of the Mir Shavot men's club. The plan was that teams of men's club members would spend the night in the temple. There would be shifts. If they couldn't get enough volunteers, they would put pressure on, call for volunteers who were not in the club. Their job would simply be to listen and sit near the phone if anyone tried to break in again. If they heard anything, any sign of a break-in, they were to call a number supplied by Leo Benishay and a Skokie police car would be at the temple door in a minute or two. There were a few younger members of the men's club but most were the same age as the Alter Cockers. In fact, many of them were Alter Cockers. A pair of them would not make a formidable force in confronting armed skinheads or Arab terrorists, though Syd reminded the group at one point that several members of the congregation, including Herschel Rosen, had actually been in the Israeli army and had seen combat. But that was a lifetime ago and, as far as everyone in the room was concerned, no one in the entire congregation with the exception of Abe Lieberman, building chairman, owned a firearm. Rabbi Wass said that he would talk to some of the younger members with families and see if he could get volunteers. At least four members of the congregation in their forties had also been in the Israeli army.

Rabbi Wass had agreed to call the other congregations, the ones in Chicago that had been attacked, and suggest that they set up an overnight watch too. There was no guarantee that the terrorists or vandals would strike again or that if they did, they would strike at the same houses of worship.

But the interview with Jara Mohammed that afternoon had not gone well. Lieberman was not at liberty to divulge everything that was said, but he definitely did not rule out the possibility that Mir Shavot might be the object of another attack of the some kind. Leo Benishay was the only one in the room besides Lieberman who knew what had gone on in the meeting at the station where Anne Crawfield Ready had definitely identified the young woman, who had a lawyer present.

The lawyer was not an Arab. Lieberman knew her well. Her name was Charlotte Warren. She had represented members of various organized black groups, including Muslims, even Martin Abdul, many times over the past twenty years. Charlotte Warren was white, Southern white with a put-on Texas accent that she should have and could have lost forty years earlier when she passed the Illinois Bar and decided to represent and defend the victims and scapegoats of a racist society. Whenever she was interviewed by the press, which was frequently, she always managed to get in that phrase about the victims and scapegoats. Coming from a white-haired former Texan, it was always impressive.

What had been the temporary downfall of Jara Mohammed was her own uncontrollable anger. Lieberman, Faye Lasher, a new member of the State Attorney's office, and Ibraham Said had sat across from Jara Mohammed and Charlotte Warren, whose badly worn briefcase rested on the desk between them.

"We have a positive identification from a witness," said Faye Lasher. "We have a photograph. We have your client with cause in a neighborhood where she says she has friends who were coming to pick her up at two in the morning, but whose names she can't remember. She can't even remember the day. We have a photograph of your client with a member of the Arab Student Response organization dressed like a skinhead coming out of the temple on the night of the attack. We have a witness, the one who took the photograph, who will testify to that. The witness has already identified your client in a lineup."

Faye Lasher was well into her forties, tall, thin, black, and perfectly groomed, never appearing at the station or on duty in anything but well-tailored suits. Faye Lasher had ambitions that looked as if they were on the way to achievement when the city had a black mayor. Those ambitions looked even more promising when a white mayor was elected who was surrounded by white Irish faces. Faye Lasher almost certainly deserved promotion in the State Attorney's office. She was sharp, had an uncanny memory for what people said, details, and she was tough. Too tough. Many was the time, once in a while with Lieberman present, that an opposing attorney across the table would simply call off the interview and threaten to file a protest over Faye Lasher's threatening behavior. One of those who had never filed such a protest was Charlotte Warren. Lasher and Warren were, in fact, friends. Lieberman knew that Warren had more than once offered to take Lasher in as a partner. Lieberman also knew it was Lasher's determination to devote her life to putting criminals in jail that had stopped her. Her brother had been the victim of a gang shooting. Her mother and father had been mugged more times than she could count. She had cousins, aunts, uncles still in the city, living afraid, afraid of their own people.

This is what Lieberman had been remembering when Hanrahan had called.

"We want a confession, names," Faye Lasher had said,

sitting next to Lieberman, her hands folded, her long fingernails painted a serious blood-dark red.

"My client is innocent," said Warren. "You give the charge. She pleads innocent. I really don't think we have anything to talk about here. You know and I know that a judge would probably throw this out, and a jury? We could sue the city for damages on behalf of a straight-A, University of Chicago graduate student in biology, with no record and no arrests, with the exception of the riot this morning in which she was a victim. We have photographs of my client's face. Just look at her."

Jara Mohammed definitely had bruises on her face and a bandage firmly in place.

"Miss Mohammed believes that some of the blows struck against her were inflicted by the police. And what do you really have here? A photograph that could have been taken any time before the unfortunate attack on a house of worship and a date on it of the day it was printed—printed, Ms. Lasher, not taken. And your witness, to whom I would like to speak should you decide to arrest my client for a crime, is old and may be quite confused. And who knows, on the witness stand, that confusion might be even more evident."

The lawyers were playing lawyer, but Lieberman and Leo Benishay were aware of another dynamic. They could feel it, had felt it before in rooms just like this.

Jara Mohammed had her eyes fixed on Ibraham Said who did not turn away. Said was maddeningly passive. The young woman grew angrier as the lawyers sparred, battled, parried, and lunged. Both sides knew what the deal would be. Jara Mohammed would be interviewed on the record on the basis of suspicion of vandalism and possibly theft, destruction of property and whatever else Lieberman and Faye Lasher could come up with. She would deny all and offer nothing.

"We are engaged in a jihad to regain our homeland, a struggle in which all Arabs should participate," Jara Mohammed said, looking directly at Said.

"In Muslim tradition," said Said calmly, "there is a greater jihad, a personal struggle to conquer one's evil impulses. It is a lesser jihad to conquer others."

Jara Mohammed gave the Muslim detective a look designed to dismiss his theory.

On the basis of the Anne Ready ID, they could probably hold Jara Mohammed for a day or two, but the case was circumstantial. Mrs. Ready's ID would probably not be enough and who knows when she took the photograph. She hadn't actually seen Howard Ramu clearly and she had not actually seen Jara Mohammed coming out of the temple.

"May I ask a question or two?" said Said calmly.

"No tape's running and I'll tell my client not to answer if I don't like the questions," said Warren. "We want to be cooperative here and then we want to walk out that door."

Warren touched Jara's arm on the table. She moved it away.

"You are a member of the Arab Student Response Committee," said Said calmly.

"I am," she answered.

"Response to what?" asked Said.

"As you know better than any in this room," she said. "Attacks are made, Arabs are blamed for terrorist acts committed by others."

"The World Trade Center explosion was an attack by Arabs," said Said.

"The Jews have the Anti-Defamation League," Jara said, now barely able to control her hatred directed across the table at Detective Ibraham Said. "They have the Jewish Defense League. We exist to counter unwarranted, unfounded attacks on Arabs. We are an official, recognized student organization at the university."

"Howard Ramu was a member of the Arab Student Response Committee?" asked Said.

"You know he was," said Jara.

"When he was found murdered, his head was shaved and he had a Nazi jacket in his closet," said Said.

"Someone put it there," Jara said. "Probably the Jews

who killed him and the two other innocent Arab students."

"The two others were innocent, but Howard Ramu was not?" Said said.

"Enough questions," said Charlotte Warren, buckling her briefcase. "You booking my client? You not booking my client?"

"Traitor," said Jara Mohammed, looking at Ibraham Said.

"Interview over," Warren insisted.

"I would suggest," said Said calmly, "that it is you who are a traitor to the cause of peace, that it is you and others like you who will cause more hatred of our people, who will take innocent lives."

"If we do not act, we are ignored by the world," Jara said.

"I advise you to stop now," Warren said, letting her courtroom voice boom out in the small room, but her client was unable to stop, unwilling to stop.

Old police ploy: Get a fanatic angry and talking and they'll eventually, proudly talk their way into a confession.

Warren looked across the table at Faye Lasher who sat back, hands folded, and shrugged.

"It is you who are the traitor to peace," Said repeated calmly, a calmness that clearly infuriated Jara Mohammed.

"Peace is treason," she said. "What you have witnessed is only the beginning."

"No more," Warren had said, moving her face in front of her client's.

"If all we've seen is the beginning," said Lieberman. "What's next?"

Jara, her lawyer's face before her, closed her eyes and nodded to her, indicating that she was now under control. She said nothing.

"No charges at present," said Faye Lasher, "but your client is a suspect and certainly a material witness who was at the scene of a felony and was seen and photographed with a murder victim hours before his death. She will give a statement, formal deposition. I don't think Judge Bright-bill will have trouble with that."

"Give me a few minutes alone with my client and we will be ready for cooperative and voluntary deposition," said Warren. "Is that all right with you, Miss Mohammed?"

Warren had tried to pry her client's eyes from Ibraham Said, who still sat passively.

"I am a practicing Muslim," said Said. "I believe in and live by the tenets of my religion."

"And I am a practicing Palestinian and I live by the tenets of history," Jara Mohammed said, appreciably calmer.

And so it had ended. Jara Mohammed had walked. And when the three policemen and Faye Lasher had left the room, Benishay had repeated Jara Mohammed's words, "What you have seen is only the beginning."

"I'll work on that," said Faye Lasher, who was distinctly taller than any of the three policemen.

"Ibraham," Lieberman said. "A cup of coffee?"

People passed them in the narrow corridor leading to the steps of the Clark Street Station.

"Some other time soon. Jara Mohammed's father and most of her family were murdered," said Said. "Murdered by a crazed Jew in Israel. Only she and a younger brother survived. Nothing will change her. Not the law and not the word of Allah."

Said walked away.

Less than an hour later, Leo Benishay and Lieberman set up the meeting in Lieberman's house. They could have gotten Maish or Yetta to sit with Barry and Melisa, but since the threat to Barry in the park, Bess had been reluctant to leave the children. Abe had assured her that the problem had been taken care of, and she believed him, but still . . . And so they were all sitting in the Liebermans' dining room drinking coffee and downing rugalah from the T & L. The pile had gone down and Lieberman had been more than tempted. He had once reached for one of the delicacies while talking about the plan. Bess had reached out and taken his hand in hers to block the move. Lieberman had been resigned, his cholesterol temporarily thwarted.

It was basically settled when the call came from Hanrahan and Lieberman had excused himself saying that the
call was related to their problem and he had to go immediately. Bess reminded him to take his heavier jacket. The
night had grown cold.

Lieberman arrived first. The little park was empty. He sat
on a bench covered with graffiti. The concrete wading pool
was dry, the rusting swings shook and squealed with each
pass of the wind. Lieberman was glad that he had taken his
heavy jacket. He also had his blue watch cap in his pocket
but he would not put it on unless his ears became seriously
cold. A new gust of wind came and the seesaw clunked
gently against the dirt.

There was an apartment building at the end of the park
which nestled in the L of two streets, neither of which was
heavily trafficked at this hour. At the other side of the park
was a small empty lot where a sign had stood for years
claiming that the choice piece of land with the park on one
side and the el train on the other was for sale.

Lieberman knew the park. He knew the neighborhood.
He also knew what to expect from the three figures that
emerged around the apartment building and headed slowly
toward him as he sat. There were two working night lamps,
chipped black iron, in the small park. The bulbs were out
on the rest of the nightlights, and the park district would
be in no hurry to repair them only to have them knocked
out by a rock or a bullet within a few days.

The three young men coming toward Lieberman were
black. They were very young and they wore zippered jackets, the color of which was hard to see in the dim light. An
elevated train heading north rattled by. Lieberman didn't
look at it.

The three young men stood in front of Lieberman who
remained seated.

"You got Alzheimer's or something, old man?" one of

the young men said. Lieberman could see now that the oldest of them was probably no more than fifteen or sixteen.

"No," said Lieberman. "Thank God, so far I've been spared that and there's no history of it in my family."

One of the boys put his foot up on the bench, his shoe almost touching Lieberman.

"Then you are fuckin' nuts or lost," said the one who was doing the talking.

"Nope," said Lieberman looking around. "This is where I want to be."

"You heard of the RP Headhunters?" asked the young man.

The third boy sat at Lieberman's side, his arms folded, looking directly at the man.

"I've heard," said Lieberman, shrugging slightly. His arms were crossed over his chest and his legs were closed protectively.

"This is our territory. Our park," the speaker said. "The sun goes down and its ours. You hear what I'm talkin' about?"

"My problems include arthritis and cholesterol," said Lieberman. "I see fine. I hear fine. It's in the genes."

The talking boy now leaned forward, his face about a foot from Lieberman who was trapped on the bench by the trio.

"Well," said the boy. "We're gonna take whatever you got in your pockets and we're gonna mark you a little and if you're alive, you're gonna walk, hobble, or run outta this park and never come back. You hear?"

"Perfectly," said Lieberman.

"Batman," said the boy, looking at the kid sitting on Lieberman's left.

Batman didn't move.

"Batman," the boy repeated. "Do him."

Batman didn't move.

Lieberman lifted his left arm and showed the talker why. The old man held a gun in his right hand and it was pressed hard against Batman's side.

"I'm a cop," said Lieberman. "If you three want to just walk back the way you came and keep walking, we can all enjoy the brisk night air and tomorrow you can have your park back. Tonight it's mine."

"You're no cop," said the boy in front of Lieberman. "You too fuckin' old to be a cop. You ain't shootin' anyone. Beach, do him."

"Hey," said Batman, who had the barrel of the gun pressing into his side.

"Beach," the leader repeated, and the boy whose foot was on the bench began to reach into his pocket.

Lieberman suddenly swung his pistol backhanded against Beach's knee. The boy fell to the ground with a scream and before he could even register what the old man had done, Batman felt the gun back in his ribs.

Beach grimaced on the dirty sidewalk next to the bench, moaning in pain. "He broke my fuckin' knee," the boy whimpered.

"Kneecap," Lieberman amended. "Get up, Batman, now."

The boy seated on Lieberman's left immediately and gladly got up. The talker had a weapon, Lieberman couldn't tell what, halfway out of his pocket. Lieberman had his gun in the boy's face pointed directly at his right eye.

"Ease it back," said Lieberman.

"Kill him, Priam," screamed Beach, holding his knee, his eyes closed in pain.

Priam eased the weapon back in his pocket.

"There's two of us, old man," said Priam. "You fast enough to shoot both of us?"

"You've seen too many junk movies," said Lieberman. "I shoot you first and then I shoot Batman. Simple, fast. Believe me."

"I believe him, Priam," said Batman.

"Kill him," Beach demanded.

"Pick up your friend," said Lieberman. "Go away and don't come back tonight. I'll be gone before tomorrow."

"You crazy or you got big balls," said Priam, shaking his head.

"Both," said Lieberman. "Now try to be retentive about what just happened here, and I'll go back to sitting alone on this bench and thinking about the meaning of good and evil."

"Re . . . ?"

"Retentive," said Lieberman, the gun still pointed at Priam's right eye. "It's your homework for tonight. Look it up in a dictionary."

"I don't need no dictionary," said Priam not backing away. "My brother's in college."

"Wish him my best," said Lieberman.

Beach groaned.

Priam pointed at Lieberman. "You here tomorrow or any other night or we catch you on our streets at night," he said, "you a dead, crazy old fart."

"I've got a lot on my mind," said Lieberman with a sigh. "Just pick up your friend Beach and go away. If you'd like, I'll count to five and shoot."

Priam shook his head and motioned to Batman, who moved to his side to help pick up the fallen Headhunter.

"Remember what I told you, old man," Priam said over his shoulder.

"I am retentive," said Lieberman, lowering his gun to his lap as the three boys slowly moved down the sidewalk and disappeared around the apartment building where not a single light had gone on when Beach had screamed.

As the three had gone away, Lieberman had seen a movement between two of the cars parked on the side street. He kept his weapon in his lap and called out, "Charles?"

Pig Sticker came out from between the two cars. His eyes followed the three boys down the street. He stood still till he was sure they were gone and then he headed toward Lieberman on the bench. The young man was big, very big, wearing a pea coat buttoned to the collar and a cap covering his shaven head. His hands were in his pockets.

"You really a cop?"

"I am really a cop," said Lieberman.

"You know my name."

"Bill Hanrahan's my partner. He'll be here in a second."

"He better hurry," said the young man. "I heard you talkin' to those niggers. You think they're not coming back with real artillery?"

"Your language is distasteful, but your logic is sound," said Lieberman.

"You always talk like that?" asked Pig Sticker.

"Depends on the company I'm in," said Lieberman. "Now take your hands out of your pockets. Slowly."

"I'm not carrying," said Pig Sticker.

"Hands," said Lieberman.

Pig Sticker removed his hands from his pockets.

"You're a Jew," said Pig Sticker.

"It shows. I know. I live with it. I'm one of the chosen people, though it baffles me why God chose us and then proceeded to torture us for centuries."

"I want Hanrahan or I've got nothing to say," Pig Sticker said, looking in the general direction of where the three boys had disappeared.

A car hurried down the street from under the elevated train viaduct and pulled into a space next to a fire plug. Pig Sticker looked as if he were going to run.

"It's Bill," said Lieberman. "I suggest you sit down. The seat's been warmed for you and I think you'd like to keep the conversation low and get it over with fast."

Hanrahan came out of his car, slamming the door behind him and hurrying across the playground.

"Sorry I'm late," he said.

"A few seconds late can mean my life, man," Pig Sticker said indignantly.

"Sit," said Lieberman.

Pig Sticker sat with a thud. He was big.

Hanrahan, wearing a coat Lieberman had bought for his partner's birthday five years earlier, hovered over Charles Kenneth Leary.

"This is fast," said Pig Sticker. "I want away from here before those niggers come back."

Hanrahan looked at his seated partner and the gun in his lap. "Several members of the Headhunters gang took umbrage at my being in their park," said Lieberman. "I gave them a vocabulary lesson and they left to work on it."

"They'll be back," said Pig Sticker. "And they'll be carrying heavy."

"Then talk," said Hanrahan.

"Something big's coming Monday," said Pig Sticker nervously. "Weapons, somebody gets hurt. I figure Berk plans to hit some Jews. He picked five of us. Said he'll tell us where to meet, when, and give us the weapons we're gonna need. He said we should be ready to kill. Big time. I'm sure, but I don't know who we're supposed to be killing. I just know I'm supposed to be somewhere to pick up a combat weapon Monday night. I'll get a call to tell me where to pick it up or if he lets us know where we're going. Then we . . . do it unless you stop us."

"OK, when you know where you're supposed to pick up the weapon, you call one of us. You memorize my number?" asked Hanrahan.

"Yeah. I'm going. One more thing. I get the same thing they all get. No special treatment. They get booked and go down, I get booked and go down with 'em. Unless it goes to a Murder One or Two and a sure conviction. Then we deal. I testify and go into witness protection."

"Everybody watches too much television," said Lieberman.

"Deal or no deal?" asked Pig Sticker.

"Fine," said Hanrahan, knowing he didn't have the power to offer Leary any such deal.

"You want to know why I wanna go down with them on anything but Murder?" asked Pig Sticker looking up at Hanrahan. "I don't want Berk or anyone else marking me and I think whatever Berk wants to do is right."

"If whatever it is does happen and you don't give us plenty of warning," said Lieberman, "I'll hug you in front of Berk, kiss your cheek, and call you *Lantsman*."

Pig Sticker looked at Lieberman with hatred and rose from the bench.

"I'm gone," he said. "You better get out of here too."

"Charles Kenneth Leary," Hanrahan sighed, watching the young man hurry between two cars and into the darkness. "You think he's straight on this Monday business?"

"Yes," said Lieberman, putting away his weapon and buttoning up.

"The Irish in him," said Hanrahan.

"The Jew in him," said Lieberman.

"We are truly blessed to belong to the two best ethnic groups in our free country," said Hanrahan. "And that's an objective truth."

"You hear me arguing, Father Murphy?"

"Let's get out of here," said Hanrahan.

Abe got up too. Not quite as quickly. The knees were not cooperating. They reveled in their arthritis when he allowed them to stay still for too long.

"Give my best to Michael," said Abe, walking toward his parked car.

"I will, Rabbi," said Hanrahan with a wave, heading back to his car.

When the Headhunters, seven of them, returned to the small park twelve minutes later, it was empty. In a rage, Priam shot out the last two lights and took a few blasts at the windows of the darkened apartment building next to the playground. No one in the building screamed or shouted. A child cried, awakened from a dream.

Priam motioned for his small troop to follow him. His anger was not satisfied. The skinny little old Jew cop had dissed him in front of two Headhunters. That skinny old Jew cop was gonna have a bad accident when Priam found him. A bad accident.

ELEVEN

BERK LOOKED AT the weapons on the table. He wore a flannel shirt with a black tie and a faded denim vest. He walked down the line of neatly laid out Uzis, handling each one, picking it up and examining it professionally while his host stood back watching, showing nothing.

"They aren't the best," Berk said putting down the last weapon and looking at the faded velvet scroll with wooden handles. "A little old."

"They don't have to be the best," his host said. "They have to leave a trail, perhaps a difficult trail, but a trail back to our mutual enemy."

Berk put his hand on the Torah. He did not like the man he was dealing with. Berk had caught the man more than once twisting his scarred face into a look of distaste when Berk's back was supposedly turned. This Arab was, in fact, not much better than the enemies they were planning to kill. Once this was over, truly over, he would see to it that this man had a fatal and painful accident. Not just because he was an Arab, but because there was no choice. The man was crazy. Berk smiled. He had often been accused of being mad himself. But he had carefully calculated that image and let his temper go when it suited him. Mr. Grits had seen through it to the man with whom he could make a deal. Here was Berk standing in front of a table of automatic weapons, planning mass murder, looking as if he could barely control his temper. Berk who had maimed and murdered and knew there had been times, many times, when he had been possessed by inspiration or madness but those times were brief. Through his normal day, even when he was making a passionate speech, Berk was in control of himself. He believed in Berk. The Arab had a cause, too; he was a true believer. But he could make mistakes and lead the police to Berk and the Mongers.

"I know," Berk said. "I want it quick, easy, and no mistakes. Better firepower would make it easier."

"But not accomplish our goal."

Berk nodded and unrolled the scroll slightly. He looked at the fancy lettering and decorations. He knew it was in Hebrew. Some of his people thought it told stories about how Jews were supposed to kill and even eat the children of their enemies as sacrifices to God. Berk was no fool. He had actually read the first five books of the Bible in English and found them not particularly interesting or threatening.

Berk was over thirty. He was growing tired of these games, this anger. It wasn't that he had given up his beliefs in the superiority of the clean, white race. That was true. That was something no one would ever change his mind about. And it wasn't that he was afraid. On the contrary, if anything he cared less about getting hurt now than he did almost eight years ago when he began. The simple high of facing down a crowd of Jews or niggers was coming less frequently. Now all he really enjoyed was the fact of his own leadership, the respect and fear of those who served under him, and the powerful, moving sound of his own voice when he spoke out. Berk didn't even know where he got the words. Mr. Grits had said that the young man was "inspired," that Christ took over when Berk spoke, that it was Jesus's voice, Jesus who wanted the white race to take back the world, whatever the cost.

Berk was strong. Berk was fearless. A dead look from his eyes could turn a listener cold with fear. He had given that look to several earlier that night, Pig Sticker, Boyce, Neville, Fallon. He had seen the fear in all of them. Not one of them, not one person in the world knew that Berk was simply tired of it all. It took too much out of a person to be mad with rage and suspicious of others all the time.

Berk had a secret plan now. He already had over $100,000 from Mr. Grits and would get $200,000 more when the job was done. He didn't think Mr. Grits would double-cross him, disappear without the final payment. Mr. Grits might think Berk could not identify him, but Mr. Grits was wrong, could be dead wrong. He had been out at a mall with Fran one night when Mr. Grits called on a public phone and the kid who answered had turned and looked around. Someone had been described to him. That someone was clearly Berk. As the kid called to him, Berk had told Fran to walk through the mall checking every public phone, the closest ones first, even the business phones in nearby shops. If she saw a well dressed man talking, she was to get as close to him as possible, listen for a Southern accent and come right back to Berk without being seen by the man if possible.

Fran had done the job. It hadn't been too hard. She had spotted him at one of the phones next to the Gap. Fran had hurried back, pleased with her success and whispered to Berk while Berk gave her a kiss and then kept talking.

"Listen to him," Berk had told Fran handing her the phone, his hand over the mouthpiece. "Don't make a sound. If he asks you a question, hang up. He'll probably keep talking a minute or two and hang up. Got it?"

She had nodded and taken the phone and Berk had hurried to where he could see the line of phones outside the Gap, being careful not to be seen. He got there just as the man hung up the phone and looked around. Berk was wearing a Bulls cap to cover his shaved head, but he didn't want to be spotted. He ducked into a vitamin store and got behind a stack of bottles of bee something.

And then he had carefully followed Mr. Grits who was smaller, older than Berk had expected. He had followed him very carefully into the parking lot and was so careful that he almost missed getting the complete license number of the rented black Lincoln.

The next day, through the crazy Arab who had connections, he had found the local address and name Mr. Grits had used to rent the Lincoln. Unwilling to trust any of his men on this one, Berk had staked out the Hilton on Skokie across from the Old Orchard Shopping Mall. He had easily found the Lincoln in the hotel lot. At the desk, he had asked the clerk if he would deliver a birthday package to Mr. Jerome Wilson. The clerk checked to be sure that Jerome Wilson was registered and then told Berk that he would see to it that the package would be delivered. Berk said the present was a surprise from Wilson's family and would arrive soon from Neiman-Marcus. The clerk said that he understood and that whoever was on duty would deliver the package.

Berk was reasonably secure now, knew what he planned to do: fake his death, become a martyr to a murderous Jew or nigger. His body would never be found. A note would be left saying that Berk's fate would be that of all who opposed Zionism or Black Nationalism. Berk would let his hair grow out, maybe grow a mustache, move to some small town, watch television, maybe get married, write a book about all he knew about the conspiracy between the police state and the impure races. He would write the book and send a copy to the Nazi press he had been corresponding with and getting books from for the last five years. They would publish it as a posthumous work discovered by a friend of the murdered Berk. The manuscript would be in Berk's own hand, undeniable, and Berk would be out fishing or shooting deer when it was published.

Another thing bothered Berk as he grew older. More and more younger members, even women, were not sufficiently frightened to keep from questioning an occasional decision. He could still beat with his fists, expel with his words, but that would not always be true.

And gnawing inside him was a fear he would not call fear. He certainly did not trust Mr. Grits. In addition, though Berk was unwilling to allow himself a clear, conscious awareness of the fact, he was becoming increasingly convinced that he had picked up HIV from a nigger woman he and two others had raped about a year ago. He hadn't raped her for pleasure. It had been to teach her a lesson, to teach them all, and it was he who had learned. He had no intention of taking a test to find out if he had the disease. What difference would it make? He'd know when it started to show. If he even had it.

Berk was highly motivated for the task ahead.

On his way home, Lieberman called the station. Nestor Briggs answered. Nestor almost always answered. He had no wife, little family, and had lost a small, smelly little white dog to simple old age more than a month ago. Nestor had always put in long hours at the desk. Now, his days were typically eighteen hours long. Nestor never put in for overtime.

Four messages. Three could wait. One . . . He pulled over next to the phone booth outside the McDonald's on Howard Street and dropped in a quarter, smelling sizzling beef and fighting the urge to pick up a Quarter Pounder when he finished his call. A man answered.

"Quien es?"

"El Viejo," said Lieberman. *"Emiliano quiere a hablar conmigo."*

"Si," said the voice and there was silence for less than two seconds before El Perro came on.

"Can you believe it, *Viejo?* Dunston homers in the ninth. Dunston. We win."

"I didn't have time to watch the game or hear it on the radio."

"*Yo se.*"

"You know?" asked Lieberman.

"Manny Guttierez tole me about what happened in the park," said El Perro. "You got guardian angels till we're sure the Korean gooks ain't gonna try anything stupid. Manny's probably watching you now."

"I appreciate your concern, Emiliano," said Lieberman, knowing that El Perro would get to the point.

"*Su cuento*, how you say it?"

"Story," said Lieberman.

"No," said El Perro. "Fuckin' bigger than that. Legend. That's the word. Someone just told me. Perez. He graduated from high school."

"Education is a privilege that should be cherished," said Lieberman.

"I don't know what you're talking about," said El Perro with a laugh, "But, Manny, he's got a carphone, told me you backed down three RP Headhunters, maybe broke one of them's knee."

"Maybe," said Lieberman, waiting for the subject of this conversation, almost certain he would not be able to resist at least a single burger with cheese.

"RP Headhunters ain't shit, *Viejo*," El Perro said. "Maybe *veinte* or *veinte y dos* with no more firepower than the nuns at St. Catherine's."

"I feel reassured," said Lieberman.

"You can't go around making enemies all the time, *Viejo*," said El Perro.

"Emiliano, you have made more enemies than the Alcohol, Tobacco, and Firearms Bureau," said Lieberman. "I know at least eight people who would risk their lives to kill you."

"Eight? Twenty. Maybe thirty," said El Perro with pride. "And is not fair. I'm a legitimate businessman now, mostly. Bingo parlor, restaurant, dry cleaner, bar, hardware store. Expanding, *Viejo*, up and down North Avenue. Pretty soon I'll have a big office and talk to IBM."

Lieberman knew that El Perro and the Tentaculos had

simply driven a string of businessmen and shop owners out by intimidation, threat, token payment, and occasional minor but distinct violence. Emiliano Del Sol might well be able to control a string of businesses in his neighborhood. He was crazy but El Perro was no fool. Someday he would lose control and not get away with it. Someday there would be too many witnesses and Emiliano Del Sol would be in Stateville, maybe even on death row. He'd make a great death-row lawyer and he had a massive, morbid knowledge about famous killers. "Gary Gilmore," El Perro had once said, "he was stupid man. Just stupid. Wrote some poetry not worth a shit. I don't see the big deal. Gacy was just nuts and lucky. Ted Bundy was smart, but crazy nuts too." El Perro could go on. His fascination with famous killers was almost matched by his passion for the Cubs, a passion shared by Lieberman.

"I need a favor, *Viejo*," said El Perro.

"Big favor?"

"Piedras got picked up again. Got in a fight with three guys. Hurt one of them pretty bad, hospital. Cops got there and Piedras hit one of them, broke his nose, the cop's. They're holding him at the North on about, who knows, twenty counts. Piedras has a record. I need Piedras. They could put him away till he's an old man on this one."

Piedras, the size of a Geo Metro, had an IQ slightly higher than a white rat, but he was El Perro's main enforcer, completely loyal, totally faithful. Piedras was too stupid to be crazy.

"Big favor, Emiliano," said Lieberman.

"You owe me, *Viejo*. We owe each other."

"I'll see what I can do, but you know one of these times, I won't have the favors to call in."

"Viejo," El Perro said. "Then call me back. If you get Piedras out, I got a free one for you."

"I'll call you back in five or ten minutes," said Lieberman. "But I may not be able to reach anyone who can help till morning."

"Then Piedras will spend a night in jail," said El Perro with a sigh. "No one will mess with him."

"You think Manny would like a Big Mac?" asked Lieberman.

"Who the hell knows?" said El Perro and hung up.

Lieberman went inside the McDonald's, got a Big Mac and a cheeseburger and a Batman glass for an extra buck. He had spotted Manny across the street while he was talking on the phone to El Perro. Manny was lounging back, windows closed, in a dark Toyota across Howard Street. Lieberman waited for a break in the traffic and crossed. Manny rolled down the window. Salsa music blared out into the night. Manny turned down the volume.

He was young, no more than nineteen or twenty, with pocked skin from a bout with some pox when he was a child in Guatemala.

"Have a Big Mac, Manny?" Lieberman said, handing him the bag and taking out the cheeseburger and the glass.

"Gracias." Manny said.

Lieberman could see the shotgun lying on the floor on the passenger side. He ignored it.

"El Perro le gusto Julio Iglesias," said Manny, turning the volume even lower. *"No me gusta."*

Lieberman nodded, patted the young man on the shoulder, and backed away.

"Quieres usar mi telefono?" Manny offered.

"No, gracias," Lieberman said, crossing Howard Street, truly enjoying his cheeseburger.

He waited till he was finished before he called the North Avenue Station. He had spent much of his time as a cop in the North Station. His old partner was still there, promoted. Lieberman probably could have been promoted by now had he remained, but he had put in for a transfer closer to home.

Lieberman was in luck. The arresting officer was a veteran named Tosconi, Vito Tosconi, and Vito was still in the building.

"Abe?" Tosconi said in his gravelly voice when he came on the line.

"It's me, Vito."

"Heard you retired."

"Not hardly," said Abe.

"This a social chat, old times?"

"I wouldn't mind knowing about the wife and kids, but I'm calling for a favor. Piedras."

"Abe, the guy is an animal. Someday he's going down for a Murder One. He should have years ago. We got him cold on a long count."

"I would consider it a personal favor if you'd let him walk."

"Walk? He broke my partner's fucking nose, sent a citizen to the hospital."

"Vito," Lieberman said, gently evoking seventeen years of friendship and favors, cover-ups, and stand-ups.

"Abe, it's a bad idea," said Tosconi.

"Nonetheless," said Lieberman.

"El Perro?"

"El Perro," Lieberman agreed.

"Ah, what the hell? My partner's an asshole kid who's gonna show off that broken shnoz like a Purple Heart and the jerk in the hospital is a drug dealer. If I don't get trouble from above . . ."

"If you do, tell Sanchez to give me a call," said Lieberman.

"Piedras will walk in the morning," said Tosconi. "The drug dealer's hurting but he'll live and he's not dumb enough to bring charges. I'll talk to my partner about the facts of life. Listen, tell Del Sol who did you the favor."

"I will. How are the wife and kids?"

"Carla is fine. Arthritis flares up once in a while. You know how that is."

"I know," said Lieberman.

"Kids are fine. Tony's teenage rebellion, which lasted almost through his twenties, is over and he's finishing a degree at UIC. And Angie is married to a cop and has two kids. You?"

"Bess is fine. Lisa's in California. Divorced. Bess and I have the kids."

"Life story. Just like that," said Vito. "Sum up almost twenty years in a few words. Take care of yourself, Abe."

"You too, Vito."

Lieberman had finished his cheeseburger and was determined not to get another when he dropped a quarter and got El Perro himself on the second ring.

"Viejo?"

"Piedras walks in the morning. Courtesy of a cop named Tosconi."

"The big old dago?"

"Same," said Lieberman. "How about you let Manny go home now?"

"I'll call him," said El Perro.

"You said you had something else for me?"

"Yeah," said El Perro happily. "A riddle. Like in *Die Hard Three* or *Batman Forever*."

"I'm not good at riddles, Emiliano. And I'm tired."

"It's only a riddle 'cause I don' know the answer," said El Perro.

"Go ahead."

"Why do six men *sin pelo* . . ."

"Bald men," Lieberman supplied.

"Yeah, bald men. Why do six bald men all buy head rugs at one of those television hair places all at once?"

"Skinheads?"

"Pienso," said El Perro. "I got a man who's got a cousin who works at the place."

"What place?"

"Harlem near Lawrence," said El Perro. "You find the answer to the riddle, you let me know, *verdad?*"

"Gracias, Emiliano."

"El mismo, Viejo."

By the time Lieberman got home it was after midnight and he was sure Manny was no longer behind him but halfway home blaring salsa music. Lieberman's street was full. He had to pull into the alley and get out to open the garage door, which was uncooperative at the best of times. Lieberman went through the back door placing the Batman glass in the cupboard in the kitchen next to Barry and Lisa's collection of cups and mugs—The Barbara Walters Specials, Hard Copy, Chicago Street Dental Group, the Save-the-Manatee mug that Melisa had painted herself. The kitchen light had been on. Not a good sign unless Bess had simply forgotten. Usually she left a table lamp on in the living room.

Lieberman moved through the dining room door, taking off his shoes as he went. The television in the living room was on but the room was dark.

"Bess?" he said softly.

David Letterman was on television. Bess never watched David Letterman. She didn't like him. Bess clicked off the television set with the remote, got up slowly. She was wearing her white silk nightgown with the white cotton robe over it. Her hair was tied in a kind of pigtail and her arms were folded.

He moved to give her a kiss.

"I'm lucky," she said in a tone that suggested she was nothing of the kind.

"We're both lucky," Abe said, kissing her gently.

"A high percentage of policemen have a drinking problem," she said. "There's even a support group for their wives and girlfriends."

"I know," said Lieberman.

"But what about policemen who eat Whoppers when they have high cholesterol," she said, her arms still folded.

"A single cheeseburger," said Lieberman holding up a finger. "It's been a hard day."

"They left at ten," Bess said. "A round-the-clock two-man watch will be at the temple every night. The police will make frequent, unscheduled stops."

"Good," said Lieberman, following Bess across the dining room and into their bedroom where she sat on the bed, unfolded her arms, and put her hands on her knees.

Lieberman slowly undressed, waiting for whatever was coming, whatever had kept his wife up waiting for him. She let him take off his jacket, remove his gun and lock it in the night table with the key he wore around his neck.

"I stand before you," Lieberman said, when he was completely nude. "One of God's conundrums."

"Lisa called," Bess said, looking at her husband and trying not to smile.

"She's coming for the kids," he said.

"No," said Bess. "And I assured her that you had taken care of the problem with the man in the park. She believed me, I think, particularly because she had something to tell me she considered important. Sit next to me, Abe."

"Without my pajamas?"

"Without your pajamas," she said.

"What did she say?" he asked, wanting to go brush his teeth and shave the white night stubble from his face.

"She's coming to Barry's bar mitzvah. She won't fight it."

"That's good news," he said.

"She is doing well at her job, whatever it is that criminologists do," said Bess. "And she has met a man."

"A man," Lieberman echoed feeling particularly naked now.

"A physician she works with, a medical examiner, someone who cuts up dead people," said Bess with a shudder. "They've been seeing each other frequently and she thinks he's going to ask to marry her."

Though Lisa was his daughter and had already been married once without success, he wondered from his own experience how anyone would want to spend his life with She Who Was Never Wrong.

"Talk, Bess," Lieberman said. "I have a feeling . . ."

She held up her right hand to quiet him. "He is in his forties, an M.D. from Stanford."

Lieberman resisted the urge to make his wife move faster.

"His name is Marvin Alexander," Bess said. "According to Lisa, he is extremely famous in his field. He wants to meet us, the children."

"Alexander?" asked Lieberman. "He's not Jewish."

"Neither is Todd, the father of our grandchildren," Bess replied.

"So, they're coming to the bar mitzvah?"

Bess nodded.

"So, fine," said Lieberman. "Now I shave, brush my teeth, take my Cardizem, and we go to bed and maybe I sleep."

"He's black," said Bess as her husband rose.

"Black?"

"African-American, negro," said Bess.

"That, my love," Lieberman said, kissing his wife's cheek, "will make for one very interesting bar mitzvah."

"Where you been?" asked Fallon when Pig Sticker came through the door shortly after midnight.

Pig Sticker shared the one-bedroom apartment in the Monger house with Fallon. The apartment was always clean. Piles of gun magazines were stacked in bookcases— Soldier of Fortune and various small circulation magazines about the rights of citizens which were being eroded and the lies the media told about history.

The furniture all belonged to the old owner. Her son had lived in the house and had been a close friend of Berk. Her son had been killed in a drive-by shooting in front of Berk's house.

Fallon was on the floor doing sit-ups, a sure sign that he was sitting on his anger or frustration or cabin fever.

Fallon was wiry thin and in great shape. He could do hundreds of sit-ups and push-ups while the television blared. Fallon had done time. He had learned a lot. Since his hair was so naturally dark, it was hard for Fallon to keep his head cleanly shaven as much as he tried.

"None of your fuckin' business," said Pig Sticker, taking off his jacket and hanging it in the closet.

An old cowboy movie with Fred MacMurray was on the tube. Fred was in a bad way, inside a burning house, fighting off a bunch of guys with beards.

"Just asking," said Fallon. "Hey, we're all brothers, right and white?"

"Yeah," said Pig Sticker, moving to a chair and siting to watch the movie, whatever it was.

"So, where you been?"

"Talking to the cops," said Pig Sticker. "I set up a meeting, went into nigger turf, met a couple of cops in a park and told them everything. I've had a change of fuckin' heart. I see that I've been wrong. I want to wipe the slate clean. Help make America the great melting pot. OK?"

Fallon laughed and kept doing sit-ups while he talked. "You are a crazy bastard," he said as Fred MacMurray shot the last bad guy, an easy target, a fat old guy.

"I went to a bar on Elston," Pig Sticker said. "Saw some of the guys there. We had a few beers, talked, and here I am. And, to tell the truth, Fallon, even though we're right and white brothers, it's none of your fuckin' business where I go or when."

Fallon shrugged and kept bobbing. "When you're right, you're right," he said. "How about we go out for another few. On me?"

"It's almost one," said Pig Sticker. "I'm tired."

"I can't stay in this room. I've got to get out for a while," said Fallon, suddenly stopping. Who knows how many sit-ups he had done. Sweat beaded on his bare chest.

Pig Sticker shook his head and got up. "One beer each," he said. "You pay."

Fallon jumped up and reached for his shirt.

"It's the waiting for whatever's coming down," said Fallon, buttoning up. "I wish it was tomorrow. I hate waiting."

Pig Sticker gave his roommate a whack in the head with his open palm. The blow had two purposes. One, it was supposedly a sign of masculine friendship. Two, it was a sign to Fallon that Pig Sticker was by far the more powerful of the two of them, that if they ever fought, it would be Fallon who would go through the window. The blow was enough. Pig Sticker put his arm around Fallon and said, "Let's go."

TWELVE

"NO PAY," THE old woman said, holding her hands folded together in front of her to keep them from shaking.

The cleaning store was small, a Lawrence Avenue institution that had gone through many hands, each reflecting a change in the neighborhood. Four Star Cleaners still got some customers from the high rises on Sheridan, especially from the Edgewater Beach Apartments, but most of their customers were neighborhood people, Korean, Vietnamese, some whites. The family of six that owned the Four Star worked long hours and delivered clothes clean and spotless for reasonable prices. They had one son in graduate school studying physics at MIT and a daughter, who now stood with her grandmother behind the counter, checking in a stack of shirts. She had just earned a full scholarship to the University of Illinois to study computer science when she finished her last year of high school.

Customers were not likely at the moment. The sky was dark, a very slight rain was falling, and rush hour wouldn't really begin for another hour or so. The three Korean men who stood across the counter were spangled with water. Their dark hair was damp.

Kim and the two men with him glanced at the girl. One of the men kept looking.

"You pay, like always," Kim said. "Or your store has an accident, a very big accident like the one that happened to Son Lee's grocery a few months ago."

"No pay," the old woman repeated shaking her head. She would have been far more comfortable talking in Korean and she had a lot to say but the young man had refused to speak the language of his birth from the first day he had come into the store months ago and demanded protection payment.

The old woman's husband was in the hospital, ill, something wrong with his lungs. He had always been a heavy smoker. Her son and daughter were away. There was just her and the girl.

"We had meeting last night," the old woman said. "We no pay. You go away. We tell police. Jew policeman say we no have to pay."

"The Jew policeman is wrong," said Kim calmly, deciding what he should do to teach this woman to pay without complaint. Things were going wrong. There had been a meeting Kim had not known about. The police were showing up. Crazy Mexicans were threatening him and someone who had been at the restaurant had probably spread the word about the visit from El Perro. Something really big had to be done. He looked at the girl who looked back at him. She was pretty with long hair, a little on the thin side for him, but this was just going to be a lesson.

"No pay," the old woman insisted, shaking her head.

Kim nodded to his right. The young man took off his sunglasses and started behind the counter toward the girl.

"No," said the old woman stepping in front of him. "You no come back here."

The young man pushed the old woman out of the way. Kim nodded to his left. The second young man went behind the counter and headed for the long rack of clothes, and took a knife from his pocket.

There was a shot. Of that Kim was sure. He had not drawn his gun nor had his two men. He reached for his weapon as the man near the girl slumped to the floor holding his stomach, as if he were praying. The man with the knife turned at the sound and another shot came. This one hit the man holding the knife in the chest. His sunglasses went flying. His knife dropped to the floor.

It was only a second or two but it had been so unexpected. It was the girl. The girl held a large, old pistol tightly in both hands. She turned it now, steady, at Kim who dropped to one knee and fired. The bullet missed the girl and went into the wall. The old woman began to scream. Kim fired at the girl once more, but as he fired, a bullet tore into his shoulder spinning him to his right. The gun fell from his hand. He reached down with his left hand for the weapon when the next shot came, hit him in his right hand.

Kim abandoned the weapon, abandoned his wounded men, and ran bleeding from the store.

The girl called 911 while her grandmother wept. She said the family cleaning shop had been robbed and that she had shot two of the perpetrators. She believed one was dead and the other badly injured. She had also shot a third robber in the arm, but he escaped.

The girl, so frightened that she had wet herself, comforted her grandmother and made a second call. This one she got from a card inside the drawer under the cash register.

"Hanrahan," came the man's voice. The girl identified herself and he said he was on the way.

The girl sat her grandmother in a chair and went to the fallen man who had the knife. She tried to be calm. She checked his pulse, opened one of his eyes and put her head to his chest being careful to avoid the blood. He was dead. The second one was slumped over in the praying position. He groaned softly. She touched his shoulder and he rolled over on his side. There was a lot of blood and the man began going into convulsions. Now that his sunglasses were off, she recognized the young man, had gone to high school with him, though he had been a grade ahead. He rolled to his back and the convulsion stopped. The girl pumped his chest and then gave him mouth-to-mouth resuscitation. He was breathing but weakly when the police car, sirens blaring, screeched to a stop in front of the shop.

The policemen had their guns out. Both were in uniform. One was black. The other was white. The police looked at the two bodies, the blood on the floor and at the calm girl.

"Extortionists," the girl said. "I have called Detective Hanrahan who knows about the case."

An ambulance pulled up, its sirens also blaring, and two paramedics came in.

"That one is dead," said the girl, handing the black policeman her gun and pointing. "The other one has lost a great deal of blood but I don't think the bullet hit his heart. And my grandmother could use some sedation."

The paramedics, both black, nodded knowingly.

"What happened?" asked one of the policemen.

"They were going to destroy our store, maybe rape me, hurt my grandmother," the girl said evenly. "I shot them. There is a trail of blood out the door from the one I failed to kill. Now, I would like to use the wash room in the back of the shop."

"Go ahead," said the black policeman.

When she was gone, the white cop said, "You ever see anyone involved in something like this so cool? Like it happens every day."

"You can't figure with these people," the black cop said.

In the small bathroom in the back of the shop, the girl closed the door, removed her panties and put on the spare pair she carried with her every day. She also changed her soiled dress, putting on one she kept on a hanger at the back of the shop. And then she sat on the closed toilet and cried. Tomorrow would be her seventeenth birthday.

*   *   *

"I'm telling you, when Tampa Bay gets the Devil Fish . . ."

"Devil Rays," Morrie Liebow corrected.

"Devil Rays," Herschel shrugged, a what-can-you-do-with-a-newcomer attitude. "Rays, fish, carp, sharks, what-ever."

"There's already a basketball team in Bradenton-Sarasota called the Sharks," said Morrie.

Herschel looked across the table at Morrie and then at the small gathering of Alter Cockers at the T & L on Devon. There was a light, slightly chilly rain falling, a cool day late in May. It wasn't even eight o'clock in the morning, but there was a concern around the table about whether the Cubs-Dodgers game would be postponed. So, Herschel, who was tired and had just finished a six-hour shift guarding Temple Mir Shavot with Bunch Levy, who cared not about sports and reserved what little passion he had for the rising cost of materials in the women's dress trade, Herschel wanted to talk a little sports before he went home for a nap.

The rest of the table, Levan, Chen, Rabinowitz, empathized with Herschel. They too had, in the month since Liebow had joined the table, felt the lash the small, white-haired man could unleash in a calm, determined voice.

Morrie Liebow used to live in Florida, had retired there from New York City where he had cut garments for half a century. He hated Florida. Too hot. He hated the beach. He hated the retirement hotel. He hated the card games. When his wife had died, Morrie had moved in with his daughter and son-in-law in Chicago. Their children were grown and out of the house. They could tolerate Morrie. The three of them lived in a large apartment right around the corner from the T & L.

"The Devil Rays," Herschel continued, looking at Morrie who adjusted the gray cap on his tilted head, "will be a powerhouse right away, immediately. They'll have the money, the draft, the experience from players the other teams have to give up. The Cubs will be embarrassed."

"So what else is new?" asked Syd Levan, drinking his coffee.

"Shame," said Herschel. "We got the Bears, the Bulls, the Black Hawks, and, though we don't give a damn, we've got the White Sox. You love the Cubs, you know they'll lose, but you don't want to be humiliated by a bunch of guys in uniforms with ugly fish on them."

"Devil Rays are not ugly," said Liebow. "They're graceful."

"That is not the issue," Herschel said with a sigh at the density of Morrie Liebow.

"I still think the Cubs are going over .500 this year," said Syd. "That's my opinion. What do you think, Abe?"

Lieberman sat at the counter, drinking coffee and coveting a Danish but avoiding it. His usual booth was taken by a quartet of produce delivery men who had their own conversation.

"I think they'll go .500," said Lieberman.

"Dreams," said Liebow.

"We live on dreams," Herschel said, leaning forward, his face turning red. "If we don't have dreams, what do we have?"

"Reality," said Liebow.

"Philosophy," Herschel said, sitting back, defeated. "We're talking baseball here and we get the cutter from New York talking philosophy. Did Hank Greenberg talk philosophy at breakfast? Max Baer? Marshall Goldberg, Sandy Koufax?"

"Old guys," said Liebow. "New guys talk money. Reality. How many bucks is a .290 batting average worth on a contract? Sixty runs batted in? Six tackles, unassisted a game? Three-pointers in the fourth quarter? Reality."

"Can I borrow your gun, Abe?" asked Herschel. "I want to shoot this old fart and put him out of my misery."

"He's not gonna give you his gun," said Liebow. "And if he did, you'd piss in your pants and give it back."

"I'm leaving," said Herschel, standing.

Urges, pleas all around the table for Herschel to sit down before he had a heart attack. He was seventy-six. He had a pacemaker. He was a leader of the Alter Cockers.

"I'm leaving," announced Liebow, standing and adjusting his hat. With his bent head, he looked as if he were perpetually peeking around a corner. "I've got things," he said, heading for the door after dropping a dollar on the table for his coffee and toasted bagel.

"Tomorrow," Syd said, his hand on Herschel's arm.

"Tomorrow," Morrie Liebow agreed. Liebow, who moved very slowly, nodded at Lieberman and went out of the T & L into the drizzle.

"He gives me terrible heartburn," said Herschel.

"He's over eighty," said Howie. "He was in a camp. He's got a number on his arm. Herschel, you know?"

"My cousin Gittel has a number on her arm," said Herschel. "She survived. She's got a sense of humor. She lives on her own, never saved money cutting cloth. Gittel's got a sense of humor. Syd, you met Gittel. What's she got?"

"A sense of humor," Syd agreed.

"So there," said Herschel, sitting with tired triumph.

"Liebow's daughter can't stand him," said Hy Hershkowitz, who had something on his mind and had said nothing till now. "He thinks she wants him to leave before he ruins what's left of her marriage. Liebow has no place to go. He's bitter."

"And I made him feel worse." said Herschel Rosen. "Now I can share the guilt with the Nazi in Brazil."

The table turned quiet for a minute till Howie Chen called out, "Got anything yet, Abe?"

Lieberman turned on his stool as Maish filled his cup, this time with decaf. Lieberman popped a Rolaids into his mouth and resisted the urge to touch his complaining stomach.

"Maybe," said Lieberman. "Can't talk about it yet, but maybe."

"Nazis," said Hershkowitz, whose fear of the Holocaust had kept him from seeing either *Sophie's Choice, Schin-*

dler's List, or anything on the subject. Hershkowitz had spent his entire life in Chicago. He had never seen a Nazi in person, only on television.

"Doesn't look that way," said Lieberman.

"Arabs," proclaimed Herschel Rosen, rejoining the conversation with conviction.

"Possibly," said Lieberman.

Herschel looked triumphant.

"Too soon to tell," said Lieberman.

Lieberman turned back to his brother behind the counter before he had to deal with more questions, questions he couldn't or wouldn't answer. "So, how's it going?"

"It's going," said Maish with a shrug, always carrying the loss of his son as a weight on his shoulders. "And you?"

"Lisa called last night," said Abe.

Maish wiped his hands on his white apron and nodded knowingly. Lisa was a problem, but at least Lisa was alive.

"She's coming to Barry's bar mitzvah," said Abe.

"She gave up fighting it?" asked Maish.

"Looks like," said Abe, taking a sip of coffee.

"And in return?" asked Maish, looking over at the Alter Cockers who were onto a new subject, sex on television.

"In return," said Abe, "she brings her new boyfriend and we are all kind and welcoming as if he were already a member of the family."

"He's an ex-con, a Sikh, what?" asked Maish.

"He's a doctor, a medical examiner," said Abe. "And he's black."

Maish nodded knowingly. "So, he's not Jewish?"

"I don't think it likely," said Abe. "But he and Lisa will be the hit of the festivities. Barry will be lost. The few family bigots will talk in corners and say things they think are particularly pithy."

"Screw 'em," said Maish, whose language had deteriorated since the death of his son. "Will Todd be there?"

"Todd will be there," said Abe.

Lieberman liked Todd in spite of the man's morbid interest in Greek tragedy.

"He won't care," said Maish. "You don't mind my saying it, he may wonder why this black biologist . . ."

"Medical examiner," Lieberman corrected. "He does autopsies."

". . . this medical examiner," Maish went on, "is interested in Lisa. Don't get me wrong, Avrum. Lisa is smart. Lisa is pretty, but Lisa is not a fun girl of the Rita Hayworth ilk."

"A more contemporary figure like Barbara Walters might be more apropos," said Lieberman, looking at his empty cup, his stomach warning him against a refill.

"Sure you don't want a bagel, no butter, toasted?" asked Maish. "It can't hurt."

Lieberman sighed and looked out the window. The drizzle was still slow, steady, the weather decidedly cold for late May. He accepted his fate, like Oedipus, he thought, and nodded at his brother to indicate that he would give in to a bagel.

"You got onion?"

"For you? You kiddin'? I've always got one tucked away," said Maish, turning.

Lieberman's beeper went off. He headed for the phone in the corner. When he came back from the quick call, he grabbed the toasted bagel from his brother's hand and hurried toward the door.

Behind him, he head a voice, he wasn't sure which of the Alter Cockers it was, saying, "Woman ice skaters are sexy. Women news anchors are sexy. Diane Sawyer, take Diane Sawyer, but these kids on TV . . ."

Michael had already been in the kitchen and had the coffee made when Bill Hanrahan went downstairs. Quite a trick. Bill was regularly up by six, started the coffee, took a shower, shaved and was dressed and ready to go while he watched "Good Morning, America," drank coffee, ate his cereal, and watched the clock. He liked Charlie Gibson. He was a cop, good at reading people. Charlie Gibson was real, sincere. Bill had met O. J. Simpson once. Simpson had a smile, a firm hand, seemed sincere enough, but Simpson had been a man distracted by other things. He was not there. He was thinking about the next place he had to be. He would always think about the next place. The world was full of people like that. But Charlie Gibson was right there, in the studio, listening, watching, feeling.

In any case, Michael was dressed in a pair of jeans and a University of Arkansas sweatshirt, an extra-large with the sleeves pulled up.

"Couldn't sleep," said Michael with a nervous smile.

"I know how it is," said his father, going for the coffee and flipping on Charlie and Joan. Bill was not obsessed with the show, but having it on might make it easier for his son to talk or not to talk.

"Last night was hard," Michael said. "Toast?" Hanrahan nodded, and Michael got it for him.

"I heard you," said Hanrahan.

Michael sat and looked at his full, dark cup of coffee. "You know what I was doing?"

"Looking for a bottle," said Hanrahan.

"My father's a detective," said Michael with a smile. He touched his face. He needed a shave. He needed a shower. He needed a shampoo and a comb, all the things his father had been through before coming downstairs. "I didn't find one."

"There isn't one," said Hanrahan. "I told you. Used to be. I'd take it out and look at it, have arguments with it and put it away. I always won, with some help from my friends. Then I got rid of the bottle. Things happened. I was afraid it would win the next argument."

"I considered going out and finding an all-night place," said Michael.

"But you didn't," his father said, digging into his shredded wheat.

"What's today going to be like?" asked Michael. "Can you see me shaking?"

"You don't look like Robert Redford on a good day, but

you're not so bad," said Hanrahan. "I'd like you to meet
Smedley, go with me to an AA meeting tonight if I'm not
working, go with Smedley anyway."

"I don't know," said Michael.

"Only way you can stay here," said Hanrahan. "It's great
to have you back. It's great to see you, but you count on
this house and me to pull you through, you won't make it
and I'll feel like its my fault. We do it my way?"

"We do it your way," Michael agreed.

"Good. As soon as I finish, I call my friend. He comes
over and you do what he says."

"What if he's not up?"

"I'll wake him," said Hanrahan. "He's been through this
before."

The phone rang. Hanrahan picked it up. It was a girl,
one of the Koreans he and Abe had talked to about the
extortion business. She told him her story quickly, calmly
and hung up.

Hanrahan took out his pen and pad and wrote Smedley
Ash's name and number and told Michael to call, that he
had to run. Michael promised to call as soon as his father
left. Hanrahan nodded and dialed Lieberman's beeper number.

While he waited less than a minute, he turned to his
sagging son, pointed a finger at him and said, "You call."

"I call," Michael agreed.

"Stay in the house till my friend tells you what to do?"

"OK," said Michael.

Hanrahan knew how much the word of an alcoholic was
worth when he felt he had to have a drink.

"I throw you out if you take a drink, Michael. I mean
it."

Hanrahan looked at his watch. The phone rang. It was
Lieberman.

Hanrahan got to the Four Star Cleaners right ahead of his
partner. They double-parked and met on the sidewalk in

front of the store where an older uniformed cop greeted them. The rain was falling lightly.

"Moonjohn," said Lieberman taking the man's hand. Hanrahan did the same.

"My partner went in the ambulance with the perp the girl wounded. The stiff is still inside. The third one took off. Blood leads that way," Moonjohn said, pointing down. In spite of the light rain the trail was clear. It wouldn't be for long. "If you didn't show up in the next two minutes, I was going after him. Girl inside says she shot him at least twice."

Moonjohn was not far from retirement. He didn't want to be a hero and run down an armed and wounded Korean gangster in an alley. Not if he didn't have to. Not if he could get two detectives to do it. Detectives got paid for doing things like that.

"Thanks," said Hanrahan. "We'll be back."

The two detectives, weapons now out and at their sides, ignored the few people who passed them on the wet morning and did their best to ignore the bloodstains and the odd pair of detectives. They had seen the police on the street before. Now they wanted to mind their own business and get to work.

The trail of blood was beginning to wash away, but the trail was so heavy that there was still plenty to follow to the corner, across the street and down the sidewalk in front of three-, six-, and twelve-flats pressed together with tiny littered lawns in front of them.

Both detectives could see that the bleeding man was not thinking straight. He should have walked or run on the grass, made it tougher to follow. The trail turned at the next corner onto a slightly bigger street not very far from where Iris and her father lived. The rain was coming down a little harder now when both men stopped and looked down three cracked concrete steps that led into a very dark tunnel. The pause was brief. Lieberman pulled his penlight out of his pocket, went down the steps. As soon as they hit the bottom step they could hear someone breathing heavily.

The detectives pressed themselves against the wall. Lieberman turned off his flashlight after getting a glimpse of the wounded man.

"Kim?" Lieberman asked. No answer.

"Kim, you're bleeding bad, very bad. You need a doctor and if you could run or walk I don't think you'd be in here. We're your hope."

The answer came in Korean, not particularly literate Korean but neither policeman knew or cared. The voice was angry, panting.

"In English," said Lieberman. "And if you're armed, throw the gun in our direction so we can hear it."

There was a pause and then a weak voice said, "Shit." Metal clattered down the passageway and the gun actually bounced off of Hanrahan's feet. Their eyes were growing more accustomed to the near darkness and Lieberman thought he could see a shape in a doorway on the left.

"I'm turning my light on now," said Lieberman. "If you've got a weapon in your hand, you die."

The light came on.

Kim was huddled in a doorway that probably led to a basement. His right arm was completely red as were his pants. His shirt seemed remarkably clean.

The detectives moved to the fallen man and looked at the wounds more carefully. Neither detective thought there was a chance of saving that arm, but they weren't surgeons.

"I'll get an ambulance," said Hanrahan.

"Yeah," said Lieberman, still holding the light on the young man's arm.

Then Hanrahan was gone.

"Am I dying?" asked Kim.

"I don't think so," said Lieberman. "I've seen people survive worse, much worse. Amazing what the human body can take."

"My arm," Kim said. "I can't feel it."

"You may never," said Lieberman, "but there too, I'm no surgeon."

"A little girl," Kim said. "And Su, Hashimi?"

"The ones who were with you? One's dead. The other is in very bad shape."

"When this gets out," Kim said, eyes tearing with pain and humiliation, "people will laugh at me. A little girl."

Lieberman didn't think people laughing at what happened would be an entirely bad thing, but he didn't say anything.

Kim's breathing became more forced. Lieberman took off his belt and used it as a tourniquet around Kim's double-wounded arm. He made it tight. Kim seemed to feel nothing. The flow of blood slowed, at least it looked that way in the beam of the flashlight. Lieberman was doing his best to keep from getting bloody. He had a decent chance of succeeding if the ambulance came fast.

There was silence, a silence in which neither man spoke but Kim breathed a bit more slowly.

"I'm going to sue," said Kim.

"Sue?"

"I went into that store to drop off some clothes," said Kim dreamily. "And the girl got frightened, thought we were coming to hurt her or try to get money. I told her we only wanted to drop off some cleaning. She started to shoot. I'm suing."

"What did you do with the clothes you brought in to be cleaned?" asked Lieberman.

"Don't remember," said Kim. "Pain. Lots of pain."

"Why did you run and hide in here?" asked Lieberman. "You could just go to a pay phone and call 911."

"Afraid," said Kim. "Thought the girl had come after me. Couldn't shoot back straight with my left hand. Looked for somewhere to hide. Came in here."

"Why were you carrying the gun?"

"I have a permit," Kim said. "You know I have enemies. I need protection."

"You also have friends who might give an old woman and her granddaughter a hard time?"

Kim shrugged.

"I can take off that belt and do some things that would

insure that you won't be alive when the ambulance comes,"
said Lieberman gently.

Kim didn't answer. Lieberman didn't remove the tourniquet. They said nothing for five minutes till they heard
footsteps in the dark.

"Abe?" called Hanrahan.

"Here," said Lieberman, turning on his light.

"He still alive?" Hanrahan stood over him soaking wet.

"Mr. Kim claims that he was an innocent customer who
got shot by a panicky kid," said Lieberman.

"Quick thinking for a dying man," said Hanrahan.

"And if I don't die?" Kim said so softly that they could
barely hear him.

"Well," said Lieberman. "We work from there." Lieberman turned the light on Kim. The Korean's eyes were
closed but he was breathing.

"A brain like that," said Abe. "He could have been a
computer whiz or something."

"Or something," Hanrahan agreed.

About a minute later they could both hear the ambulance
siren through the lightly falling rain.

Rene Catolino found the hairpieces El Perro had told Lieberman about. The team started with the neighborhood El
Perro had given them, though none but Lieberman, Hanrahan, and Captain Kearney had known the source of the
information.

It was Kearney who had insisted that the team go out to
ask and carry photographs from the rally. The telephone
would be the last resort if they started running out of time.
Monday was two days away. It was Saturday. Lieberman
was excused from duty on Saturdays and Friday nights.
Hanrahan usually covered for him as Lieberman did for his
partner on Sundays, especially now that Hanrahan was actually going to services at St. Bart's. Of course, when something big was coming down or a lead just couldn't wait,
God was asked to understand. It was both Lieberman and

his partner's belief that their respective gods did not much care if the policemen worked on the Sabbath. What they were doing was more important than the repose, worship, and solace they would have sitting or standing with their congregations.

But it was Rene who found the hair, in the fourth stop she made. It was in a hair consultation shop for men where transplants were one of the options. Rene spoke to a receptionist who assured her that women were welcome as clients and that there were quite a few in spite of the masculine nature of the business.

"Women are understandably more sensitive," the full-headed red-haired receptionist old enough to be Rene's grandmother, had said softly out of the hearing range of a lone man with a receding hairline pretending to read a *People* magazine in the waiting room.

"I'm not sensitive," Rene assured her in her most confident Chicago accent, showing her badge. "I want to see whoever's in charge."

"If you'll just have a . . ." the woman began.

"Now," said Rene. "One minute."

"Is it really necessary to . . ." the woman tried again.

"Absolutely," said Rene. "One minute."

The old woman was clearly shaken now. Rene could have handled it various ways. This was the one she had learned from her father. It seemed especially effective coming from a tough-sounding, good-looking young woman with an attitude.

The old woman said something on the phone and hung up.

"Mr. Churchill will be out in a moment," the woman said, glancing at the man reading *People* magazine, who tried hard to mind his own business.

The walls of the waiting room were tastefully covered with photographs of men with white, toothy smiles and heads of wonderful hair that looked as if they needed no grooming, just occasional admiration. A door not far from the receptionist opened and a man emerged. He was small, wore a gray suit, a concerned smile, and a head of dark hair that deserved a picture on the reception room wall. In fact, Rene looked back at the wall and confirmed her memory that a photo of this man was there, though in the photograph he wore a much bigger smile.

"My office?" he said, holding the door open for Rene Catolino who stepped in.

"I am Randy Churchill," he said as if he expected her to recognize him.

She didn't, even when they were seated in his office, Churchill behind a big desk. She sat in a modern black leather and chrome chair before it. The walls were covered with bookshelves. Identical books, large, black.

"Styles, satisfied customers," Churchill said, seeing her eyes scan the walls.

His desk was completely clear except for a telephone and two photographs which were turned just far enough so Rene could see them. One was a trio in color, a small blonde girl with a ribbon in her hair on the knee of a pretty, dark-haired, smiling woman in her thirties. A young teenage boy with dark hair stood next to the woman. The other photograph was much smaller, black and white, an old man and woman.

"Last week," said Rene. "Six, maybe seven wigs . . ."

"Hairpieces," Churchill jumped in.

"Hairpieces," she said. "Six or seven. The buyer wanted good ones. Wanted them without you seeing the people they were for."

"Officer . . ."

"Catolino," she said. "Six or seven hairpieces. Do you know what I'm talking about?"

"You have a definite tendency toward abrupt behavior."

"You haven't seen my behavior yet," she said. "Just a small sign of my attitude."

"You know who I am?" he asked, sitting up.

"Winston Churchill," she said.

"Randy Churchill," he said. "Most people recognize me from the ads on television. You know, I was my first customer. I show a picture of me when I was bald."

"Different guy did it first," Rene said impatiently.

"Well, he did it first, but mine is different. He . . ."

"Six or seven hairpieces," said Rene.

"Our services, I'm afraid, are confidential," he said. "You can understand that."

"You're no lawyer, you're no doctor, you're no private detective, or psychologist," she said. "You're not even a fucking chiropractor or acupuncturist. I leave anything out?"

"Your manners," he said, obviously shaken.

"These photographs," she said, reaching for the one of the woman and two children. "Your family?"

"Well . . . actually, no. A member of my staff. I'm very fond of them."

"No wife. The old man and woman?"

"I bought it," he said with irritation and just a bit of bravado in the presence of this aggression.

"Hairpieces," she repeated.

Churchill touched his fine head of hair to be sure it was still there.

"If I have to take you to the station or we have to start calling your lawyer, I'm going to be very upset because lives may be on the line here, and the clock is moving, and your hair will definitely suffer."

Churchill sagged, defeated. "Seven pieces," he said softly. "Very good ones. All male. All dark. Since I wasn't allowed a fitting, I didn't give my usual warranty. Payment was in cash."

"Paid well?" Rene pressed on.

"Yes," Churchill admitted.

"With a warning to keep your mouth shut about the sale?" she said.

"I don't want to get in trouble with the police," he said. "I have a sensitive clientele."

"Who bought them?"

"A man, in his thirties," Churchill said.

"Bald?"

"No," said Churchill. "Full head of hair. All natural. I can tell."

"Describe him," she said, taking out her notebook.

Churchill shrugged. "Hard to remember."

"It's your job to remember how people look before and after," she said. "Exercise your professional skills and give me a goddamn description."

"I intend to report your bellicose behavior," Churchill said.

"Bellicose," Rene repeated, pursing her lips and nodding her head in appreciation of his vocabulary. "Describe the person who bought the hairpieces."

"Dark, not very tall. Male. Slight accent perhaps."

"What kind of accent?"

"How do I know?" Churchill said with a sigh.

"Look at these photographs," she said placing the pile from the rally on the desk facing Churchill. "Slowly. Stop if you see anyone familiar, even if it's not the man you sold the hair to."

Churchill sighed and began to go through the photographs. He started to go through them quickly. Rene told him to slow down and look carefully or they could do it in the peaceful solitude of an interrogation room.

Churchill went more slowly. There were thirty-six photographs. He pulled out three and pointed to a man in the small crowd.

"Him," he said. "At least I'm sure in that photograph and fairly certain in this one. He's moving in the last one but I think . . ."

"Thanks," said Rene, gathering the photographs.

"I won't be asked to testify about this, will I? I mean if this man is in trouble?" asked Churchill as Rene stood.

"It's possible," she said. "But I doubt it."

"You mean," he said, "there isn't much chance of my getting involved in this? After all, all I did was sell a man some hairpieces."

"He must have been a real sweetheart," she said.

"It was not comfortable to be with him," Churchill admitted. "He was very determined and filled with something, maybe rage. He told me distinctly not to discuss this transaction and I had a strong impression that I was being threatened with great harm. He actually picked up the photograph of Santiago's family and looked at it when he told me to keep the transaction very private."

"Thanks for your help," Rene said. "I'll know where to find you if we need you." She went out the office door, closing it behind her.

Randy Churchill began to shake. He had already started perspiring and he could feel his hairpiece growing warm and slipping back. He had four hairpieces, all human hair from the same person, each a different length to simulate daily growth and authenticity.

Randy had been trained as a barber. Barbers didn't make money. He had worked briefly as a hairdresser, but he simply didn't have the eye or the talent. He had not exactly grown rich in the hairpiece business but he was far from poor.

What he wanted most, however, was to remain among the living.

THIRTEEN

"THIS MAN," LIEBERMAN said, showing Jara Mohammed the clearest of the three photographs taken at the
rally.

They were seated in a coffee shop on Hyde Park Boulevard, the two policemen and the young Arab girl. Jara
drank nothing. The policemen drank coffee.

She looked down at the photograph briefly and then up
at the Jew policeman.

"Will you tell us who that man is?"

"I don't know," she said defiantly.

"He's your brother," said Hanrahan. "A few years younger.
Big boy. Walks with a decided limp."

The identification had been made by Ibraham Said. The
problem was that the known address of Massad Mohammed
was, as the police had discovered before dawn, empty and
abandoned except for a few cardboard boxes and some rusting kitchen utensils. The landlord, a defensive and angry
old man, did not know when Massad had moved out, but
he was sure he wasn't renting to any more Arabs, providing

the goddamn government didn't force him to.

The girl didn't answer. She pushed the photograph back toward the policemen and sat erect. There were few other customers, mostly students, in the coffee shop. They sat in a high-backed wooden booth and talked in a normal tone.

"Your brother bought seven hairpieces last week, expensive ones," said Lieberman. "Have any idea why?"

It was just a flicker, perhaps the hint of a tic but both policemen noticed it.

"What bald men does your brother know?" asked Hanrahan.

"Or women," added Lieberman.

"He is my brother," Jara said with a sigh. "We seldom speak. I do not know his friends."

"Skinheads," said Hanrahan softly. "White supremacists. They hate Jews, blacks, Asians, and Arabs. They hate anyone who doesn't claim to be white, Christian, and as bigoted as they are. To put it simply, these sons-of-bitches hate you and your brother. Why is he buying them hairpieces?"

"It is a mistake," she said, a few more signs of nervousness appearing, primarily her look downward at the table and the deliberate slowness of her words, as if she were trying to believe what she was saying.

"No," said Hanrahan. "Reliable source in a group of skinheads, positive ID from the people who sold the hair. You ask me, your brother is planning to do something very stupid."

"You don't understand," she said. "He wouldn't . . ." Her voice trailed off and then picked up to say, "He is all that is left of my family. Our politics are different, but we are a family."

"How are your politics different?" Lieberman asked.

She looked at him, bit her lower lip. She was, Lieberman thought, a remarkably beautiful young woman.

"I believe in the political or military destruction of the State of Israel," she said, looking directly at Lieberman. "I believe Arab nations should band together and fight war after war with Israel till we win. I am against the PLO land agreement. The land is ours. It should never have been an empty garbage sack for countries to get rid of their Jews who would want ever more land."

"So you hate Jews," said Lieberman.

"No," she said. "I hate Israelis. I do not hate Jews. I told you, my motives are political, never to let the world forget that we will get back that which was stolen from us, that we exist."

"Terror," said Lieberman.

"I don't believe in killing," she said. "I have seen enough killing. A day or two ago after the rally, after Howard Ramu's murder, I advocated local violence. I thought about it. Then I changed my mind. Attacks on American Jews are not the answer. That will only make it worse. Innocent Jews will suffer and then innocent Arabs."

She looked at an original painting on the wall not far from where she sat. It was abstract, light, something bright and yellow in the corner like the sun.

"When I was a child," she said, "my family was massacred by an Israeli, a doctor. We were on our way home. Our family, my uncle and his family. The Israeli had an automatic weapon. We had no chance. He didn't know us, knew only that we were a van filled with Palestinians, little children. The Israeli shot me. I was six. He shot me in the shoulder and was going to shoot again and then . . . an off-duty Israeli border guard, just a boy wearing glasses, shot the mad Jew. The madman went down, the *kepuh* on his head rolled into the darkness, blown by a night breeze I didn't feel. The Israeli soldier was crying. He checked my wound, wrapped it quickly with something from his pack, looked at my fallen, dead father and went back to the van. I remember that one of the lights of the van was still on, flickering, trying to stay alive. The soldier came back with my little brother in his arms. Massad's face was covered in blood. He still wears scars from the overturning of the van. The border guard said nothing. He was not a big man but he picked me up on one shoulder and carried my brother on the other. I don't know how far we walked along the road and then down a smaller road, one mile, two. I remember a breeze and the weeping of the soldier who kept telling us in Hebrew that we would be all right."

She stopped speaking.

"And?" asked Hanrahan.

"And," she said. "I do not hate Jews. A Jew saved my life. Saved my brother's life. For me it is politics."

"And for your brother?"

"He blames all Jews," she said, looking at Lieberman again. "Just as Jews hate Arabs."

"Temple Mir Shavot," Lieberman said. "The temple you and your friends defiled. Most of the members, almost all of the members don't hate Arabs. But there are a few, a few can't be changed. Jews who you don't hate suffered."

"In politics and terror people suffer."

"You said you don't believe in killing," said Hanrahan. "How about your brother?"

She didn't answer. Lieberman considered calling the waitress over for some more coffee. But the coffee was awful and his stomach was upset.

"Help us find him," said Lieberman. "Before he kills someone. Before someone kills him. Both sides have had enough martyrs. We need families."

Jara looked at the old Jew. He meant it. What he hadn't said was there was a very good chance that Massad Mohammed had already killed, ironically it had not been Jews but Howard Ramu and two innocent Arabs.

"Monday," she said. "Afternoon. Night. He has something planned ... something, but Massad said he would play no more Halloween pranks, that he had allies who would fire shots heard all the way to Syria and Israel."

"Where can we find him?" Lieberman asked.

"Mustafa Quadri was close to him," she said.

Quadri, Lieberman remembered, was the thin Arab with glasses who had been stripped of his bullhorn at the rally. Jara gave the policemen Mustafa's address. It made no difference. They could have obtained it from the university directory.

"I don't want my brother hurt," she said, sitting up with dignity.

"We don't want anybody hurt," said Hanrahan.

Jara thought about this for a moment and looked around the room. Her eyes fixed on a thin, young boy with a recent home haircut and a pair of glasses on his nose.

"That boy," she said. "He's a Jew. He reminds me of the soldier who carried me and my brother, saved our lives. The soldier was just a boy." She stood up and left without another word.

"So?" asked Hanrahan.

"We see this Quadri," said Lieberman, fishing in his pocket for his wallet for three dollars, which he laid on the table. The wallet was open to a photograph, a year out of date, of Barry and Melisa. Lieberman looked at the photograph for an instant and put the wallet away.

"Berk?" asked Hanrahan.

"Let's call the Pig Sticker," Lieberman suggested.

Hanrahan agreed, moved to a phone near the men's room with a bile green door, took out his notebook, and dialed a number.

Leary answered.

"What the fuck you callin' me here for?" Pig Sticker said with a hiss. "I room with a Monger. You're goddamn lucky he's out. We have a deal. I call you, you don't call me."

"Consider me chastised, Charles," said Hanrahan. "But you've taken a long time to get back."

"Nothing much is new," said Pig Sticker, nervous and angry.

"Nothing much?" asked the detective. "I've got another source that says something's going down on Monday for sure. You got something to add?"

The pause was long. Fallon might come back any second. Berk might even have the phone line tapped.

"Monday afternoon," said Pig Sticker. "Just the word. Nothing definite."

"You'll let me know when everything's definite," said Hanrahan.

"I'll let you know," said Pig Sticker, hanging up the phone with a bang.

"Monday p.m. confirmed, Rabbi," said Hanrahan. "We pick up the Monger, Berk?"

"Last resort. We won't get anything out of him. Might make him put off what he's planning for Monday. But it'll be another Monday or Tuesday. Agreed?"

"Agreed," said Hanrahan. "But the question is what kind of deal can this Arab kid Massad have with a guy like Berk who goes around saying Arabs should have their heads cut off and hung on schoolyard fences."

"We'll see," said Lieberman.

"Better we don't see, Rabbi," said Hanrahan. "Better we stop it before we see. Give me another second."

Hanrahan made another call. The phone rang nine times. Michael didn't answer. It wasn't even noon.

On the way out, past the tables and booths of earnest children and the bustling of teenage waitresses, Lieberman moved ahead to the door to give his partner something approaching privacy.

"It's a miracle," said Rabbi Wass.

In some things, Rabbi Wass was ideal. He worked hard, far beyond what was required of him, attending almost every interdenominational lunch and breakfast to which he was invited, meeting with other rabbis, priests, ministers. He knew Torah. He had a likable helplessness about him. But he didn't have his father's intellect. Rabbi Wass's sermons were not really disasters. They were tributes to a tradition that had become, for Congregation Mir Shavot, almost as much of a ritual as the Shabbat services.

"It's not a miracle," said Bess.

They were sitting around the table in the rabbi's office with Ida Katzman and Irving Hamel, who had announced at this very table moments ago that he was definitely running for state representative for his district, which included the land on which Temple Mir Shavot rested. This announcement came after three weary days of cleanup, mounting bills, and an outpouring of sympathy, indignation, and money from Jews and Gentiles alike. It was a good time for Hamel to throw his *kepuh* in the ring and run on a platform of community harmony and unity against hatred.

"Not a miracle," said Ida Katzman.

"This is the biggest campaign we've ever had," Rabbi Wass exclaimed, looking down at the computer printout in front of him. "Money came in from every suburb, all over the United States, some of it divided between the vandalized temples, some of it earmarked directly to us, over one hundred thousand dollars just for us, to redeem our Torah."

"One hundred thousand thirty-seven dollars and some change," said Hamel with a smile that showed his vital position on the temple board might be a very visible asset in his campaign, which would include a sturdy plank on tolerance and the need for anti-hate legislation throughout the state.

"In Florida," said Bess Lieberman, morning elegant, her silver hair set fashionably in place, her thoughts on many things, "a Jewish radio show on a small alternative station was having its annual campaign for a few thousand dollars. A foulmouthed anti-Semite called and said the Holocaust was a fraud and said that any decent American would cut his throat rather than give a penny to a Jewish radio show, a show, by the way, that made community announcements and played American and Israeli Jewish music. As soon as the anti-Semite hung up, the phones went wild, pledges rolled in. The host pointed out the irony of the caller's making the campaign a success."

"So?" said Rabbi Wass. "It's like what happened to us. Almost half is from non-Jews."

"About twenty-six percent," Hamel corrected. "Some from Christian organizations, some from individuals who definitely do not have Jewish names."

"Each donor will have to be sent a letter of thanks and a reminder that their gift is tax deductible," said Bess.

"Of course," said Rabbi Wass.

"I'll do the letters," said Bess. "They should have my name and Rabbi Wass's at the bottom. I can use the computer."

"We can ask some of the Sisterhood to help," said Rabbi Wass.

"If we get more than enough for the Torah, then some of that money that's pouring in should be spent on another computer, one from this century," said Bess.

It was Lieberman's opinion, confirmed by Said, that the vandals had no intention of returning the Torah. Money was not the issue.

As they moved down the agenda and Ida Katzman looked as if she were about to doze off, Bess came to the last item, New Business.

"We should continue to have volunteers here at night," said Bess.

"For how long?" asked Rabbi Wass.

"I don't know," said Bess. She hesitated and then went on wondering how she was not going to cross the line of Abe's confidence. "Another few weeks, maybe more. And Monday, Monday I think we should have people at the doors during services."

"Monday?" asked Rabbi Wass. "Why Monday?"

"Intuition," said Bess.

"Intuition is usually borne of subtle signs picked up by an alert but not necessarily logical individual," said Hamel, playing with his law school class ring. Unsaid was that the subtle signs had probably come from Detective Abraham Lieberman.

"People on the doors," said Ida Katzman, who wasn't sleeping. "Extra men all night Monday."

Rabbi Wass shrugged. When Ida Katzman spoke, it was law.

The man who Berk knew as Mr. Grits stood inside a public phone booth, the doors closed to traffic and possible intruders. He had a huge stack of quarters piled on the metal ledge. He looked at his watch and when the hour hand hit eleven he placed his call.

After two rings, the person on the other end, who was standing in a phone booth in Bedford, Montana, picked up the phone and said nothing.

"Monday afternoon or night," said Mr. Grits. "Everything set. I'll be out of here within one hour of the event, unidentified, on the means of transportation arranged. Be watchin' CNN."

The other person didn't answer. The other person in Bedford, Montana, tapped the phone twice, the signal to go ahead with the plan. And then the person in Bedford hung up the phone.

Mr. Grits was excited and ready. He had been through one military action in Panama. He hadn't been called up for Desert Storm and he didn't volunteer. By then, he didn't want an FBI check on his activities since his release from the service. He didn't want to be turned down for a chance to legally shoot down crazy Arabs, but he didn't want government computers humming about him. They probably had enough on him already, even as careful as he had been.

He hung up the phone, pocketed the remaining coins, and stepped out of the phone booth. He did his usual check, scanned the street and sidewalk and nearby cars with eyes hidden by tinted glasses. No one. Nothing.

He would spend an hour in the mall across the boulevard, making sure he was not being followed. They were close now. He had to be very careful. He had to play Berk like a steel guitar. Mr. Grits's favorite song was Creedence Clearwater Revival's "Bad Moon Rising." He hummed it as he waited for a break in the traffic.

Mustafa Quadri was home. He was really in no condition to be anywhere but home or in a hospital. His skull, he explained to the two policemen who had come only seconds before, was cracked like a coconut. Walking to the door to open it had made him dizzy. Sitting on the straight-back chair made him dizzy.

"Were I to sit in one of the more comfortable chairs," Quadri explained, "It would be a major event for me to rise. I take little yellow pills, Meclazine, but I remain dizzy. The price to be paid for one's principles."

Neither policeman had done anything so far but identify himself and take a seat in the chairs Mustafa Quadri had described as comfortable. The studio apartment was little more than the size of Lieberman's living room. There was a small round table with three chairs in one corner near the alcove that served as a kitchen. Bookshelves, simple wooden planks held up by concrete bricks, lined the walls. Books were everywhere. There was, however, no bed. Lieberman was certain one of the comfortable chairs opened into a single bed or there was a futon in the closet.

Quadri's head was heavily bandaged, the bridge of his glasses held together with Scotch tape.

"So," said Quadri folding his hands. "You wish me to identify the man who you have arrested, the Jew who hit me."

"You filed charges?" asked Hanrahan.

"Of course, is that not why you are here?" asked Quadri.

"No," said Lieberman. "My guess is the Hyde Park police are following up on that. We'll be happy to check with them to see what progress they've made."

Quadri shifted uneasily and winced from the pain. He folded his hands in front of him and looked from policeman to policeman.

"Then what do you want?"

"Who do we want," Hanrahan amended.

"Massad Mohammed," said Lieberman.

"I do not wish to discuss him," said Quadri. "I am deeply upset with him. The Arab Student Response Committee has been almost destroyed by his defection."

"Defection?" asked Hanrahan.

"He quit. Walked out."

"Why?" asked Lieberman.

"My head hurts," said the young man, closing his eyes.

Neither policeman thought Quadri was lying about the pain. So, they waited.

"I am considered something of a genius," Quadri said, eyes still closed. "I have read every book in this room and much more. But I cannot read now. It makes me dizzy. The words dance. The one who did this to me should be given the full punishment of the law."

"I agree," said Lieberman.

"I know everything in these books," said Quadri. "They are my life. Almost all are in English. Some are Arabic. Some German. Some French."

"Deuteronomy, chapter 13, verse 2," said Lieberman, vaguely remembering the passage from Rabbi Wass's last sermon.

Quadri smiled and opened his eyes saying, "If there arise in the midst of thee a prophet or a dreamer of dreams— and he give thee a sign or a wonder, and the sign or the wonder come to pass, whereof he spoke unto thee—saying: Let us go after other gods, which thou hast not known, and let us serve them; thou shalt not hearken unto the words of that prophet, or unto that dreamer of dreams. Enough?"

"Enough," said Lieberman. "Anything like that in the Koran?"

"Very much like that," said Quadri. "Would you like . . . ?"

"No," said Lieberman. "Are you a devout man?"

"Yes," said Quadri.

"May I suggest to you that Massad Mohammed is a false prophet, a dreamer of nightmares," said Lieberman. "He has given a false sign and follows one of the false gods."

"Yes," said Quadri with a sigh and a squint to keep his glasses from falling.

"We think he killed Howard Ramu and his two room-mates, all Arabs, all Moslems," said Lieberman. "And he tried to blame it on a Jew by leaving a bloody yarmulke in the room. He is following a false prophet following a false dream, making alliances with enemies. Do you know where he is?"

"No," said Quadri, putting a hand to his aching, bandaged head. "He moved. He hides such information from us all now."

"What is going to happen Monday?"

"I do not know," said Quadri. "Massad did say something about Monday when last we met, but it was without detail or substance. But I fear it will be violent. I fear that it will create even more contempt for our movement. Our leader . . ."

"Jara Mohammed," said Lieberman.

Quadri nodded and said, "She was angry after the rally. Had a moment of such anger that she suggested great violence, but she quickly changed her mind. Massad, however . . ."

"When did you last see Massad?" asked Hanrahan.

"Several days," said Quadri. "I cannot recall. My head, you see. It . . ."

"Well, thanks for your cooperation," said Lieberman, getting up. Hanrahan joined him.

"Please forgive me if I do not walk you to the door and forgive the fact that I've offered you no refreshment," said Quadri.

"We understand," said Lieberman.

"You are a Jew, are you not?" asked Quadri.

"Yes," said Lieberman. "And a member of Congregation Mir Shavot where you, Jara Mohammed, and Howard Ramu desecrated our temple."

Quadri looked away. "Does he have the Torah?" Lieberman asked.

"I will deny saying this in public. I will say that you coerced me, but it is my understanding that Howard Ramu was in possession of the Torah when he was murdered. I do not know who murdered Howard. I do know you should catch Massad. Stop him. He does follow a false god of vengeance."

"We plan to," said Hanrahan. "Get some rest."

In the hall, with the door closed behind them, Hanrahan said, "You were good in there, Rabbi."

"I liked him," said Lieberman.

"Yeah," said Hanrahan, looking at the door. "Yeah, and you liked the girl. They tear up your church, crap on your prayer shawls, and you like them."

"A paradox," said Lieberman.

"World's full of 'em," said Hanrahan. "You think Massad has your Torah, killed three Arabs to get it?"

"I don't know," said Lieberman. They walked down the stairs and out the front door of the musty apartment building.

"You don't know but you've got an idea," said Hanrahan, moving to the car.

"Maybe," Lieberman agreed, getting into the passenger side of the car.

Hanrahan got behind the wheel and closed the door. He looked at his partner's beagle of a face and said, "Well?"

"OK, let's say it. Why pick a Monday?"

Hanrahan shrugged wanting to find the nearest phone and hoping that Michael would answer this time, say he'd fallen asleep or was on the toilet when Hanrahan had called last.

"Random," said Hanrahan.

"Maybe," said Lieberman. "And maybe something's happening on Monday. If they're planning to attack Jews on a non-holiday Monday night, they aren't going to find a lot of victims at prayer."

"A restaurant," said Hanrahan. "Kosher restaurant."

"Possible. Very possible. Pattern?"

"Not enough information," said Hanrahan. "Only MO we've got is his killing the three Arabs with an automatic weapon and leaving one of those little Jewish caps to make it look like a lunatic Jew did it."

"What if we add in the attacks on the temples?" said Lieberman. "Tried to make it look like neo-Nazi or skinhead stuff. What if the Monday plan is to make the attack look like Jews against someone else."

"Arabs?" said Hanrahan. "This Massad is going to co-operate in killing more Arabs?"

"Looks like he's already killed three," said Lieberman. "Kill more Arabs, make it look like a vendetta of murder by Jews. Maybe they're holding onto the Torah to leave it at the massacre site."

"Maybe," said Hanrahan. "It feels slim, but it feels right, maybe. So who do we warn?"

It was Lieberman's turn to shrug. "You know," he said. "Sometimes you get a taste for something, a craving. Won't go away. Drives you crazy."

Hanrahan knew the drill. He started the car and drove slowly down the street.

"Where are we goin', Rabbi?"

"Kosher hot dog with everything," said Lieberman. "Fluky's."

"You're on a diet," Hanrahan said.

"Occasionally, a moment of respite and sustenance gives us the power to forge ahead," said Lieberman.

"It doesn't work that way, Rabbi," Hanrahan said.

"I know, Father Murphy, but as far as I know there's no place called Kosher Hot Dog Lovers Anonymous."

Kim lay in the hospital bed, thinking, planning, refusing to answer the pain, to acknowledge it.

He had received but three visitors. That was all that was allowed. The visit from the black woman named Lasher from the district attorney's office did not count. She had been brief and informative. First, both of Kim's men were dead. Second, the girl was a hero. Third, Kim should call his attorney as soon as he was up to it, and the attorney should call Lasher, who left her card. She had been pleasant. She had listened to his story of the girl making a murderous mistake. She had taken notes and then she had risen and said, "You better get a lawyer. You were up for extortion last week and this one could be pushed up to attempted murder."

"Two of my men were murdered. My arm . . . and I could be accused of attempted murder?"

"You want a public defender?"

He shook his head. Lasher left.

His parents had come to visit, had said almost nothing. His mother cried. Kim said he would be fine. They spoke in Korean. Kim was glad when they left. So were they.

Finally, Chung Lee came looking uncomfortable. Kim had closed his eyes and found Lee standing next to the bed when he opened them. Chung Lee was decidedly nervous.

"Who is still with us?" asked Kim weakly. "How many?"

Lee held up four fingers and then put one down.

Kim closed his eyes again. Three. They would probably all drop out, go on their own, join another gang if one would take them after this disgrace.

Lee wouldn't go. He was hulking, laughed too easily, was sad too easily, and was incredibly stupid. He would, however, do what Kim told him to do. He worshiped Kim. A time would come. Now, he told Lee where he had hidden a great deal of cash. He told Lee to call his lawyer and to bring two thousand dollars of the cash to the lawyer and to tell the lawyer to come see Kim tomorrow.

It was a lot for Lee to remember.

"What do I do with the rest of the money?" asked Lee.

"Put it back. We'll take it as we need it till it runs out. I must sleep now."

"Will you die?" asked Lee, his eyes moist.

"No," said Kim, closing his eyes.

"Will you lose your arm?"

"Yes," said Kim.

Lee left, and Kim went back to thinking. He had been informed. He had consented. The arm would be removed in the morning. The pain was bitter. Why couldn't it have been his left arm not his right? Now he would have to learn to write, shoot, do everything with his left hand. Can you drive with one hand? Would he have to go to prison, defend himself in prison with one arm?

It certainly wouldn't be soon, Kim thought, but there

would be a day when the pain and humiliation the girl caused him would be returned to her one hundred times over and if that meant killing the two policemen, then he would kill them too. In fact, he might have no choice. For when he killed the girl, the two policemen would obviously come looking for him.

If he were to cover his scars, those inside and out, the girl and the two policemen would have to die. He tried to wiggle the fingers on his right hand. His arm hurt just above the elbow even though he was filled with pain-killing medication. But he felt nothing in his fingers. He expected to feel nothing.

Kim stopped trying and went back to his thoughts. He had a great deal of time to plan.

FOURTEEN

ELI TOWSER WAS seated at a table in the library awk-wardly and, perhaps, painfully, turning the pages of a book. It was still early and the library was not yet teeming with the aged, bored, and parents and children.

Lieberman had found Towser by going to the young man's apartment on Peterson Avenue where Mrs. Towser, a slight, pale, blonde woman with short hair and a not particularly becoming green dress, reluctantly let him in when he showed his badge and gave his name.

The apartment was small and the woman young, nervous, and defensive. Lieberman liked her. For one reason, regardless of her fear, her eyes met his.

"What has Eli done?" she had said. "Eli is a good man, Detective Lieberman."

"I know," said Lieberman.

"Oh," she said. "I'm sorry, please sit. I'll get coffee, tea?"

"Neither," said Lieberman, sitting.

The room was rather grimly decorated, from the heavy

dark couch and almost matching armchair to the pair of unmatched bookcases against the wall. There was a copy of a painting on the wall, a painting Lieberman had seen once before and which had haunted him for years, three little girls swinging solemnly around on a schoolyard thing that looked like a swing. Behind the girls were the ruins of a devastated city with buildings torn apart. Lieberman thought it was by Ben Shahn. He forced himself to look away from it.

"I need to talk to Eli," he had said.

"If you leave your number, when he returns . . ." she began.

"I don't have the time. Tomorrow is Monday. Do you know what's going to happen tomorrow?"

Towser's wife was sitting on the sofa, her legs together. Lieberman was on the chair, leaning forward. The girl looked genuinely puzzled by the question. "No," she said.

"Eli might," said Lieberman. "He might be able to save lives, keep Jews from being accused of an atrocity."

She smiled in disbelief, but stopped when she realized the man with the look of a sad dog was serious.

"How could Eli do that?" she said.

"Maybe he can't. I'll know when I ask him," said Lieberman.

"He's at the public library," she said. "His arm was broken at a rally. He can't go far without pain and he had something he said he had to look up. It's very hard to do one's prayers with one hand. Eli is not in a good mood."

"Thanks for the warning," said Lieberman, rising.

She had risen too. "Eli is a good man," she repeated.

Lieberman nodded. He would withhold judgment. "You were at the rally," Lieberman said, remembering a blonde in a dark dress near Eli Towser. He did not, however, remember seeing her in any of the photographs.

"Yes," she said.

Lieberman thanked her and left, heading for the library, where he would have no trouble spotting Towser even had he not known him. The cast was on his left arm in such a way that it was bent at the elbow and resting in an awkward sling. He was sitting alone, his *kepuh* clipped to his curly dark hair.

Lieberman sat opposite Towser and waited patiently, hands folded. Towser was either too absorbed in what he was reading or refused to acknowledge the presence of his former employer.

Towser went on reading awkwardly. Lieberman was fairly sure from the young man's eye movements that he was not reading at all, just pretending. Finally, Towser put a pencil in the book as a marker and looked up at Lieberman. Towser touched his beard and waited, showing nothing and looking directly into his eyes as Sarah Towser had done.

"Tomorrow is Monday," said Lieberman softly, though there was no one near their table.

"Thank you for coming all the way here to inform me of this important fact," whispered Towser with a sincerity that made his sarcasm all the more biting.

He would, Lieberman thought, make an effective rabbi.

"Something is going to happen tomorrow," said Lieberman.

"Something happens every day," said Towser.

Lieberman touched his mustache and nodded his head.

"Tomorrow," he said, "something bad is going to happen. We have reason to believe that a group of skinheads, perhaps with the help of a fanatic Arab individual or group, is going to do something violent, something they plan to blame on Jews, possibly, if they can, blame on your group."

Towser shook his head. "My 'group' is the Jewish people which is also your 'group.'"

"OK," said Lieberman, holding up his hands. "I thought it was worth a try. The FBI hasn't come up with anything. Our informants haven't come up with anything. We're not even sure, to tell you the truth, that they plan to attack a non-Jewish group. They might be going after a Jewish restaurant or a temple while people are worshiping."

Towser sat thinking for a moment while Lieberman tried

to see what book the young man was reading. Towser turned the book around so that the detective could read it. The book was *Rejoice O Youth: Comprehensive Jewish Ideology* by Avigdor Miller. "This book made a great impression on me when I was younger," Towser said, trying to shift his cast to a less uncomfortable position. "I had an urge to revisit it. I have no copy of my own."

"And?" asked Lieberman.

"If one keeps an open mind," said the young man, "one finds that the past is constantly changing and a book or person revisited may not be the entity we thought it before. It is the price we pay for spiritual growth. It is the reason the Talmud exists and why scholars continue to debate it."

Lieberman waited. Eli Towser was not just lecturing. He was coming to a decision. "Wait," he said, rising. "I have a phone call to make."

Towser moved past the check-out desk toward the two phones near the front door of the library. Lieberman could see him awkwardly fish out a quarter, insert it, dial, and wait. Then someone came on the line. Lieberman couldn't hear it, but the discussion was apparently heated for the first minute or two and then moved to a calm with Towser listening. He hung up the phone after about three minutes and returned to the table.

People were coming into the branch library now, children holding their parents' hands, anxious to pull away and explore, a few of the homeless, and a dozen or so old men and women who came to spend a morning off the streets or away from the loneliness of their apartments.

Towser said, "You'll need to write this down," making it clear that his own memory was sufficient so that he had not felt the need to write down the information while on the phone. It was also questionable, given his disabled arm, that he could have written down the information.

Lieberman took out his notebook and pen.

"Temple Emanuel in Albany Park is having an evening meeting of the Sisterhood. Muslims will meet for prayer in the following three locations."

Lieberman wrote as Towser spoke softly.

"And," Towser said, "the most likely target is a meeting of the so-called Honorable Martin Abdul and the board of the African Muslim Church, militantly anti-Semitic. Should be about sixteen senior members of the advisory board and maybe a guest or two. Abdul has, as you may have noted in the newspapers and on television, increased his verbal attacks on the Jewish people and his attempt to incite black people to attack Jews. He has furthered the division between two peoples who should be working in concert, political and defensive, from our mutual enemies."

"A perfect target for a partnership of Arab terrorists and neo-Nazi skinheads," said Lieberman.

"Kill them and blame it on us," said Towser. "Get rid of a group of blacks who they hate and fear and blame it on the Jews, who they also hate and fear. And then the union between Arab militants and Nazi skinheads will end in war between the two allies. The repetition of history."

"Anything else?" said Lieberman.

Towser shook his head. Lieberman closed his notebook and put it away.

"Thanks, Eli," he said.

"I gave you this information to try to protect Jews," said the young man. "And as much as I despise Martin Abdul and what he represents, I do not wish him dead until his spewing forth of hate results in the first attack on a Jew. Though at the moment," he continued, holding up his heavily cast arm, "there is little I can do in the way of retaliation."

Towser awkwardly opened the book he had been reading and made it clear that the discussion had ended.

"We've looked at the photographs," said Lieberman. "The man who broke your arm may be the Arab working with the skinheads, the Hate Mongers." Towser looked up at Lieberman, blinked once, and went back to his book.

Lieberman went into the children's room, directly to the line of books by Roald Dahl and picked out the only two he had not read to Melisa. His own daughter, Lisa, had

read the Dahl books over and over. Her favorite had been
Matilda.

Lieberman walked past Towser, who did not look up as
the policeman checked out the books, and left.

When Hanrahan had come home late the night before, his
son Michael was sitting in the kitchen, a half-full cup of
coffee in his hand, watching CNN on the small black-and-
white next to the refrigerator. Michael was wearing a pair
of white undershorts with a DePaul Blue Demon printed
on the right leg. His T-shirt was a match, white with a Blue
Demon in the center.

Hanrahan had already left his jacket neatly hung in the
front closet. He still wore his holster and gun. He turned
off the television and poured himself a cup of coffee.

"Not hot," said Michael. "I microwaved this."

Hanrahan's son held up his cup and gave a small smile.
Hanrahan nodded and put his cup of coffee in the microwave. While it hummed, he turned toward his son who was
clean shaven, hair still wet from a very recent shower.

"CNN was talking about military spending," Michael explained after taking a sip of coffee.

Hanrahan, standing near the refrigerator, nodded once
again. The microwave stopped humming and Hanrahan
took out the mug. It was white, his old "Hill Street Blues"
cup. Michael had given it to him on Father's Day a long
time ago. The writing on it in dark blue said, "Let's be
careful out there."

Hanrahan sat across from his son and took a sip of the
coffee. It was hotter than he liked, but he drank.

"How was your day?" Michael asked.

"I chased bad guys, tried to ignore aching knees, and
called my son who wasn't here," said Hanrahan, looking at
Michael who forced himself to face his father.

"Must have been in the shower," said Michael with a
shrug.

"I called around noon," said Hanrahan. "and then at two. How many showers do you take a day?"

"I was on the back porch reading part of the day," Michael said. "Short story collection I brought with me. I think you might like some of it. I can mark the ones I think are especially good."

Hanrahan nodded and said, "Which chair did you take out there?"

"I don't know. One of these. The one you're sitting on, I think, why?"

"Not a great day to be outside reading," said Hanrahan. "The rain and all. And the eave leaks. But it accounts for your not answering the phone."

"I felt cooped up in the house," Michael said with a sigh "A little rain wasn't bad."

"Michael," Hanrahan said, leaning forward. "We stop the bullshit right now or you go upstairs and pack. You get dressed. I shake your hand, give you a hug, wish you luck and say 'goodbye.' I'm a cop and I'm an alcoholic and I'm your father. Lying to me is a humiliation to you and an insult to me."

Michael rose, moved to the sink, poured out what remained of the coffee in his mug, rinsed the mug, and put it in the dishwasher. His father waited patiently, quietly, drinking his coffee.

"It was just a couple of beers, for Chrissake," said Michael, looking down at the familiar linoleum on the kitchen floor. It was well worn in front of the refrigerator and around the table. Michael remembered thinking when he was a kid that you could see the pattern of white with blue lines as squares or diamonds depending on where you stood. "You said you'd be home early and we'd . . ."

"Michael," Hanrahan said. "You were drinking in the morning and afternoon."

His son's head jerked up as if he had been dozing.

"Last chance," said the father.

"The two beers were chasers," said Michael. "For my

first real day, compared to where I was a week ago, I'd say that's not too bad."

"It doesn't work that way, Mike," Hanrahan said, motioning for his son to sit back down. Michael obeyed. "You stop. You get help and you stop. You decide that you want to stop. You may not be off it forever and you may need help the rest of your life, but you start by stopping."

Michael glanced up at his father, back at the table, and then up again before saying in an angry whisper, "Where were you when this started, when I needed you? You were deeper in the bottle than I am."

"True, but I'm out now and trying to make me feel guilty about the past isn't going to do you any good in the present or future. I was a half-assed, nonpresent alcoholic father. I never hit you or your mother or your brother, but I wasn't here. We're talking about you, Michael. You want to stop, give Smedley Ash a call. You come to an AA meeting with me tomorrow night. You stay in the house and you don't have a drink during the day."

"Is that part of the AA code?" asked Michael.

"The part about staying home alone all day is all my own idea," said Hanrahan. "It's the deal. Last chance. Take it or not. If you decide to leave, I'd rather you did it in the morning so I can say goodbye, but . . ."

"Tough love," said Michael.

"All love is tough," said Hanrahan. He gave a single, short laugh. "I've turned second-rate Irish philosopher in my middle age. Pretty soon I'll bore myself." He looked at his son for a response. "You know what I'm aching to do, Mike? I'm aching to tell you to get dressed so we can go to one of the bars I used to get drunk in. We could get happy, loving, remember the few good times when you were a kid, and I could tell you parts of my life story you don't know. We'd be pals, buddies, drunks together. It has its appeal, Michael, but it's not worth the price."

Michael Hanrahan rose and brushed back his hair. "What time's the meeting tomorrow?"

"Seven."

Michael nodded and left the room. Hanrahan listened to the stairs creaking. There were twelve of them. He had counted them a thousand times, mounted them in the dark, counting out loud and thinking he was being silent. Maureen had always heard him coming up in darkness, drunk. He only had to count when he was really drunk. The light was out in the hall. He wondered if his son was counting.

Twenty minutes later, Bill Hanrahan had taken a shower, shaved, and brushed his teeth. He smelled good even to himself from the shampoo Iris had given him, something from China. It reminded him of Iris. He placed his gun on the night table near his hand where he always put it since Maureen and the boys had left. Before that, if he were sober enough, he put holster and weapon in the night table. He put on his orange terrycloth shorts and plain, white T-shirt and got into bed. He slept on top of the blankets unless it got really Chicago winter cold. He slept with a pillow in his arms. He looked at the gun and turned off the light on the table.

When he had been alone for three days, he had taken to putting the weapon within reach. He told himself that with no other people in the house, a burglar might think it was easy pickings. The neighborhood had gone down. What did it hurt to be extra careful?

Smedley Ash had suggested that he kept the weapon within easy reach so he could suddenly one night put the barrel in his mouth and pull the trigger, do it all quick, barely thinking.

Hanrahan had come to the conclusion that Smedley was right. Now he kept the weapon nearby to remind him how close the bottle had come to actually killing him. Had he pulled that trigger one night in the dark, there would have been no Iris, no Michael in the next room, no more job, no more banter with Lieberman, no meeting Father Parker.

Hanrahan checked the clock. It was a little after one. He set the alarm for seven. Now that he was sleeping more or less normally that was all the rest he needed. He had called Iris earlier, arranged for her to join him and Michael for late dinner the next day, actually that day, Sunday.

Hanrahan lay listening. He heard his son pacing slowly, the radio in his room tuned softly enough so that Hanrahan did not know if the gentle vibration was talk or music. He wondered if Michael would be there when he woke up in the morning. He lay on his back and fell asleep.

Before he had gone to find Eli Towser at the public library, Lieberman had spent one of his many nearly sleepless nights. He had chronic insomnia, had it since he was a boy. His father had suffered from it before Lieberman, and his father thought the malady had gone on for generations.

Bess was a sound sleeper, accustomed to her husband getting in and out of bed, taking baths in the middle of the night, dozing off in the hot water and occasionally destroying one of her *Architectural Digest*s or one of his own *Atlantic Monthly*s.

There were occasional times when Lieberman could sleep all night, fall asleep in an instant. This could go on for a week, even two and then, the insomnia would return.

Lieberman had locked his weapon in the side drawer next to his and Bess's bed with the key he wore around his neck all night. Lieberman slept best during the day when he was on all-night shift, but now he was a senior detective, day shift, worked extra hours if the job needed it.

Abe Lieberman had learned that fighting his insomnia did no good. He went along with it, read, sometimes watched an old movie on AMC, tried not to think about work, his daughter, his wife, his grandchildren. He sought a meditation in the mindlessness of television, a magazine, a book. He had even played Tetris on Barry's Game Boy at three in the morning. Lieberman was terrible at the game, but time passed and he could sometimes fall asleep in his chair, the game in his hand.

Abe had simply learned to live with sleeplessness. The hardest part was staying out of the kitchen, keeping himself from the refrigerator and the shelves of cans and boxes of

matzoh and almost-healthy cookies. Occasionally, he wondered why his brother had escaped the curse of insomnia.
Maish slept soundly, eight hours every night, always had.
Retained the nickname "Nothing Bothers Maish" through
the Alter Cockers, even though he had earned it almost half
a century ago at the free-throw line. During a routine, required annual medical exam a few years ago, the doctor
had suggested that the weary look Abe wore was partially
due to his insomnia. Abe had pointed out that his brother,
who could sleep through the coming of the Messiah, looked
just as weary as did Abraham Lieberman. The doctor had
refused to withdraw his tentative conclusion. Lieberman did
it for him. He knew the difference between heredity and a
lack of sleep. His mirror reminded him every morning and
frequently in the middle of the night.

The idea of finding Towser had come to him while he
sat in his chair in the darkness of the living room watching
Claudette Colbert step out of a black-and-white bath, her
body hidden by the huge towel held up by her ladies in
waiting to hide Claudette's body from the camera.

By the time he had moved to his chair, Lieberman had
already bathed, read an entire six-month-old *Architectural
Digest*, trying to make out the titles of the books on the
shelves of the wealthy and famous, and shaved. He had
also read some poetry in old issues of his *Atlantic Monthly*.
It had been about a man driving to work who couldn't get
the word "Pondecherry" out of his mind. It rang true. Lieberman had laid out all of his clothes for the coming day,
considered trying to get back into bed, and decided against
it.

That's when he had found *Cleopatra* on AMC and that's
when the Eli Towser idea had come to him. He didn't remember clicking off the television or falling asleep.

When he awoke, he felt a weight on his chest. Light was
coming through the window. It was just past dawn. And
for an instant, Lieberman concluded that he was having a
heart attack. Well, what better place than in his chair and
what better attire than his pajamas. The instant thought was

gone and then he considered that he was dreaming of his daughter Lisa, little Lisa as she had been when she was no more than seven, lying in his arms, sleeping against his chest, wearing the white nightgown he and Bess had given her for one of her eight Hanukkah presents. And then Lieberman was awake and realized, that it was his granddaughter asleep against him breathing gently. He sat there enjoying the feeling, remembering that Lisa had done the same thing almost thirty years before. He had forgotten till this moment that when Lisa had awakened in his arms, she had reluctantly admitted that she had a bad dream.

Lieberman rose, gently cradling his granddaughter whose eyes flickered as he carried her up the stairs to her bedroom.

"Is it morning?" Melisa asked.

"It's morning, butterfly," he said. "But you could use a little more sleep."

Melisa closed her eyes. Lieberman put her in bed and stood looking at her for two or three minutes while she clutched her Simba and slept. Then he had gotten dressed, kissed his sleeping wife who muttered something unintelligible, and headed for the T & L. He arrived fifteen minutes before the deli officially opened but Maish was there and showed not the least surprise at looking up from mopping the floor to see his brother.

"Coffee's ready," Maish had said. "Help yourself. I'm mopping."

Abe went behind the counter and found a cup. The dishes, utensils, napkins, everything was lined up, spotless.

"You mopped last night?" Abe said, coming around the counter with his coffee.

"Every night," said Maish.

"Now every morning," said Abe.

Maish, who had given up all hope of diet after his son David's death, was now devoted to making his small part of the world clean and orderly. Maish's wife said he did the same thing at home and was driving her crazy, though she knew why he was doing it.

"Nothing Bothers Maish," Lieberman had said, sipping the hot coffee.

Maish had let out a sardonic laugh that was closer to a grunt as he continued mopping. "The temple looks good," said Maish. "Maybe better than before."

Maish had helped with the cleanup. When David had died, Maish had not lost his faith. He had simply refused to talk to God. There was no reason, no excuse, nothing about the mystery of God's actions, that Maish could consider. He would go to services. He would be a temple member. He would give to the poor, but he would sit there ignoring God and his word until the Lord actually appeared before him to explain the inexplicable. Maish very much doubted that God would ever make such an appearance.

"Eli Towser," Abe had said.

Maish knew all in the Jewish community. Pieces of that community moved in and out of the T & L. Maish listened, his sagging face a mask, his memory a better source of information than anyone else in the community. He knew a great deal about Eli Towser.

"Bitter young man," Maish said still mopping. "That's why you stopped his giving bar mitzvah lessons to Barry."

Abe was seated at the counter on one of the swivel chairs facing his brother, drinking his coffee. "You think I was wrong?"

"You didn't ask me," said Maish. "Your decision. I think Towser has a right to be bitter. I think we all do. Between us, Towser is smarter than Rabbi Wass. Barry was learning more from Towser than Wass."

"But what was he learning, Maish?"

"The truth," said Maish pausing and leaning on the mop handle as he looked at his brother. "That you have to protect yourself, your people. That we're surrounded by hate and all we have are less than the tip of a toothpick compared to the tubful of people in this world."

Maish had spoken without passion. Abe had nodded. "You did what you believed you had to do," said Maish, resuming his mopping.

"Towser," said Abe.

"Eli Towser," Maish said, finishing the floor and standing back to see if there were some spot he may have missed. "He's a member of the Jewish Salvation Movement, small, well informed. I give them information sometimes. They keep track of hate groups. The Anti-Defamation League is minor league compared to the Jewish Salvation Movement, which believes in taking its own action when they know a group or individual plans to attack Jews with words or actions. Can you believe it, Abraham? When we were kids on the West Side, we lived in what most of the city called Jew Town. We thought half the world was Jewish. No one attacked us for what we were or believed. That's what we thought. We were wrong."

Abe finished his coffee and started around the counter being careful not to step in places that were still wet.

"Leave the cup," Maish said. "I want to clean it myself."

Abe nodded and made his way to the door as Maish put his mop away and said, "Leave the door open. It's time."

Lieberman turned to look at his brother who was already behind the counter, scrubbing Abe's coffee cup. Lieberman went outside. The sky was reasonably clear, his light windbreaker just right for the slight nip of late spring weather.

He had a slight but definite queasiness in his stomach. He should have eaten something with his coffee.

Abe headed for his car and waved at Herschel Rosen who was making his way slowly down the street. The first of the Alter Cockers. Maish's day could begin.

FIFTEEN

THEY HAD MOVED to the large interrogation room, the largest space in the station that would hold everyone at the meeting. The squad room across the hall was teeming with the sound of arrivals, departures, complaints, not-particularly-inventive foul language, and the rest of a normal Sunday's activity.

There was a new white board in the interrogation room. Captain Alan Kearney wrote on it with a red marker that squeaked down everyone's back. Kearney wore a suit and tie and looked dressed for a wedding. In fact, he had gone to church that morning with his parents for the christening of his cousin's new baby. Only this emergency meeting had saved Kearney from a day of family politeness, frequent toasts, and a vast array of cookies, cakes, and candies followed by a massive dinner featuring his mother's famous ham, and his Aunt Megan's equally famous apple cake, both of which Alan Kearney had always hated.

"OK," said Kearney, looking hard at what he had written and then turning to the people seated around the table. No one at the table was a smoker, though half of them had been at one time. Still, the room smelled of cigarettes and the smell was sure to stay in their clothes. "What do we have?"

Harley Buel, who looked like a forty-year-old bald school principal, said, "Our source is supposed to call as soon as he knows what's going down?"

"Right," said Bill Hanrahan, seated next to his partner who drank water from a Styrofoam cup. Lieberman's stomach had been bothering him all the time he had talked to Eli Towser at the library that morning. He was sure it was the coffee he had drunk at the T & L. Lieberman had now come to the conclusion that whatever was wrong with his stomach, coffee made it worse. He remembered watching a 2 a.m. taped interview with some sexy movie star.

Lieberman had gone home after talking to Towser and called Kearney, who set up the meeting. Abe had picked up Bess and the kids and headed for Lincoln Park. Barry and Melisa argued in the back seat. Bess touched his hand in the front seat. She knew something was bothering him and she knew where they were going and why.

When they got to the zoo, Lieberman headed directly for the ape building. Bess took the kids promising them overpriced, tasteless hot dogs from a vendor and visits to tigers and the children's zoo. Lieberman had sat watching the gorillas. Crowds moved past him, children whined, a few wondered about the old man who sat there mesmerized by the apes. There was one gorilla, Abe didn't know its name, who would occasionally meet the detective's eyes. They would stare knowingly at each other for a few seconds and then the ape would turn away. When Bess and the kids came to pick him up, Abe felt better.

"Why do you do that, grandpa?" Melisa asked.

"Your grandpa finds gorillas soothing," said Bess, guiding the brood through the crowd. They had already eaten. The sky was overcast but not enough to promise rain. They had gone home where Lieberman ate a bowl of potato barley soup and played a game of Uncle Wiggly with Melisa.

Barry had felt confident enough with his grandfather's promise, that it was definitely safe to play baseball at the JCC. Barry had left and Bess had gone to some temple committee meeting. Sunday was a good day for meetings if you weren't Christian.

Bess had changed since the attack on Mir Shavot. It was slight and Lieberman knew that he was the only one who noticed. She was a drop more serious, and an atom more determined with a protected darkness, a sadness inside her. Only Lieberman could see it. It was the Torah. The missing Torah. Who had it? What were they doing with it or what had they done to it? She had said nothing to Lieberman about it. He knew and had stopped just short of promising its return.

And now Lieberman sat listening at the table in the interrogation room, drinking a cup of water from the cooler, and wanting a cup of coffee.

The only person in the room wearing a suit and tie besides Captain Kearney was Special Agent Triplett of the FBI, who sat erect drinking real coffee, at least the stuff Nestor Briggs made every morning that many swore was from a special supply of cheap coffee beans that had been rejected by Juan Valdez.

Rene Catolino wore a dress and sweater. The dress was a brown knit. The sweater was a muted green. Lieberman, Hanrahan, Said, and Tony Munoz all wore lightweight zipper jackets, slacks, and shirts of various colors.

"Summary," said Kearney. "A group of skinheads led by William Stanley Berk with the help and possible participation of Massad Mohammed either working on his own or with one or more dissident Arabs is going to dress up like Jews and stage a raid on a meeting of Martin Abdul's black Muslims. They're going to leave definite clues that the raid was conducted by Jews who may or may not blame them for the synagogue attacks. That it? Anybody see it any other way?"

"Lots of ways to see it," said Triplett. "Information is leaking all over the place, from your source inside the skinhead group, a guy who sells hairpieces, Massad's sister. I can see Massad doing this, taking this chance, though I think he'd prefer the direct approach of simply killing a group of Jews and blaming it on black Muslims."

"I agree," said Said. "Massad claims that his principal goal is to discredit Jews and drive them from Israel. I think his goal is to purge his anger by killing Jews."

"Berk?" asked Kearney.

"Similar problems," said Hanrahan. "Why does he need to work with Massad? Why a massacre? Why not kill Jews and blame Arabs or blacks?"

"Detective Hanrahan has a point," said the FBI man. "Berk has managed to spend no more than a few hours in jail his whole life. He has no criminal record other than a long sheet of arrests for disturbing the peace. None of the arrests resulted in convictions. He's smart. Whatever violence he's done before, it's probably always been short of murder, at least as far as we know."

"A new incentive," said Lieberman.

"New incentive?" asked Kearney. "What 'new incentive?' "

"Sex, money, fame," said Lieberman with a shrug. "Maybe he has a brain tumor or stomach cancer and he wants to go out in a flash, a martyr, betraying his Arab partner, killing who knows who, a bunch of uppity blacks."

"That what you really think, Abe?" asked Kearney.

"Money," said Lieberman. "That's my guess."

"Money? From where?" Kearney asked. "From who? Massad?"

Lieberman looked at the FBI agent, who paused for a long beat and finally said, "There are well-funded groups, white supremacists, who we think have been making payoffs to small groups around the country to spread anti-Jewish and anti-black feelings. It's a small coalition. They don't use phones that can be easily tapped. They don't keep books. They don't use fax machines and they don't put anything in writing. They send dispatchers who make deals with groups like Berk's, pay off, and disappear without giving their names or even letting themselves be seen by the people they're paying."

"And what makes you think that might be happening here?" asked Kearney.

"One of the dispatchers for one of the bigger, wealthier groups is in the area," said Triplett. "Been here for about five weeks. He may be the one who brought the plan, whatever it is, and is making a pay-off to Berk, probably a personal pay-off. We've got an informant in this dispatcher's group. Low ranking but reliable. We haven't been able to pinpoint the exact location of this dispatcher yet, but he's here and he may be handing Berk cash, maybe a lot of cash."

"And you wait till now to tell us?" asked Kearney.

"We're following up on it," said Triplett. "We're not certain this is the situation, but . . ."

"When do we move?" asked Tony Munoz. They all looked at Triplett, who looked at Kearney. "Do we pick up Berk now, maybe some of his people? Massad?" Munoz said. "Let 'em know we know what's going on. Make 'em uncomfortable."

"We'd like a felony in progress," said Triplett. "A felony and the clear breaking of civil rights law."

"Then we're playing with the lives of—if we're right— Martin Abdul and his buddies, not that I'd send flowers to their funeral," said Rene Catolino.

"Since Detective Lieberman's information came to us this morning," said Triplett, "we've alerted Martin Abdul. He doesn't particularly trust the federal government in general and the Bureau in particular and insists that he can take care of any problems that might arise. Our man dealing with Mr. Abdul believes Abdul thinks we're setting up a trap for him, that we've concocted a government plot to kill him and blame Jews, Arabs, skinheads, whoever."

"So," said Lieberman, "we save him in spite of himself."

Kearney looked at the FBI man.

"I'd like to talk to Agent Triplett alone," said Kearney. "We'll work out response details. This room is headquarters, direct phone line, operational with a live officer twenty-four hours a day till this is over. Detective Hanrahan calls as soon as his informant gives some information. Then we move. All my people are on duty from four till who knows when. In or near this room. Objections, Agent Triplett?"

"None," said Triplett. "The Bureau will have a team ready. Low profile. It's your show."

"So I've been told by my chief," said Kearney.

Lieberman didn't look up but he read the subtext. It was Kearney's squad that had come up with this plot. It was crazy, but it was possible. Downtown didn't want to touch it in case it was a fizzle and the media found out. The FBI wanted a low profile for the same reason. Captain Alan Kearney was out there alone and if he read the information wrong and there was some kind of deadly attack that he missed, it would be all his. Once Kearney had been the department's Irish hope. Then things had gone wrong and now he was high on the list of department scapegoats. He looked tired all the time and Lieberman could see that the man was in a constant battle with himself to keep from losing control.

"Agent Triplett?" Kearney said. It was the sign for everyone else to leave. They did. Rene was the last one out. She closed the door and resisted the urge to pause for a few seconds to try to catch part of the conversation. She had a date with her dentist, named Marty Stevenson. He was divorced, had a good practice, and was in great shape, ranked among the top ten squash players in the country in the over-fifty group. Marty had nice hands.

Hanrahan and Lieberman went back to their face-to-face desks near the window of the squad room. Sundays were busy. Sundays were loud. People weren't working. They got into trouble. Hanrahan was sure someone had vomited in the squad room in the not-distant past.

"You want a coffee, Rabbi?" asked Hanrahan.

Lieberman said no and looked around the room as

Hanrahan got himself a cup. Victims bleeding, angry, perps feigning innocence, maybe even a few of them innocent. Most of them in this district were Hispanic, though it had its share of blacks and poor whites. One of the black guys, a big man who looked a little like George Foreman, sat at Roper's desk bleeding from a cut deep on top of his shaved head. He was trying to staunch it with a towel that may have been slowing the bleeding but, depending on where the towel came from, might be infecting him with viruses undreamed of except in the recesses of a Chicago district station.

Hanrahan returned. "Well, Rabbi?" he asked.

Lieberman watched his partner drink the coffee. His stomach immediately told him not to consider what he was considering.

"Took Bess and the kids to the zoo this afternoon," said Lieberman.

"Gorillas?" said Hanrahan, knowing his partner.

"Even when they're shitting right in front of dozens of people, locked up for no crime they committed, they have dignity," said Lieberman. For Lieberman it was either the great apes or, during the baseball season, the Cubs. "Got a call from Lisa on the machine when we got home. She's coming tomorrow for a few days, bringing a friend. We thought we wouldn't see her till Barry's bar mitzvah."

"A friend?" asked Hanrahan, now certain that someone had vomited in the squad room and someone else had done a half-assed job of cleaning it up.

"A black guy, doctor, medical examiner," said Lieberman. "They'll talk to each other and I won't understand a word they're saying. Then she'll tell me they're getting married."

"You sure?"

"Why else?" said Lieberman.

Hanrahan nodded. He knew his partner was right. "How's the family going to take it?" he asked.

"They'll get used to it," said Lieberman. "They'll talk

when we're not around, make 'Guess Who Came to Dinner' jokes, feel sorry for me and Bess. It'll come. It'll pass, not completely, but with time, it'll pass."

"Iris and I have a date," said Hanrahan. "We're going out for dinner with the priest to talk it over. Michael's coming too. Maybe Smedley if he can get away."

Lieberman nodded.

"I thought he was going to leave last night, Rabbi," said Hanrahan, looking out the window at the parking lot full of cars. "But he stayed. I think he's got a chance, but . . . ?"

"But, indeed, Father Murphy. You think I can talk this guy into becoming a Jew?" asked Lieberman.

"The black doctor? I think you're going to try," said Hanrahan. "Iris won't turn Catholic. She wants to try to have a kid. I think it's too dangerous at her age, but she wants to try. Says we can raise him or her as a Catholic."

"Doctor say?"

"Iris has the body of a thirty-year-old and the health of an aerobics fanatic," said Hanrahan. "Doctor says there's a chance we could pull it off."

"You want to, Father Murphy?"

"I want to get a chance to do it right, Abe. This time I want to do it right."

Lieberman nodded and wondered if a Diet Coke with caffeine would be tempting the gods. He decided to tempt the gods. "You think Leary will come through?" asked Lieberman.

"I don't know, to tell the truth," said Hanrahan. "You think?"

"I had a good feeling about him," said Lieberman. "Anti-Semitic bastard, but he's got something that passes for a conscience."

"If he doesn't," said Hanrahan, throwing his empty cup in the overflowing wastebasket, "it's gonna come down the ladder and land on us."

"Not the first time," said Abe.

"Not the first time," agreed Hanrahan.

*   *   *

On Sunday, Robert Kim lost his right arm. The surgery went quickly but there were complications caused by a loss of blood and shock. The surgeon, a near-retirement physician named Stringman, saved enough of a stump so a prosthetic arm could be more easily fitted and manipulated.

After almost two hours of surgery, Dr. Stringman, after changing into his slacks and sports jacket, combed his silver hair, and went out to talk to Kim's parents and sister who listened without comment or emotion.

"I understand your son does not have medical insurance," said the doctor.

"Cash, he can pay dollars," said Kim's father.

"So I understand," said Dr. Stringman, who had heard from one of the nurses that the young Korean had been involved in a shootout and belonged to a gang. "I'm not concerned about getting paid. I was concerned about how you'd be able to manage."

"We manage," the father said.

The sister was young, looked angry, arms folded.

"He will live?" asked the mother.

"He'll be fine," said the doctor. "We'll have him working with a therapist in a week. He'll be fitted for a prosthetic arm and hand soon, depending on his recovery time."

"And he will be back on the streets and holding a gun in that hand," the sister said. "He would be better dead."

Kim's mother bit her lower lip and tried not to weep. She had done a lot of weeping in the past two days, in fact, during many of the days they had been in the United States. Most of the weeping had been because of her son.

"Maybe this will change him," said the father. The sister turned away.

"When he was going under the anesthetic, he mentioned a girl," said the doctor. "Said he wanted to see the girl with the gun. Does that make sense to any of you?"

"He was shot by a girl trying to protect her grandmother," said the sister. "When you and your nurses and therapists spend all your hours and days saving his life, he will, at the first possible moment, murder that girl. You would be better to have let him die."

Dr. Anthony Stringman had been performing surgery for more than thirty years. With rare exceptions, when the patient was saved and he informed the family, he was blanketed in praise and thanks. It was, he assumed, something like what an actor must feel when he takes his curtain call. There had been exceptions—particularly, one abusive husband who had been in a drunk-driving accident and whose life insurance would have been a blessing to a wife and children, and whom Dr. Stringman had saved with no thanks from the prospective widow who foresaw even more abuse in her future and that of her children.

Dr. Stringman, whose fees were high and whose sense of worth even higher, was quite uncomfortable in the presence of this sister who wished her brother dead. It was equally clear that the mother and father had rather mixed feelings about the successful surgery.

"Well," said Stringman, looking at his watch. "I must go. I'll check on Robert in the morning on my rounds unless some problem develops, and you can check as often as you like with the surgical nursing station. He'll be in recovery for a few hours and then in intensive care for probably no more than a day."

Dr. Stringman gave them his most reassuring smile of perfect white teeth. He was a big man and for years he had run into patients and families who connected his name to the University of Michigan Rose Bowl team on which he had played, a blocking back of some distinction who had been drafted by the NFL but had chosen medical school instead, a fact made possible by a father who was a very successful cardiac surgeon. It was a rare event now to be recognized for his football success.

Dr. Stringman left after patting Robert Kim's mother on the arm. The Kims began speaking quickly in Korean before he could leave and there was clearly a disagreement among them.

The sister looked up at Stringmam and said, "Can other visitors be kept away? Others besides us?"

"Well," said Stringman. "If the patient wants to see someone and is capable of the visit, there's not much that can be done. Visitors are generally considered beneficial and your brother is an adult."

More talk in Korean and the father said "thank you," extending his hand and shaking the doctor's. Both men had powerful grips, but the strength in the Korean's surprised Stringman.

"I've got to go," the doctor said with his smile suggesting that he had more lives to save when, in fact, he was meeting his latest mistress, a young surgical nurse who worshiped him and was five years younger than Stringman's eldest son. Stringman had told his wife that he had to spend the afternoon working out his surgical schedule for the week with members of his surgical team. She knew better but said nothing.

It was raining again when Stringman got into his car. He had a bad feeling and, in fact, had lost his desire for the assignation, but he was committed now to an afternoon of lies and the hope that he was up to the challenge of the young nurse's lust.

Anne Crawfield Ready had a Sunday visitor, a cousin from Salt Lake City who was in town for the day and promised the family he would look in on her. He was not really a close cousin, perhaps twice removed by marriage, but he was a decent man doing his duty. His name was Carleton Jackson and he owned a garage in Salt Lake City that specialized in both body work and problems with custom-made and expensive cars. He was actually in Chicago to personally pick up a 1984 Lamborghini engine that had come out of a car wreck completely unscathed. Jackson had a customer for it in Salt Lake, the heir to a well-known line of jams, jellies, and preserves. Jackson had driven the carefully padded covered pick-up truck down and it was parked downstairs of Anne Crawfield Ready's apartment right now.

Jackson was fifty-two and brawny, with a full head of the Crawfield family red hair, and a desire to get this chore over with as soon as possible and get on the road. The engine was well protected and covered but it was raining and there might be a leak in the customized metal rooftop on the pickup.

Jackson ate his piece of cake across from Anne at the little table, drank his coffee and told Anne about her relatives, many of whom she didn't remember ever meeting. When they were finished and Anne had told him about her exciting visit from the police, Jackson made the mistake of asking politely, "Is there anything I can do for you before I head back, Anne?"

"Give my love to everyone. Tell them they're welcome here any time, and take me to the new mall on McCormick to shop for an hour. If that wouldn't be too much trouble?"

"No trouble at all," said Jackson, seeing no way out and feeling guilty about wanting one. "One hour and then I'll have to get on the road."

In a car parked in the closed Shell station across from Anne Crawfield Ready's apartment, Massad Mohammed sat with his engine off, watching. He had arrived an hour earlier. He did not read. He did not listen to music. He hardly paid attention to Temple Mir Shavot across the street, the temple he had helped to vandalize two days earlier, the temple whose sacred Torah was stored safely with the automatic weapons far from his old apartment in an empty, recently closed supermarket just off of Western Avenue. The supermarket shelves were empty. A large sign in the front window told prospective buyers who to call if they were interested.

The supermarket was in a small mall where none of the shops were open on Sunday. Massad had a key to the back door, a key obtained through threat, coercion, and an appeal to Arab patriotism from an Arab who worked in the real estate office. The man's name was Fred Starr. No one in the office had the slightest idea that Fred was an Arab. Given the political climate of the United States, Fred Starr had not chosen to share this information, but other Arabs knew and one of them was Massad Mohammed.

Now, Massad sat in the car making up his mind, wondering who the big red-haired man in the flannel jacket was who had parked his car and gone up to Anne Ready's apartment over the photography store. The photography store was closed but the baseball card store next door was doing a brisk Sunday business. There were more bicycles than there was space for on the metal rack. Kids went in and out.

Were the woman alone, as he had reason to believe she always was, Massad would have simply gone up to the apartment, made her tell him if there were any photographs of him taken from her window on the night of the vandalism of Mir Shavot. Jara had told him of the woman she had seen in the window, had told him of the photographs the police had of her. It was Jara who quickly concluded that the old woman in the window had taken the photographs and she had shared this with her brother and others, though the information seemed now to be of no use to Jara.

Massad thought that the old woman with red hair would have been frightened if he came through her door, gun in hand, scarred face, on a Sunday afternoon. She was an old woman. She wasn't a Jew. He would take no pleasure and have little satisfaction in what he would have to do. Finding incriminating photographs or not, he would have to kill her. Then, to insure that there were no hidden negatives or photographs of him, he would burn the apartment. This had to be done today. Tomorrow, Monday, was the attack. He would have to leave as soon as the attack was successfully completed. He had a false ID that said he was a Saudi Arabian. He had some money. The FBI would be after him and if they found him, he wanted as little evidence left behind as possible. Jail didn't frighten him. But if he were in jail, he could not carry out his lifetime mission. The old woman might have taken a photograph of him on the night they attacked the temple that he could now clearly see. It would be part of a chain of evidence. Who knew what others were already saying about him? He knew there were those who might even suspect him of being the killer of Howard Ramu and the other two Arabs. They might suspect it but they would not say it. It was too terrible a possibility to be uttered. Massad Mohammed, however, was committed to the terrible, had been since his father, mother, uncle, aunt, and cousins had been slaughtered on a dark road by a mad Jew.

He could wait no longer. If necessary, he would also kill the man with the red hair. In a war there are sometimes innocent victims. Arafat had said that before he betrayed the Palestinians. It was still true.

He started to get out of the car in the very light drizzle when the door across the street opened and Anne Ready and the red-haired man came out, got in the small truck, and drove away.

Massad had no idea how long they would be gone. If they returned too soon, the gun he carried would kill them silently, a single bullet in the head before the victim had any idea of what was going on. He would shoot the red-haired man first because he was the bigger threat and then, with his body on the floor, he would question the woman who would be too frightened to lie. Then he would kill her.

Massad got out of the car, locked the door, and limped across Dempster Street. In front of the card shop, three boys were talking about something called a Cal Ripken card and showing it around. Massad didn't care for any sport but soccer, which he could watch dreamily and without enthusiasm on television. The three boys didn't look up at Massad, who did his best to hide his limp in case these children were questioned later and one of them remembered a man going through the door.

When he got to the top of the stairs, Massad could see that the apartment door was no problem. The lock was a joke. There was an apartment across from Anne Ready's. No sound came from it. Still, Massad opened the door carefully and quietly. His search was thorough. The problem was the overwhelming vastness of the collection of photographs and negatives of Anne Crawfield Ready's life. He went through books, boxes, held negative strips up to the window. Twenty minutes. Too long. He could simply sit and wait, gun in hand, and carry out his other plan, but he decided against it. Too much risk. Suppose they came back with friends? Suppose the police came to ask her more questions? Not likely, but possible. Massad knew what photographs the police had of him at the rally. That couldn't be helped, but there might be more, better, something in this room that connected him directly to the crime across the street, something she had overlooked or held back.

He could find nothing. He strewed negatives and photographs around the small apartment. Negatives and photographs are highly flammable. Massad started the fire in three places and the effect was immediate. Flames spread quickly, scorching the walls, igniting books. Massad did not care if the fire investigators concluded, as they surely would, that it was arson. Nor did he care if the police considered the photographs as a possible motive. It was Sunday. This was Skokie. It would take them days. It would all be over by then.

Massad backed out of the blazing room, closed the door gently, and limped down the stairs as quickly as he could. There were no children standing outside when he went into the light rain. He moved slowly, but steadily back across Dempster and got into his car.

Across the street, the window of Anne Ready's apartment blew out, showering glass, some of it as far as the sidewalk in front of Mir Shavot, which struck Massad as pleasant irony.

He put the car in gear, looked up at the smoke now billowing through the broken window, and started his engine. He took a right turn out of the parking lot, and a car almost ran into him but skidded to a near stop. Massad headed toward the expressway. People were already looking up at the window of the apartment. He wondered if there were some frightened Jew in the temple hearing the noise who would come to the door, see the blaze, and cower in fear of another attack.

Massad smiled.

Officer Edward Munger was driving his marked car down Dempster, making his rounds, double-checking on the temple, when he heard the windows of Anne Ready's apartment break. He looked up, knowing that the woman who lived there had been questioned and had provided information to the task force. Officer Munger caught a glimpse of a man who took two limping steps and climbed into an Oldsmobile parked in the closed Shell station across from the blast. Something clicked. A report about a possible terrorist with a limp had just come in that morning or the night before. Still, Munger was about to pull into the small mall parking lot, run up the stairs, and see if there was anyone, particularly the old woman, who needed help.

Then Munger saw a blue Ford Escort almost hit the Oldsmobile, which pulled out of the Shell station. Munger had to hit his brakes behind the Escort. The Olds sped down the street. Munger watched it for a second and then made his call on the radio. He shouted the location of the fire and added, without fully knowing why at the moment, "I'm in pursuit of the possible arsonist. He's in a late eighties blue Olds Cutlass."

Munger had been a police officer for five years. Two years back home in Zachary, Louisiana, after he graduated from Grambling, and three years here in Skokie when he moved his wife and two children north, looking for some promise of advancement. The Mungers lived on the south side of Skokie just off of Howard Street on Kedvale, an area of whites, Asians, and a few African-Americans like the Mungers. The schools were good. The neighborhood was safe, and Munger was due for a promotion.

He moved now on instinct. A car pulling out of an empty station across from the crime, the driver hardly looking

back when he was almost hit by another car, not even slowing down to see why there was a police car whose lights
were now flashing two cars behind him, the profile of the
driver who with a brief glimpse looked foreign. Munger
had decided this was enough to warrant pursuit. If the
woman was still in the apartment and in trouble, he was
making a big mistake, but his radio gave him slight comfort
as he followed the Olds by saying that another patrol car
was already arriving at the fire site. Behind him, Munger
could hear the siren of a fire engine. The closest station
was only a few blocks away.

Foot traffic on Dempster was heavy in spite of the light
rain and unusual chill. People were out visiting with their
families, going to movies, lunch, relatives, friends, rides to
keep from being cooped up in the house with the kids. It
wasn't like a rush hour morning, but it wasn't clear either.
Munger ran his siren and weaved through the traffic past
the Escort, keeping an eye on the Oldsmobile, which was
now switching lanes and definitely taking chances to move
ahead in the traffic. No doubt. The guy in the Olds was
running. Munger felt better. He also felt a bright surge of
adrenaline. He took a chance and moved into the oncoming
lane, which had no traffic at the moment. He made up three
car lengths before he had to pull back into the westbound
traffic.

He was right on the Olds's tail now, siren going, lights
flashing. The Olds paid no attention and suddenly made a
right turn from the left lane, almost hitting a Toyota. Munger watched the Olds go down the side street. He called it
in and was told that a police car was on duty at the fire
site and two kids had said that the old lady and a red-
headed fat man had gone out a while earlier and not come
back. It appeared, according to the fire unit chief on the
site, that there were no fatalities. They were trying to con-
tain the fire and keep it from the photo store below that
probably had enough chemicals, film, and negatives to
cause an explosion.

Munger took a deep breath and did what was definitely

not acceptable procedure. He too turned right far too close to the Toyota, which clipped Munger's fender sending the patrol car into a spin on the wet side street. Munger righted the car, took another deep breath, and went down the side street, trying to remember the neighborhood he was in. The Oldsmobile was going north on the next street. Munger was heading north. The Olds could do a lot of things including pulling into a driveway and heading back to Dempster. Munger's instincts told him it wasn't likely. The man in the Olds hadn't seen Munger make the same dangerous move he had and probably thought there was a cop back on Dempster trying to find a way to go after him down the street. If the man in the Olds behaved the way Munger thought he would behave, he would get away from the neighborhood, from Skokie, as fast as he could. The problem was, the Olds driver probably didn't know the streets. Munger called in his location, turned off his siren and flashing light and sped up. On these side streets no one but a woman in a yellow raincoat with a little dog on a leash was walking in the rain. The real danger was cars on the cross streets. At the first corner, Munger looked right and saw nothing. He took a chance, went even faster and came to the street in front of the park and the school at the T intersection. He turned right. If the Olds had kept going he would hit this T and have to turn right or left. Left might lead him into the police car that was following him. Munger bet on a right turn.

The policeman turned and thought he caught sight of a car turning down another street a few blocks down. Munger pursued looking down each street as he went, seeing no Olds. When he got to the street where he thought he had seen a turning car, there it was, a block ahead, moving slower, inside the speed limit, trying to avoid notice. Munger drove to the next block, turned left and went north, paralleling the Olds on the next street but going well above the speed limit.

If the timing was right . . . Munger made a sharp left turn, drove the short block and then turned left again. The Olds

was right in front, facing him, maybe thirty yards away.
The man in the car stopped. Policeman and suspect looked
at each other through the swishing of their windshield wip-
ers. The Olds began to back down the street but the driver
couldn't control the car at the speed he was trying to move.
He hit a parked car and stalled. Munger gave his location
on the radio, said he was in foot pursuit of the suspect, and
got out, shielding himself with the open door of his patrol
car, window rolled down, weapon in his dark hands leveled
at the driver's door of the Oldsmobile.

Munger screamed, "Come out with your hands up."

He wasn't sure if the suspect heard him. He reached into
his car for the bullhorn, and spoke into it after switching it
on, "Come out of your vehicle. If you cannot do so, open
your window, and put both arms out where I can see them."

There was no movement from the stalled Oldsmobile but
a few faces did appear at the windows of the small brick
homes on either side of the street. Munger wanted to keep
his weapon leveled at the Olds but he reached for the bullhorn again and said, "Will all of you in your homes get
away from the windows? Move to the back of your homes."

He threw the bullhorn onto the seat. People moved away
from the windows. Sweat mixed now with the drizzle and
Munger's blue uniform was getting decidedly wet. He had
not had time to put on his raincoat that lay in the back seat
of the patrol car.

Suddenly the door of the Oldsmobile opened. A man
stepped out. He was around thirty, maybe younger, dark,
wearing a raincoat, and carrying an automatic weapon of
some kind in his hands.

"Stop," Munger shouted, taking aim.

Massad fired. A burst of shots hit the patrol car, breaking
windows and lights, penetrating the hood. One shot went
right through the door behind which Munger was crouched.
It missed him by the width of a palm. Munger fired as the
man moved across the street, still firing his weapon. The
man ran with a definite limp. And then the man stopped
for an instant, but just an instant, and Munger was certain

he had hit him. The next burst from the limping man sent two rounds through the door, both less than a foot from officer Munger, who felt fear and anger. This man meant to kill him. The feeling was now mutual. Munger stood up to fire. The street was empty. He looked at the sidewalk.

Empty. He looked back at the Olds for an instant but knew that the limping man would not head for the stalled car.

Police sirens came from the south. Munger, firearm at the ready, moved to the site where he thought he had hit the suspect. The rain had almost stopped now but it hadn't washed away the splatter of blood on the street. The blood trailed to the right. Munger followed and when he hit the sidewalk, the bloody trail stopped. The limping man had done something to halt the bleeding, a piece of cloth, a torn shirt.

There were passageways between houses, leading, Munger knew, to small backyards and one-car garages. It was not only insane to pursue alone with only a handgun, it was against departmental rules. Two more patrol cars came up the street from the south. Munger knew the officers who stepped out of each. One was holding a shotgun. Both were white.

"Automatic weapon," Munger said. "I got him, don't know how bad. Went that way."

The other two officers nodded. Now he could pursue. There were families in these houses. Shotzman, the senior of the three officers on the scene, motioned to Munger and the other officers to comb the nearest cement sidewalks next to the nearest brick houses. They did. When they got to the yards, they looked both ways, weapons ready, fearing attack. There was no sign of the limping man. The officer with the shotgun panicked and fired at a bush that moved in the breeze. There was no one behind the bush. They moved to the alley. It was empty. They carefully tried garage doors on both sides of the alley, all locked. More cars arrived, marked and unmarked. Leo Benishay had heard the call in his own car. He was pulling out of the parking lot of Wok Fu's Restaurant. He told his wife and daughter to go back inside and have a dessert. His wife knew better than to argue.

The search went on for two hours. Doors were knocked on, roofs climbed, bushes moved. Signs of blood searched for. The limping man was gone.

Leo Benishay told Munger he had done a good job and ordered him back to the station if he was in shape to drive and his car could still move. As it turned out, twenty-one rounds from Massad's weapon had torn into it and the car wouldn't budge. More rounds had hit nearby cars and made holes in the street. Munger got in the passenger seat of Shotzman's car, happy to be alive, wondering what had happened to the limping man.

Leo Benishay found Lieberman at his desk. The call was quick, information clear. It looked as if Massad Mohammed had torched Anne Ready's apartment and been pursued by an officer who was sure he hit him with at least one shot. Suspect's car had been examined. There were no weapons, no Torah. Suspect had not yet been found.

Massad's shoulder was bleeding and time was passing. The old couple, who said their names were Tabitha and Arnold Shultz, sat quietly on the bed while Massad sat on the floor. No one outside could see them in this room. The only problem had come when the police had knocked at the door.

Massad had sent the woman to answer. She had seemed the calmer of the two. He had told her, "You have seen nothing. You heard some sounds, noise outside, but you and your husband are just about to watch television. You convince them and they go away. You fail, and I kill your husband and then come out shooting, probably killing us all. You understand?"

Tabitha Shultz had nodded that she understood and she had left the bedroom and gone to the front door. Massad had listened to her through the partly open bedroom door while he watched Arnold sitting erect and frightened on the bed. The police had gone away.

It had been surprisingly easy to get into the Shultz house. He had simply knocked at the back door, his weapon under his coat, turned sideways to keep his wound from being seen. Arnold had immediately opened the door and asked, "What's wrong?"

He and his wife found out.

These were not Jews and he had no desire to hurt them, but they were Americans and if he let them live, he wanted them afraid. Under Massad's direction, Tabitha, her white hair in a bun, had tended Massad's wound. The shot from Officer Munger had torn through Massad's shoulder just below the right collarbone.

"I can see the tip of the bullet," Tabitha Shultz had said looking at Massad's back when he took off his coat and shirt revealing a large handgun in addition to the automatic weapon he cradled in his arms.

"Pull it out," Massad ordered, aiming his weapon at Arnold.

Tabitha disappeared and returned in a few minutes. She had a pliers in her hand.

"Heated it over the flames from the gas range," she said. "No point in telling you this is dangerous and you should see a doctor."

"Take it out and put a bandage on the hole," Massad ordered.

She did. The pain was monstrous. Massad fought to keep from passing out.

"I think you'll live," Tabitha said after bandaging the wounds. "I was a nurse in World War Two. I saw worse."

"You're not afraid?" he said long after the police had left and darkness was coming.

"Not for me," said Tabitha Shultz. "I have cancer. Pretty soon I'll be in the hospital and start my dyin'. Arnold doesn't talk much, accident years ago, hurts his throat, but he's a good man. Never hurt anyone. Well read. Machinist, retired."

She touched her husband's head lovingly, and he took her hand.

"He'll go live with our daughter in Des Plaines when I'm gone," she said.

Massad had said nothing. He had gulped down half a bottle of Tylenol and two tablets of a stronger pain reliever prescribed for Tabitha Shultz. He was afraid to take more. The bandage seeped a bit of blood, but not much. He went to the closet and found a shirt, a dark brown shirt. He put it on carefully, watching the Shultzes but sure they would give him no trouble.

"You have a car?" he said.

Tabitha Shultz nodded.

"You both drive?"

"Take turns."

"Good," said Massad. "Go to your car, open the garage, start the engine. Arnold and I will come out behind you."

Tabitha rose, touched her husband's cheek, picked up a small brown purse on the corner of a dresser and went out to start the car.

Massad asked Arnold for a gym bag or shopping bag. Arnold, zombielike, went to the closet and came up with a white canvas shopping bag with a full-color picture of Michael Jordan smiling on the side. Massad folded the handle of his weapon and fit it into the bag. He took out his handgun, led Arnold to the kitchen. Arnold sat. Massad waited no more than a minute and told Arnold it was time to go. Arnold rose. The yard seemed clear as they moved to the garage. Inside, Tabitha sat in the driver's seat. Massad told Arnold to get in the front passenger seat while he kept down in the back seat with his canvas bag and gun. Tabitha drove out into the small alley and closed the garage door with the automatic opener.

"Where are we going?" asked Tabitha.

"To the city," Massad said. "Slowly. If you see police, smile. If you know a way out through alleys, take it. If we are stopped by the police, people will die. You understand?"

"Yes," said Tabitha. "Have you ever killed anyone?"

Massad hesitated and answered, "I think so. Once. An Israeli soldier. I was a boy. One of my friends had hit him with a rock. When I got to him, he was groaning and reaching for his glasses. He was not much older than I was. I hit him with a tree branch. I don't know if he died. And there have been others."

He had Tabitha drive him down the Kennedy Expressway to Division Street and park not far from the elevated train tracks.

The neighborhood businesses—restaurants, hardware stores, pawn shops, used bookstores—were closed. Traffic was light.

"You can stop," said Tabitha. "Stop killing people."

"No," Massad said. "I cannot. I will not. My people are oppressed."

"Sounds familiar," said Tabitha with a wry wry chuckle. "When it really comes down to it, it isn't the big stuff, countries, causes, history that counts. It's people, one-on-one. Like me and Arnold. You wanting revenge."

"Now you are a philosopher," Massad said with slight derision as he peeked over the top of the seat to check the traffic.

"Read a lot," she said. "Always have. I'd say the coast is clear."

"I assume you plan to tell the police," he said, reaching for the door handle.

"Soon as I can find a phone," she said. "No point in lying to you."

Massad never even considered shooting the old couple. It was what he should have done, have them park even further away, parked on a side street where their bodies might not be discovered until Monday had passed and he was far away. But Massad had to admit to himself that he liked the old couple, particularly the dying woman who did not panic.

"Good luck," he said, getting out of the car with his canvas Michael Jordan bag.

"And to you," said Tabitha without emotion, though Massad knew that she meant it. Arnold turned to face Massad, who stood next to his window now. A small sad smile touched Arnold Shultz's face.

Massad motioned for Tabitha to drive. She headed slowly down Division Street east toward the lake. When he was sure she could not see him in the rear view mirror, he entered the shadows of the overhead elevated train as one rumbled above. The space between the pillars of rusting metal was a tunnel of junk and weeds. Massad entered the long tunnel between the pillars.

On each side of the train tracks were fences, most high and wooden, a few of stone, neither safe from gangs of children or the homeless who often found shelter below the tracks. They lived in property that was limited in value because of the rumbling noise of the trains.

Massad did not want to run, but he had little choice. Complicating this escape was his limp, which slowed him down and marked him for identification. He knew Tabitha would find the nearest phone and that police would be all over the area within minutes. Running caused his shoulder great pain, but it didn't seem to be bleeding. Tabitha Shultz had been a good nurse. The canvas bag with the folded automatic bounced against his leg. He held the handgun with the silencer in his other hand, his hand that throbbed with the pain of the shoulder wound.

Massad ran four blocks under the tracks, tripping once on an empty beer can, pausing as an animal, perhaps a cat or large rat, raced across the strip of filth in front of him. Then he turned onto the street he was looking for. The rain had stopped and the sky was actually clearing. A few children were out playing. He put the handgun in the canvas bag and moved slowly on the opposite side of the street from the children, four girls absorbed in jumping rope and arguing.

The houses were small, reasonably cared for. Here and there a small apartment building sat, red brick, dirt courtyard where bushes and grass had once grown, one larger apartment building boarded up and scheduled, according to the sign, for demolition.

When Massad got to the apartment building he searched for, he heard no sirens, not yet. He had moved far and, considering his limp, his wound, and the weapon he carried, he had moved quickly. He was panting now as he entered the small hallway of one of the apartment buildings and rang a bell. No one answered but he could hear a door open beyond the inner door and footsteps coming down the stairs. Through the barred glass he could see the face of Yasar, who did not look happy to see him. Yasar hesitated for only a second and opened the door.

"Massad?" he asked.

Massad nodded, breathing heavily.

"It's been a long time," Yasar said. "Two years."

"Almost three," said Massad. "I need your help. For the cause."

Yasar, who bore a small resemblance to the actor Don Knotts, nodded, knowing that he had no choice. He stood back to let Massad enter.

SIXTEEN

IT WAS MONDAY morning. The children had four more days before school ended. Bess and Abe blessed those four days as they waited for the passengers at the gate at O'Hare. The 10:40 A.M. plane from Los Angeles had arrived. Bess and Abe searched for Lisa. She was one of the last to exit. She looked younger to Abe, still serious but not quite so serious as he had remembered. And she was wearing a yellow dress. Lisa did not wear yellow. She wore black, dark browns, somber blues. Lisa was holding the hand of a black man who wore slacks, a light tweed sports jacket, and a black turtleneck sweater. The man looked nothing like what Bess expected, nothing, she admitted to herself, like a young Sidney Poitier. Lieberman had learned to expect nothing.

As they approached and Lisa recognized her parents, the man at her side smiled. He was slightly taller than Lisa, on the thin side, and decidedly older than their daughter. His hair was definitely showing signs of gray.

Lisa gave her mother their usual quick hug with Bess

trying to hold on just a bit longer. Then Lisa turned and hugged her father. Unprecedented. He had expected the usual handshake and solemn smile. Granted, the hug was fleeting, but it was a hug. People hurried past, greeting others, racing for the baggage claim counter, an automated feminine voice in the not great distance informing people that they were about to enter the moving walkway and should be careful.

Lieberman and Bess shook the hand of the black man whom Lisa introduced as Marvin Alexander. The handshake was firm, the smile sincere. There was a hint of something deeper than initial awkwardness behind Dr. Marvin Alexander's smile.

"Shalom," said Alexander, taking Lisa's hand.

Lisa beamed nervously.

"You don't have to overdo it, Marvin," said Lieberman.

"You were right, Abe," Bess said.

"Right?" said Lisa.

"You're already married," said Lieberman.

"Yes," said Marvin Alexander taking both of Lisa's hands in his.

An image came unbidden to Lieberman. Lisa would have more children. They would be black children. When Lieberman was almost eighty, his teenage grandchildren would walk down the street and people would be afraid of them. He didn't want people to be afraid of his grandchildren, grandchildren probably not yet conceived and maybe not even contemplated. He put the image from his mind. Lieberman had enough to worry about, a bad stomach, cholesterol, a bar mitzvah, the telling of Barry and Melisa that their mother had not only remarried but married an African-American. Before he could stop himself, something made Lieberman ask, "Are you an American?"

Alexander smiled. "Yes. But my parents were from Jamaica."

"Marvin got his M.D. from Stanford," Lisa said.

The crowd had thinned. Lieberman nodded.

"He's won the Flexner Prize, the . . ." Lisa began.

"Married before?" asked Lieberman.

"This can wait, Abraham," Bess said firmly.

"Yes," said Alexander. "I was married before. My wife died."

"Children?" asked Lieberman.

"Abe," Bess insisted.

"None," said Alexander, "to my regret. She died young. And before you ask your next question, I am forty-nine years old and I do not mind the questions."

Lieberman nodded, satisfied for the moment, liking the man who made his morose daughter smile. They headed for baggage claim, Lisa holding Marvin Alexander's hand and talking.

"Marvin is considering converting to Judaism," said Lisa. "He speaks Hebrew, spent almost two years at Hebrew University in Jerusalem."

"Did he run into your Aunt Fanny there?" asked Lieberman.

Bess nudged her husband and said, "That's not funny, Abraham."

"We're all more than a bit nervous," Alexander said.

"If you want to stop in the bathroom and take the contacts out," said Abe as they headed for baggage claim, "we'll wait."

"Lisa said you were a good detective," said Alexander.

"She did?" asked Lieberman with slight surprise.

"I wore the contacts . . ."

"At my request," Lisa confessed.

"I wore the contacts in the hope that I would look a bit younger," Alexander said. "I do not, as you noted, find them comfortable."

"Take them out," said Lieberman. "We'll sit here."

There was no discussion. Lieberman simply sat in an empty waiting area where the board indicated that the next plane was arriving from Seattle in an hour. Lisa touched Alexander's cheek and he moved toward the nearest restroom. Bess sat next to her husband. Lisa hovered over her parents.

"Well?" she said.

"We just met the man," said Lieberman. "He makes a good first impression, but so did Irving Spoderman."

"Irving . . . ?" Lisa asked.

"Murdered his wife with a small, slightly dull ax back in '79 or '80," explained Lieberman. "Couldn't meet a nicer guy. Wrote poetry, loved movies, could quote from *The Wild Bunch*, Ibsen, *It's a Wonderful Life* nearly as well as Iris Huang's father. Did a pretty good Jimmy Stewart. Had a good job, editing trade magazines about welding, machine equipment. Had no explanation for what he did. Just got up one morning, said, 'the hell with it,' and was decidedly unkind to his wife of almost thirty years."

"Abe, this is too much," said Bess.

Lisa was close to tears.

"Sorry," said Abe with a sigh. "I've had a bad week and a long night to look forward to on the job. Truth is, so far I like him and, since we're being honest, I am impressed that he likes you. Lisa, you're my daughter and I love you, but your mother and I and your former husband, not to mention several of your employers and brief friends, have found you a bit too critical and somber."

"Marvin's changed me," said Lisa. "Give him a chance. Give us a chance."

"You got it," said Lieberman. "Besides, do I have a choice?"

"He's really considering converting?" asked Bess as she saw Alexander returning.

"Yes, Mother," said Lisa. "And he really is a doctor."

"Mother?" Lieberman said. "Not Bess? You going to start calling me 'Father' or 'Dad' instead of 'Abe?' "

"We'll see," Lisa said with a smile, moving to meet her husband.

"Rimless glasses," Lieberman said to Bess. "Now he looks like a professor."

"What do you think, Abraham? First impression. I'm your wife, remember, not your district captain."

"I said I like him," said Lieberman, rising. "Let's go get the luggage. I've got to get to work."

Hanrahan checked his watch. He had about half an hour, maybe a little more before he went to the station to wait for the call from Pig Sticker. He was carrying the cellular phone he shared with Lieberman on which Pig Sticker could reach him, but he might have to move fast. He'd be more comfortable back at the station, but he sat back and watched as Michael and Smedley Ash talked on the other side of the living room. Hanrahan had chosen not to listen, but he was sure his very presence was putting pressure on Michael who was listening to Smedley, nodding, and talking very softly.

Smedley was not an imposing figure, a small, bald man with a little round gut who wore suspenders and now worked as a leather cutter in a luggage factory. Monday was Smedley's day off.

Hanrahan got up and moved into the kitchen to bring them both more coffee. The discussion in the other room was only the first step. Next, they'd go to a meeting tonight where Michael would decide whether to go on.

Hanrahan had made a full pot. Michael had been consuming it at an enormous rate, possibly a good sign. Hanrahan poured two cups, black, and sugared Michael's.

Earlier that morning, Maureen had called. It had been a shock. Hanrahan had convinced himself that he was over his ex-wife, that he had put her in a deep but cherished box of his memory, that if they met, it would be a polite conversation, if she would allow it to be, and that it would be conducted with slight nervousness but, he hoped, cordiality. Maureen was aware of Iris and probably knew about the wedding plans. That was fine. But her voice had taken him by surprise. Memories collapsed inside him. He had to sit down.

He had been at the kitchen table when she called, reading the *Sun-Times*, which had been delivered at the door, waiting for Michael to get up and Smedley to arrive. The call was early, before Maureen had to go to work.

"Bill?" she repeated when she didn't get an immediate answer.

"Yes," he said after a long pause. "How are you, Maureen?"

"I'm fine, Bill. Michael's with you?"

"Yes."

"How are you doing?"

"Still sober, approaching two years," he said, understanding her question quite clearly.

It was Maureen's turn to pause. Bill had waited.

"Can you help him?"

"I may be able to help him help himself," said Hanrahan. "I'm trying. I'll try."

"It's a disease," she said. "Inherited from you."

It hadn't been an accusation. Just a statement sadly, pensively made in a tone he recognized.

"Something like that," Hanrahan had said. "Yes."

"Does he want to . . . Will he see me?" she had asked.

"I'll ask," he had said. "I think so, but not this week, maybe not for a week or two."

"Quite a reversal," Maureen had said. "When he came to town with his wife and new baby, it was you he didn't want to see. Now . . ."

He had almost said, "Now you know how it feels," but he didn't because he really didn't feel it. Instead, he had said, "I'll tell him you called. It's up to him. Let's have some faith in our son."

"Take care of yourself, William," Maureen had said softly.

"I'll try," Hanrahan had said and she had hung up.

He sat at the table after the call trembling. God help him, the deep demon told him he needed a drink, but the demon was deep in a locked box and he knew he could and would resist it. Stopping had been too horrible. Starting again with the prospect of going through the whole process again would probably lead him to the suicide he had once considered.

No, the demon could speak but it was in a tight box.

Hanrahan had a bowl of Frosted Flakes and milk after Maureen's call. He had read the paper, sports first, comics, editorials, and then the news. He skipped the obits and wondered why Lieberman always read them first. And then Smedley had come.

He brought the mugs into the living room and handed one each to his son and Smedley who nodded their thanks.

"I've got to go," said Hanrahan. "I don't know if this is a good time, but there won't be another till tonight or tomorrow morning. Michael, your mother called before you got up. I told her I wasn't sure if you'd want to call her for a while. She understood. You do what you want."

Michael nodded and Smedley gave Hanrahan a reassuring look. No one had come back from deeper than Smedley, who had lost family, friends, job, and was among the homeless before he found AA. "A lot of God and mumbo-jumbo, I'll admit," Smedley had once told Hanrahan, "but it saved me. And I believe in it."

It had taken time and Smedley's help for Hanrahan to believe in it. Hanrahan went to meetings with only a few reservations, carrying the deep demon that Smedley had said he would never be rid of.

"You learn to live with it," Smedley had said one night. "When it wants to converse, don't talk to it. Don't even tell it to shut up. Just ignore it."

Smedley had been right. He had known. His own deep demon was probably stronger than Hanrahan's, and Michael's was not even in a box yet, but sitting on his shoulder, invisible, urging. Hanrahan wondered if all diseases were like that, an AIDS demon, a cancer demon, a hepatitis demon, a different demon for every disease saying there was no hope.

Hanrahan left his son and Smedley and went to work. They hardly noticed him leaving. On the whole, Hanrahan felt pretty good. The air was unseasonably cool. He had weathered a call from Maureen. Michael looked as if he had a chance. Iris had held his hand especially tight the night before and it was clear she and Michael had gotten along. They had eaten at Rodity's, Michael's favorite restaurant in Greek Town on Halsted Street. There had been no wine and the waiter hadn't pushed it. Michael had ordered the combination plate, Bill the mousaka, and Iris the leg of lamb. If he lived through this day, the future looked brighter than it had in a long, long time.

Lieberman was seated at his desk when Hanrahan arrived. The squad room was reasonably quiet. A few typewriters taking complaints, booking moody suspects, one a white woman with wild white hair and a face that said she was probably younger than she looked. She was in outer space, dreaming, and Roper was trying to get a rape report. The day janitor was trying to clean up. Word was that there were budget cutbacks and they were going to lose the day man. He wasn't going to lose his job, just get transferred to night duty at the North Avenue, much closer to where he lived. The night man there was retiring after almost forty years. Lieberman knew the night man at the North. He was a black man everyone called Solly. Lieberman wondered if they were going to have a retirement party for Solly. He'd call Rodrigucz tomorrow and find out. However, there would be no replacement when the Clark Street Station lost the day janitor. Budget cutbacks. In a few weeks, it would be next to impossible to breathe the daytime air in the squad room no matter how hard the night man scrubbed and cleaned, carted, sprayed, and emptied.

"Lisa's friend," Hanrahan asked immediately.

"They're married," said Abe.

"You were right," said Hanrahan. "First impressions?"

"I like him," said Lieberman with a shrug looking at the cup of coffee in front of him, afraid to drink it but already feeling the first stages of the agony of withdrawal which ed him to ask, "Michael?"

"Holding his own," said Hanrahan sitting.

"Good, I like Michael. You want this cup of coffee? Just poured it. Still hot. Haven't touched it. Stomach's acting up."

"Sure," said Hanrahan, reaching over to accept the cup.

"How did the kids take it?" Hanrahan asked.

"Barry was OK," said Lieberman. "Asked him if he liked the Cubs. If he played basketball, baseball."

"Does he?" Hanrahan asked.

"A little, not enough to be very impressive, at least according to my new son-in-law. Seems to be good for Lisa so far. Melisa reminded all present that Todd was her daddy. No one contradicted her. Lisa handled it reasonably well. Alexander said he understood everyone's discomfort if not its degree."

"So far, so good," said Hanrahan.

"He says he's considering turning Jewish," said Lieberman. "Speaks Hebrew. Spent almost two years in Israel. I can't speak Hebrew. Bess can't speak it."

"Something you're not saying, Rabbi," said Hanrahan.

"Maish," Lieberman said, shaking his head. "A black man killed David. I think it may be a problem with Maish. We'll see. Dr. Marvin Alexander will have the opportunity to meet the entire family and Rabbi Wass tomorrow night. You're invited. So is Michael. I advise you to stay away."

"We may come," said Hanrahan, drinking the coffee and ignoring the advice.

The call came at four in the afternoon. Before Pig Sticker even told them, they both knew. The time was right. It was to be the board meeting of the African Muslim Church, Martin Abdul, meeting to start at 5:30 P.M. at the mosque in plain sight from the Dan Ryan just south of the Loop.

"Six of us," Pig Sticker whispered. "Automatic weapons. Uzis. We've got wigs, little Jew hats. I don't know where we're going, but Berk said we had some niggers who needed killing. All I got for you."

He hung up.

"They've got some niggers to kill," said Hanrahan, hanging up the phone and standing up.

Lieberman stood too. There were things to be done very quickly and plans to be confirmed.

It was Ibraham Said's job to call Martin Abdul. Said did not consider Abdul's people true Muslims. Fortunately, that was not an issue that need come up now. Said got through to Abdul via a highly suspicious man who answered the phone after ten rings. Abdul said in his famous, or infamous, deep voice that he was well aware of who Ibraham Said was, well aware that he was a police officer, well aware that he was a devout Muslim, well aware that he had a reputation for honesty. It was a bit surprising to both men that they had not spoken to each other before this moment.

Said went through brief amenities and said, "We have reason to believe that a small group of neo-Nazis disguised as Jews and carrying Uzis intend to crash into your board meeting and murder you, blaming it on the Jews."

"I knew of the possibility. A good plan," Martin Abdul said calmly. "Murder me and fifteen or more of their black enemies, blame the Jews, start a race war, and stand back to watch the results."

"Precisely," said Said.

"I assume you know that with your warning we are quite capable of protecting ourselves, of surprising these enemies, of killing them within our walls in self-defense," said Abdul.

"I know," said Said.

"We would welcome the opportunity," said Abdul.

"I know," said Said.

"But you have something else in mind," said Martin Abdul.

"I do. We do," said Said. "We wish to place a SWAT team inside your mosque with some police officers. We wish to surprise the assassins, take them in the act of attempted murder, perhaps get them to reveal those who support them. A link to information about neo-Nazi and other racist groups and possible statements of crimes they have committed would be more valuable than simply killing them, though I understand what you would gain psychologically by protecting yourselves. I believe you would gain more politically, however, by allowing us to trap the intruders. If you do not agree, we will take them outside your mosque and have more difficulty with indictments for attempted assassination."

"The opportunity to gain national publicity and sympathy for *our* cause will be very valuable in either case," said Abdul.

"It would appear so," said Said.

"Then come. And bring your people. I plan to go ahead with our meeting, inside of which will be four heavily armed men who will be prepared to act if you fail. I want no charges brought against my men, who have permits for their weapons. I want no charges brought if they are forced to protect us."

"You have my word," said Said.

"I hear that your word is good. *Salaam Alechem.*"

"*Alechem Salaam,*" said Said, hanging up the phone and looking at the people assembled in the squad room.

Kearney looked at Special Agent Triplett of the FBI, who nodded his approval. And the plan went into action.

Charles Kenneth Leary sat in the rear of the car Fallon was driving. Berk sat next to Fallon in the front seat. Leary sat in the center of the back seat flanked by two young men who did not look appreciably different from him. Each had a wig and little cap on his lap. Each had an Uzi between his legs. It was not a weapon that any of them was particularly familiar with, but the Arab, Massad, who looked like death, had demonstrated how easy it was to use the weapon. He also said that in the confined space of a boardroom, five Uzis firing at the same time would need no great accuracy; just pulling back the trigger and spraying would take care of business.

The five in this car would do the killing.

The car behind was being driven by Massad, who Berk had decided would not join in the massacre. Massad had protested, but Berk had said given his condition, he would be a liability. He was wounded. When the killing was over, Massad could enter the boardroom and have the pleasure of placing the stolen Torah in the center of the table of dead niggers.

Massad, now full of painkillers, was really given no choice. He had turned over the weapons, demonstrated them, and barely had the energy to get to the car Berk had told him to drive. The blue velvet Torah lay on the seat next to Massad. He had handled it with care and in spite of himself admired the object and felt that something sacred did live within it. The scroll, after all, was not inconsistent with his own religion.

He drove behind the other car, fighting to stay alert, awake. His shoulder ached, a dull pain. The old Shultz woman who was dying of cancer had done a remarkable job. The bleeding had stopped. He should, of course, see a doctor, go to a hospital. He was well aware of the dangers of infection, the possibility that internal, permanent damage had been done, but that would have to wait. It might have to wait forever. Though there was little religion left in him, he told himself that if it was the will of Allah that he should die, then it would be so. Others would soon be dying too.

The two cars drove within the speed limit. The sun was out. They had hoped for rain, but that couldn't be helped. It took them almost forty minutes to get to the mosque. They parked next to the iron mesh fence across the street. Beyond the fence was a grassy hill that went down sharply to the expressway, where cars were jammed but moving in Monday rush hour, the start of the evening traffic rush. The Mongers had purposely avoided the expressway and its possible delays.

There was time. Fallon stuffed the keys to the car in the space behind the driver side cushion and the men in the first car got out, wigs and caps already on their heads in case someone appeared on the street. The Uzis were held discreetly at their sides. Except for Muslims coming to the mosque early the street was not in great use, and the mosque, the adjacent headquarters building, and offices took up most of the remaining street. On the block to the south was an empty lot and to the north was an abandoned ironworks. Martin Abdul had made a fair bid for the property and was now waiting for an answer. He expected it to be affirmative. He planned to build a school on the site, a large building, accredited for grades from kindergarten up to as high as he could obtain official certification. African-American children of members would get the best secular and religious education. There would be a big campaign. There would be no tuition or fees and lunches would be free. They would learn the basics and they would learn the truth of the world, including who should be hated and why.

Massad watched the five armed men move across the street looking both ways. They moved to the large door up twelve stone steps. The door was ornate. It was always open to worshipers. The men who burst in were not worshipers. Berk knew the layout of the mosque. He had paid a black junkie forty dollars for it and paid another junkie fifty dollars for his version of the interior layout of the mosque. The two junkies had posed as potential converts and had been welcomed, shown the mosque, and directed toward the drug rehabilitation room in the next building. Both versions of the layout of the mosque coincided.

The first room was more than a room. It was a huge domed space with colors beaming down from the richly colored glass in the dome. There were no chairs or pews in the room, just a floor tiled in a massive and beautiful mosaic with white as the dominant color and shapes suggesting the moon, stars, and planets.

The five men moved to the door on the right and opened it. They were in a long corridor with doors on either side. The boardroom was directly ahead of them. All five men wore soft-soled shoes instead of their usual boots. Berk was in back, Fallon in front, single file. In front of the boardroom door, they would line up side by side. Fallon was about ten feet from the door when the doors on both sides of the corridor opened and men began springing out, more than a dozen, rifles at the ready, each man wearing a cap and flack jacket indicating that they were a SWAT team. Two men aiming directly at each of the lined up Mongers.

"Drop the weapons," one of the SWAT men said. "Now."

One thing that Charles Kenneth Leary had decided was that when this moment came he did not want to be the first to put down his weapon. Fallon saved him from that, not only lowering his Uzi but letting it drop to the floor and putting his hands behind his head. Pig Sticker immediately did the same. Berk was last, at the end of the line nearest the door they had come through to get into the corridor. He dropped his weapon and ran for the open door. Two bullets were fired. Neither hit Berk, who threw the heavy doors closed behind him. Another bullet thudded into the wood near his hand as he turned the bolt. The men behind the door could get a key from Martin Abdul but that would take them half a minute, maybe longer by the time they actually got the heavy door open.

Betrayed. No doubt. No other answer. But no time to think about it now. Berk ran for the front door of the mosque, opened it and ran into the street, wondering if they had thought to cover the exit. No policeman or woman was there with a gun. Berk ran for his car glancing at Massad in the car behind, but not pausing.

There was a Mauser under the seat of the car. Berk was going to need it if he got away. He had already decided that if he were pursued and surrounded, he would give up. He looked in the rearview mirror as he screeched away. At that time, a car pulled out from what must have been the driveway on the other side of the headquarters building.

Massad was confused, fighting delirium, not certain of why Berk had come out alone and was fleeing. Something had gone wrong. Massad started his car, seeing Berk make a

dangerous tire-squealing left turn at the next corner. Just as
Massad started, another car pulled out behind him, a flashing light on top. Massad pressed the gas pedal to the floor.

Lieberman was in the driver's seat. The order from Kearney
through the FBI was that they should stay back. This was
going to be an FBI bust in cooperation with the Chicago
police. The Clark Street Station detectives were now officially out of what was sure to be a front page, TV news
lead-in story. That wasn't necessarily bad. What was bad
was that from where they sat in their car, they saw Berk
dash from the mosque and jump in the car. A moment later,
Massad's car, parked directly behind Berk's, took off as if
it were going for a new acceleration record.

"Which one?" Hanrahan said, since the second car was
going straight and the other had turned.

"The one we can see," said Lieberman. "We've got the
ID on Berk. It's the other fellow who didn't go in who has
me worried. Besides, I think we can catch him."

"Drive away, Rabbi," said Hanrahan.

Mr. Grits was packed. He was watching the news. It was
unlikely that anything would come on till ten, not even a
bulletin, but it might. He checked his watch. A little after
eight. He'd give it ten more minutes and then go out and
call Berk from a mall phone. He'd browse for a few
minutes, put something expensive on the counter, and ask
if he could use the store phone, local call, very quick to
ask his wife about the purchase. He wouldn't be turned
down. If all had gone well, Berk would be at the gas station
on Touhy and Sheridan waiting in front of the outdoor pay
phone.

There was a knock at the door. Mr. Grits placed his gun
between the pillows of the small hotel sofa. "Who is it?"
he asked.

"Plumber," came a bored voice. "Leak. Bad. Both floors up. Checking lines."

Mr. Grits got up, walked over to the door, looked through the peephole, saw an engineer's cap, and opened the door. Berk burst in.

"Surprise, Mr. Grits," he said, taking off his cap and pointing his Mauser at the well-dressed man.

"This is not a good idea, Mr. Berk," Grits said sadly.

"Aren't you going to ask how I found you?" Berk said.

"Later," said Grits calmly. "I have your money. I was going to deliver it as promised. I have exactly eleven hundred and twenty dollars beyond that. Are you risking your life for an extra eleven hundred and twenty dollars, Mr. Berk?"

"Lift the jacket," said Berk. "In fact, take it off slow."

Mr. Grits took off his jacket. He wasn't wearing a weapon, at least not one Berk could see.

"Hands against the wall, spread eagle."

Mr. Grits calmly complied and Berk patted him down. He was clean. Berk lifted the eleven hundred from the wallet. He left twenty dollars and the credit cards and checked the driver's license.

"Luckenbill," said Berk. "Harold Luckenbill. That your real name?"

"No," said Mr. Grits, pushing away from the wall and moving to the sofa. He offered his guest the armchair in the corner. Berk took it, Mauser still in his hand.

"You're a piece of work, Mr. Grits," Berk said, shaking his head.

"You're not here because you distrust me," Mr. Grits said. "You're here because you've failed and you know you will not be paid."

"We were set up," Berk agreed. "I'm here to take that money from you."

"And then kill me?" asked Grits.

"No," said Berk. "You dead, the money gone, the job a bust? No. Your friends will figure me right away. Killing you won't help. Doesn't mean I won't if you're not cooperative."

Mr. Grits smiled confidently, though he was beginning to feel his own fear, a fear almost equal to that of the piece of trash across from him. He would have to call his own people as soon as possible, tell them that the plan had gone wrong. It had happened before, but not to Mr. Grits and not to anyone in the link at this level, not a dispatcher. But Mr. Grits smiled confidently. He would not be physically punished, simply given an unofficial demotion. He had worked hard for his present position and now this creature across from him had ruined it. Mr. Grits kept smiling as he said, "On the table, in the briefcase, just as I promised you."

Berk got up, still watching Mr. Grits, who crossed his legs and uncreased his pants as Berk tried to do a quick count of the money. The television was going, a nondistraction.

"There aren't many places you can hide where we can't find you," said Mr. Grits calmly.

"I'll just have to try," said Berk. "I don't see any choice, do you? And with the money you already gave me and this briefcase full, I should be able to get pretty far away."

"Not sufficiently far," said Mr. Grits. "What now?"

"Like I said, I tie you up, gag you, and get as far away as fast as I can," said Berk. "I'm a rich man. Life's full of fuckin' little ironies, you know?"

"I know," said Mr. Grits, lifting his weapon from between the cushions of the sofa.

Berk's gun was only loosely aimed in Mr. Grits's direction. He didn't get off a shot. Four silenced bullets struck Berk before he could shoot and, fortunately for Mr. Grits, the dying Berk's finger did not tighten around the trigger. Two shots had hit Berk in the face. One to the right side of his nose. The other on a spot just above his right eye. The other two were body shots aimed at and entering the heart. Berk went down hard.

Mr. Grits got up with a sigh, checked to be sure Berk was dead, and then looked at the blood. He was in a hotel room with a man he had just shot. People from the hotel had seen him. Not often, not clearly, but they had seen him and might be able to identify him from a photograph. Mr. Grits had been in situations not unlike this in the past. He thought he had risen above it. Now he was back. He put his weapon down on the sofa, went to the door, locked it behind him and put on the "Do Not Disturb" sign. He had a very difficult call to make after which he would have to return to this room, clean up the mess, decide which of several ways to get Berk's body out of the hotel and into the trunk of Mr. Grits's rented car, without leaving traces of blood. The process would require some purchases. The whole task would be thankless.

SEVENTEEN

LIEBERMAN AND HANRAHAN had removed the flashing light. They had not turned on the siren. The man in the car in front of them—it looked like only one man—was driving much too slowly and erratically for a major felon fleeing the scene of a possible murder. Something was wrong.

"You want to get in front of him?" asked Hanrahan. "Stop him?"

"Let's see where he's going," said Lieberman.

And so they drove, across the expressway bridge, to Western Avenue and north directly behind the man in the car.

"Call it in?" asked Hanrahan.

"We are in slow pursuit of a suspect heading north on Western," Lieberman suggested. "At present, no backup is needed. We'll keep them informed."

Hanrahan made the call. It took longer than Lieberman anticipated.

"They patched me through to Kearney," he said when he

hung up. "I got the impression this was one collar he wanted his people to get the credit for."

There really was no place for Massad to go. He knew he was being followed. Streams of marked police cars could appear on the street any moment. And he was growing more weak and tired with each block.

He had one last plan, not much of one. He shared it with the Torah, asked its advice, and grinned madly when it did not answer. When he was within three blocks of where he was going, Massad got in the left lane. The men in the car behind followed. He had chosen carefully. He would do precisely the same thing he had done to elude the black policeman in Skokie.

In spite of his near delirium, it was much easier this time than it had been the last. Massad in the left lane signaled for a left turn. So did the car behind. He slowed down and then suddenly a break came in the lane on his right. He put his foot to the floor, went through the opening and had no idea if he would hit something in the lane nearest the sidewalk.

As it was, he didn't. A woman with three arguing children in the back seat had slowed down so she could look at them over her right shoulder and threaten them with early bedtime. At that instant, Massad had skidded through the narrow space and down the street.

"Son of a bitch," shouted Hanrahan.

"Get out, Father Murphy, and stop the traffic," said Lieberman.

Hanrahan got out, took out his wallet to show his shield and held up his hand. The car in the right lane came within four inches of hitting the big man before it stopped.

"Stay right there," Hanrahan shouted.

The driver, a man who had been absorbed in listening to a talk show about abortion, froze. The next lane was already moving slowly. Hanrahan had no trouble stopping traffic there.

Abe burst through, leaving his partner in the middle of Western Avenue directing traffic. The car they had been following was nowhere in sight. Since they had been going north, Lieberman made a left turn. It paid. There next to the sidewalk was the car crookedly parked behind a badly rusted Pontiac. There was no one visible in the car he had been following and the driver's side door was open.

Lieberman called for backup now, gave his location, and hung up. He got out of the car, weapon ready, and moved to the passenger side of the parked car, ready to fire if anything moved. It didn't. There was no one and nothing in the car he could see. Lieberman looked around. A run-down apartment building next to an alley across the street, a boarded up supermarket on the curb side of the parked car. Lieberman moved to the front door of the supermarket. Locked tight. He tried to peer between the wooden boards that covered the windows, most of which were broken. He thought he saw a movement.

Lieberman moved around and down past the loading dock of the supermarket stepping over bits of debris on the cracked concrete. There was a rear door. It was locked. It took two bullets to shoot the lock to pieces.

Lieberman went in low. There was some light coming through the boarded up windows around the building. Empty aisles and shelves lined the building. He moved to his left, ready at each aisle.

When he came to the last aisle, he saw the man crouched at the far end. He was holding something in his hands. It was aimed directly at Lieberman who half expected to be torn to pieces, but nothing happened. The man with the object was weeping softly.

Lieberman advanced slowly and said, "Put it down." Instead the man held it out.

"Down," Lieberman insisted.

The man continued to hold the object out and Lieberman seriously considered shooting him, but something about the object, something in the dim light, caught his eye. It was blue, but not a metallic blue.

Ten steps closer and Lieberman recognized the Torah. There was nothing else in the man's hands. Lieberman moved closer and took the Torah. It took both arms. Lieberman held it awkwardly still pointing his weapon at the man who was on his knees, weeping and blinking his eyes.

"I was going to destroy it, but you saved my life. You saved Jara's life," he said. "You carried us. You found the doctor. You should have this sacred object."

The man slumped to the floor. Lieberman carefully put down the Torah on one of the steel shelves and went to the man. He was conscious. He had a gun, which Lieberman took and shoved down the aisle.

"Massad Mohammed?" he said.

Massad's eyes were closed but he smiled.

It took fifteen minutes to get Massad to the hospital and another hour for Hanrahan and Lieberman to get to the main police station downtown where the skinhead Mongers were being booked. Pig Sticker exchanged no looks with Hanrahan or Lieberman. They had a deal. He would do his time if he had to. Hanrahan and Lieberman were confident that with the help of some people they knew in the district attorney's office, some way would be found to get Charles Kenneth Leary out of prison very early should he be convicted along with the others.

"A long day, Rabbi," said Hanrahan.

"A long day, Father Murphy," Lieberman agreed.

Their shift was over. Lieberman drove Hanrahan home. Michael's car was parked in front and something was frying in the kitchen when Hanrahan went through the door.

"Michael?"

"In the kitchen," his son called.

Hanrahan hung up his coat and moved into the kitchen where Michael was at the oven, a skillet in his hand.

"Right on time," said Michael. "Did you know I have a great recipe for blackened fish?"

"That I did not," said Hanrahan, looking carefully at his son.

"I haven't had a drink, Dad," he said. "I'll get there."

"I'm gonna wash up," said Hanrahan. "It's been a long, dirty day."

Lieberman was home a little over half an hour later. He thought the kids might be asleep. They weren't. They were at the dining room table listening to Marvin Alexander telling a ghost story his own father had brought from Jamaica. The children were enthralled. Melisa was in Marvin's lap, drowsy but listening carefully. Even Lisa at the end of the table was listening to the tale, Lisa who thought anything but nonfiction was a waste of time, even in children's books. Both children wore their pajamas. Abe wondered what sleeping arrangement Bess had made.

Bess was at the head of the table, her back to him. She nodded back and waved, not really getting a look at him.

"Grandpa," Barry said excitedly. "You know what Marvin does? He cuts open dead bodies, even looks in their stomachs. He said I could watch sometime if it was all right with you."

Dr. Marvin Alexander looked up at Abe apologetically. Abe had seen autopsies. He had never forgotten his first, had never forgotten any of them.

"We'll see," Abe said as he approached the table, stopped in front of his wife. Marvin stopped his story. Abe carefully placed the Torah on the table in front of his wife. Silence at the table as Bess looked at it and then at her husband. She stood, almost knocking down the chair, and gave Abe a hug and kiss.

Marvin Alexander knew what a Torah was and thought this was an especially fine example of one, but what he did not understand was why his mother-in-law sat down again, put her forehead against the blue velvet covering and began to cry softly.

When his doorbell rang the next morning, Eli Towser had just awkwardly finished his morning prayers and was carefully and ritually putting away the headpiece and narrow black bands that he had wrapped around his hands and fingers during his devotions before the rising sun.

It was very early, and because he had heard about what had taken place the day before he approached the door carefully, his heavily cast arm resting awkwardly in a sling. Doing his prayers three times each day was going to prove difficult, but he was quickly learning to make adjustments.

Eli looked through the peephole. There was no one there. Carefully, leaving the heavy chain in place, he opened the door an inch or two and tried to scan the corridor. No one. A mistake? A wrong bell rung so early in the morning and an embarrassed visitor hurrying away? Eli knew the chain could not keep out a determined violent intruder and no one had yet kicked open the door.

He looked down and thought he saw something leaning against the partly open door. A brown package. He released the chain and opened the door. The package was shaped like many things, including a bomb. It had his name on it, printed, no address.

Eli pulled the package in and locked the door. It didn't have the heaviness of metal. He took it to the kitchen, took the wrapping off carefully, found a white box inside, and lifted the top of the box.

Inside the box was a pristine copy of *Rejoice O Youth: Comprehensive Jewish Ideology* by Avigdor Miller.

Eli opened the first page and saw written in small letters in blue ink: "To Eli Towser and all of his children yet to be. *Shalom*. Peace. *Salaam*." It was signed "Avrum Lieberman and Ibraham Said."

Tel Aviv, Israel, Today

FROM TIME TO time, especially when he was at a meeting at which someone was making a speech that had been made thousands of times, Tsvi Ben Levitt would wonder what had become of those two children he had carried so many years ago. They had lived. He knew that. And they had been sent to relatives. He had tried to find them again but they had been swallowed into the Palestinian population of Jordan and he could get no cooperation from the relatives no matter how sincerely he asked.

He remembered that night. That he had killed his cousin, that women and children and a man trying to protect his family from a madman had died. The death of his cousin, who was beloved in the community, had forced the young border guard to leave the kibbutz.

He had moved to the city as soon as his tour of duty had ended. He had gotten a job in a factory and gone to school. He had gotten his degree in history and then two more degrees in political science specializing in and becoming a respected expert on Arab politics.

He had married, had children, run for public office after

three years of teaching, and had been elected to the *Knesset*, where he was appointed to committee after committee, got to make an occasional speech, and was looked on as the hope of his party, perhaps a future prime minister.

The chairman of this committee called for further discussion. Tsvi Ben Levitt had learned to rise only infrequently at committee meetings when he spoke. Rising suggested that he would deliver a long speech to which his colleagues would listen with as much indifference as he listened to them. So, he learned to sit and control his passion. Very little came out of these committee meetings of politicians so diverse in their views as to defy reason or the belief that they could ever come up with anything upon which they could show the slightest agreement. But, he had learned, with enormous, exhausting patience, decisions could be reached, recommendations could be passed upward for discussion and possible acceptance and passage.

Tsvi spoke calmly, emphatically, and with a great confidence that demanded at least the eyes of the men who sat around that table, pads before them, eyes weary.

The subject was the part Israel would play in the education of Arab children in Israel, whether they were being given an inferior education, and whether more money should be spent on their education.

Tsvi adjusted his glasses and began to present a chain of logic for improving the education of Arab children, the advantages it would have to the state. He said nothing at this point about the moral rightness of the proposed bill. He had done that many times in the past. These men of diversity would be moved only by a chain of logic that convinced them that the bill would best serve Israel and its continued sovereignty.

So, as he spoke, Tsvi could see himself, a frail, frightened border guard carrying two children in the dark toward a distant light. He saw and felt but did not speak of it. Instead he was the perfect image of professorial logic.